Void's Enigmatic Mansion

4

HeeEun Kim
JiEun Ha

Yen Press

Void's
Enigmatic
Mansion

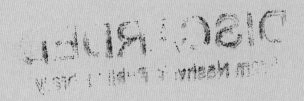

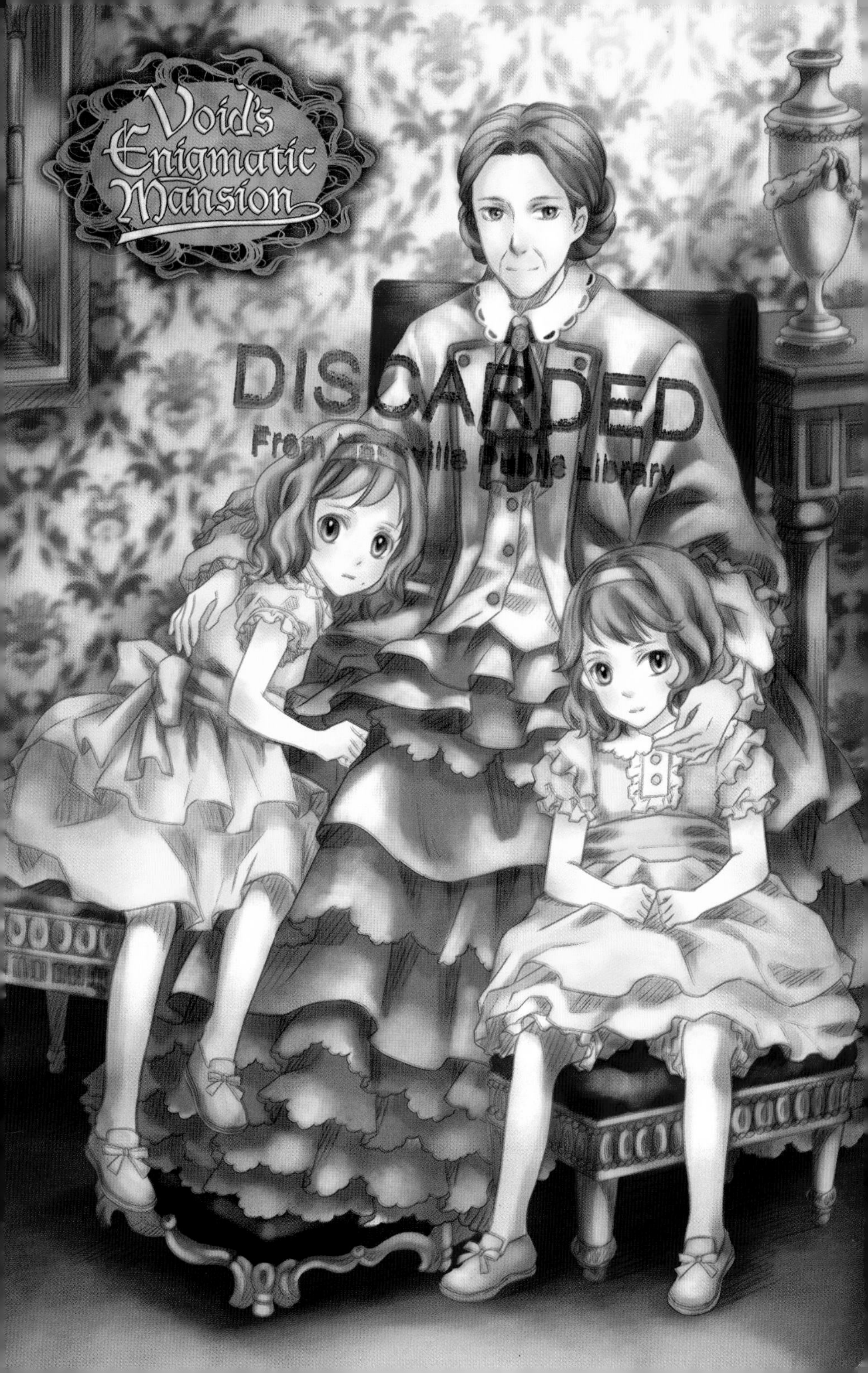
Void's
Enigmatic
Mansion

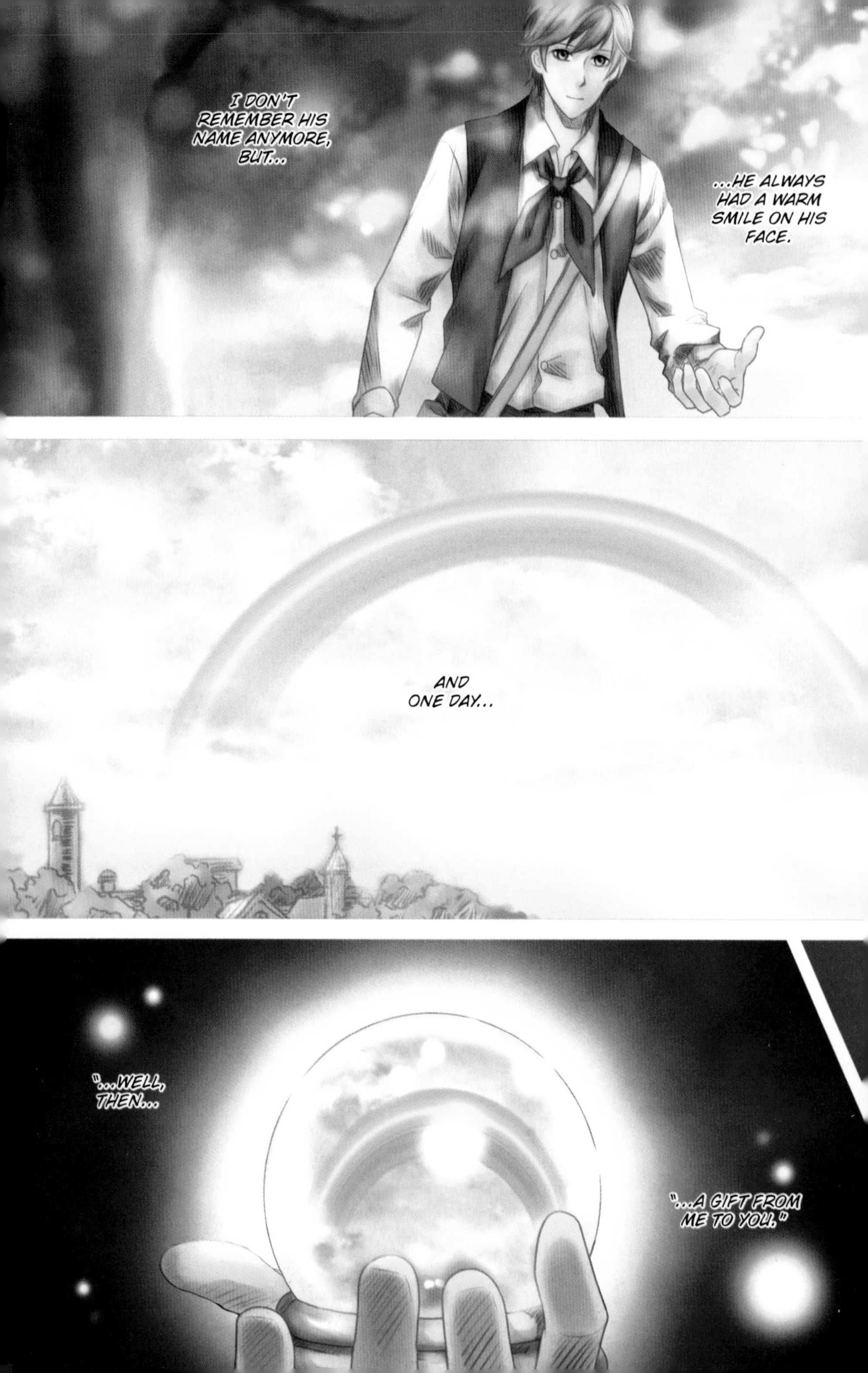
I DON'T REMEMBER HIS NAME ANYMORE, BUT...
...HE ALWAYS HAD A WARM SMILE ON HIS FACE.
AND ONE DAY...
"...WELL, THEN...
"...A GIFT FROM ME TO YOU."

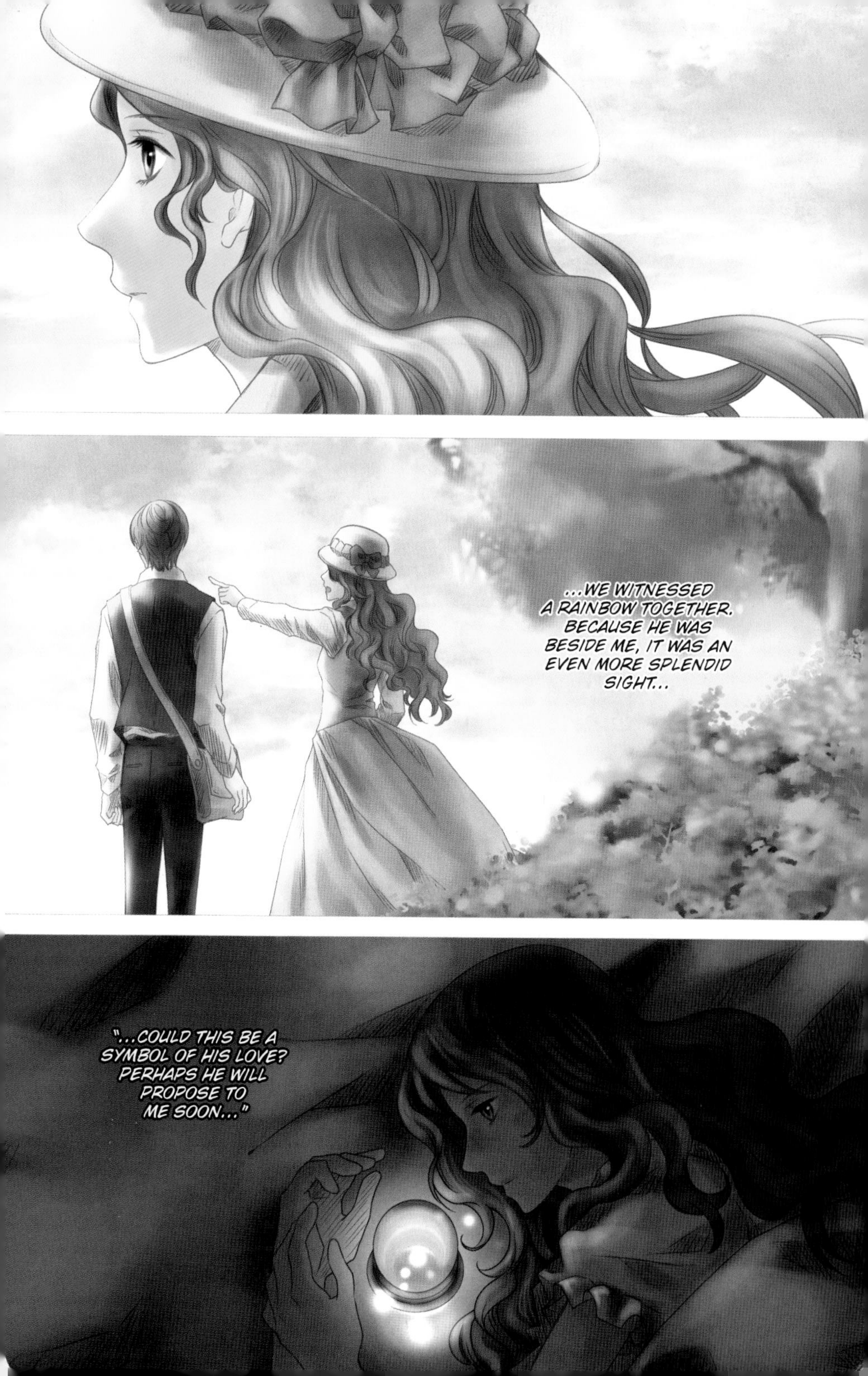
...WE WITNESSED A RAINBOW TOGETHER. BECAUSE HE WAS BESIDE ME, IT WAS AN EVEN MORE SPLENDID SIGHT...
"...COULD THIS BE A SYMBOL OF HIS LOVE? PERHAPS HE WILL PROPOSE TO ME SOON..."

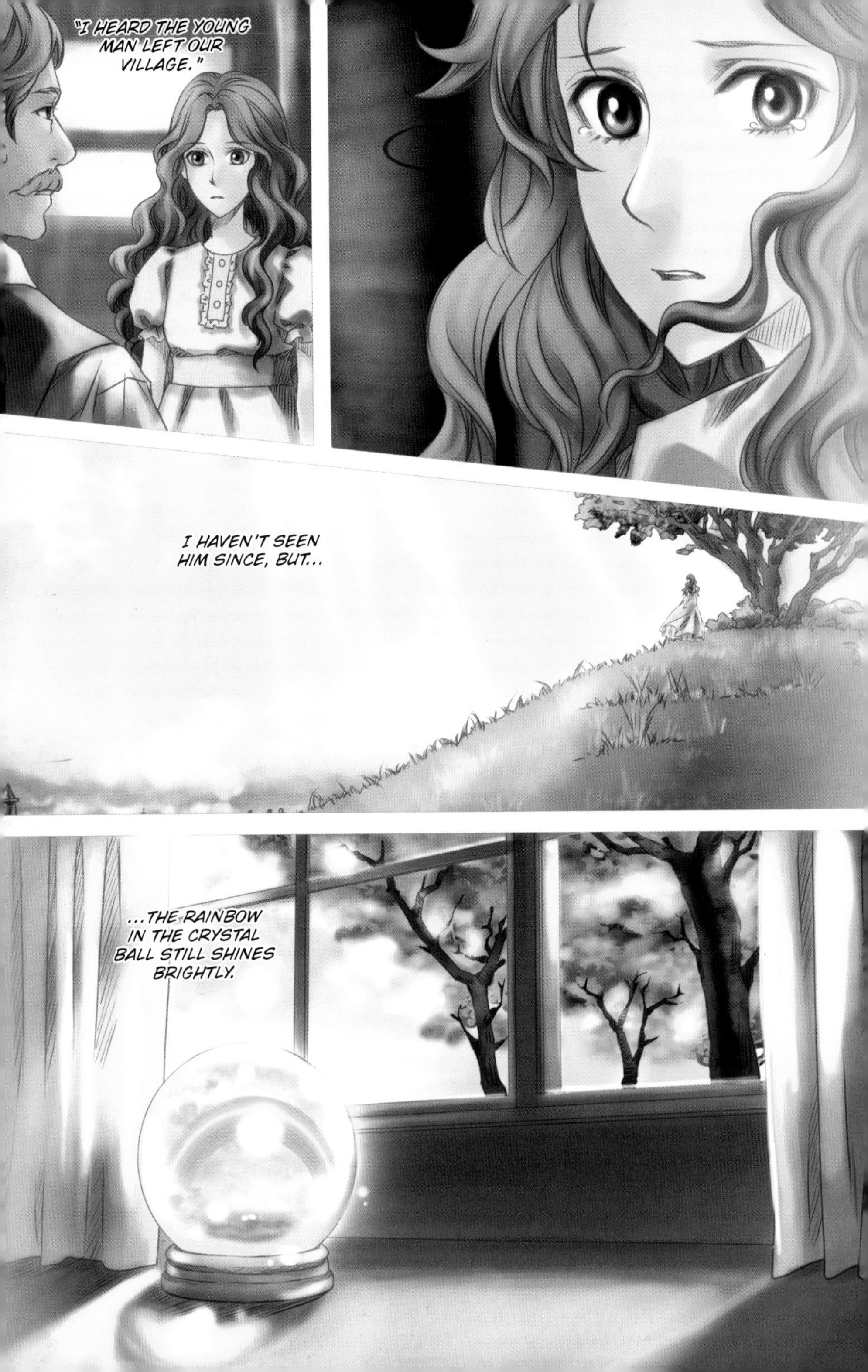
"I HEARD THE YOUNG MAN LEFT OUR VILLAGE."
I HAVEN'T SEEN HIM SINCE, BUT...
...THE RAINBOW IN THE CRYSTAL BALL STILL SHINES BRIGHTLY.

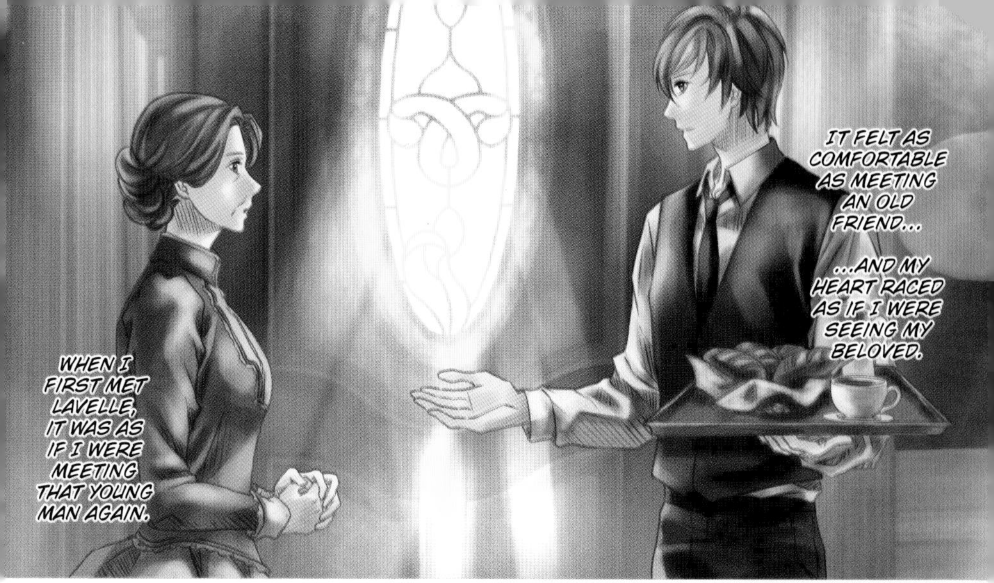
WHEN I FIRST MET LAVELLE, IT WAS AS IF I WERE MEETING THAT YOUNG MAN AGAIN.
IT FELT AS COMFORTABLE AS MEETING AN OLD FRIEND...
...AND MY HEART RACED AS IF I WERE SEEING MY BELOVED.

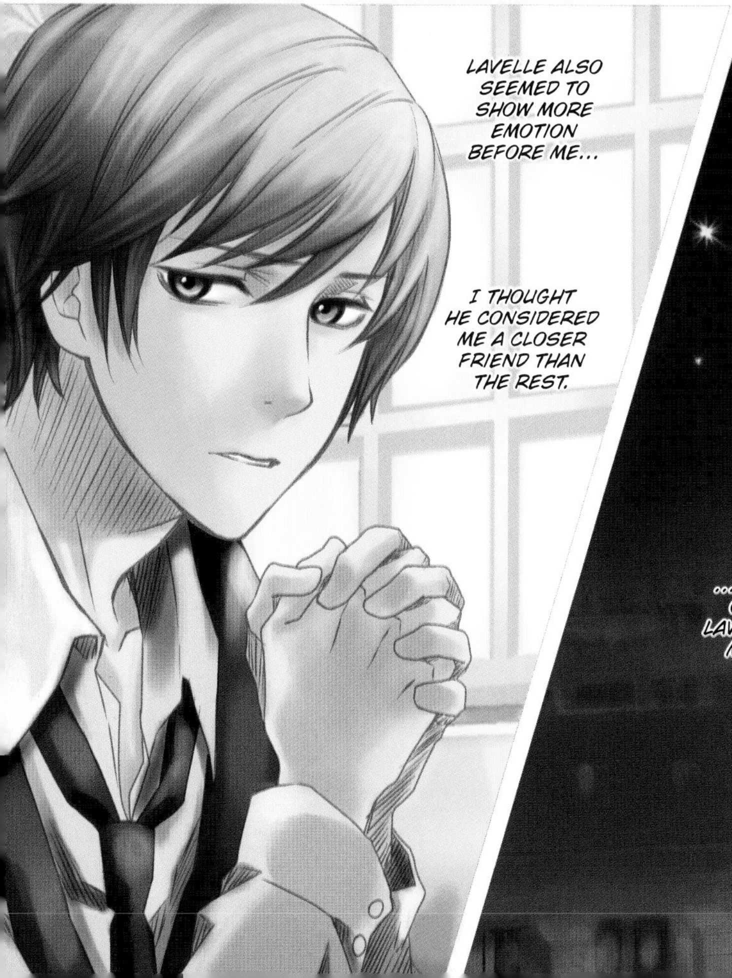
LAVELLE ALSO SEEMED TO SHOW MORE EMOTION BEFORE ME...
I THOUGHT HE CONSIDERED ME A CLOSER FRIEND THAN THE REST.

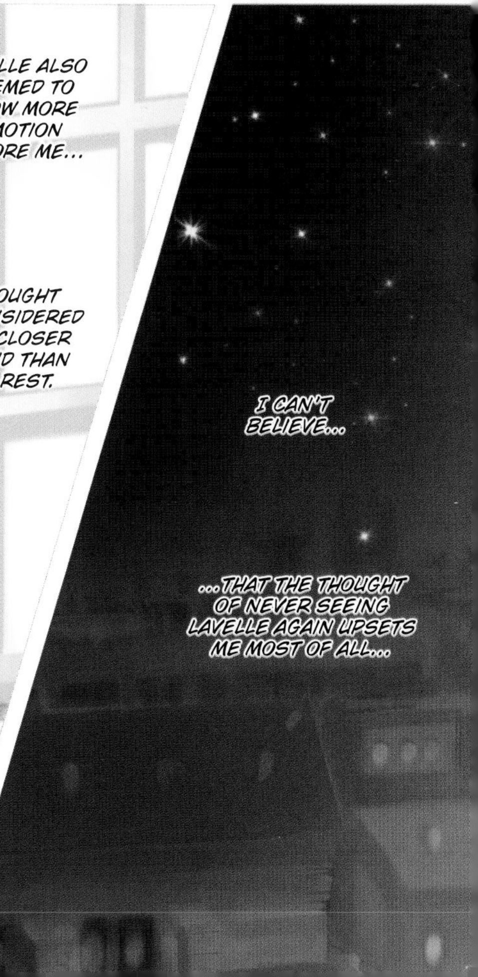
I CAN'T BELIEVE...
...THAT THE THOUGHT OF NEVER SEEING LAVELLE AGAIN UPSETS ME MOST OF ALL...

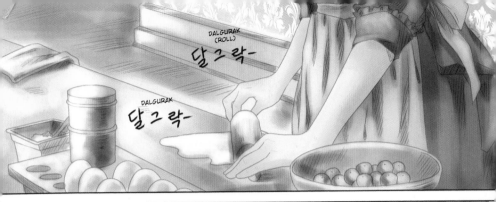

DALGURAK
(ROLL)
달그락-

DALGURAK
달그락-

WHAT ARE YOU DOING?

YOU'RE UP?

BREAKFAST IS NEARLY READY, SO WAKE JANE AND THE CHILDREN.

ALREADY? THEY'RE STILL FAST ASLEEP...

DO YOU WAKE UP AT THIS LATE HOUR EVERY DAY? IT SEEMS LIKE A BAD HABIT.

WHY NOT HAVE PIERRE TUTOR YOUR CHILDREN?

THAT DILETTANTE TEACHING MY CHILDREN? I THINK NOT.

PIERRE IS SUITABLE FOR THE SON OF AN ARISTOCRAT, YOU KNOW. BESIDES, THEY SEEM TO BE HAVING SOME FINANCIAL DIFFICULTIES. YOU WOULD BE DOING THEM A FAVOR TOO.

WORD HAS IT THAT YOUR CHILDREN COULD USE SOME LESSONS IN MANNERS.

IT'S NOT NECESSARY. K AND KARIN A FINE WITHOUT THAT NONSEN

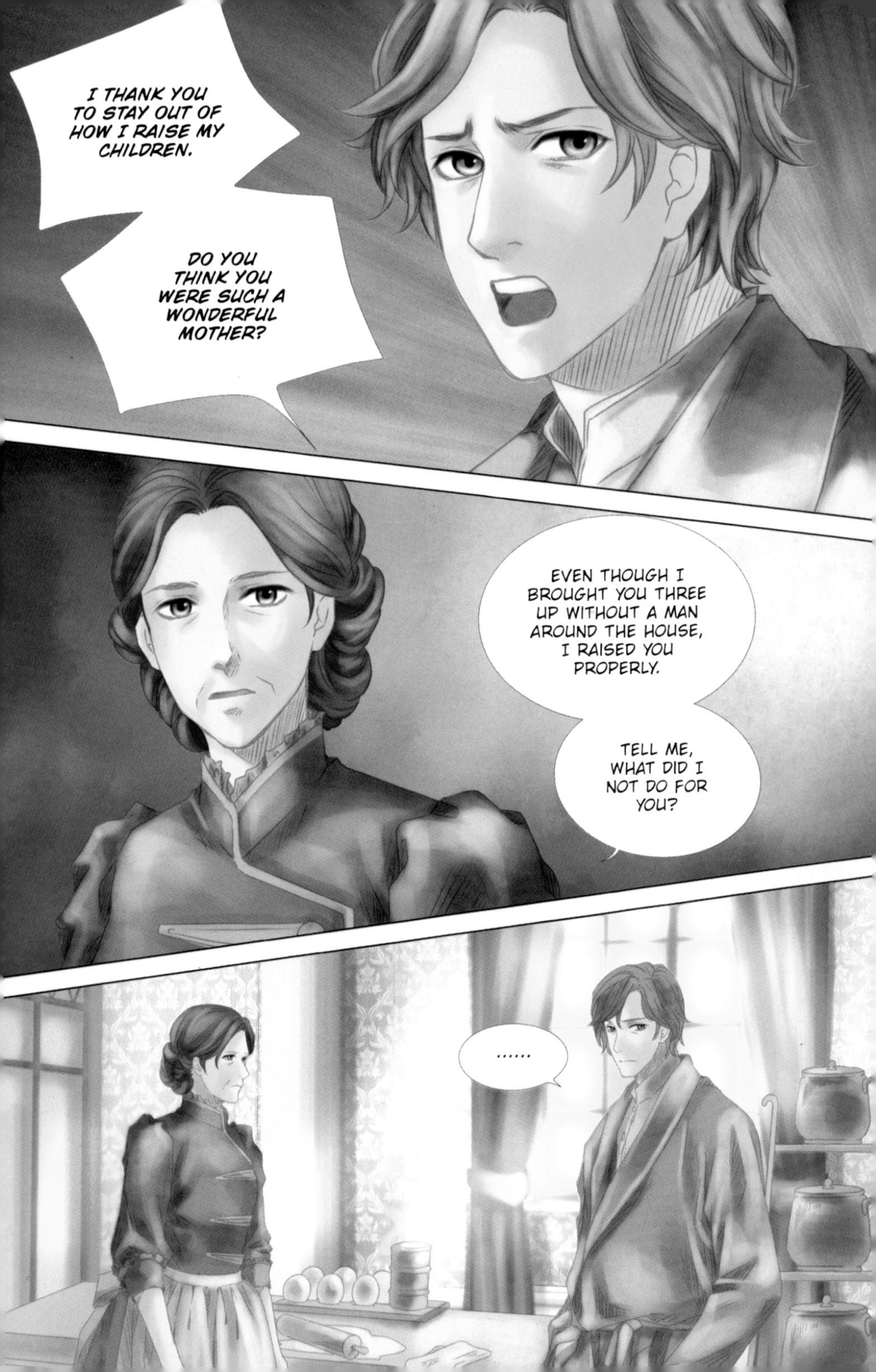
I THANK YOU TO STAY OUT OF HOW I RAISE MY CHILDREN.
DO YOU THINK YOU WERE SUCH A WONDERFUL MOTHER?
EVEN THOUGH I BROUGHT YOU THREE UP WITHOUT A MAN AROUND THE HOUSE, I RAISED YOU PROPERLY.
TELL ME, WHAT DID I NOT DO FOR YOU?
......

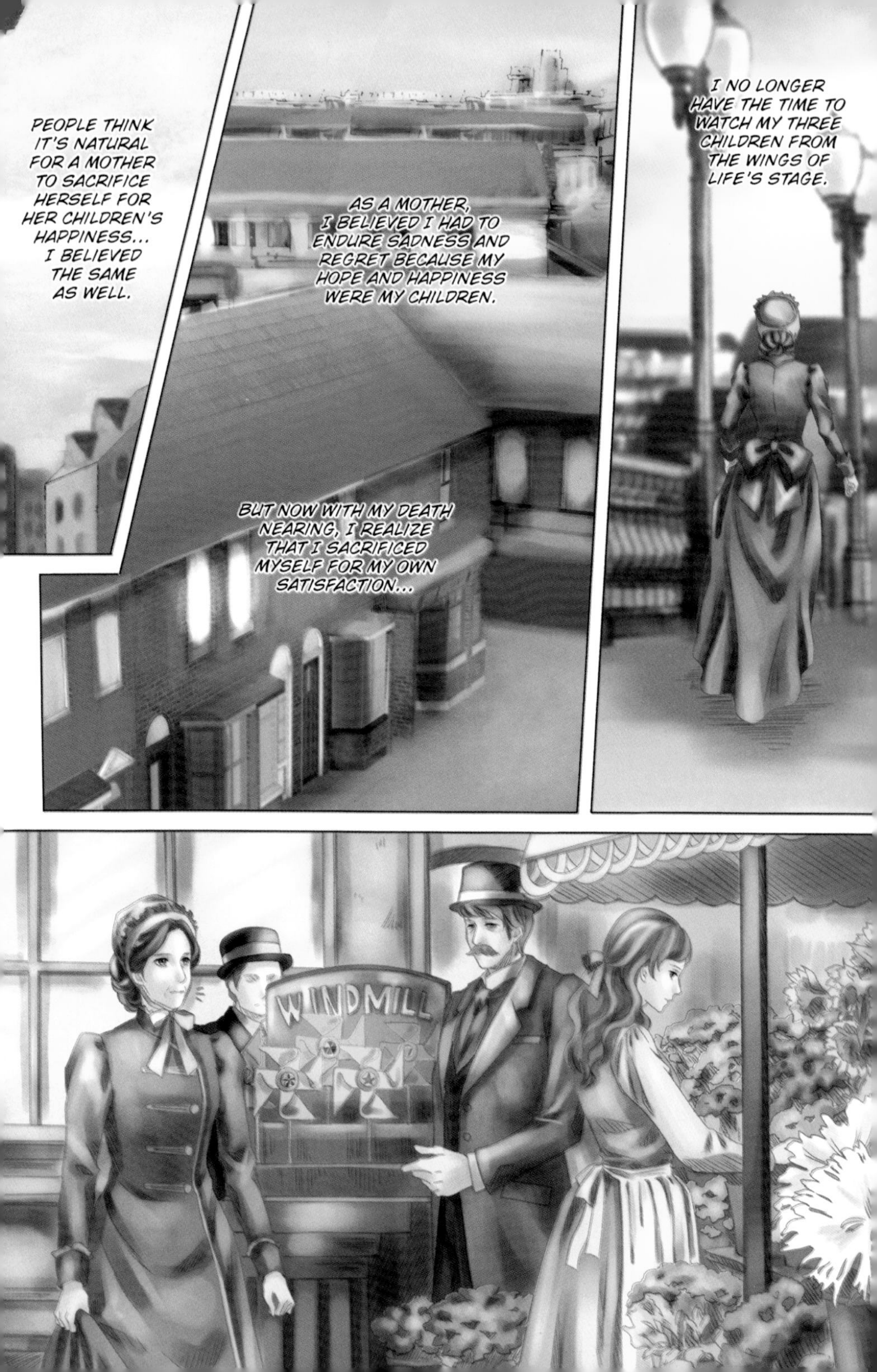
PEOPLE THINK IT'S NATURAL FOR A MOTHER TO SACRIFICE HERSELF FOR HER CHILDREN'S HAPPINESS... I BELIEVED THE SAME AS WELL.
AS A MOTHER, I BELIEVED I HAD TO ENDURE SADNESS AND REGRET BECAUSE MY HOPE AND HAPPINESS WERE MY CHILDREN.
BUT NOW WITH MY DEATH NEARING, I REALIZE THAT I SACRIFICED MYSELF FOR MY OWN SATISFACTION...
I NO LONGER HAVE THE TIME TO WATCH MY THREE CHILDREN FROM THE WINGS OF LIFE'S STAGE.
WINDMILL

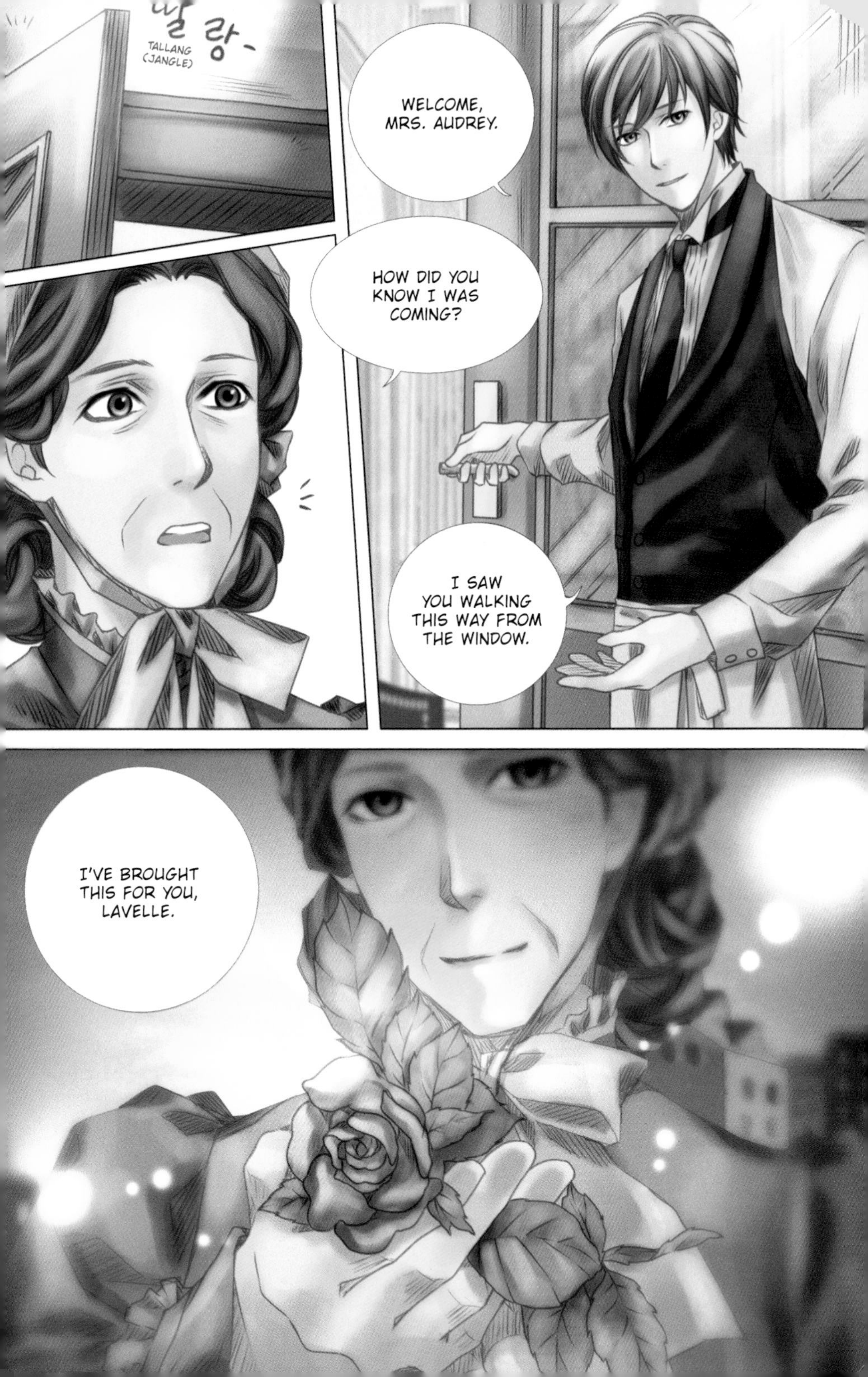
딸랑-
TALLANG (JANGLE)
WELCOME, MRS. AUDREY.
HOW DID YOU KNOW I WAS COMING?
I SAW YOU WALKING THIS WAY FROM THE WINDOW.
I'VE BROUGHT THIS FOR YOU, LAVELLE.

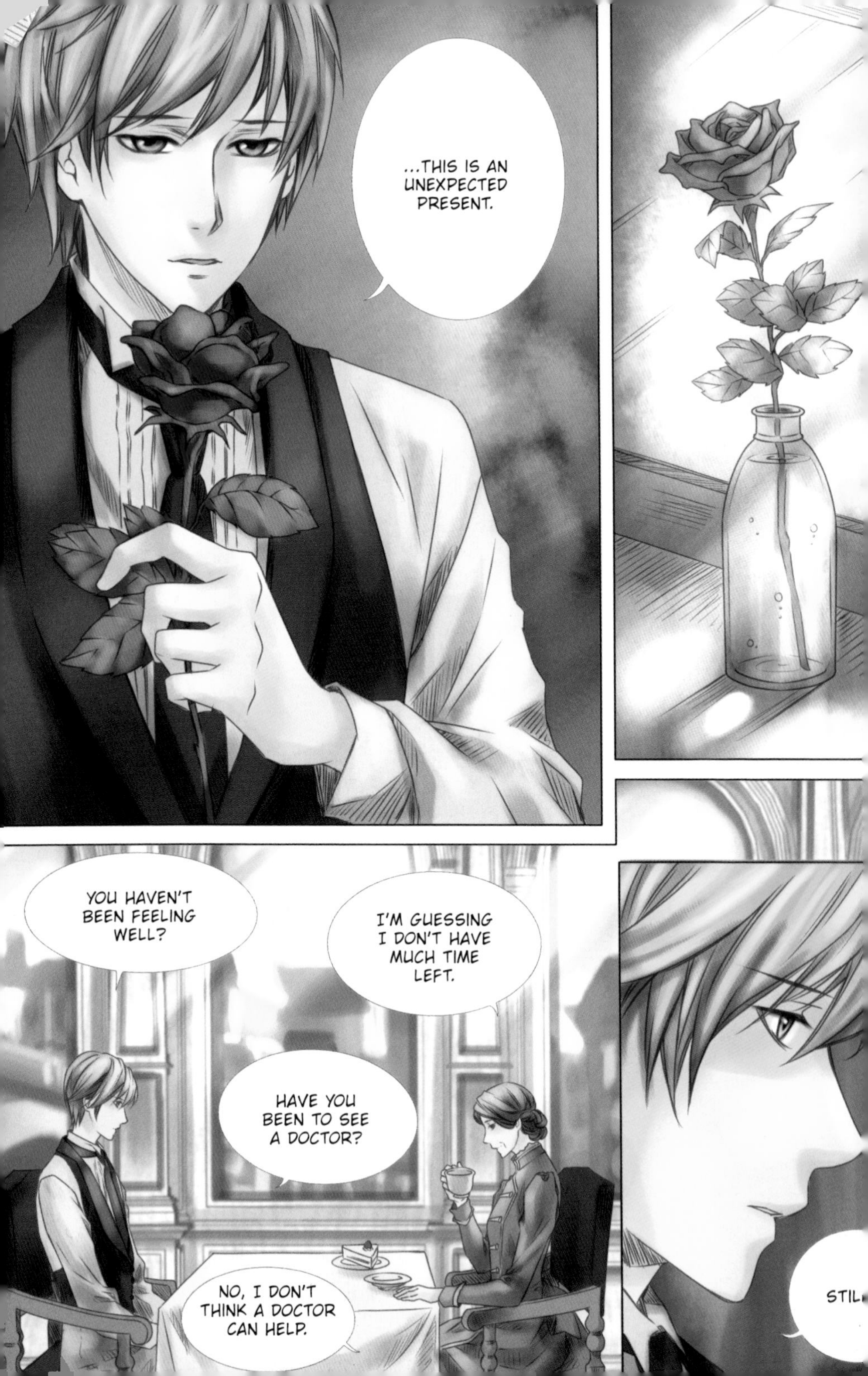
...THIS IS AN UNEXPECTED PRESENT.
YOU HAVEN'T BEEN FEELING WELL?
I'M GUESSING I DON'T HAVE MUCH TIME LEFT.
HAVE YOU BEEN TO SEE A DOCTOR?
NO, I DON'T THINK A DOCTOR CAN HELP.
STIL

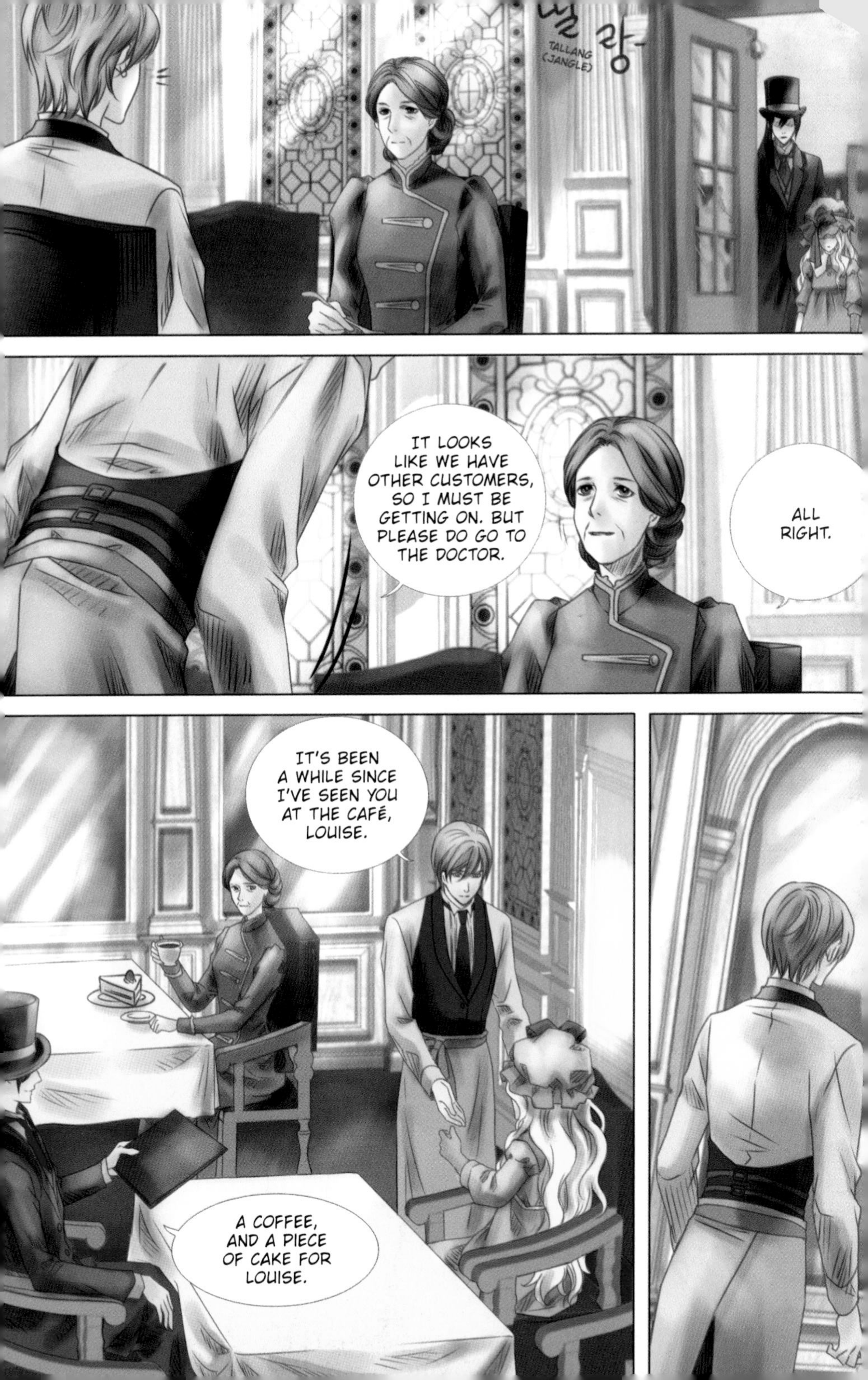

랑
TALLANG (JANGLE)
IT LOOKS LIKE WE HAVE OTHER CUSTOMERS, SO I MUST BE GETTING ON. BUT PLEASE DO GO TO THE DOCTOR.
ALL RIGHT.
IT'S BEEN A WHILE SINCE I'VE SEEN YOU AT THE CAFÉ, LOUISE.
A COFFEE, AND A PIECE OF CAKE FOR LOUISE.

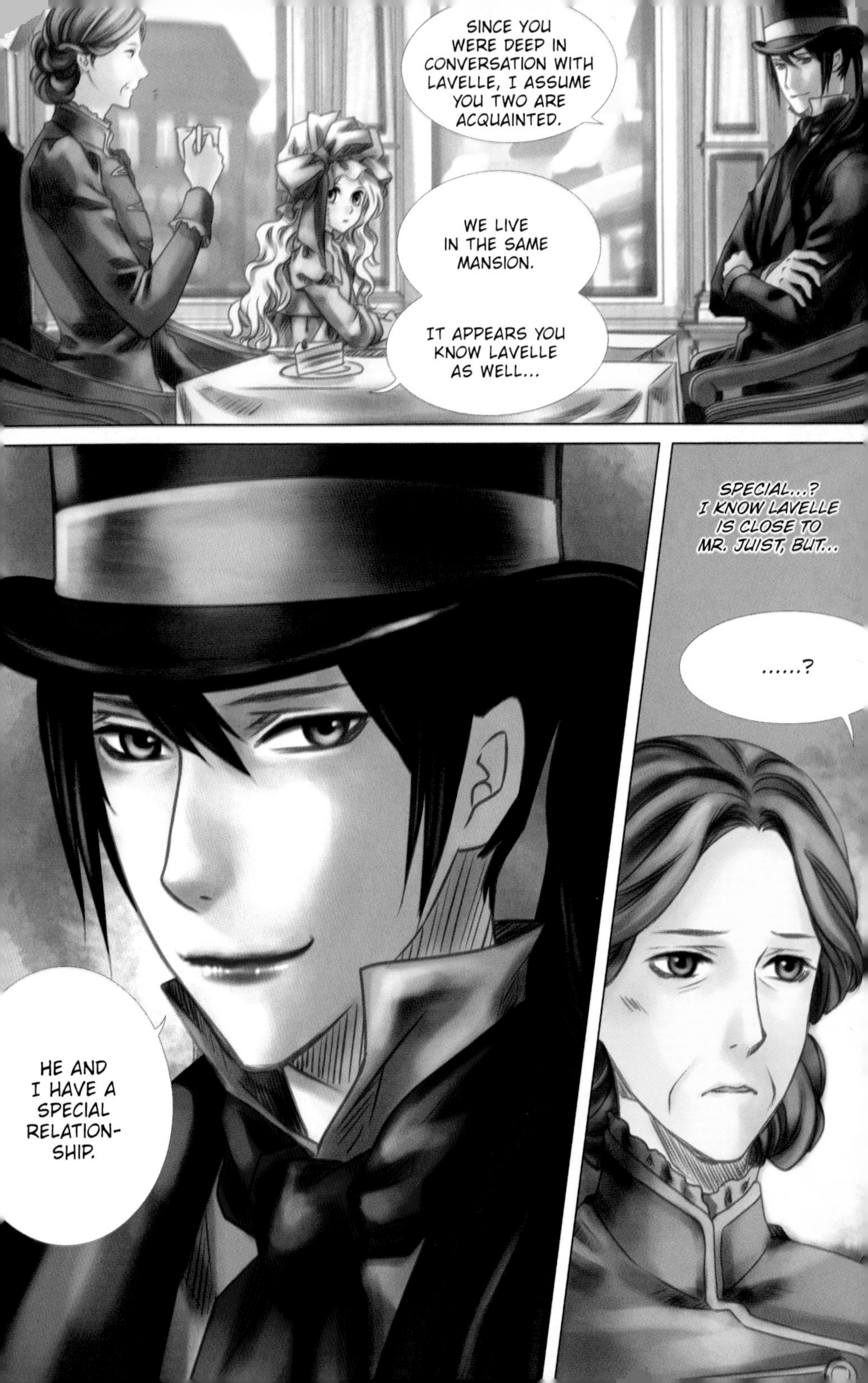

SINCE YOU WERE DEEP IN CONVERSATION WITH LAVELLE, I ASSUME YOU TWO ARE ACQUAINTED.
WE LIVE IN THE SAME MANSION.
IT APPEARS YOU KNOW LAVELLE AS WELL...
HE AND I HAVE A SPECIAL RELATION-SHIP.
SPECIAL...? I KNOW LAVELLE IS CLOSE TO MR. JUIST, BUT...
......?

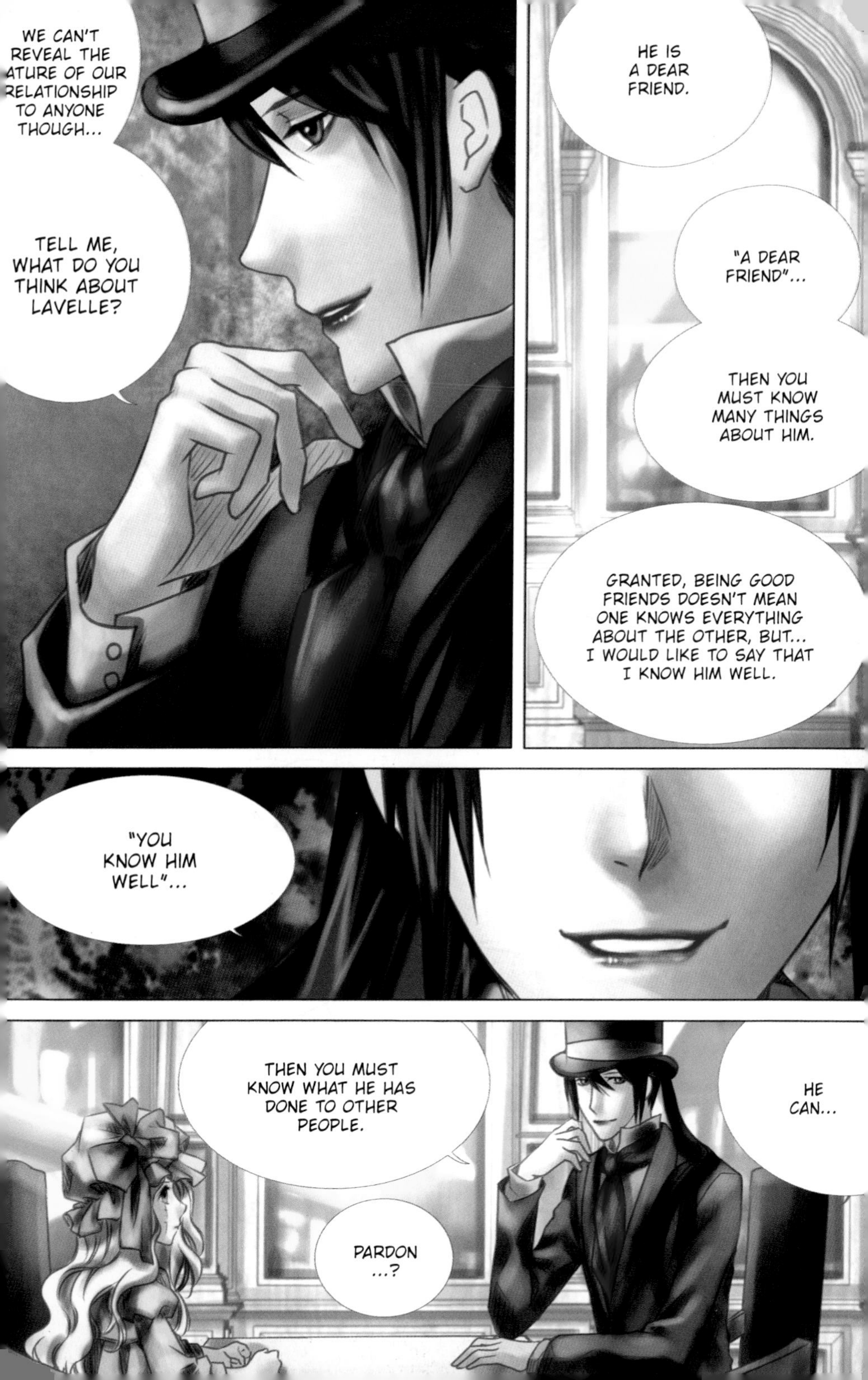
WE CAN'T REVEAL THE ATURE OF OUR RELATIONSHIP TO ANYONE THOUGH...
TELL ME, WHAT DO YOU THINK ABOUT LAVELLE?
HE IS A DEAR FRIEND.
"A DEAR FRIEND"...
THEN YOU MUST KNOW MANY THINGS ABOUT HIM.
GRANTED, BEING GOOD FRIENDS DOESN'T MEAN ONE KNOWS EVERYTHING ABOUT THE OTHER, BUT... I WOULD LIKE TO SAY THAT I KNOW HIM WELL.
"YOU KNOW HIM WELL"...
THEN YOU MUST KNOW WHAT HE HAS DONE TO OTHER PEOPLE.
PARDON ...?
HE CAN...

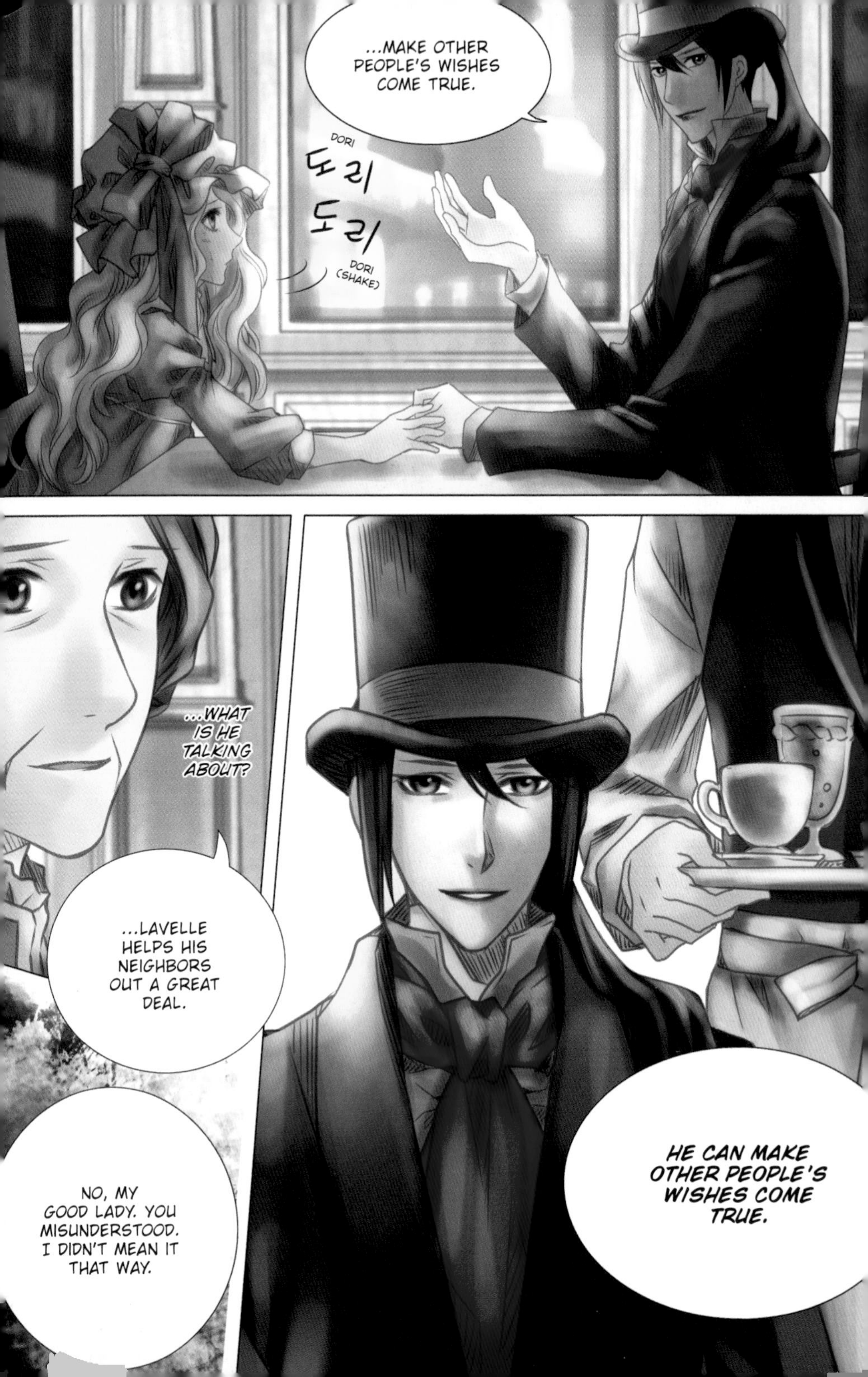
...MAKE OTHER PEOPLE'S WISHES COME TRUE.
DORI
도리
도리
DORI (SHAKE)
...WHAT IS HE TALKING ABOUT?
...LAVELLE HELPS HIS NEIGHBORS OUT A GREAT DEAL.
NO, MY GOOD LADY. YOU MISUNDERSTOOD. I DIDN'T MEAN IT THAT WAY.
HE CAN MAKE OTHER PEOPLE'S WISHES COME TRUE.

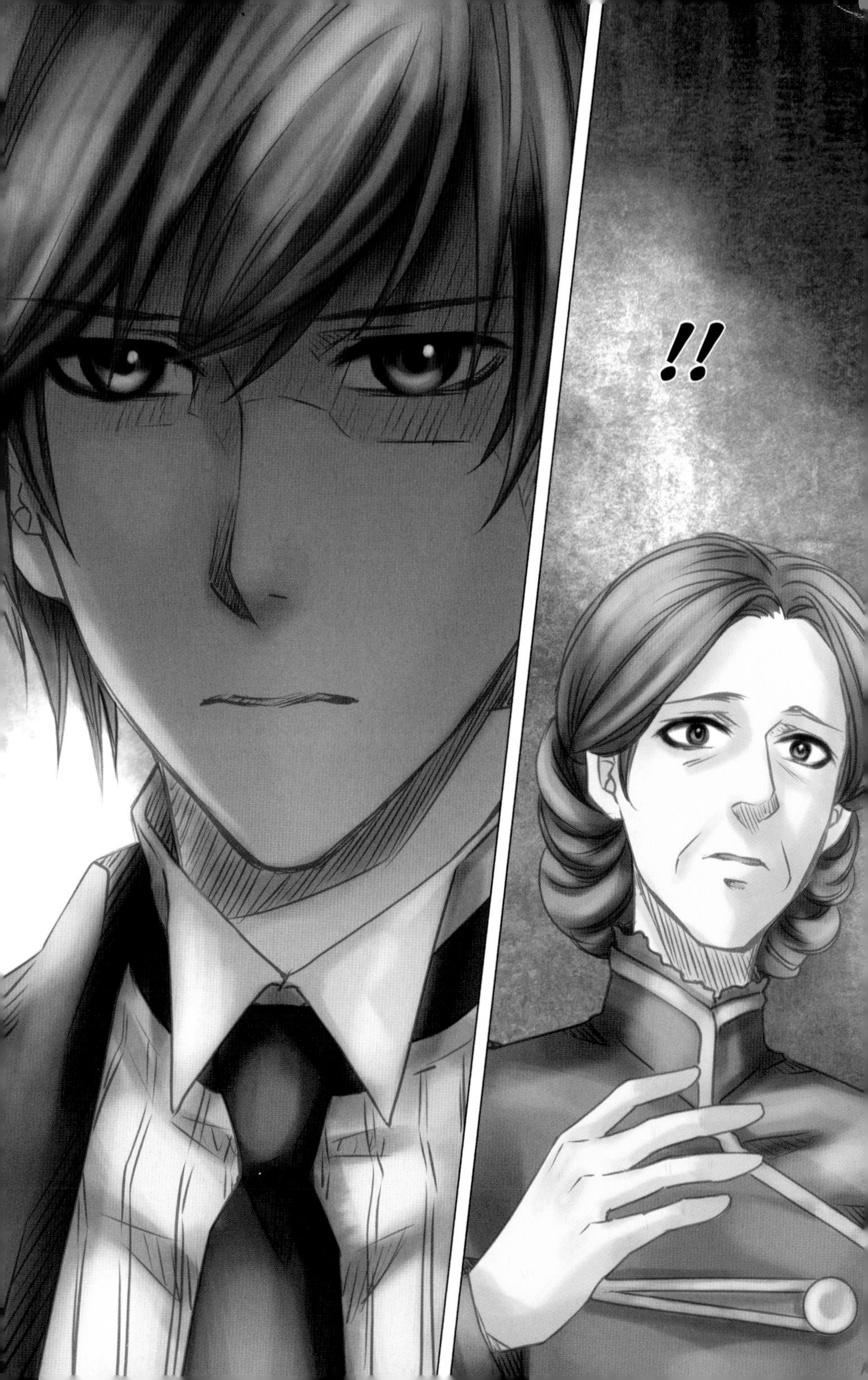
!!

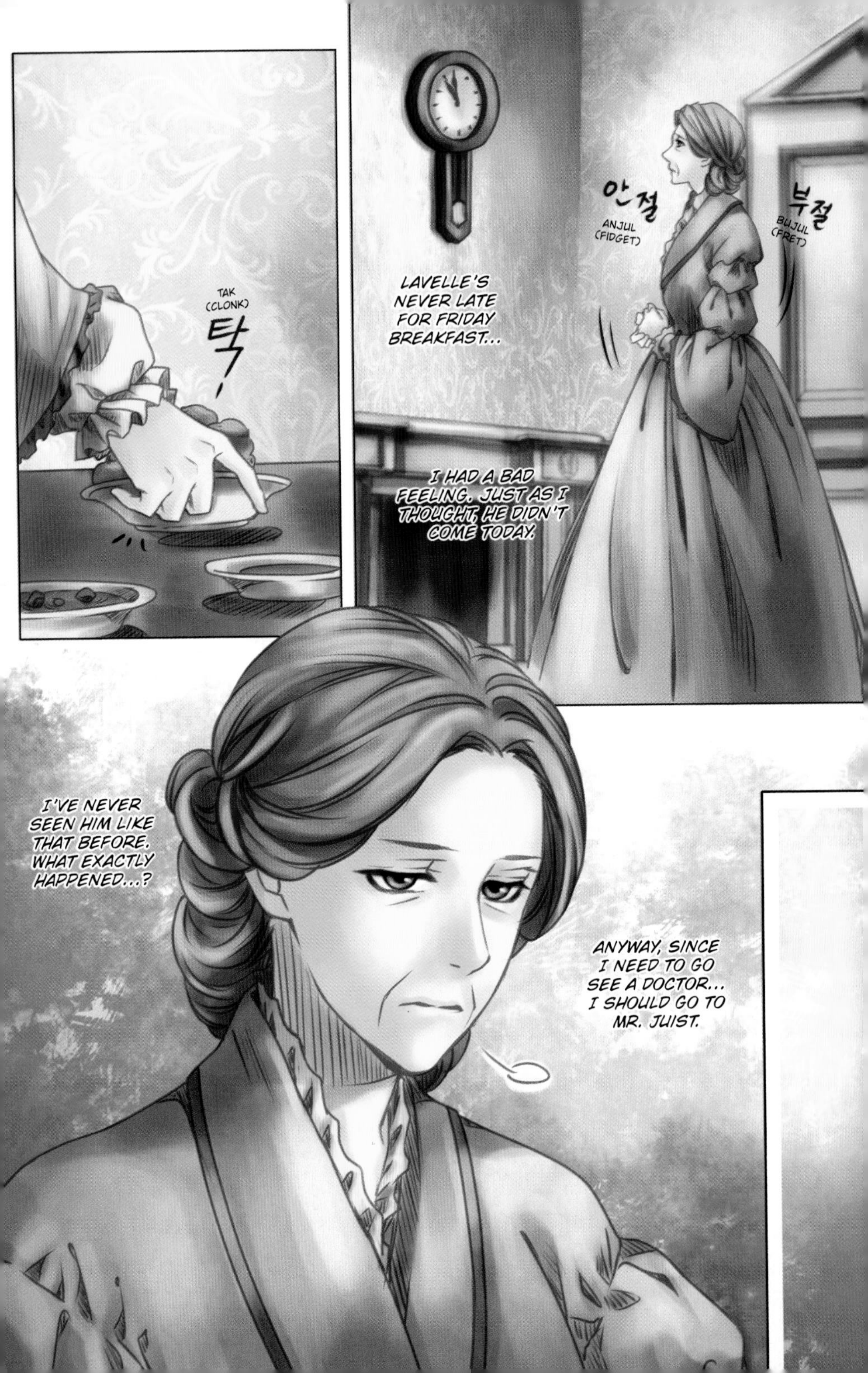

TAK (CLONK)
탁
LAVELLE'S NEVER LATE FOR FRIDAY BREAKFAST...
안절
ANJUL (FIDGET)
부절
BUJUL (FRET)
I HAD A BAD FEELING. JUST AS I THOUGHT, HE DIDN'T COME TODAY.
I'VE NEVER SEEN HIM LIKE THAT BEFORE. WHAT EXACTLY HAPPENED...?
ANYWAY, SINCE I NEED TO GO SEE A DOCTOR... I SHOULD GO TO MR. JUIST.

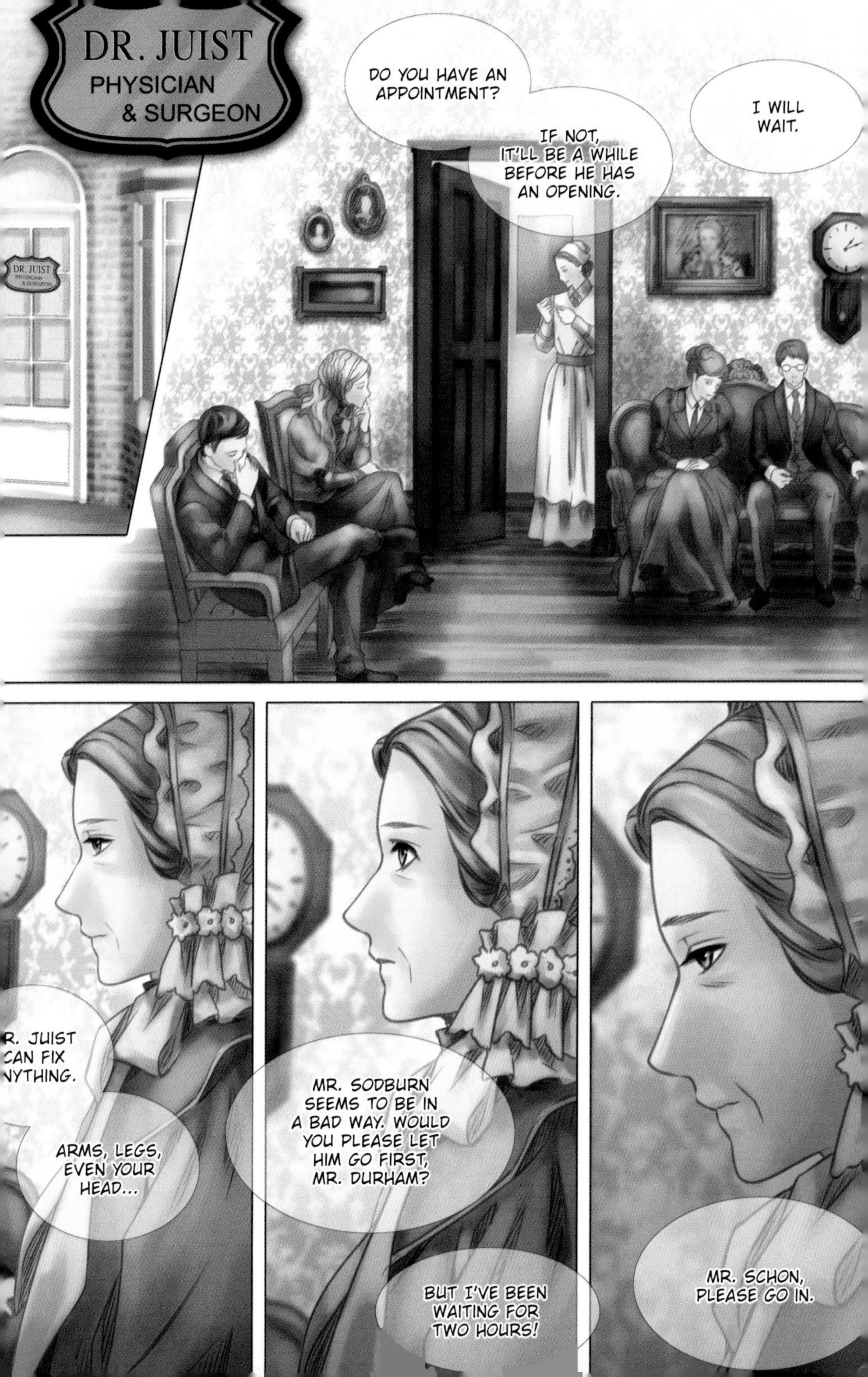
DR. JUIST PHYSICIAN & SURGEON
DO YOU HAVE AN APPOINTMENT?
IF NOT, IT'LL BE A WHILE BEFORE HE HAS AN OPENING.
I WILL WAIT.
R. JUIST CAN FIX NYTHING.
ARMS, LEGS, EVEN YOUR HEAD...
MR. SODBURN SEEMS TO BE IN A BAD WAY. WOULD YOU PLEASE LET HIM GO FIRST, MR. DURHAM?
BUT I'VE BEEN WAITING FOR TWO HOURS!
MR. SCHON, PLEASE GO IN.

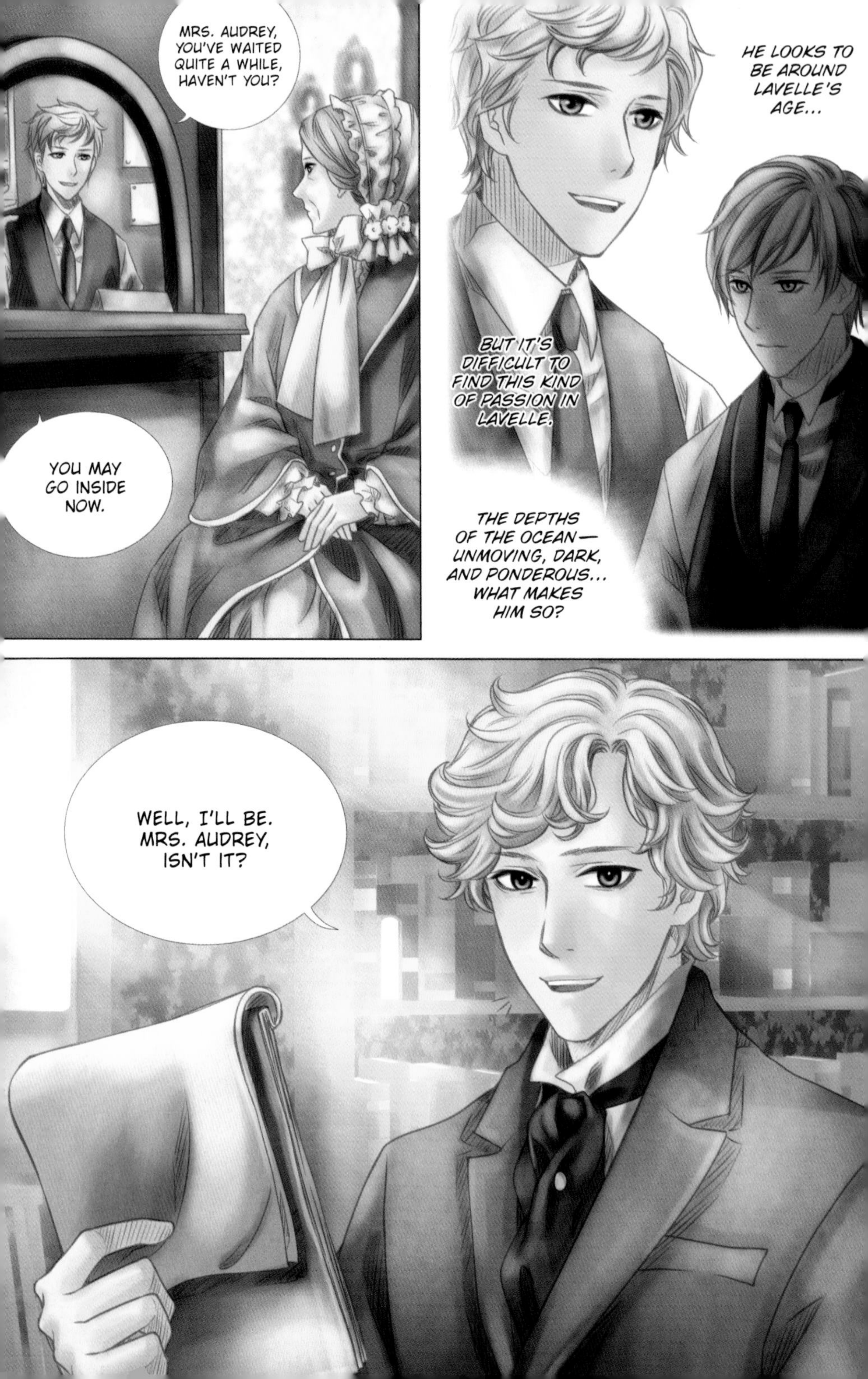
MRS. AUDREY, YOU'VE WAITED QUITE A WHILE, HAVEN'T YOU?
YOU MAY GO INSIDE NOW.
HE LOOKS TO BE AROUND LAVELLE'S AGE...
BUT IT'S DIFFICULT TO FIND THIS KIND OF PASSION IN LAVELLE.
THE DEPTHS OF THE OCEAN—UNMOVING, DARK, AND PONDEROUS... WHAT MAKES HIM SO?
WELL, I'LL BE. MRS. AUDREY, ISN'T IT?

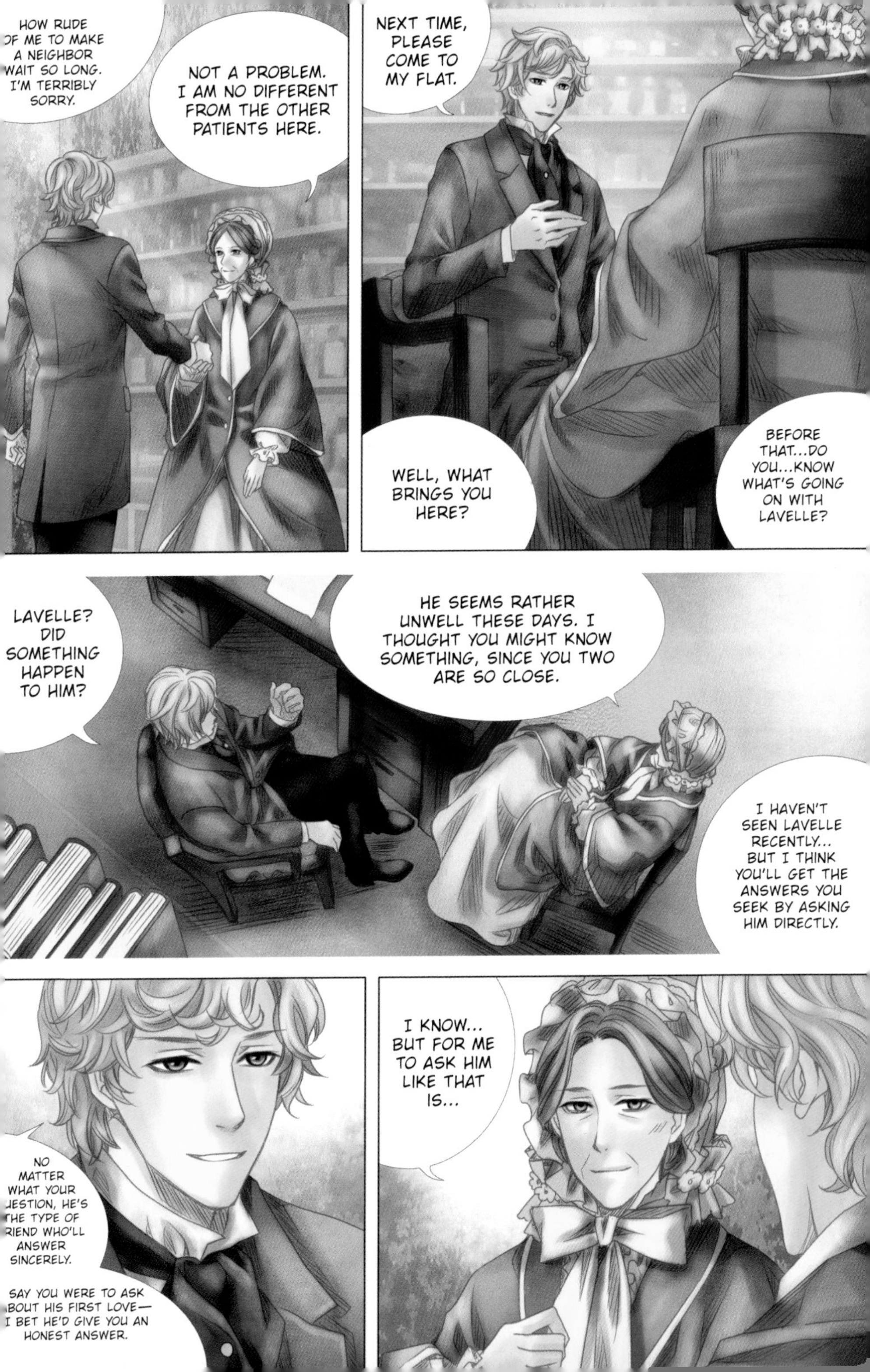
HOW RUDE OF ME TO MAKE A NEIGHBOR WAIT SO LONG. I'M TERRIBLY SORRY.
NOT A PROBLEM. I AM NO DIFFERENT FROM THE OTHER PATIENTS HERE.
NEXT TIME, PLEASE COME TO MY FLAT.
WELL, WHAT BRINGS YOU HERE?
BEFORE THAT...DO YOU...KNOW WHAT'S GOING ON WITH LAVELLE?
LAVELLE? DID SOMETHING HAPPEN TO HIM?
HE SEEMS RATHER UNWELL THESE DAYS. I THOUGHT YOU MIGHT KNOW SOMETHING, SINCE YOU TWO ARE SO CLOSE.
I HAVEN'T SEEN LAVELLE RECENTLY... BUT I THINK YOU'LL GET THE ANSWERS YOU SEEK BY ASKING HIM DIRECTLY.
NO MATTER WHAT YOUR UESTION, HE'S THE TYPE OF RIEND WHO'LL ANSWER SINCERELY.
SAY YOU WERE TO ASK BOUT HIS FIRST LOVE— I BET HE'D GIVE YOU AN HONEST ANSWER.
I KNOW... BUT FOR ME TO ASK HIM LIKE THAT IS...

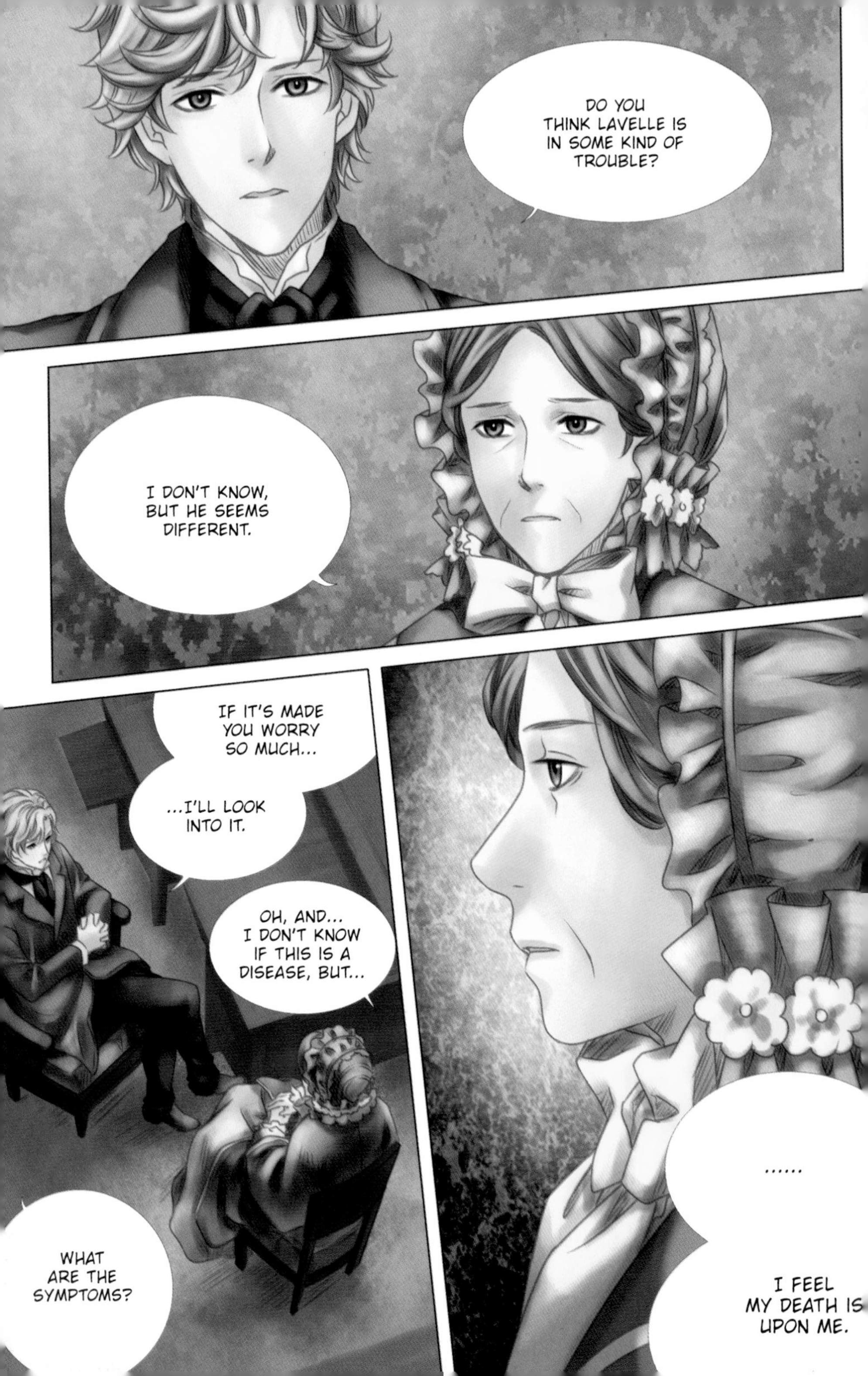
DO YOU THINK LAVELLE IS IN SOME KIND OF TROUBLE?
I DON'T KNOW, BUT HE SEEMS DIFFERENT.
IF IT'S MADE YOU WORRY SO MUCH...
...I'LL LOOK INTO IT.
OH, AND... I DON'T KNOW IF THIS IS A DISEASE, BUT...
WHAT ARE THE SYMPTOMS?
......
I FEEL MY DEATH IS UPON ME.

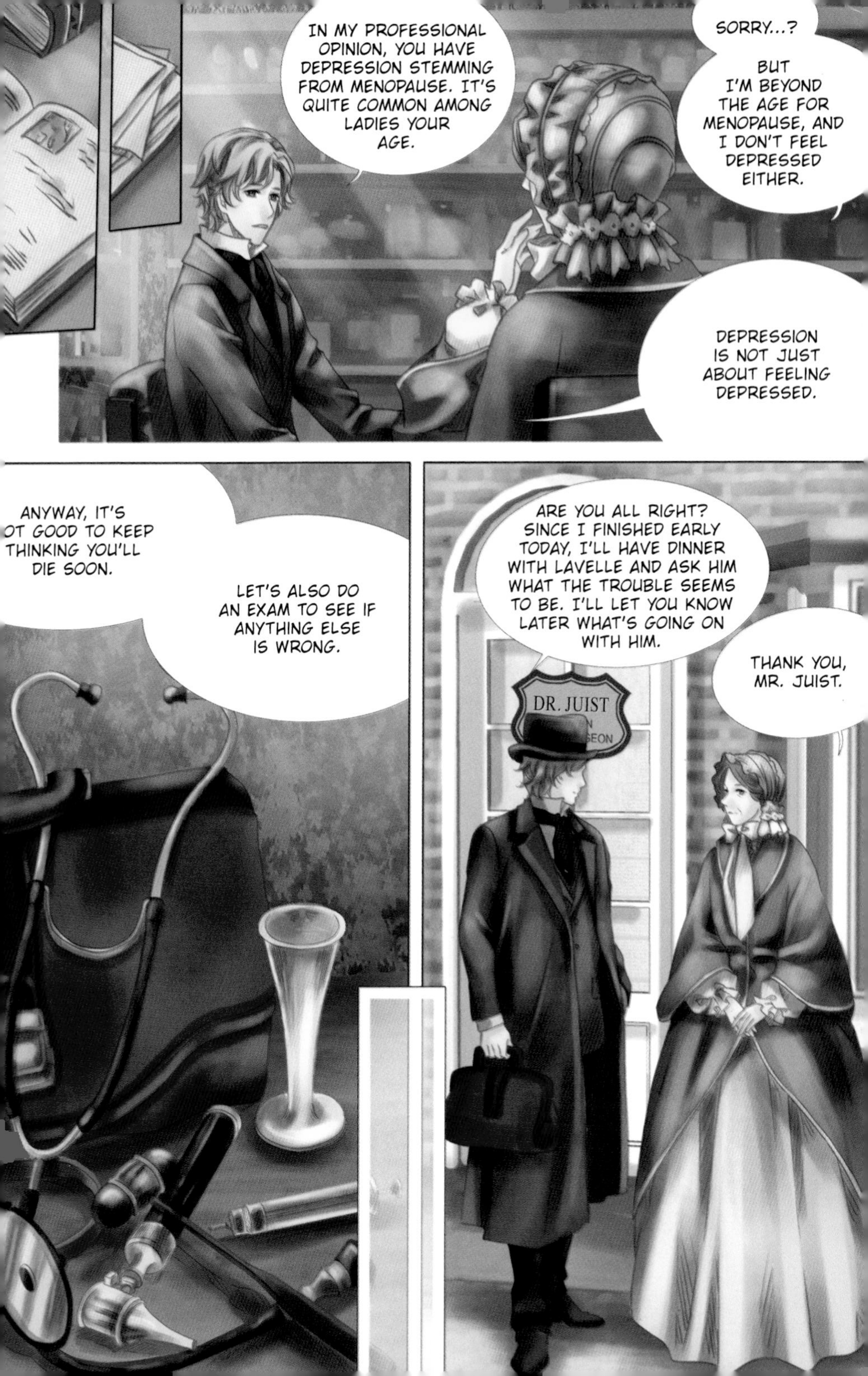
IN MY PROFESSIONAL OPINION, YOU HAVE DEPRESSION STEMMING FROM MENOPAUSE. IT'S QUITE COMMON AMONG LADIES YOUR AGE.
SORRY...?
BUT I'M BEYOND THE AGE FOR MENOPAUSE, AND I DON'T FEEL DEPRESSED EITHER.
DEPRESSION IS NOT JUST ABOUT FEELING DEPRESSED.
ANYWAY, IT'S OT GOOD TO KEEP THINKING YOU'LL DIE SOON.
LET'S ALSO DO AN EXAM TO SEE IF ANYTHING ELSE IS WRONG.
ARE YOU ALL RIGHT? SINCE I FINISHED EARLY TODAY, I'LL HAVE DINNER WITH LAVELLE AND ASK HIM WHAT THE TROUBLE SEEMS TO BE. I'LL LET YOU KNOW LATER WHAT'S GOING ON WITH HIM.
DR. JUIST
THANK YOU, MR. JUIST.

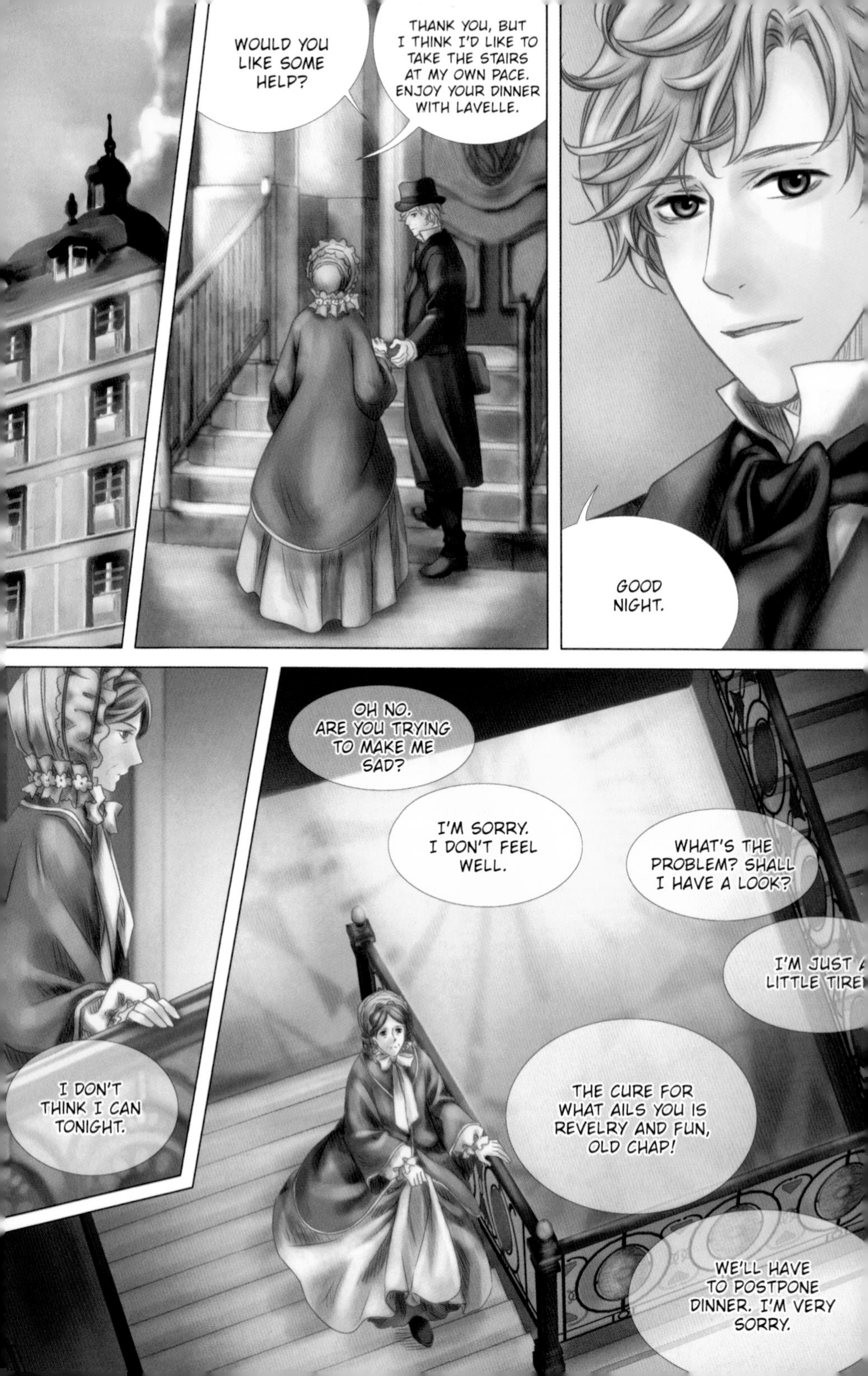
WOULD YOU LIKE SOME HELP?
THANK YOU, BUT I THINK I'D LIKE TO TAKE THE STAIRS AT MY OWN PACE. ENJOY YOUR DINNER WITH LAVELLE.
GOOD NIGHT.
I DON'T THINK I CAN TONIGHT.
OH NO. ARE YOU TRYING TO MAKE ME SAD?
I'M SORRY. I DON'T FEEL WELL.
WHAT'S THE PROBLEM? SHALL I HAVE A LOOK?
I'M JUST A LITTLE TIRE
THE CURE FOR WHAT AILS YOU IS REVELRY AND FUN, OLD CHAP!
WE'LL HAVE TO POSTPONE DINNER. I'M VERY SORRY.

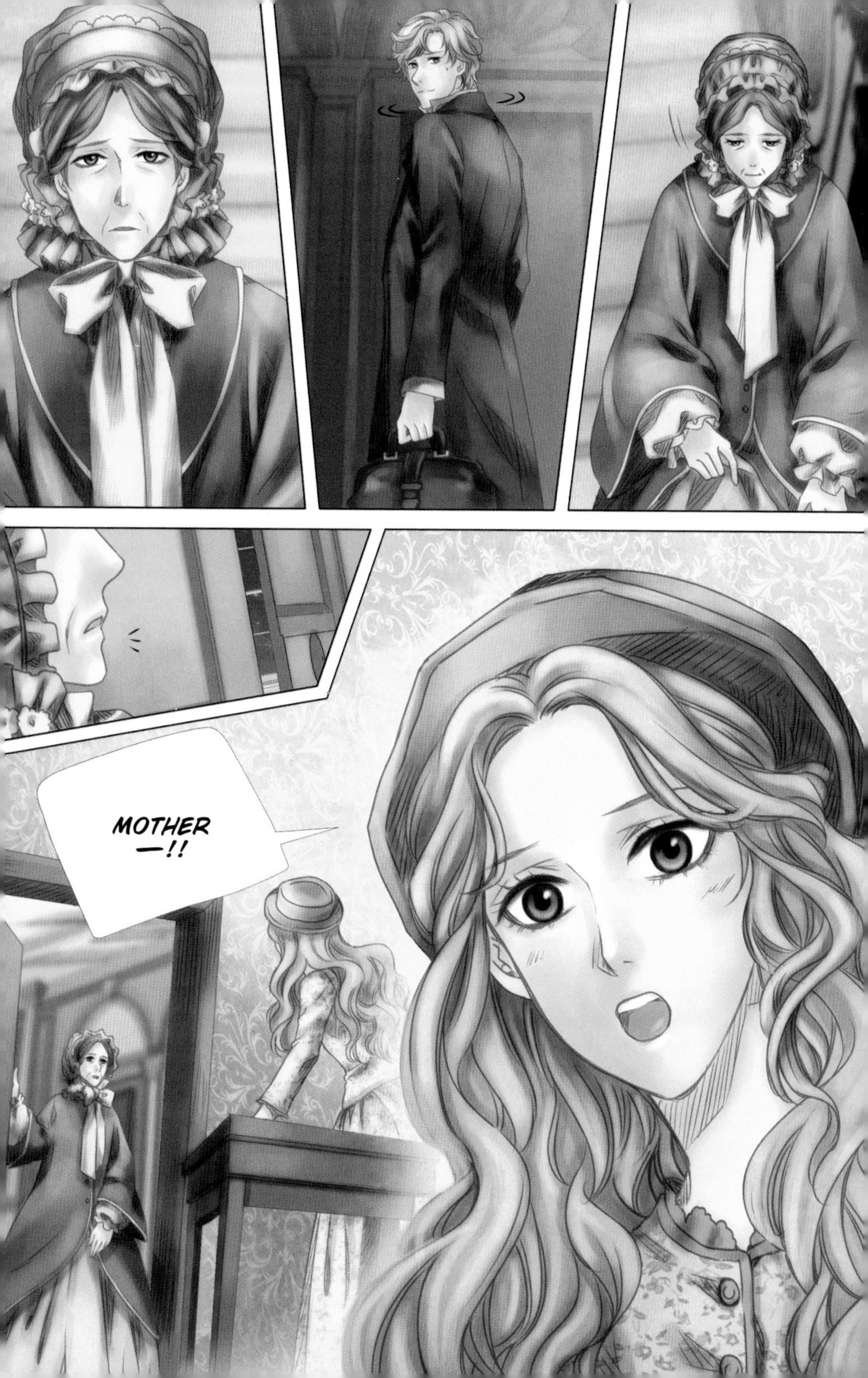
MOTHER
—!!

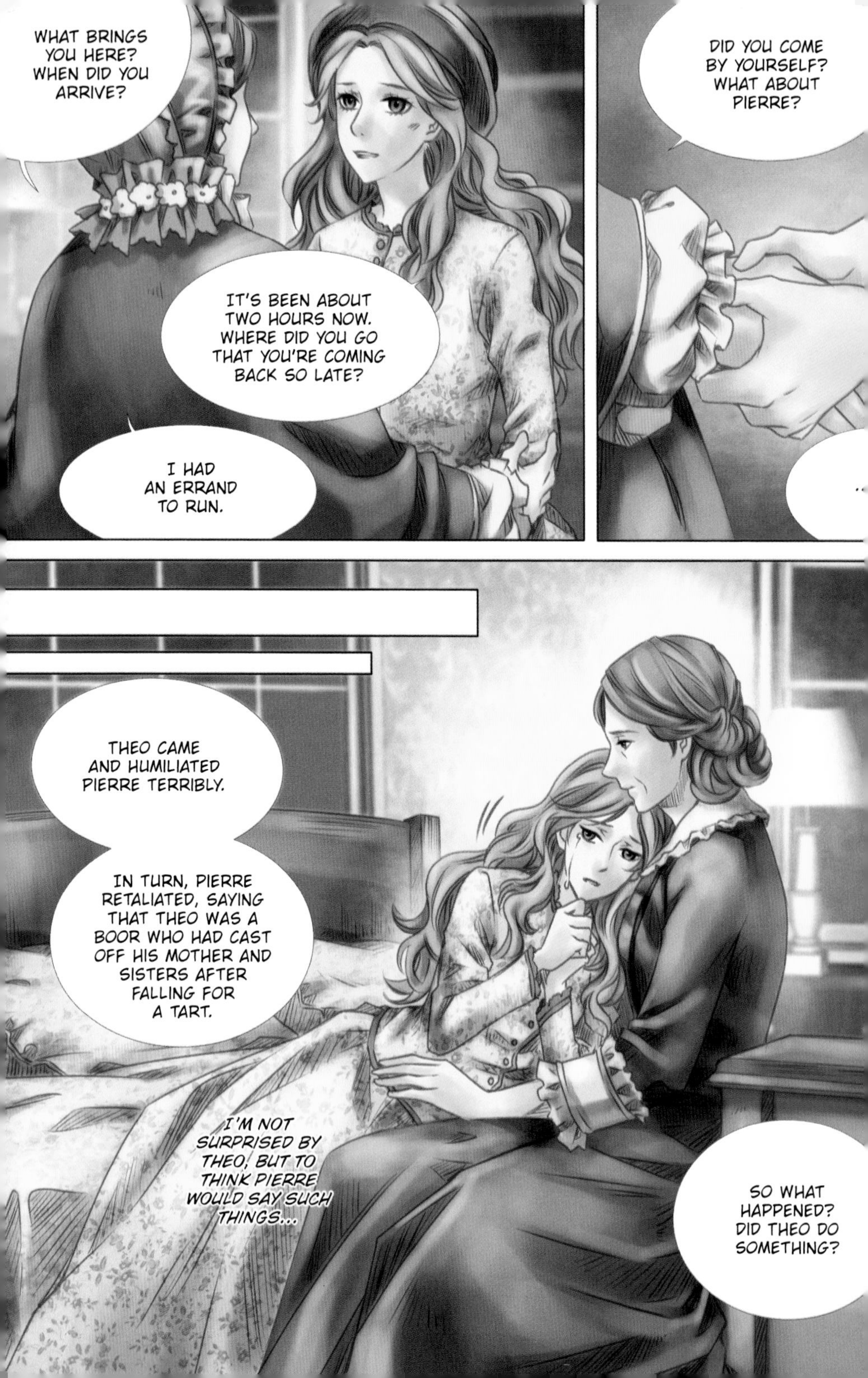
WHAT BRINGS YOU HERE? WHEN DID YOU ARRIVE?
IT'S BEEN ABOUT TWO HOURS NOW. WHERE DID YOU GO THAT YOU'RE COMING BACK SO LATE?
I HAD AN ERRAND TO RUN.
DID YOU COME BY YOURSELF? WHAT ABOUT PIERRE?
THEO CAME AND HUMILIATED PIERRE TERRIBLY.
IN TURN, PIERRE RETALIATED, SAYING THAT THEO WAS A BOOR WHO HAD CAST OFF HIS MOTHER AND SISTERS AFTER FALLING FOR A TART.
I'M NOT SURPRISED BY THEO, BUT TO THINK PIERRE WOULD SAY SUCH THINGS...
SO WHAT HAPPENED? DID THEO DO SOMETHING?

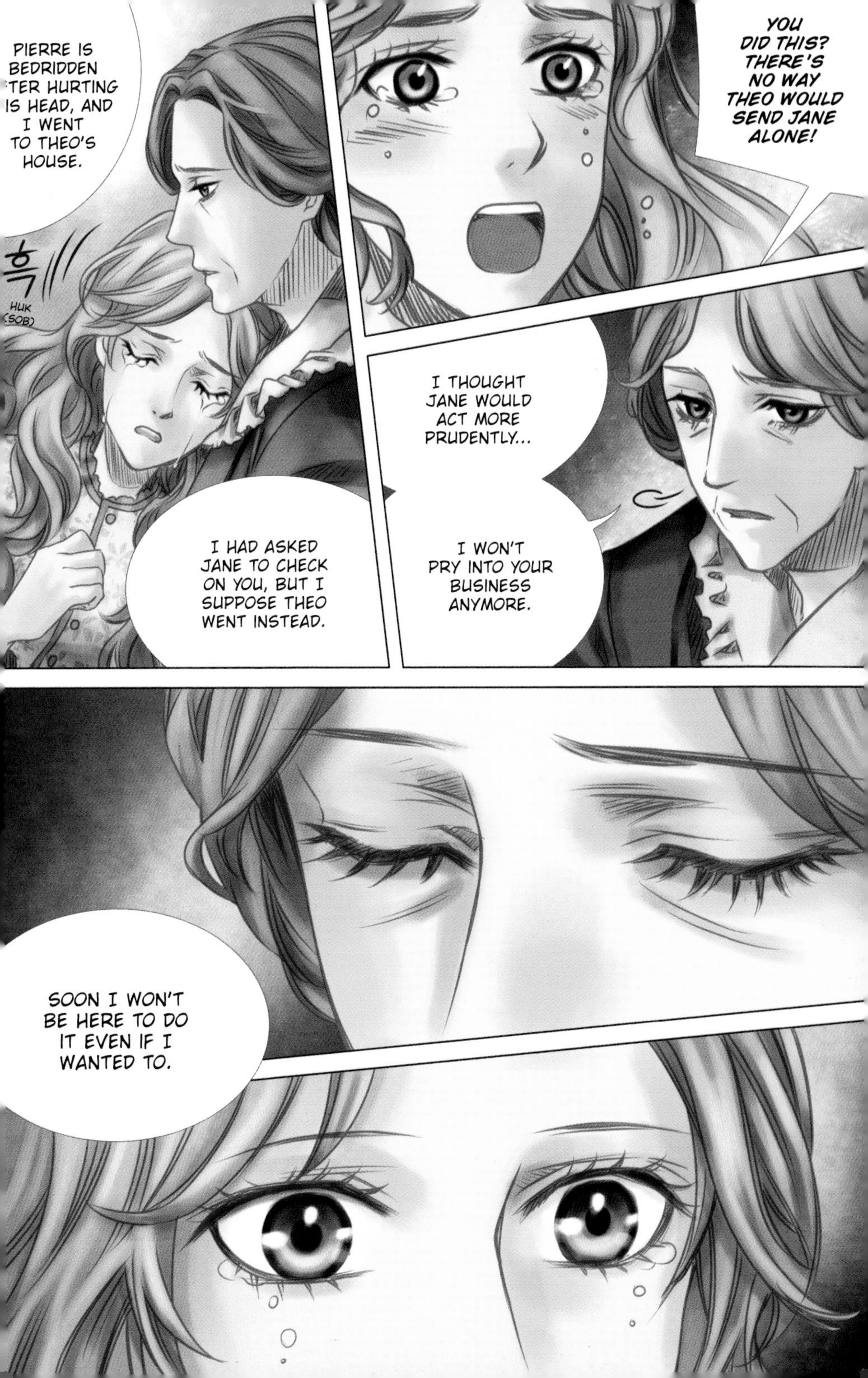
PIERRE IS BEDRIDDEN FTER HURTING IS HEAD, AND I WENT TO THEO'S HOUSE.
흑
HUK (SOB)
I HAD ASKED JANE TO CHECK ON YOU, BUT I SUPPOSE THEO WENT INSTEAD.
YOU DID THIS? THERE'S NO WAY THEO WOULD SEND JANE ALONE!
I THOUGHT JANE WOULD ACT MORE PRUDENTLY...
I WON'T PRY INTO YOUR BUSINESS ANYMORE.
SOON I WON'T BE HERE TO DO IT EVEN IF I WANTED TO.

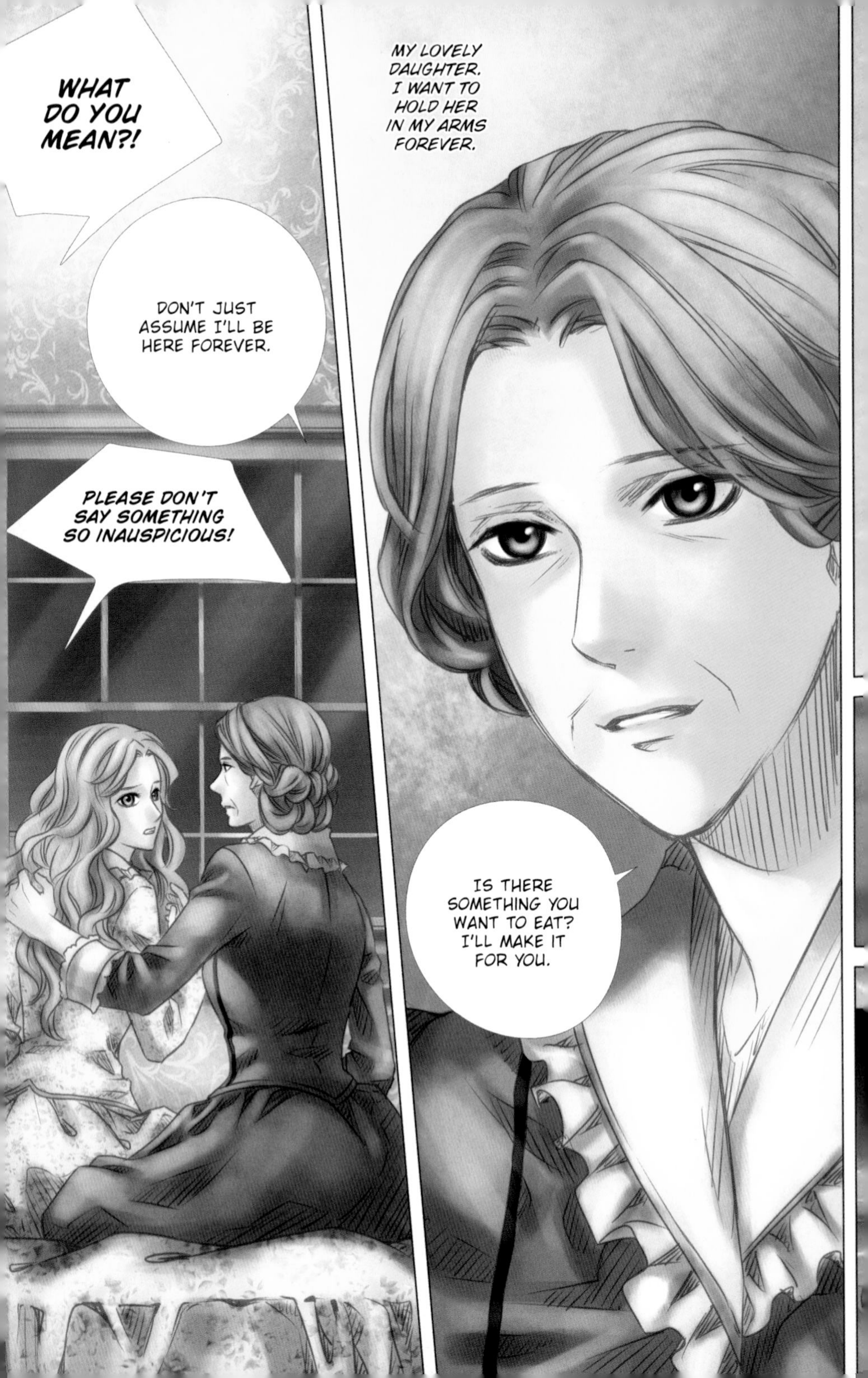
WHAT DO YOU MEAN?!
DON'T JUST ASSUME I'LL BE HERE FOREVER.
PLEASE DON'T SAY SOMETHING SO INAUSPICIOUS!
MY LOVELY DAUGHTER. I WANT TO HOLD HER IN MY ARMS FOREVER.
IS THERE SOMETHING YOU WANT TO EAT? I'LL MAKE IT FOR YOU.

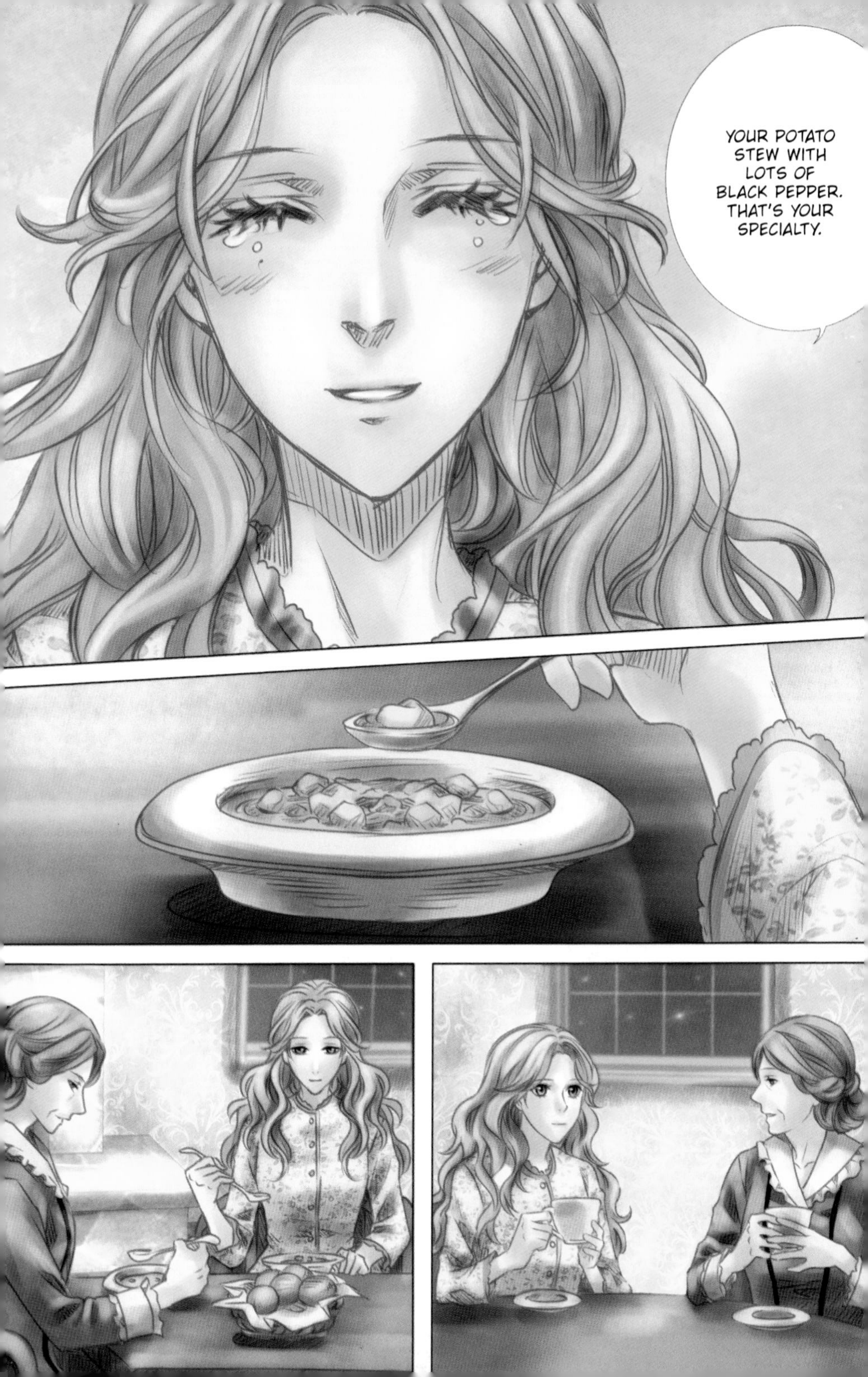
YOUR POTATO STEW WITH LOTS OF BLACK PEPPER. THAT'S YOUR SPECIALTY.

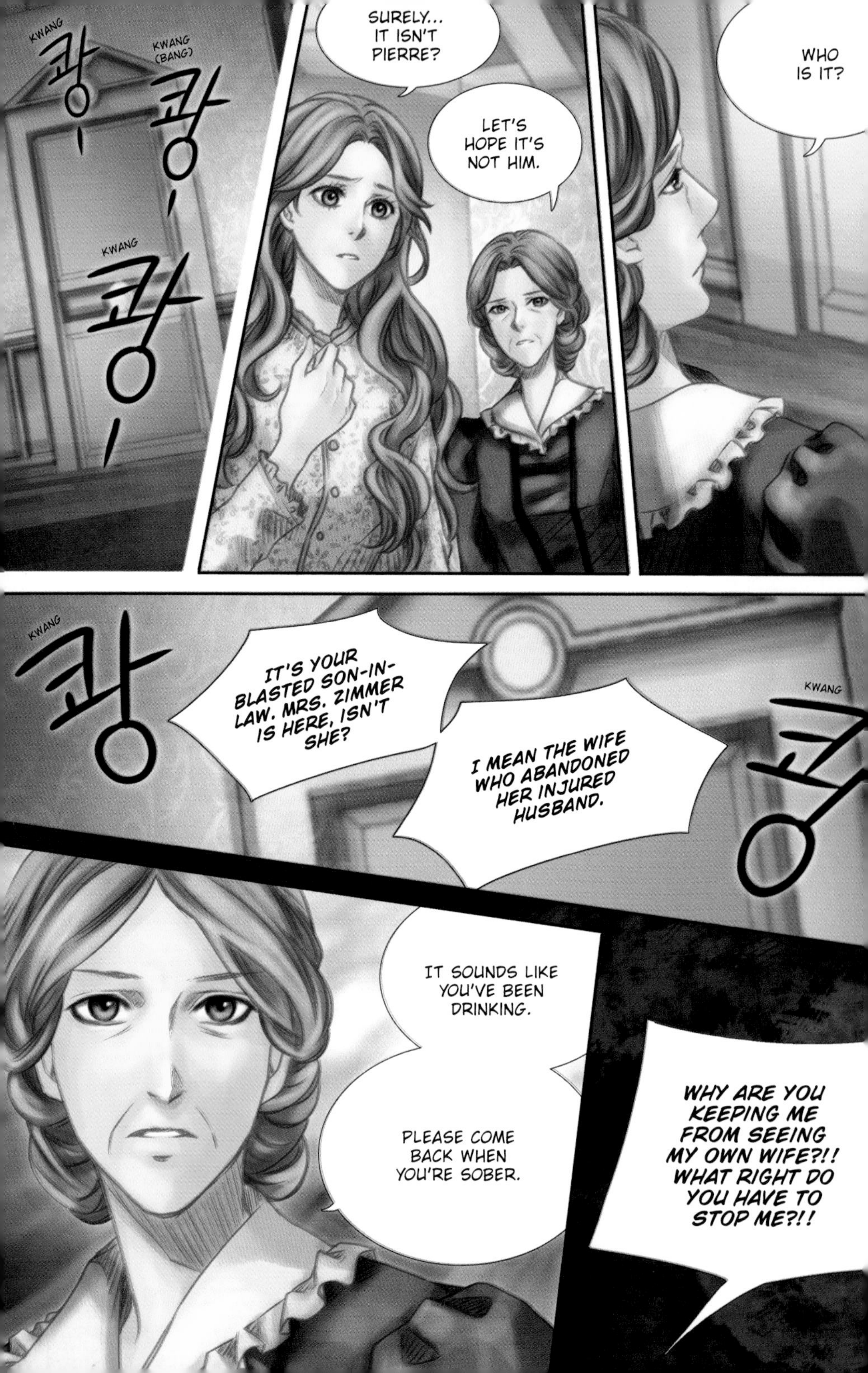
KWANG
KWANG (BANG)
KWANG
SURELY... IT ISN'T PIERRE?
LET'S HOPE IT'S NOT HIM.
WHO IS IT?
KWANG
IT'S YOUR BLASTED SON-IN-LAW. MRS. ZIMMER IS HERE, ISN'T SHE?
I MEAN THE WIFE WHO ABANDONED HER INJURED HUSBAND.
KWANG
IT SOUNDS LIKE YOU'VE BEEN DRINKING.
PLEASE COME BACK WHEN YOU'RE SOBER.
WHY ARE YOU KEEPING ME FROM SEEING MY OWN WIFE?!! WHAT RIGHT DO YOU HAVE TO STOP ME?!!

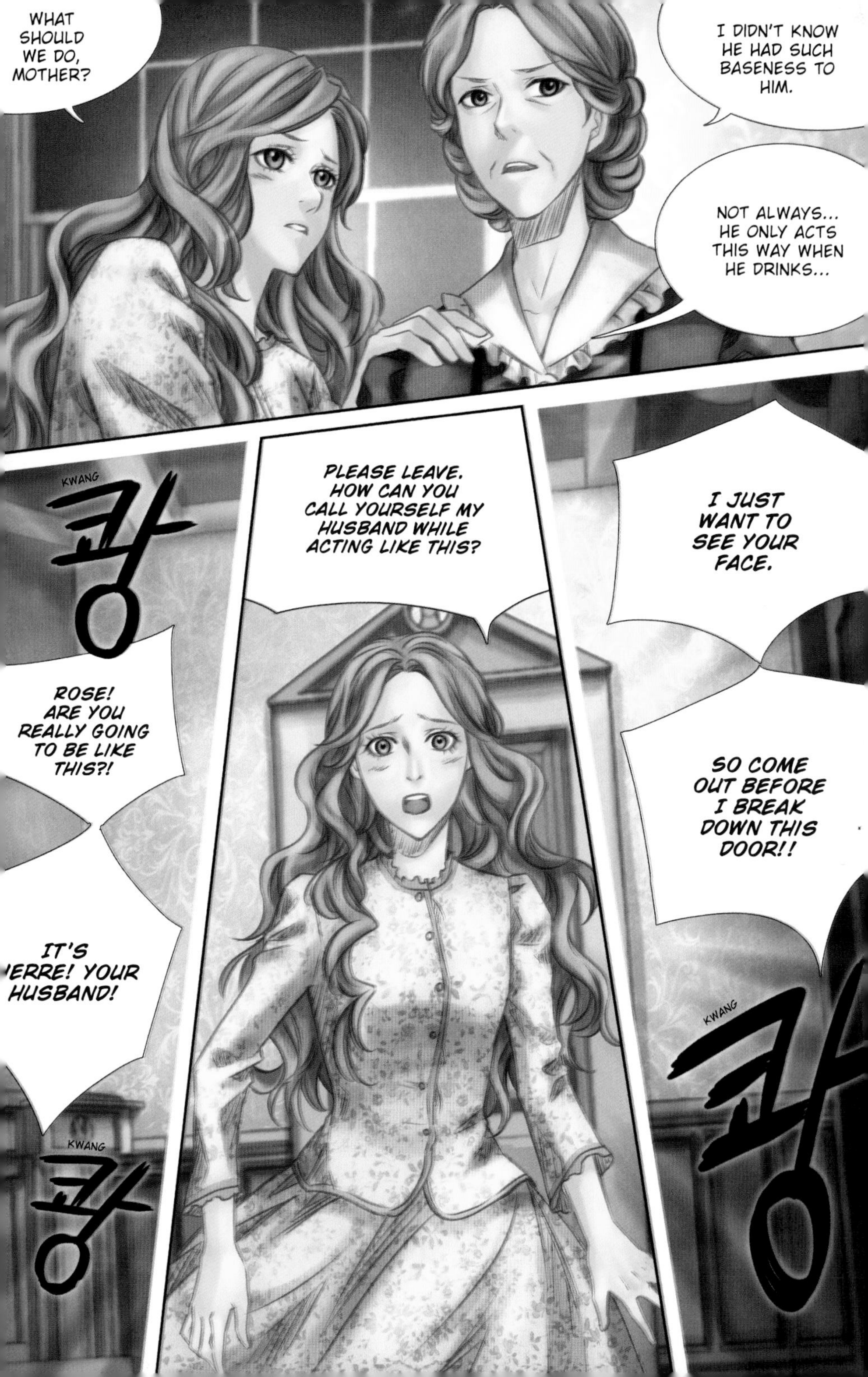
WHAT SHOULD WE DO, MOTHER?
I DIDN'T KNOW HE HAD SUCH BASENESS TO HIM.
NOT ALWAYS... HE ONLY ACTS THIS WAY WHEN HE DRINKS...
KWANG
ROSE! ARE YOU REALLY GOING TO BE LIKE THIS?!
IT'S 'ERRE! YOUR HUSBAND!
KWANG
PLEASE LEAVE. HOW CAN YOU CALL YOURSELF MY HUSBAND WHILE ACTING LIKE THIS?
I JUST WANT TO SEE YOUR FACE.
SO COME OUT BEFORE I BREAK DOWN THIS DOOR!!
KWANG

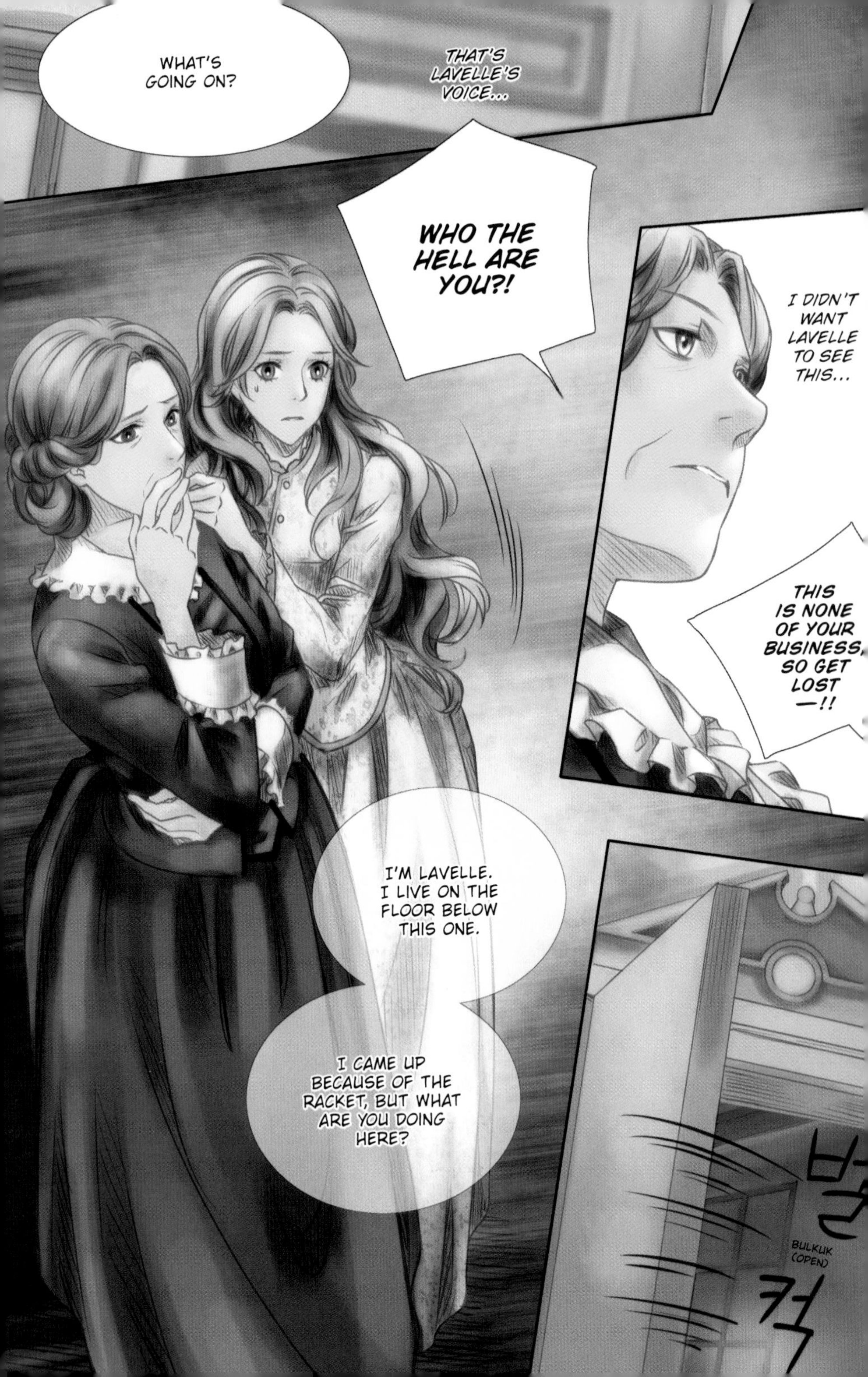
WHAT'S GOING ON?
THAT'S LAVELLE'S VOICE...
WHO THE HELL ARE YOU?!
I'M LAVELLE. I LIVE ON THE FLOOR BELOW THIS ONE.
I CAME UP BECAUSE OF THE RACKET, BUT WHAT ARE YOU DOING HERE?
I DIDN'T WANT LAVELLE TO SEE THIS...
THIS IS NONE OF YOUR BUSINESS, SO GET LOST—!!
벌컥
BULKUK (OPEN)

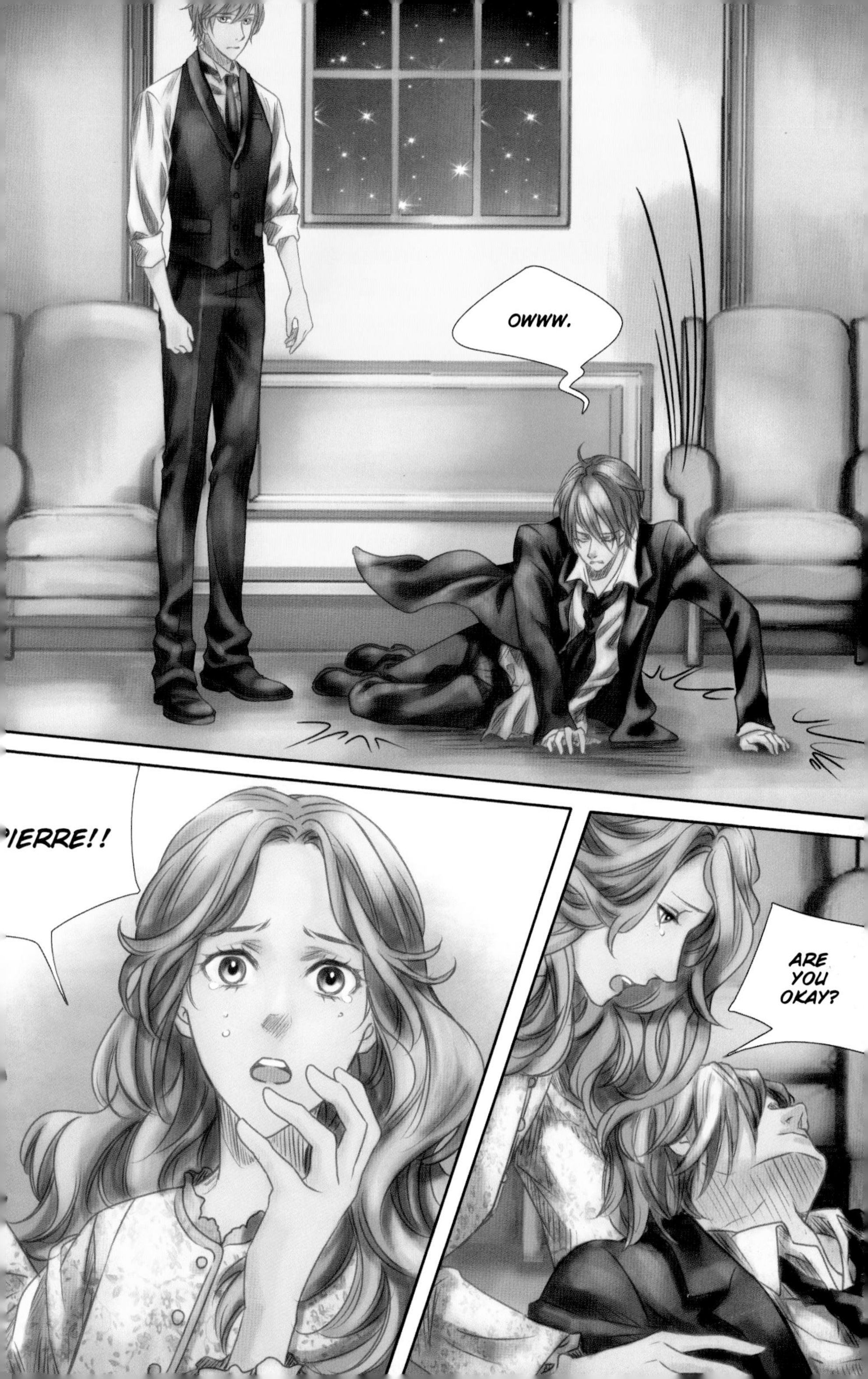
OWWW.
IERRE!!
ARE YOU OKAY?

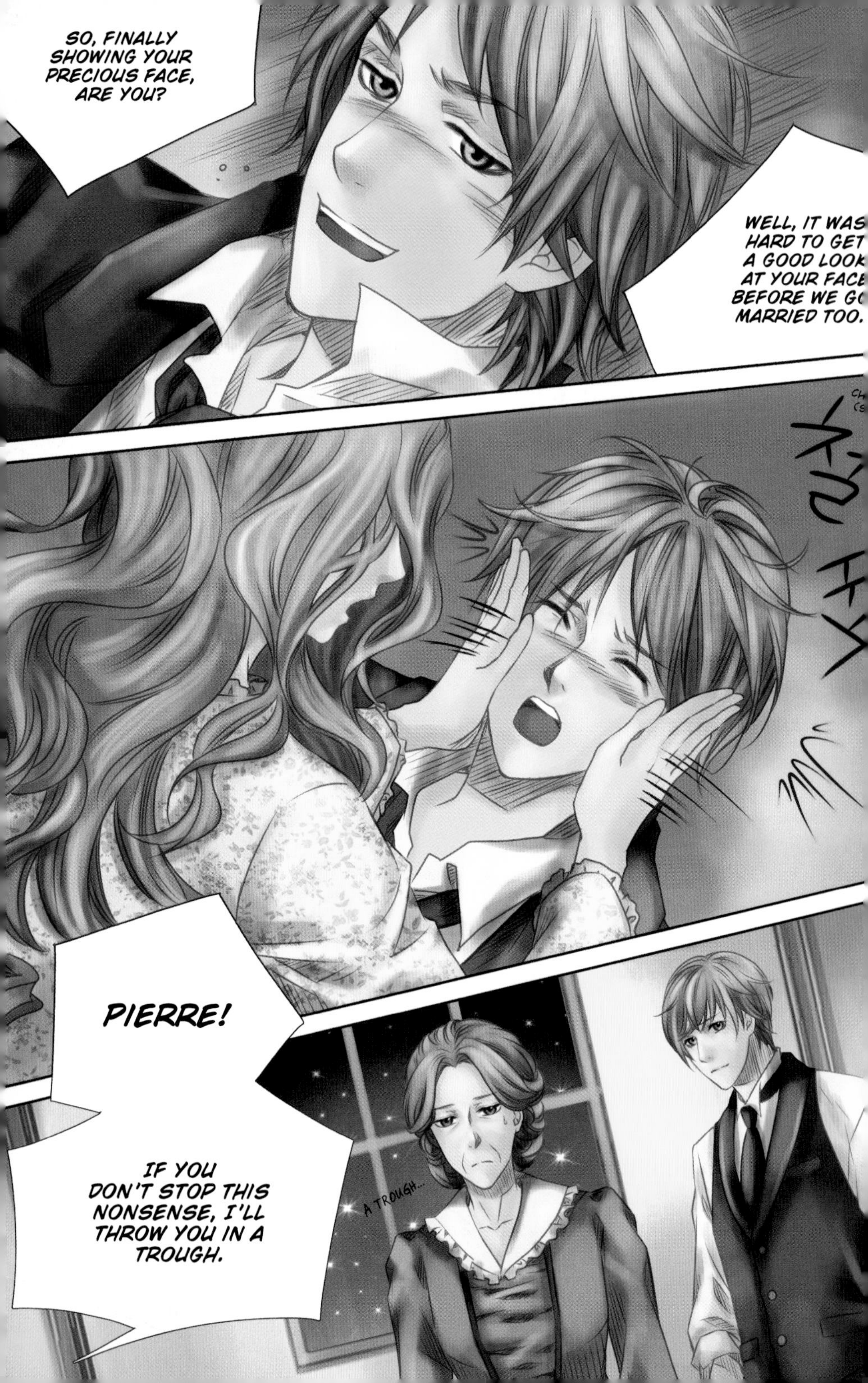
SO, FINALLY SHOWING YOUR PRECIOUS FACE, ARE YOU?
WELL, IT WAS HARD TO GET A GOOD LOOK AT YOUR FACE BEFORE WE GO MARRIED TOO.
PIERRE!
IF YOU DON'T STOP THIS NONSENSE, I'LL THROW YOU IN A TROUGH.
A TROUGH...

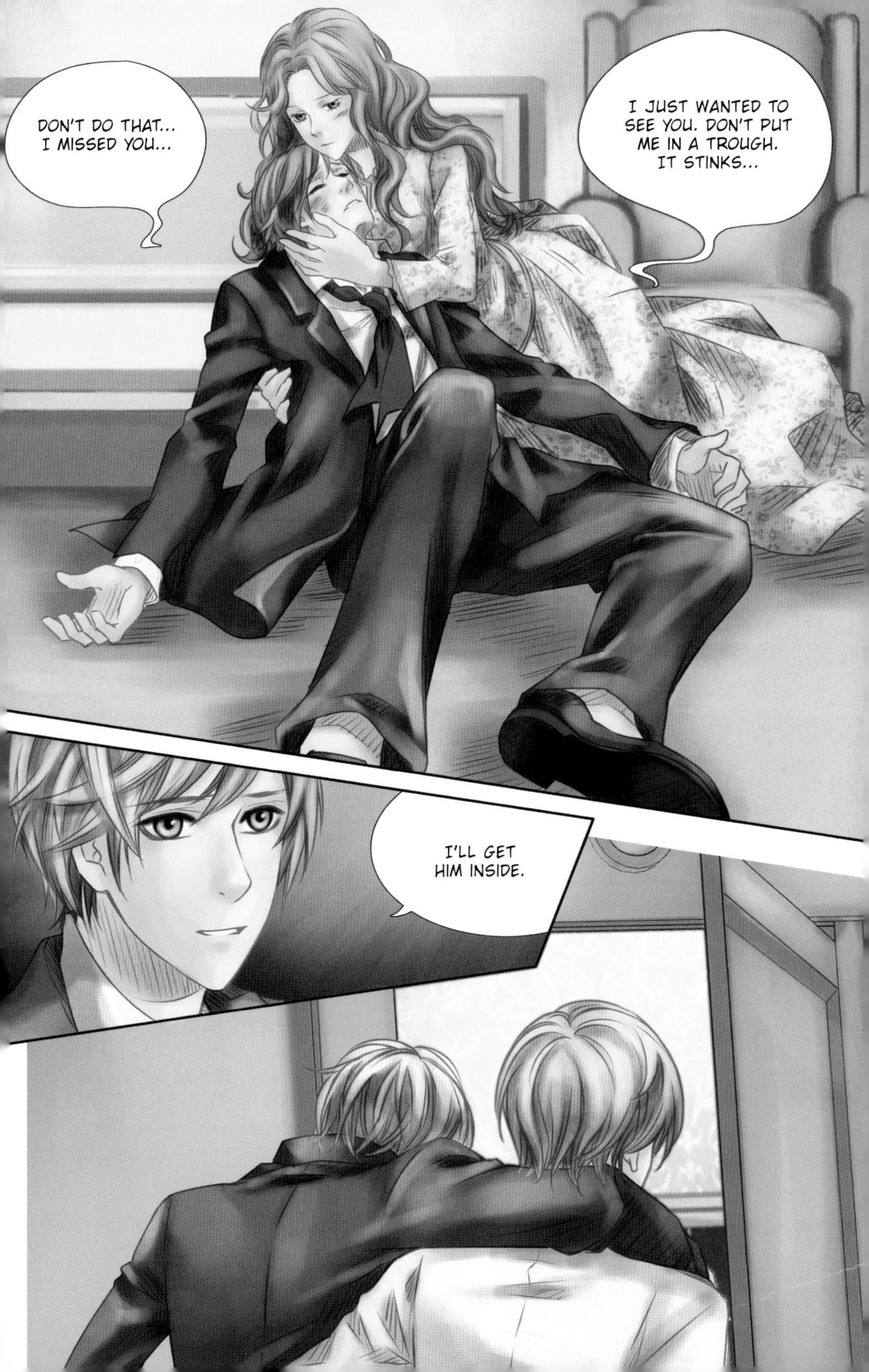
DON'T DO THAT... I MISSED YOU...
I JUST WANTED TO SEE YOU. DON'T PUT ME IN A TROUGH. IT STINKS...
I'LL GET HIM INSIDE.

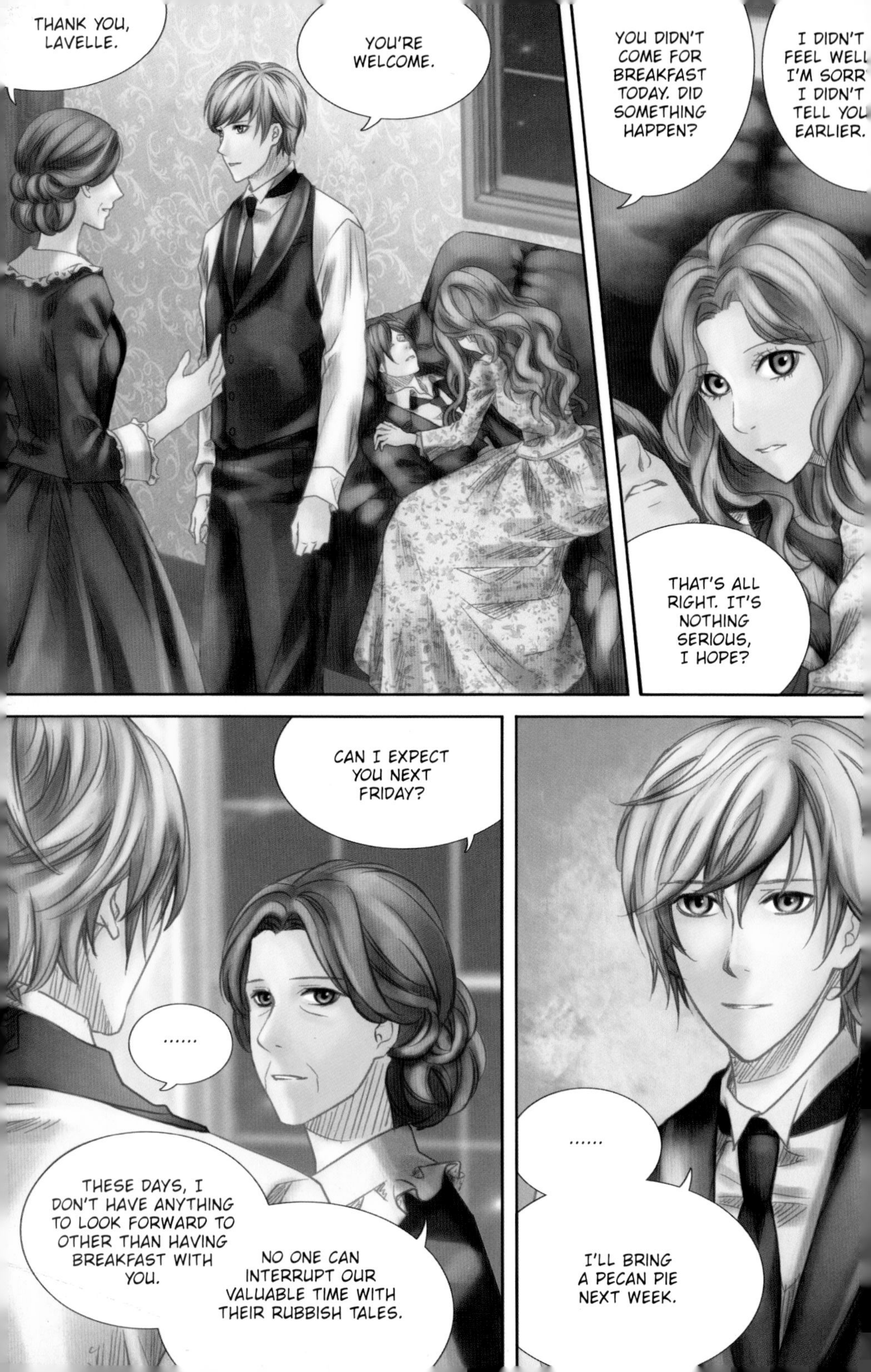

THANK YOU, LAVELLE.
YOU'RE WELCOME.
YOU DIDN'T COME FOR BREAKFAST TODAY. DID SOMETHING HAPPEN?
I DIDN'T FEEL WELL. I'M SORRY I DIDN'T TELL YOU EARLIER.
THAT'S ALL RIGHT. IT'S NOTHING SERIOUS, I HOPE?
CAN I EXPECT YOU NEXT FRIDAY?
......
THESE DAYS, I DON'T HAVE ANYTHING TO LOOK FORWARD TO OTHER THAN HAVING BREAKFAST WITH YOU.
NO ONE CAN INTERRUPT OUR VALUABLE TIME WITH THEIR RUBBISH TALES.
......
I'LL BRING A PECAN PIE NEXT WEEK.

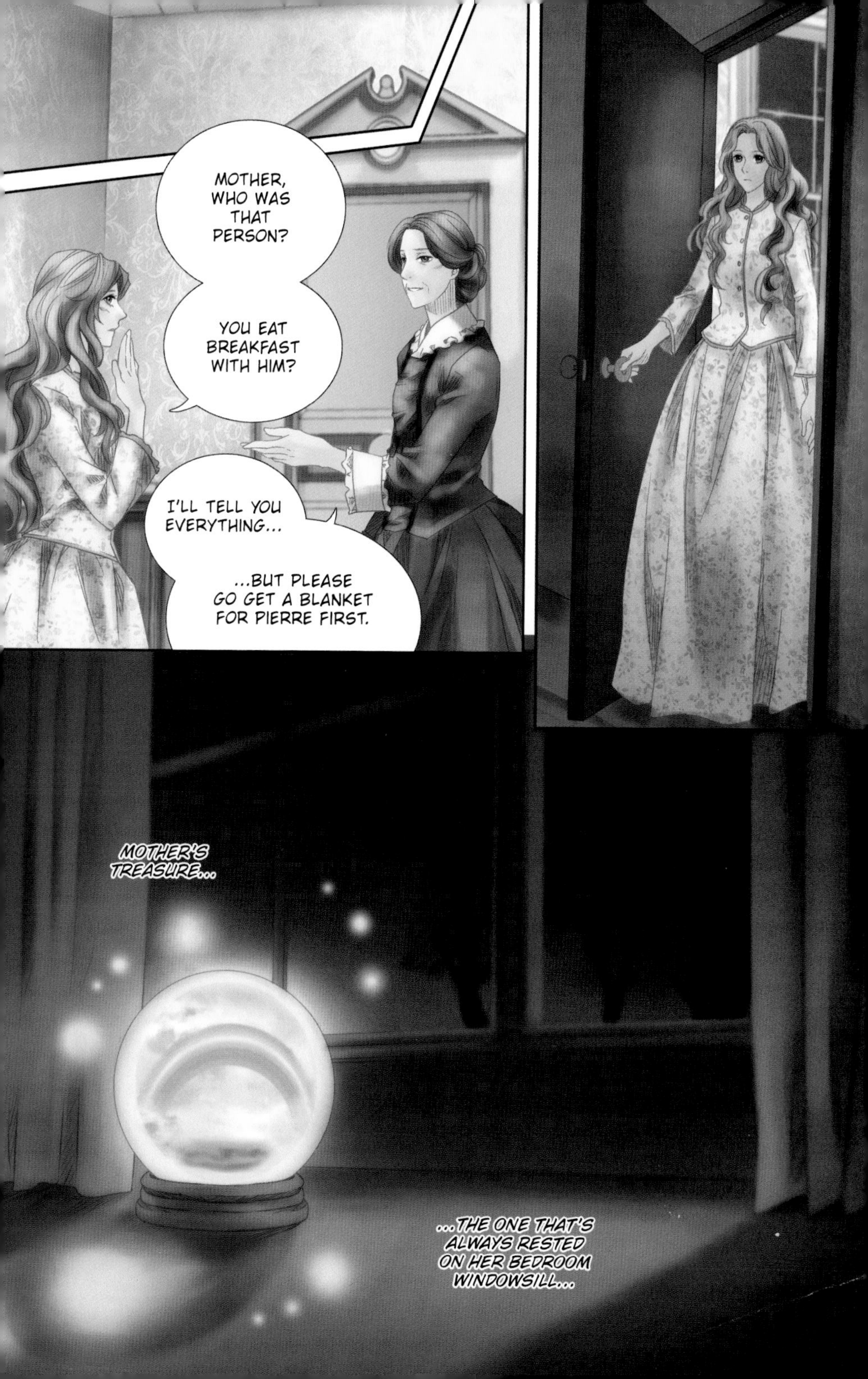
MOTHER, WHO WAS THAT PERSON?
YOU EAT BREAKFAST WITH HIM?
I'LL TELL YOU EVERYTHING...
...BUT PLEASE GO GET A BLANKET FOR PIERRE FIRST.
MOTHER'S TREASURE...
...THE ONE THAT'S ALWAYS RESTED ON HER BEDROOM WINDOWSILL...

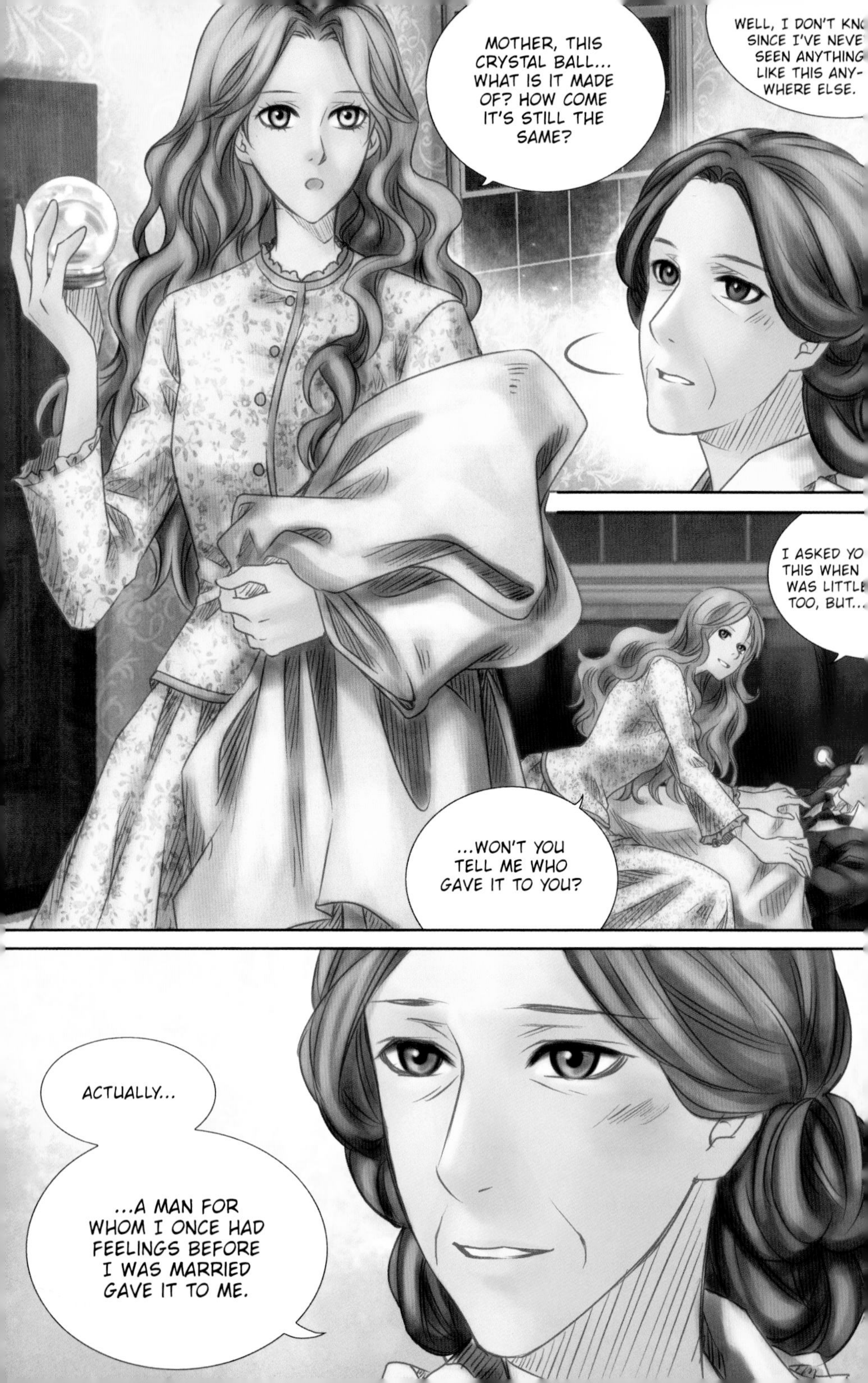
MOTHER, THIS CRYSTAL BALL... WHAT IS IT MADE OF? HOW COME IT'S STILL THE SAME?
WELL, I DON'T KN SINCE I'VE NEVE SEEN ANYTHING LIKE THIS ANY-WHERE ELSE.
I ASKED YO THIS WHEN WAS LITTL TOO, BUT...
...WON'T YOU TELL ME WHO GAVE IT TO YOU?
ACTUALLY...
...A MAN FOR WHOM I ONCE HAD FEELINGS BEFORE I WAS MARRIED GAVE IT TO ME.

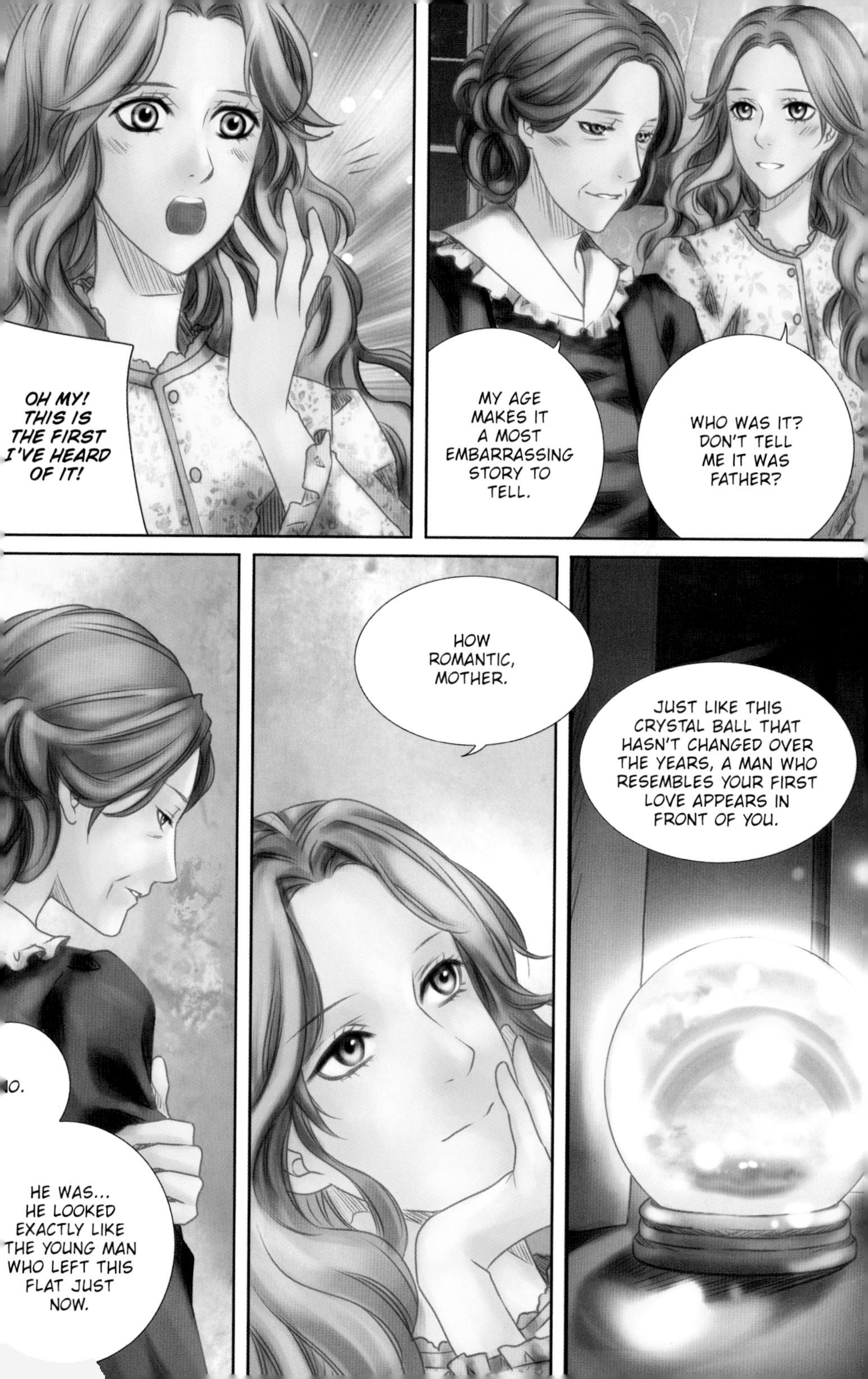
OH MY! THIS IS THE FIRST I'VE HEARD OF IT!
MY AGE MAKES IT A MOST EMBARRASSING STORY TO TELL.
WHO WAS IT? DON'T TELL ME IT WAS FATHER?
HE WAS... HE LOOKED EXACTLY LIKE THE YOUNG MAN WHO LEFT THIS FLAT JUST NOW.
HOW ROMANTIC, MOTHER.
JUST LIKE THIS CRYSTAL BALL THAT HASN'T CHANGED OVER THE YEARS, A MAN WHO RESEMBLES YOUR FIRST LOVE APPEARS IN FRONT OF YOU.

AHEM, AHEM...

THANK YOU SO MUCH FOR LETTING ME SPEND THE NIGHT, MRS. AUDREY.

WE'LL TAKE OUR LEAVE NOW.

I'LL VISIT YOU AGAIN, MOTHER.

IT'S BEST TO PRETE... I DON'T REMEMBE WHAT HAPPENED LAS NIGHT...

...YES, PLEASE DO.

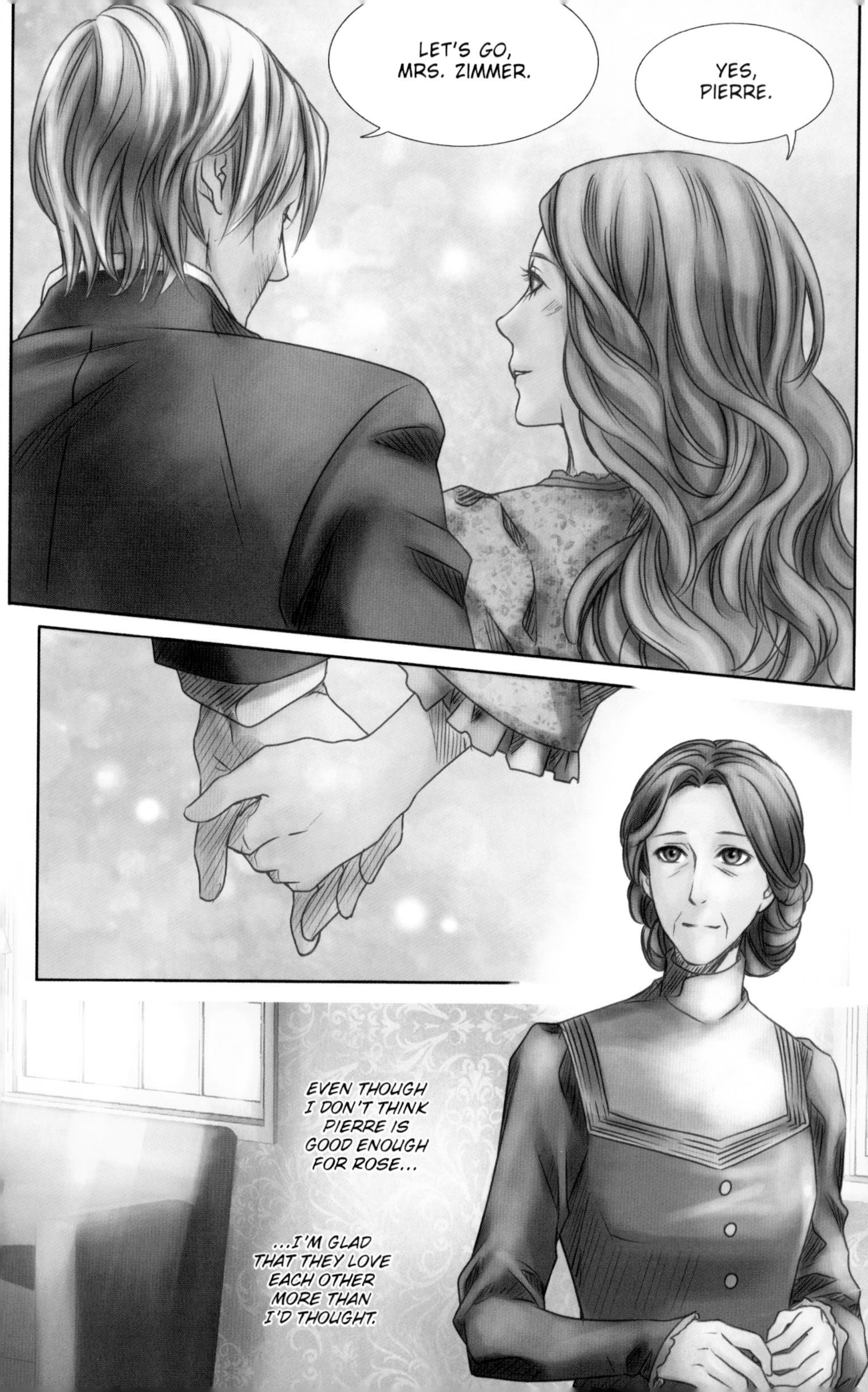
LET'S GO, MRS. ZIMMER.
YES, PIERRE.
EVEN THOUGH I DON'T THINK PIERRE IS GOOD ENOUGH FOR ROSE...
...I'M GLAD THAT THEY LOVE EACH OTHER MORE THAN I'D THOUGHT.

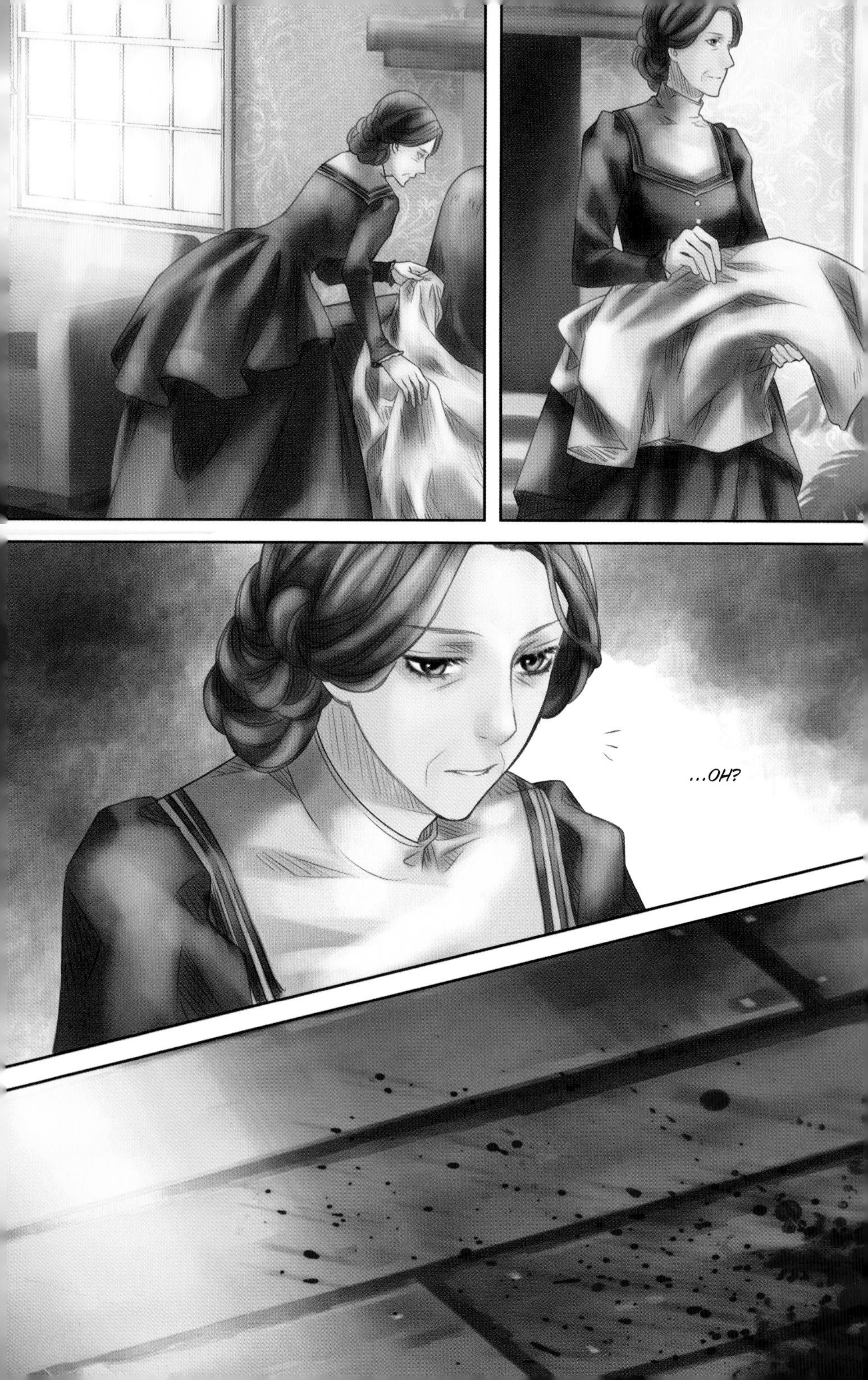
...OH?

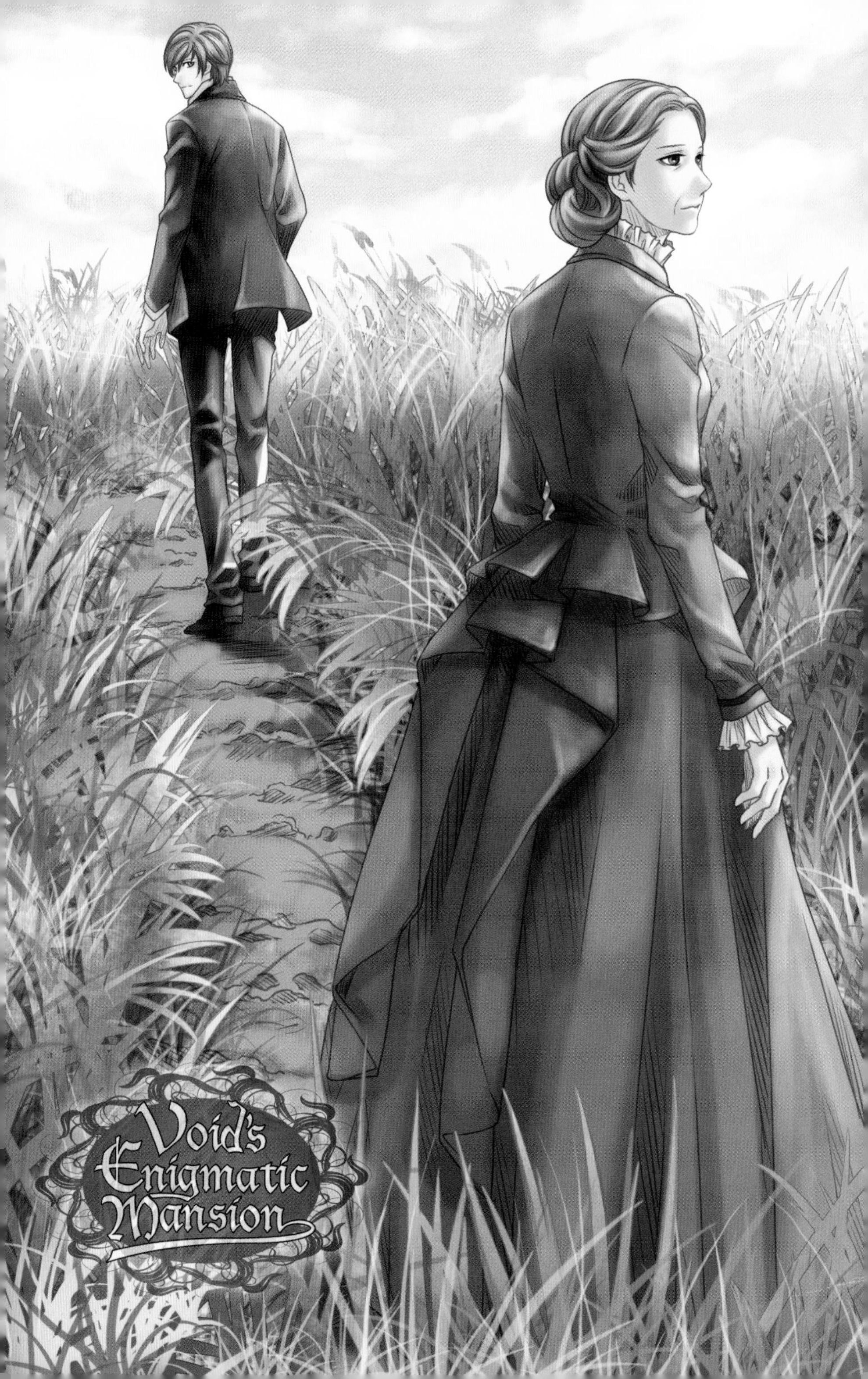
Void's Enigmatic Mansion

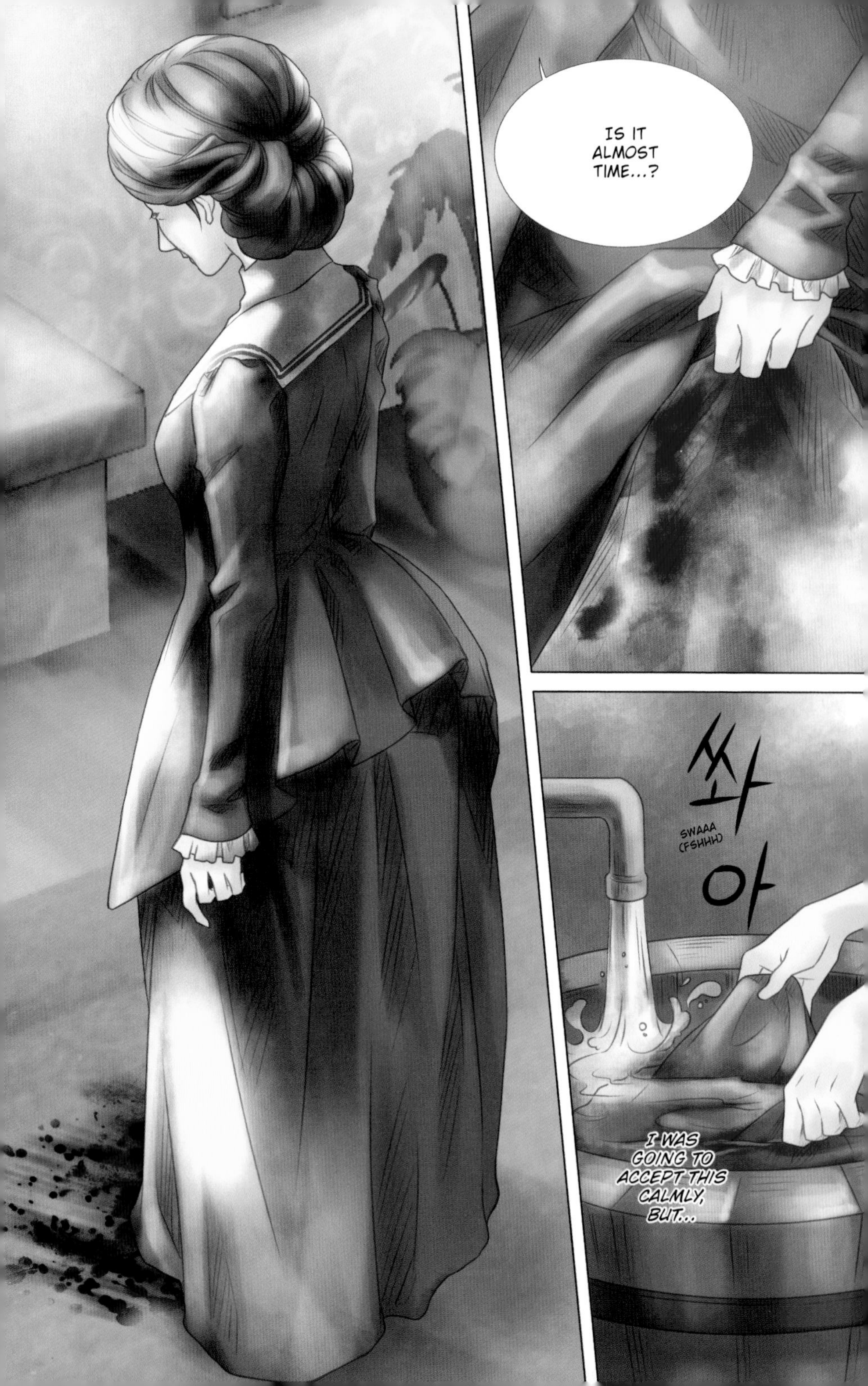
IS IT ALMOST TIME...?
쏴아
SWAAA (FSHHH)
I WAS GOING TO ACCEPT THIS CALMLY, BUT...

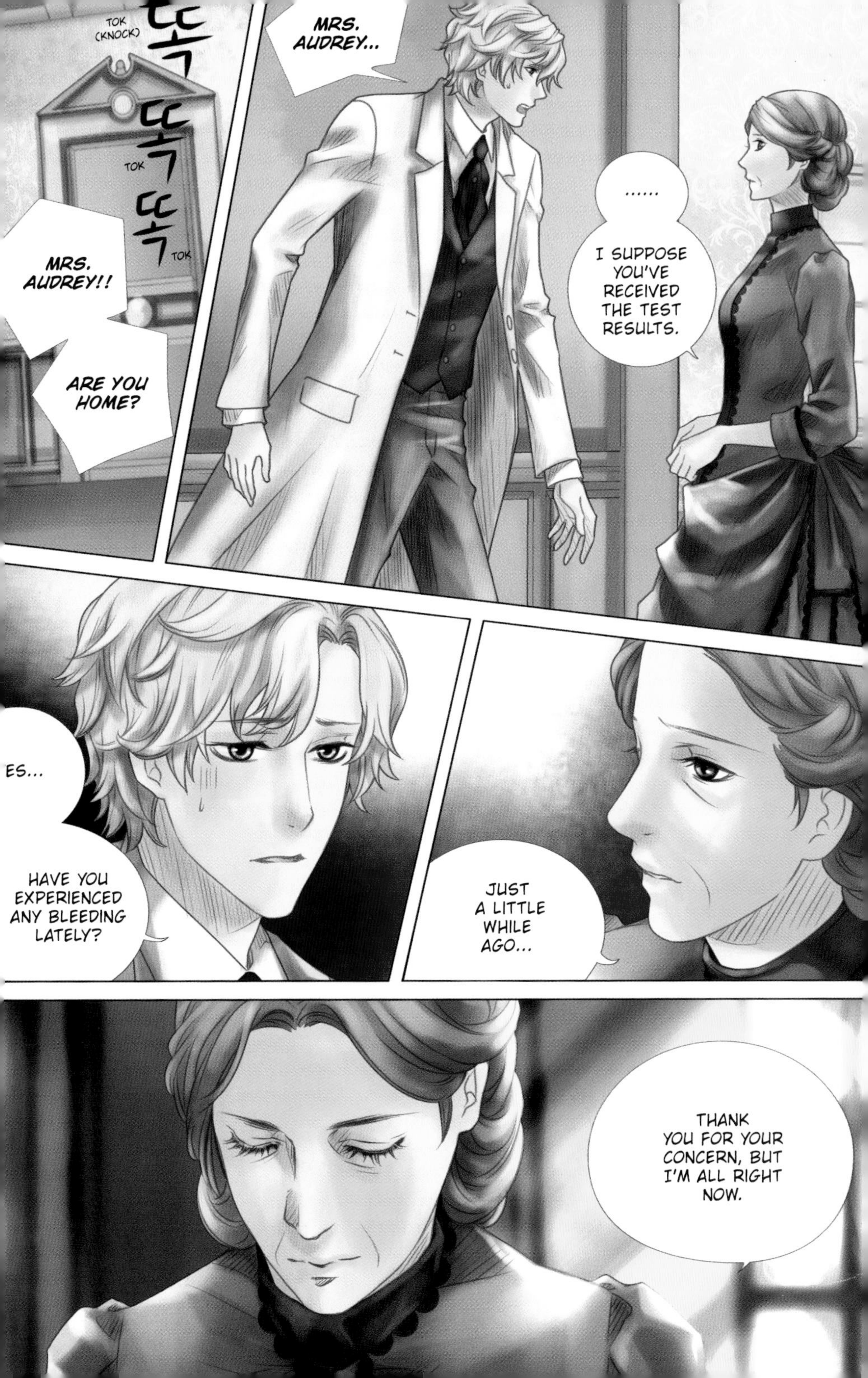
똑
TOK (KNOCK)
똑
TOK
똑
TOK
MRS. AUDREY!!
ARE YOU HOME?
MRS. AUDREY...
......
I SUPPOSE YOU'VE RECEIVED THE TEST RESULTS.
ES...
HAVE YOU EXPERIENCED ANY BLEEDING LATELY?
JUST A LITTLE WHILE AGO...
THANK YOU FOR YOUR CONCERN, BUT I'M ALL RIGHT NOW.

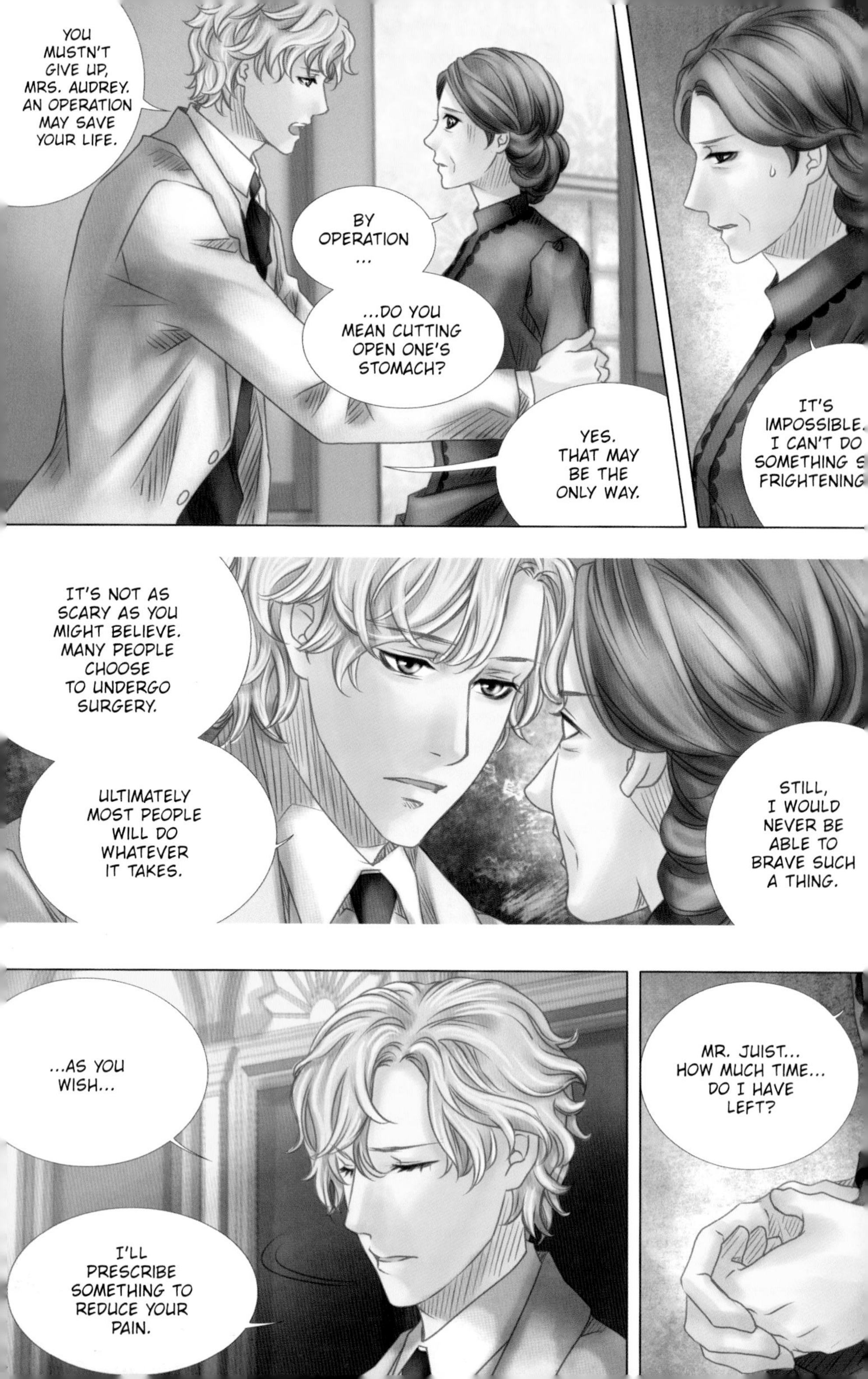
YOU MUSTN'T GIVE UP, MRS. AUDREY. AN OPERATION MAY SAVE YOUR LIFE.
BY OPERATION ...
...DO YOU MEAN CUTTING OPEN ONE'S STOMACH?
YES. THAT MAY BE THE ONLY WAY.
IT'S IMPOSSIBLE. I CAN'T DO SOMETHING S FRIGHTENING
IT'S NOT AS SCARY AS YOU MIGHT BELIEVE. MANY PEOPLE CHOOSE TO UNDERGO SURGERY.
ULTIMATELY MOST PEOPLE WILL DO WHATEVER IT TAKES.
STILL, I WOULD NEVER BE ABLE TO BRAVE SUCH A THING.
...AS YOU WISH...
I'LL PRESCRIBE SOMETHING TO REDUCE YOUR PAIN.
MR. JUIST... HOW MUCH TIME... DO I HAVE LEFT?

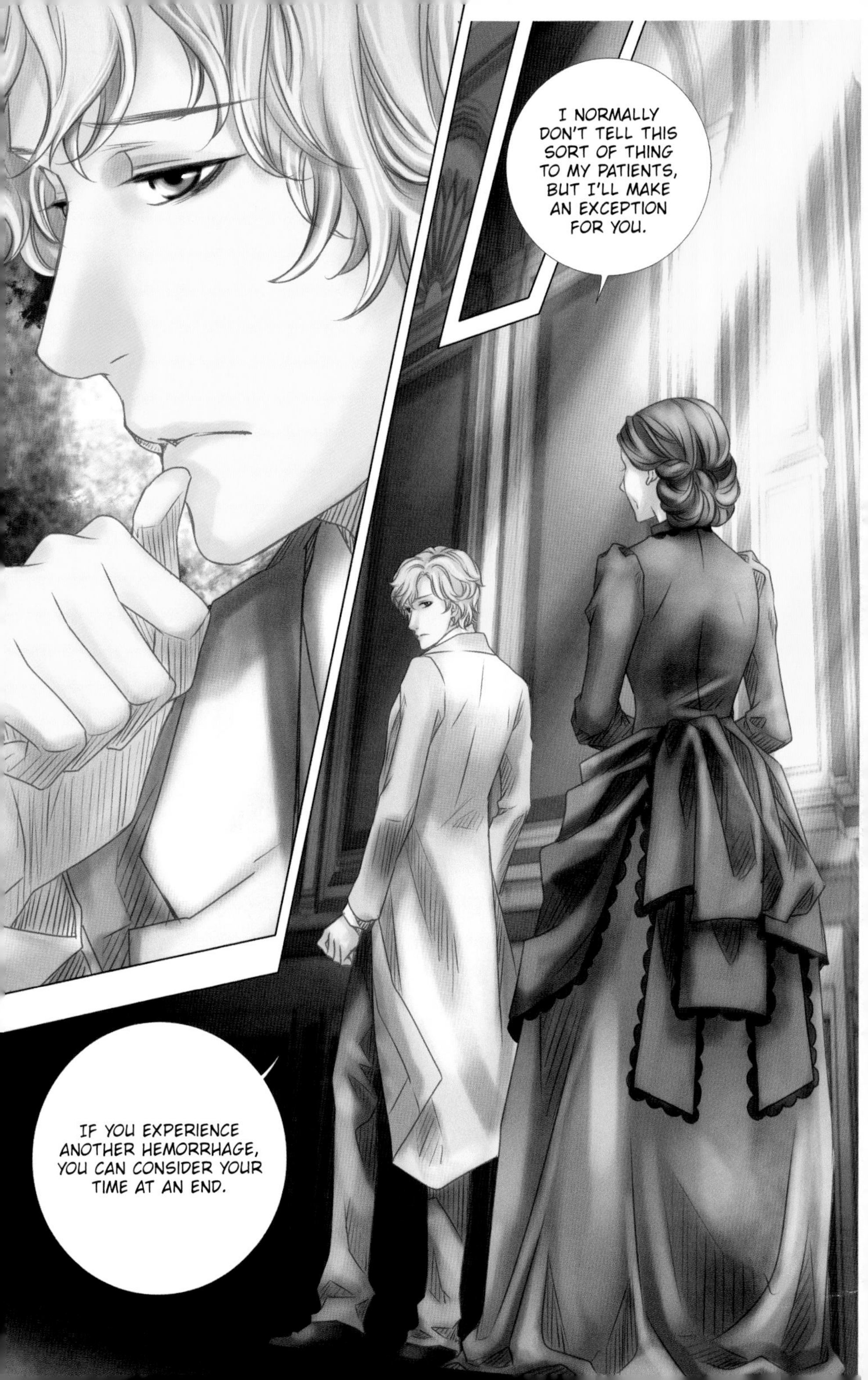
I NORMALLY DON'T TELL THIS SORT OF THING TO MY PATIENTS, BUT I'LL MAKE AN EXCEPTION FOR YOU.
IF YOU EXPERIENCE ANOTHER HEMORRHAGE, YOU CAN CONSIDER YOUR TIME AT AN END.

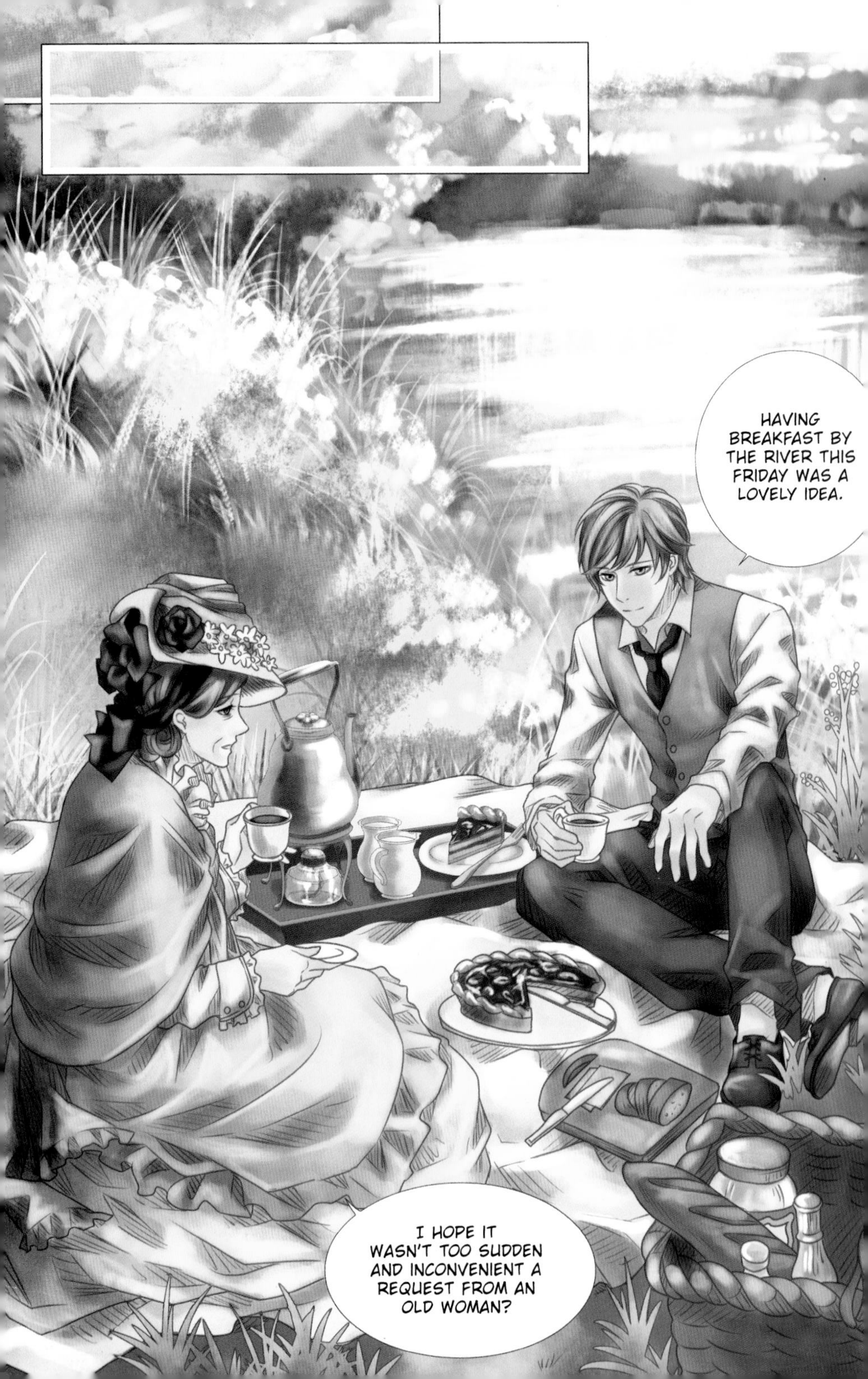
HAVING BREAKFAST BY THE RIVER THIS FRIDAY WAS A LOVELY IDEA.
I HOPE IT WASN'T TOO SUDDEN AND INCONVENIENT A REQUEST FROM AN OLD WOMAN?

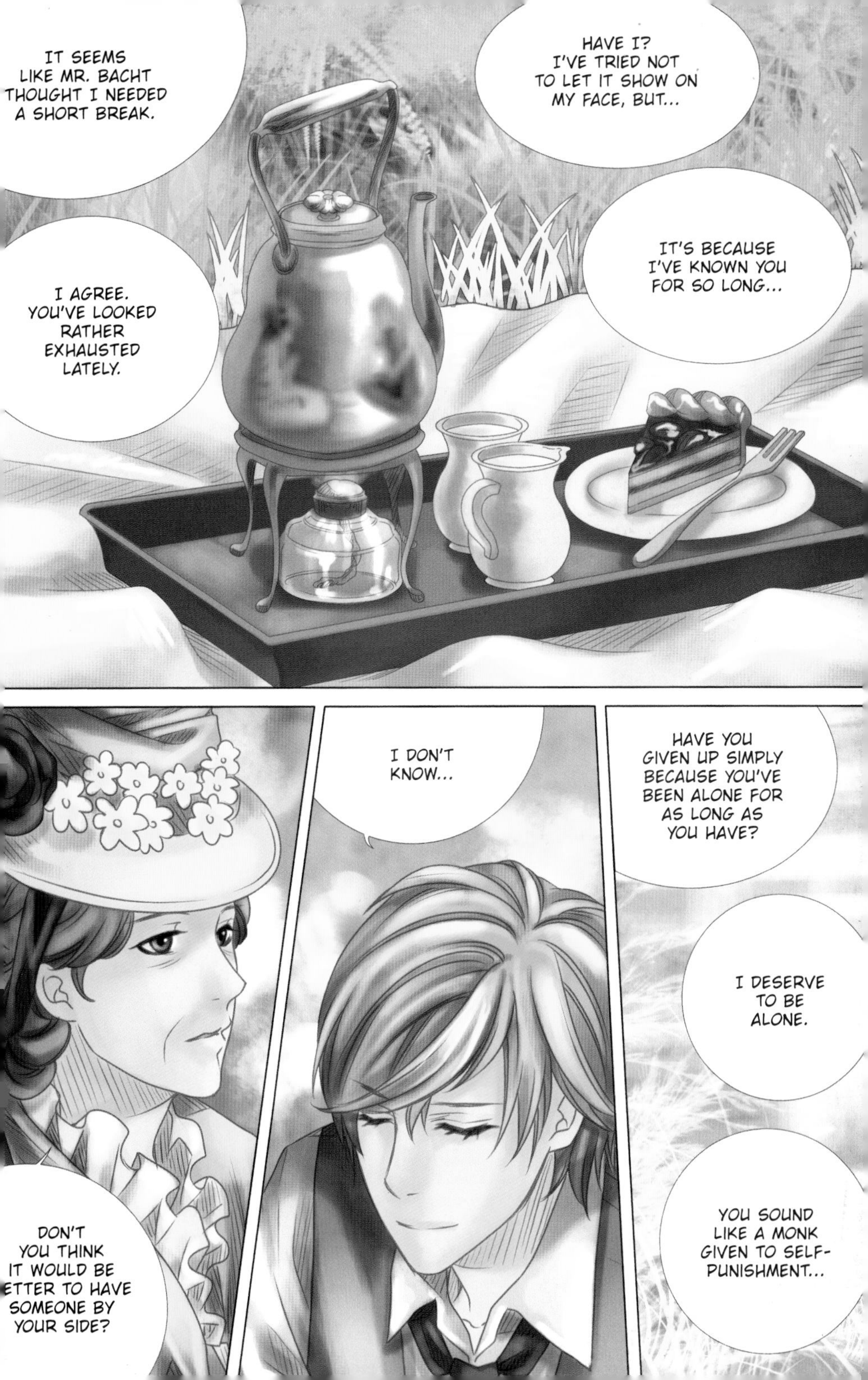
IT SEEMS LIKE MR. BACHT THOUGHT I NEEDED A SHORT BREAK.
I AGREE. YOU'VE LOOKED RATHER EXHAUSTED LATELY.
HAVE I? I'VE TRIED NOT TO LET IT SHOW ON MY FACE, BUT...
IT'S BECAUSE I'VE KNOWN YOU FOR SO LONG...
DON'T YOU THINK IT WOULD BE ETTER TO HAVE SOMEONE BY YOUR SIDE?
I DON'T KNOW...
HAVE YOU GIVEN UP SIMPLY BECAUSE YOU'VE BEEN ALONE FOR AS LONG AS YOU HAVE?
I DESERVE TO BE ALONE.
YOU SOUND LIKE A MONK GIVEN TO SELF-PUNISHMENT...

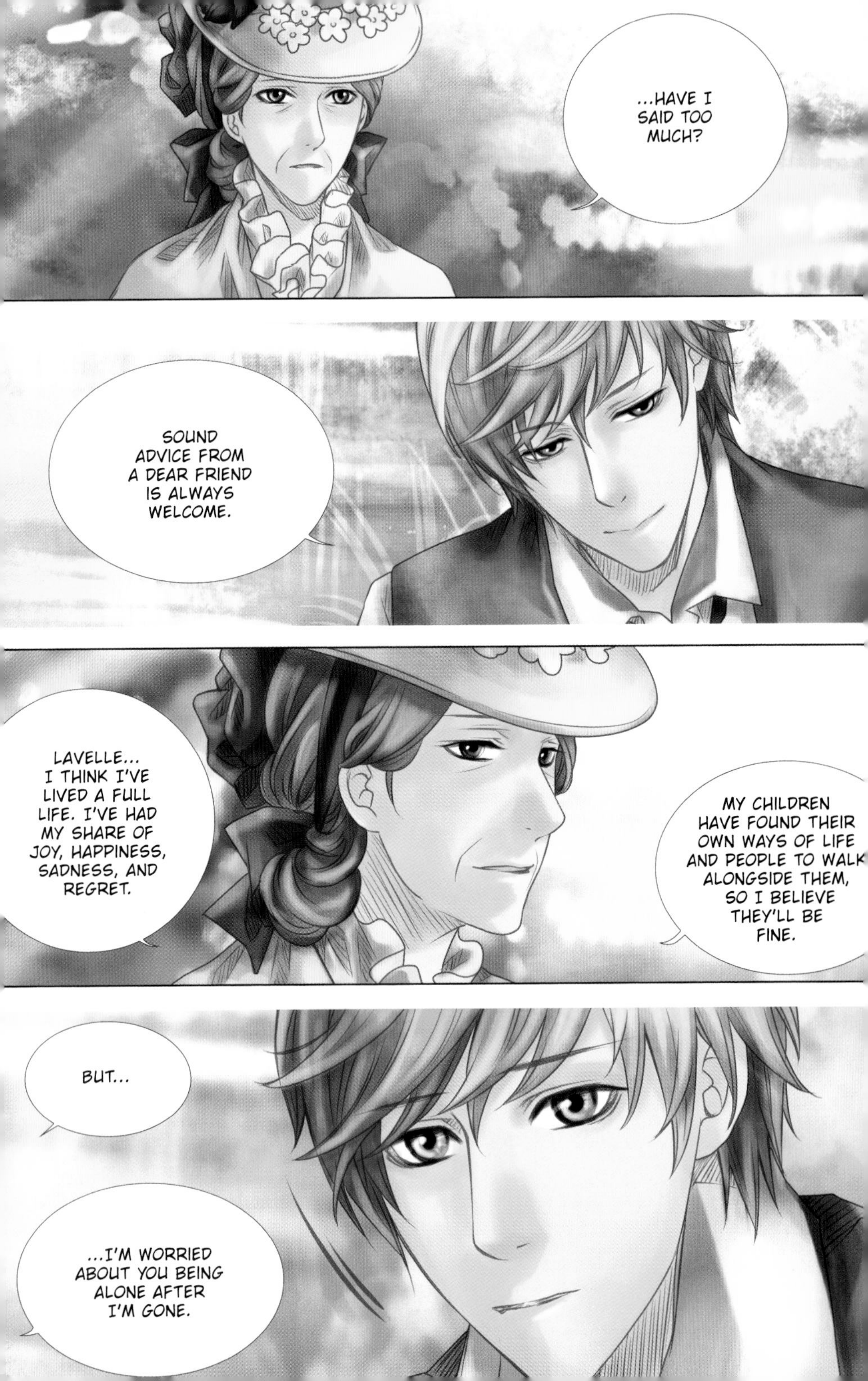
...HAVE I SAID TOO MUCH?
SOUND ADVICE FROM A DEAR FRIEND IS ALWAYS WELCOME.
LAVELLE... I THINK I'VE LIVED A FULL LIFE. I'VE HAD MY SHARE OF JOY, HAPPINESS, SADNESS, AND REGRET.
MY CHILDREN HAVE FOUND THEIR OWN WAYS OF LIFE AND PEOPLE TO WALK ALONGSIDE THEM, SO I BELIEVE THEY'LL BE FINE.
BUT...
...I'M WORRIED ABOUT YOU BEING ALONE AFTER I'M GONE.

I'M GOING
TO DIE SOON,
LAVELLE.

NO...

IS
THERE...
NOTHING
THAT CAN
BE DONE?

MR. JUIST
SAYS I DON'T
HAVE MUCH
TIME LEFT.
I FEEL IT
TOO.

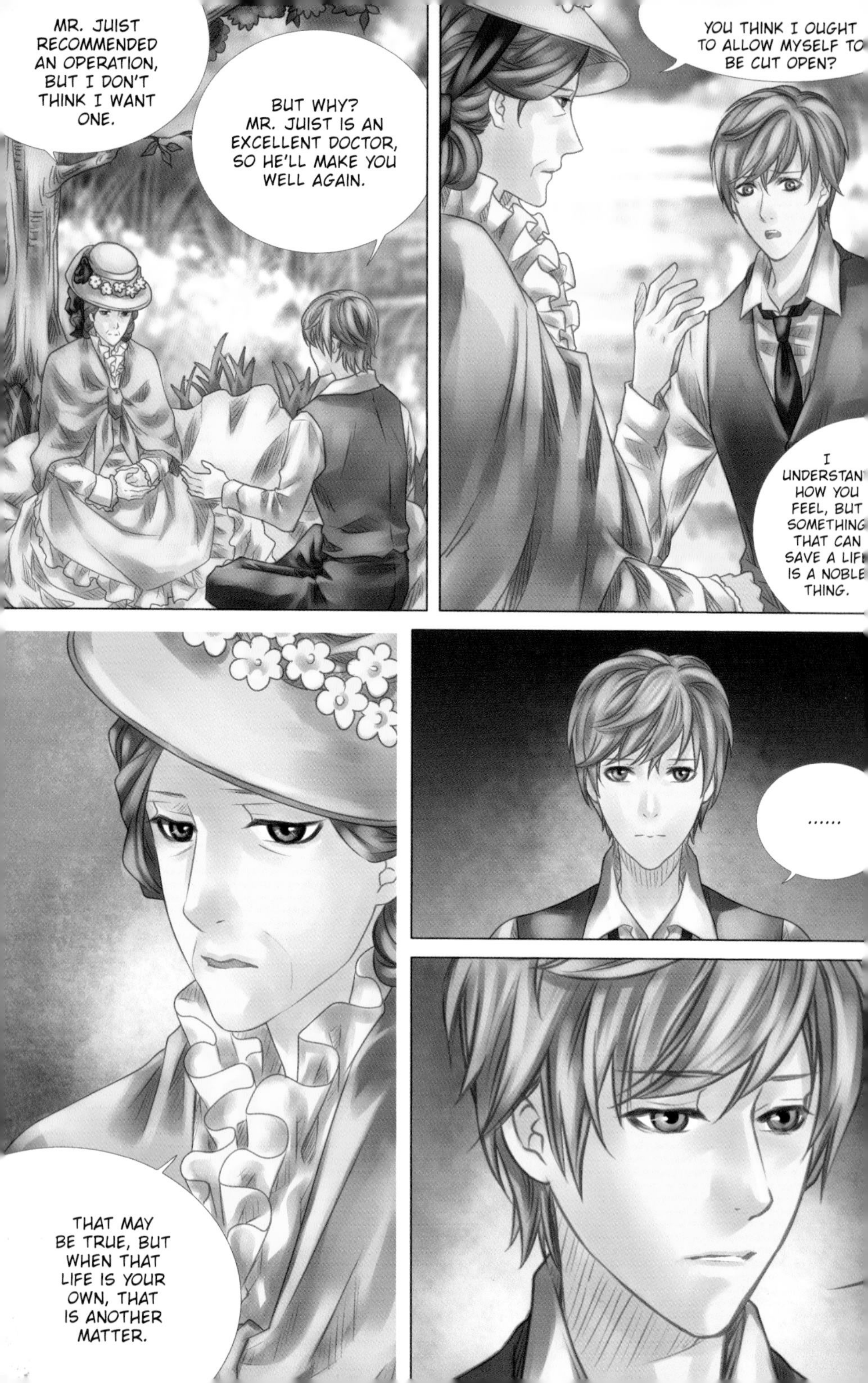
MR. JUIST RECOMMENDED AN OPERATION, BUT I DON'T THINK I WANT ONE.
BUT WHY? MR. JUIST IS AN EXCELLENT DOCTOR, SO HE'LL MAKE YOU WELL AGAIN.
YOU THINK I OUGHT TO ALLOW MYSELF TO BE CUT OPEN?
I UNDERSTAN HOW YOU FEEL, BUT SOMETHING THAT CAN SAVE A LIF IS A NOBLE THING.
THAT MAY BE TRUE, BUT WHEN THAT LIFE IS YOUR OWN, THAT IS ANOTHER MATTER.
......

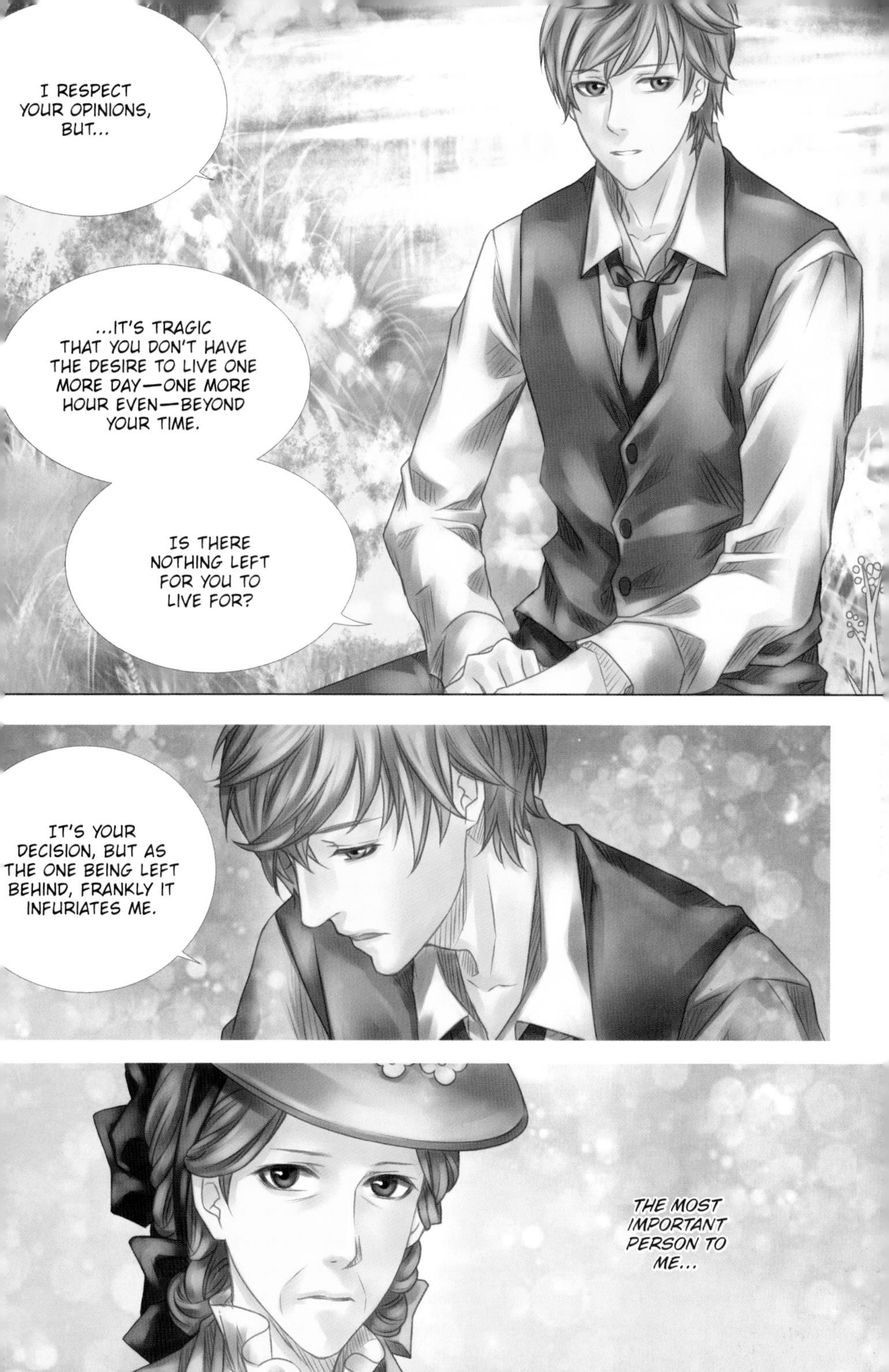
I RESPECT YOUR OPINIONS, BUT...
...IT'S TRAGIC THAT YOU DON'T HAVE THE DESIRE TO LIVE ONE MORE DAY—ONE MORE HOUR EVEN—BEYOND YOUR TIME.
IS THERE NOTHING LEFT FOR YOU TO LIVE FOR?
IT'S YOUR DECISION, BUT AS THE ONE BEING LEFT BEHIND, FRANKLY IT INFURIATES ME.
THE MOST IMPORTANT PERSON TO ME...

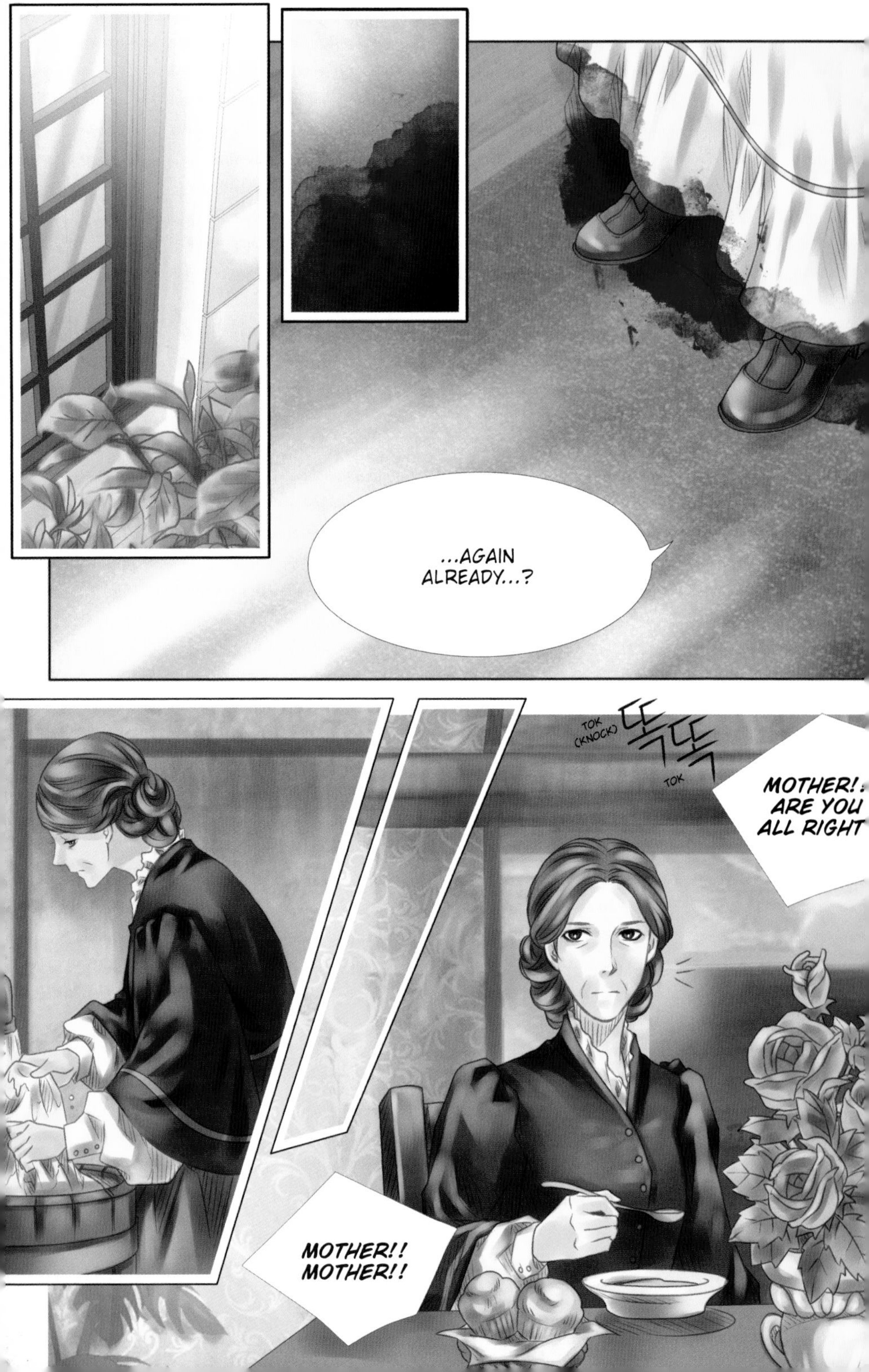
...AGAIN ALREADY...?
TOK (KNOCK) 똑똑 TOK
MOTHER!! ARE YOU ALL RIGHT
MOTHER!! MOTHER!!

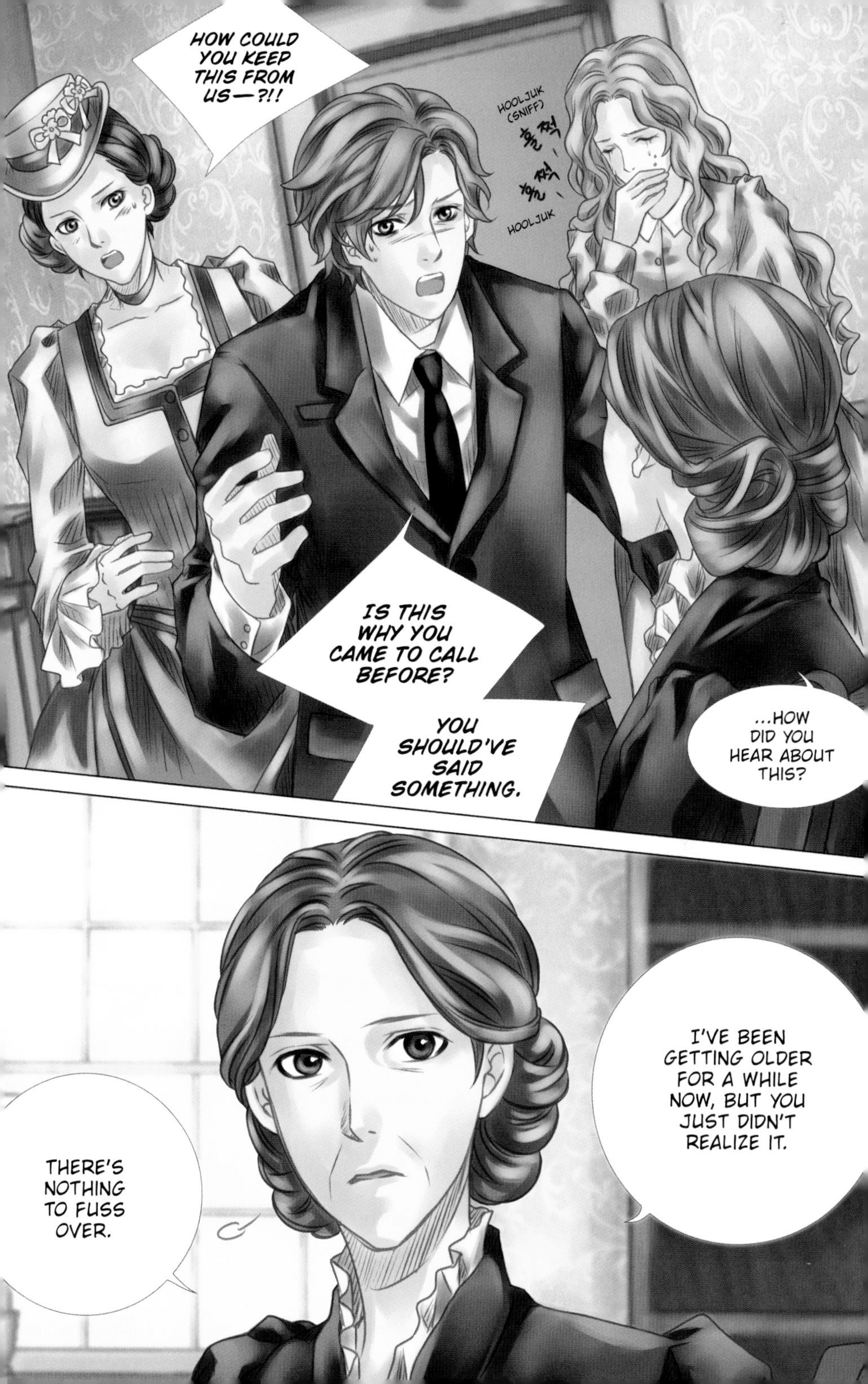
HOW COULD YOU KEEP THIS FROM US—?!!
HOOLJUK (SNIFF)
HOOLJUK
IS THIS WHY YOU CAME TO CALL BEFORE?
YOU SHOULD'VE SAID SOMETHING.
...HOW DID YOU HEAR ABOUT THIS?
THERE'S NOTHING TO FUSS OVER.
I'VE BEEN GETTING OLDER FOR A WHILE NOW, BUT YOU JUST DIDN'T REALIZE IT.

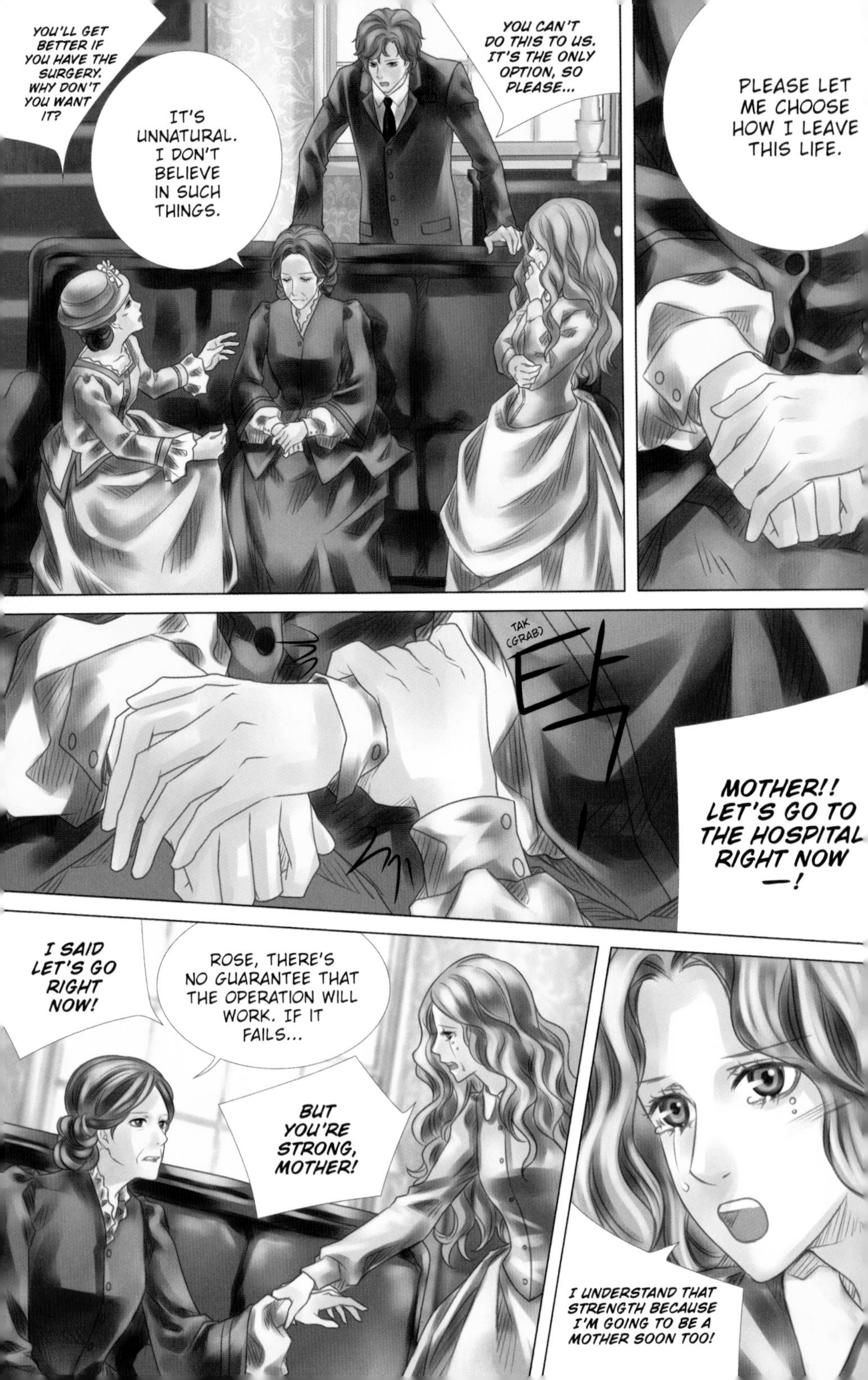
YOU'LL GET BETTER IF YOU HAVE THE SURGERY. WHY DON'T YOU WANT IT?
IT'S UNNATURAL. I DON'T BELIEVE IN SUCH THINGS.
YOU CAN'T DO THIS TO US. IT'S THE ONLY OPTION, SO PLEASE...
PLEASE LET ME CHOOSE HOW I LEAVE THIS LIFE.
TAK (GRAB)
MOTHER!! LET'S GO TO THE HOSPITAL RIGHT NOW —!
I SAID LET'S GO RIGHT NOW!
ROSE, THERE'S NO GUARANTEE THAT THE OPERATION WILL WORK. IF IT FAILS...
BUT YOU'RE STRONG, MOTHER!
I UNDERSTAND THAT STRENGTH BECAUSE I'M GOING TO BE A MOTHER SOON TOO!

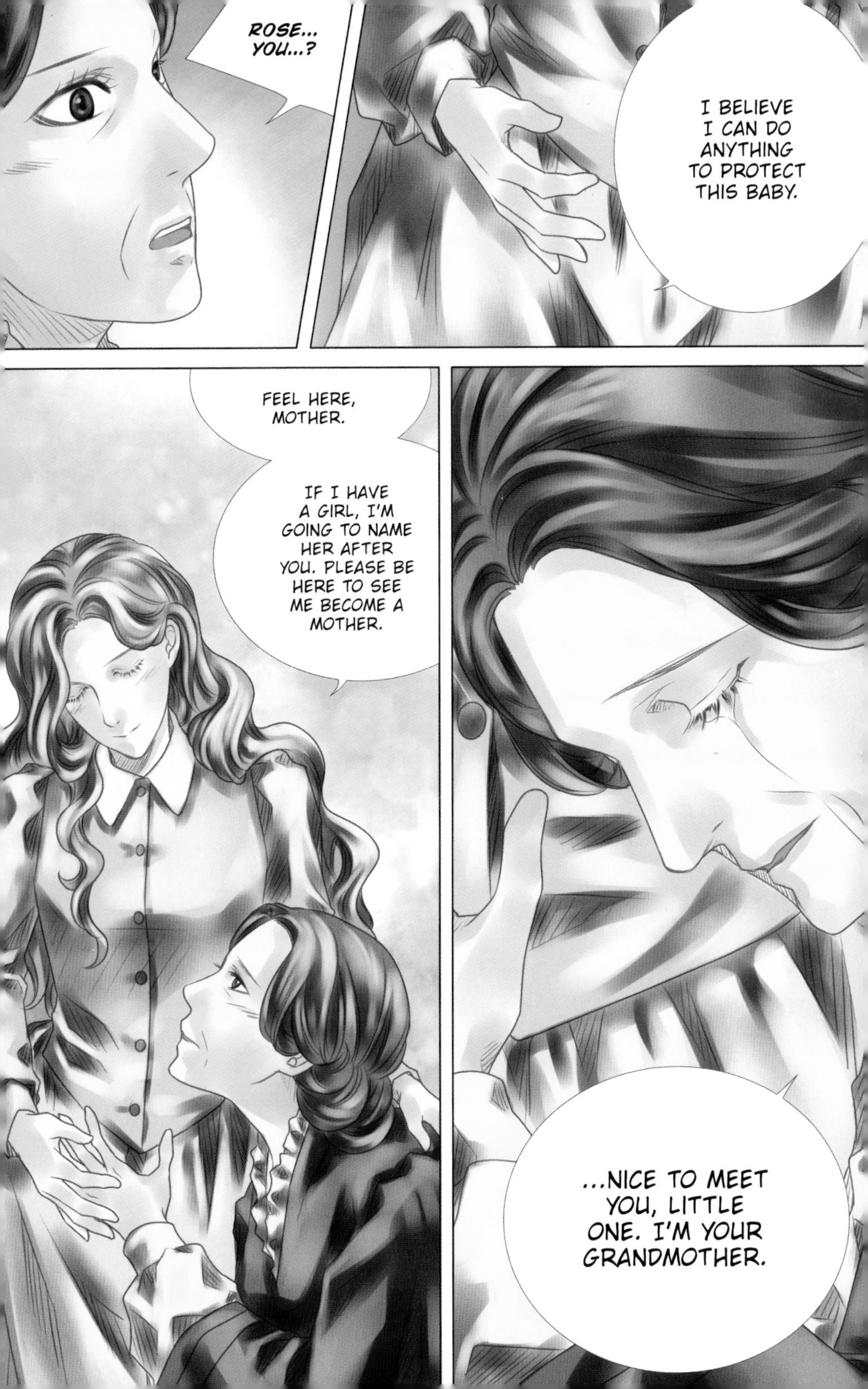
ROSE... YOU...?
I BELIEVE I CAN DO ANYTHING TO PROTECT THIS BABY.
FEEL HERE, MOTHER.
IF I HAVE A GIRL, I'M GOING TO NAME HER AFTER YOU. PLEASE BE HERE TO SEE ME BECOME A MOTHER.
...NICE TO MEET YOU, LITTLE ONE. I'M YOUR GRANDMOTHER.

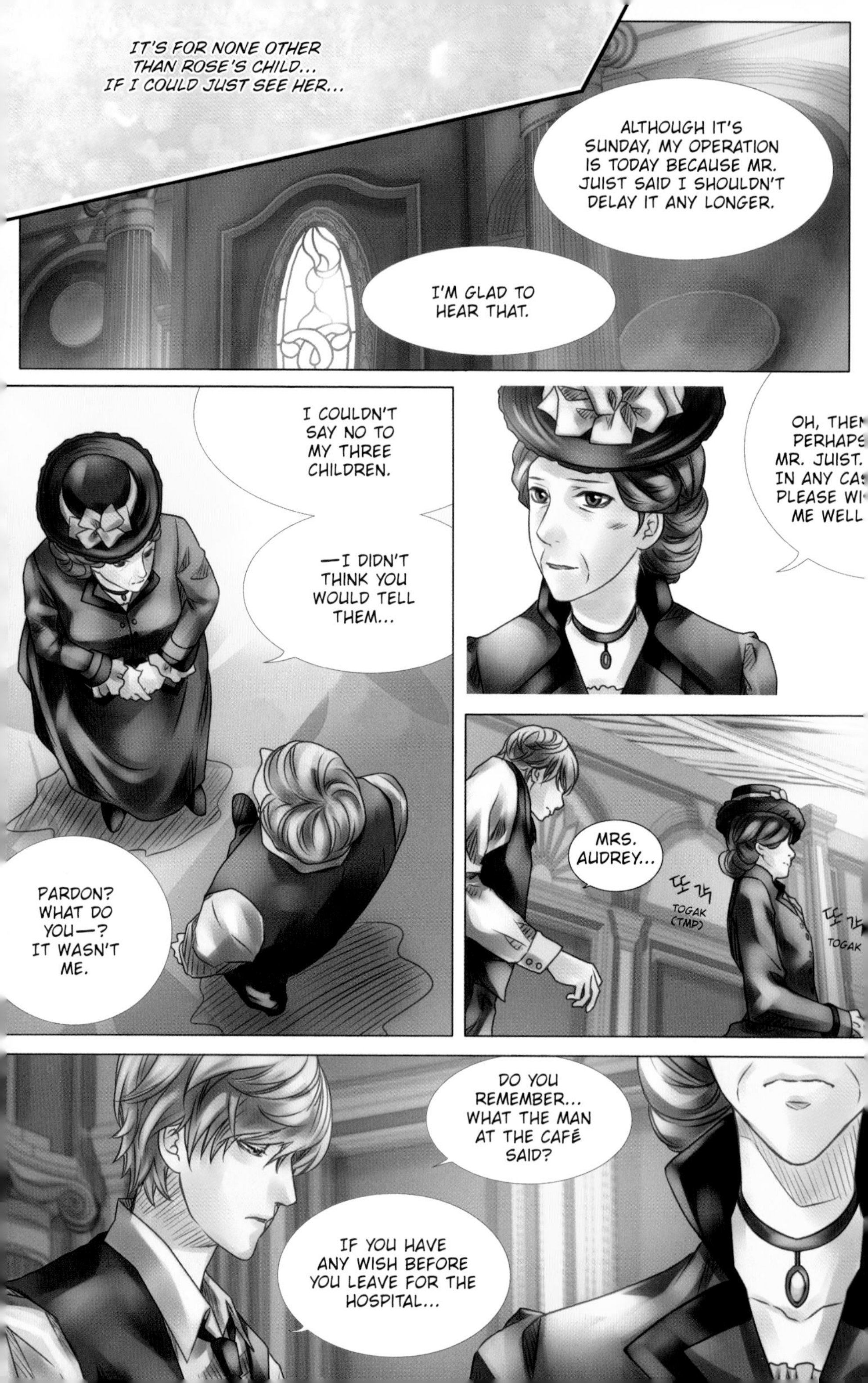
IT'S FOR NONE OTHER THAN ROSE'S CHILD... IF I COULD JUST SEE HER...
ALTHOUGH IT'S SUNDAY, MY OPERATION IS TODAY BECAUSE MR. JUIST SAID I SHOULDN'T DELAY IT ANY LONGER.
I'M GLAD TO HEAR THAT.
I COULDN'T SAY NO TO MY THREE CHILDREN.
—I DIDN'T THINK YOU WOULD TELL THEM...
PARDON? WHAT DO YOU—? IT WASN'T ME.
OH, THEN PERHAPS MR. JUIST. IN ANY CA PLEASE WI ME WELL
MRS. AUDREY...
또각
TOGAK (TMP)
또각
TOGAK
DO YOU REMEMBER... WHAT THE MAN AT THE CAFÉ SAID?
IF YOU HAVE ANY WISH BEFORE YOU LEAVE FOR THE HOSPITAL...

THERE'S NO REASON FOR YOU TO GO TO ANY TROUBLE, LAVELLE.

WHAT I NEED RIGHT NOW IS A GOOD DOCTOR AND THE WILL TO SURVIVE THIS SURGERY.

IT'S NOT DIFFICULT FOR ME, BUT...

AND YET YOU SAY THAT WITH SUCH A PAINFUL EXPRESSION ON YOUR FACE.

IF I HAD ONE WISH... IT WOULD BE TO SEE MY FIRST LOVE AGAIN AND TELL HIM THAT I LOVED HIM...

BUT THAT'S IMPOSSIBLE. SO PLEASE DON'T LIVE YOUR LIFE THINKING YOU HAVE TO HELP EVERYONE.

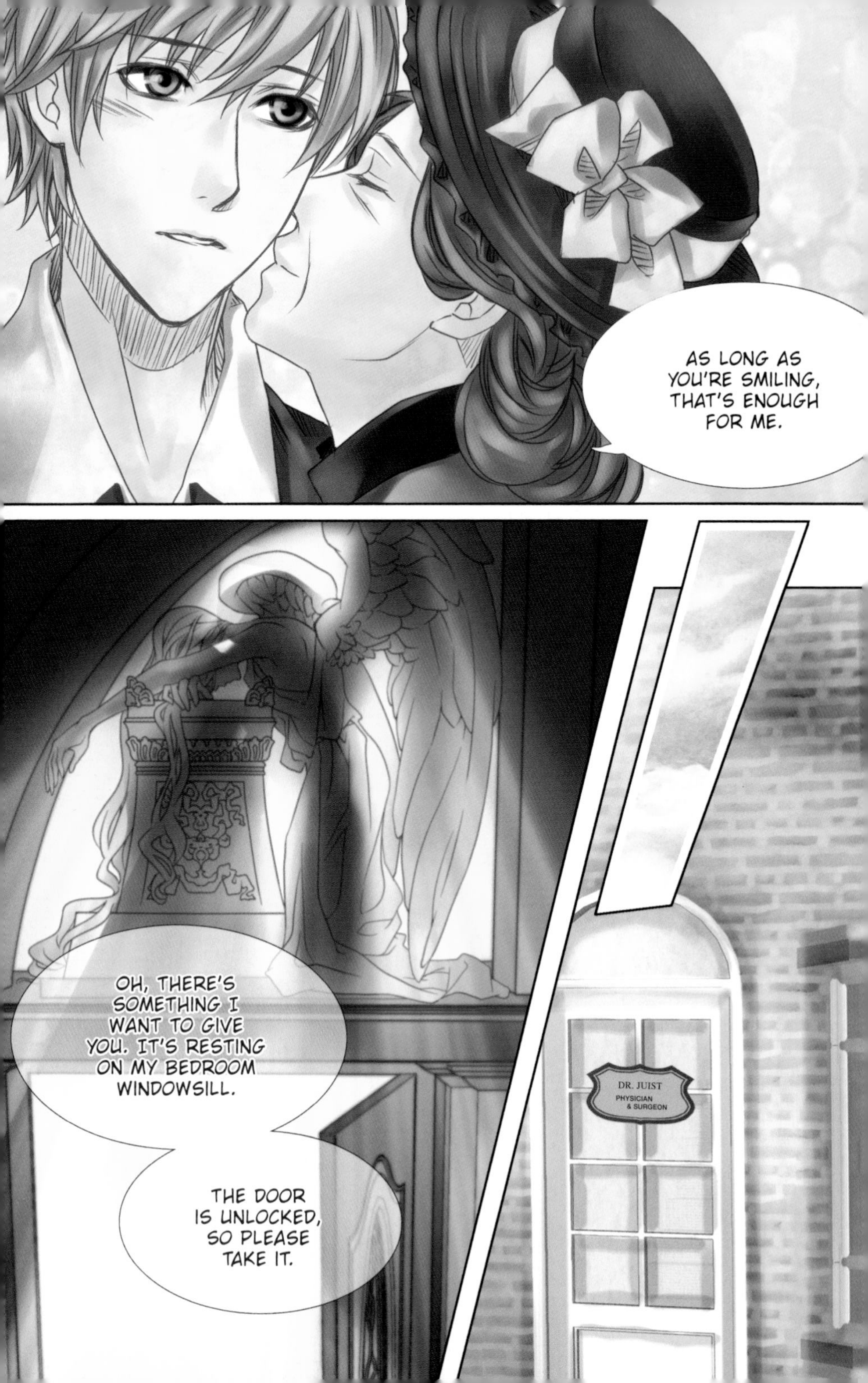
AS LONG AS YOU'RE SMILING, THAT'S ENOUGH FOR ME.
OH, THERE'S SOMETHING I WANT TO GIVE YOU. IT'S RESTING ON MY BEDROOM WINDOWSILL.
THE DOOR IS UNLOCKED, SO PLEASE TAKE IT.
DR. JUIST
PHYSICIAN & SURGEON

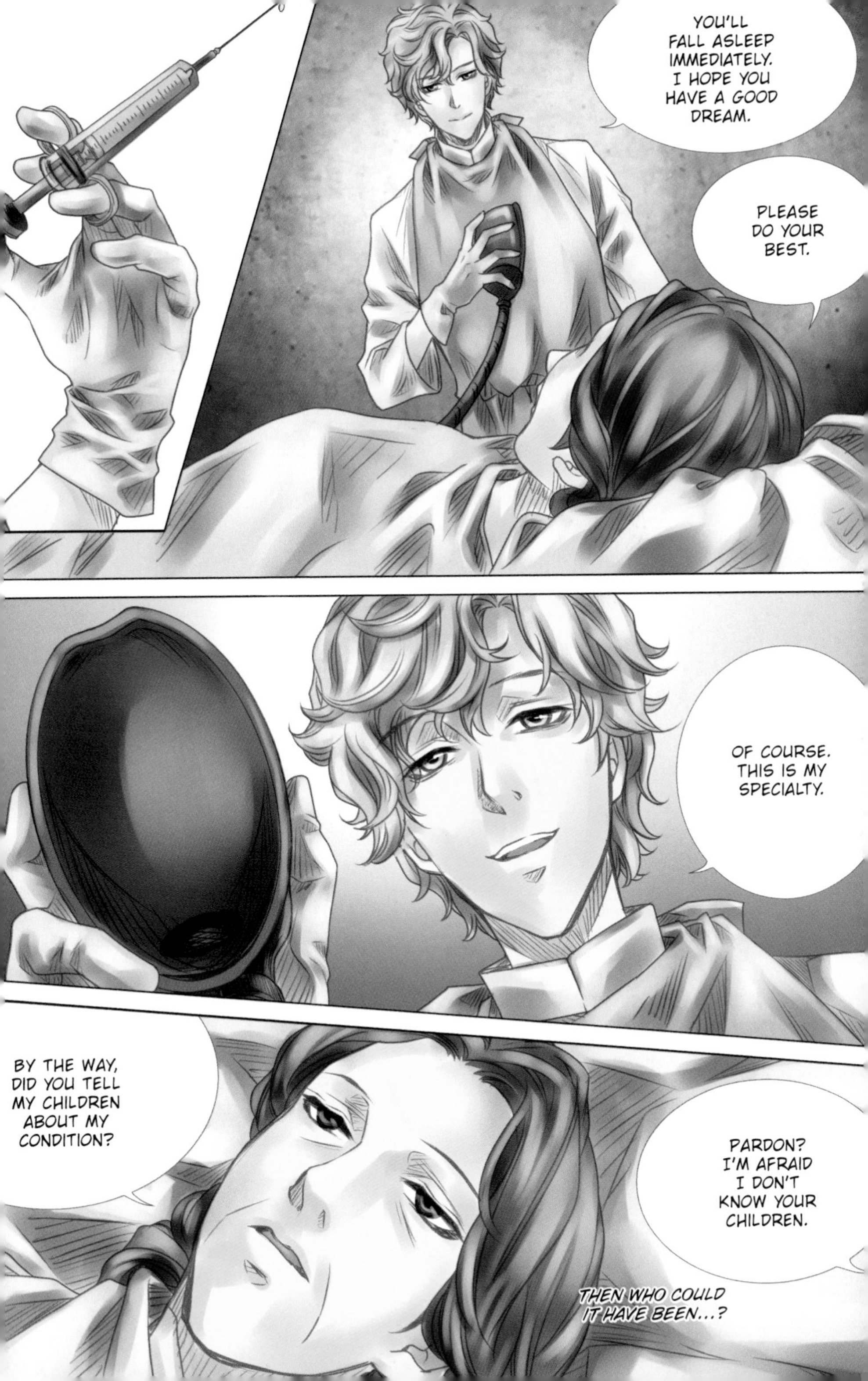
YOU'LL FALL ASLEEP IMMEDIATELY. I HOPE YOU HAVE A GOOD DREAM.
PLEASE DO YOUR BEST.
OF COURSE. THIS IS MY SPECIALTY.
BY THE WAY, DID YOU TELL MY CHILDREN ABOUT MY CONDITION?
PARDON? I'M AFRAID I DON'T KNOW YOUR CHILDREN.
THEN WHO COULD IT HAVE BEEN...?

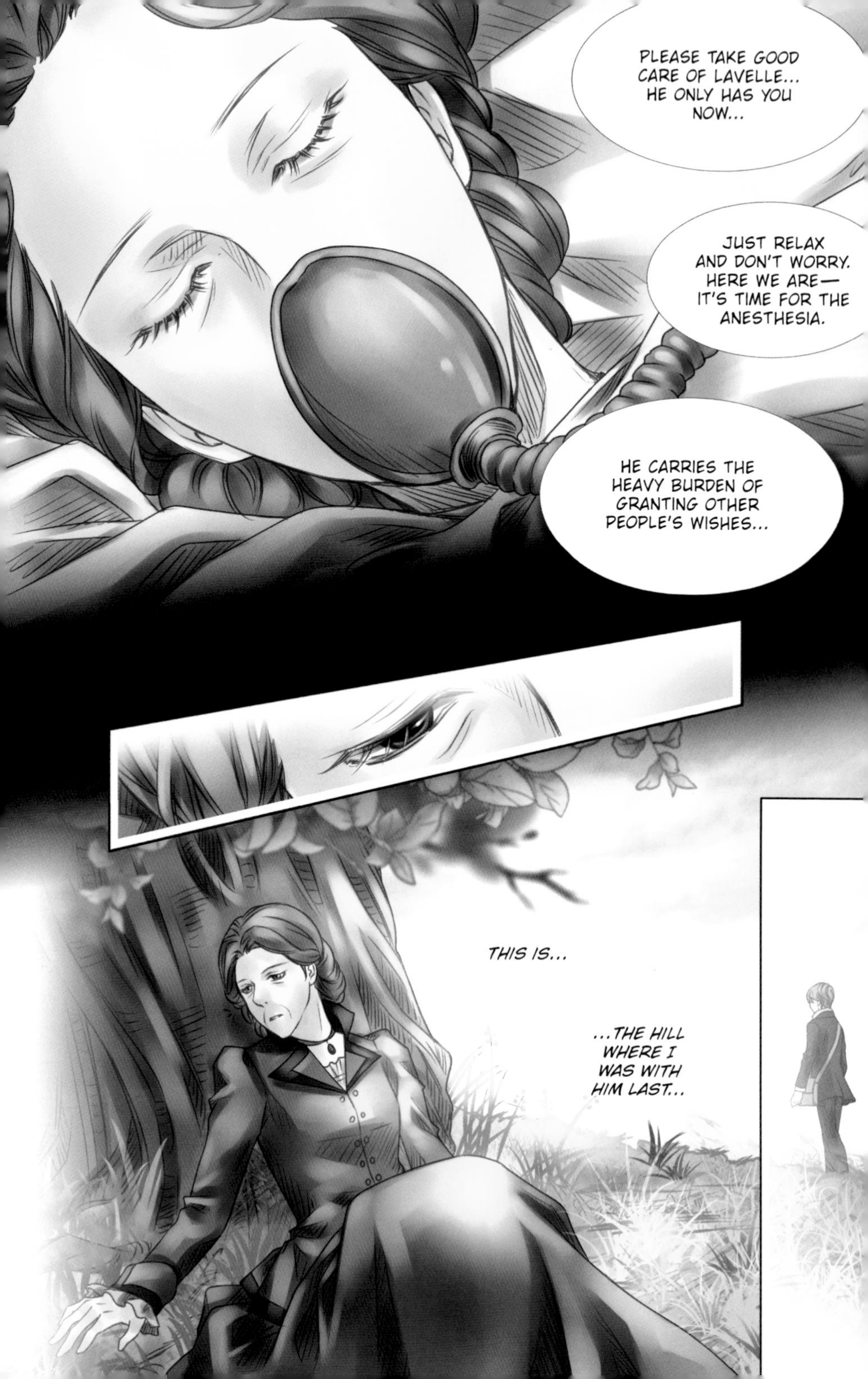
PLEASE TAKE GOOD CARE OF LAVELLE... HE ONLY HAS YOU NOW...
JUST RELAX AND DON'T WORRY. HERE WE ARE— IT'S TIME FOR THE ANESTHESIA.
HE CARRIES THE HEAVY BURDEN OF GRANTING OTHER PEOPLE'S WISHES...
THIS IS...
...THE HILL WHERE I WAS WITH HIM LAST...

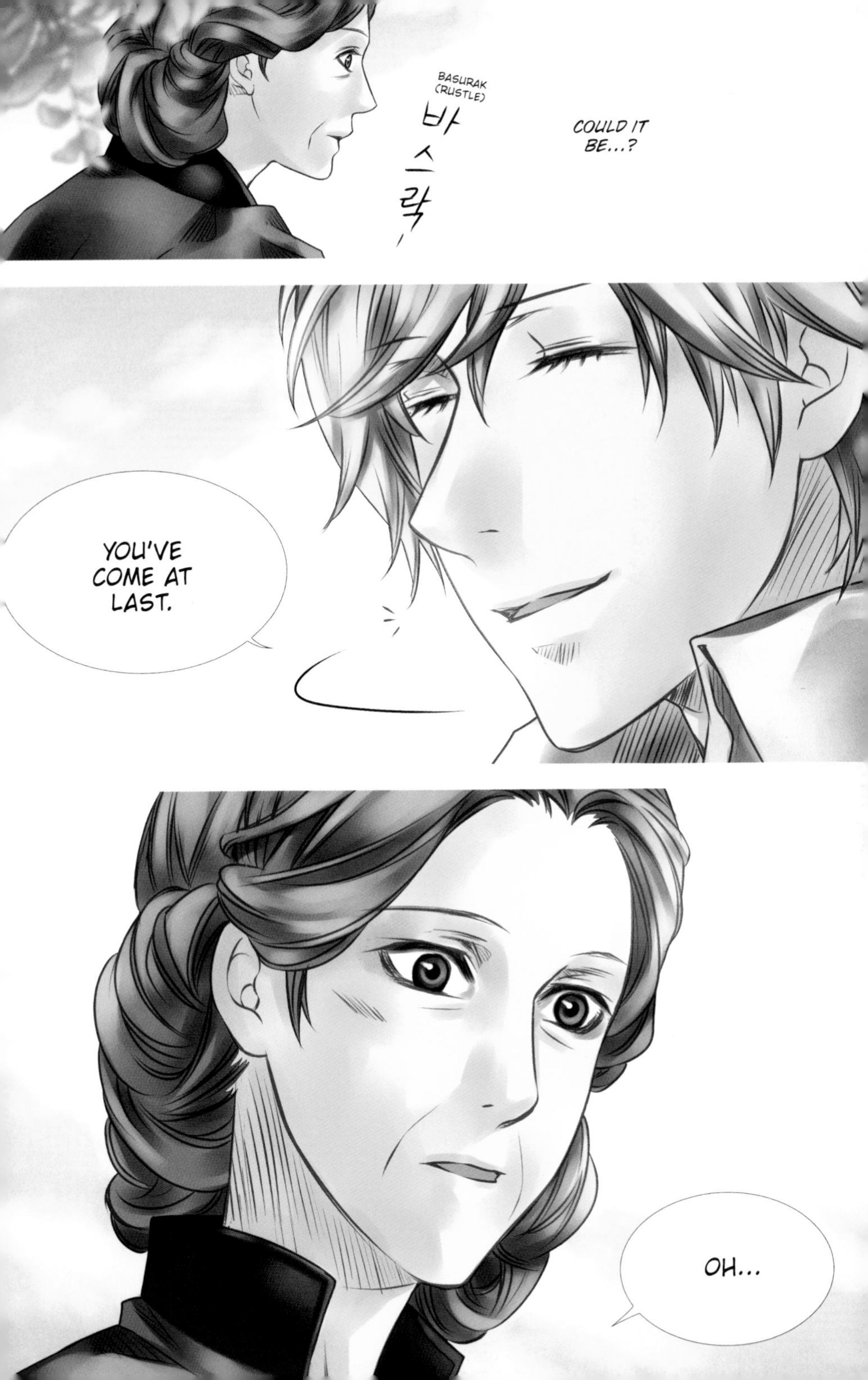
BASURAK (RUSTLE)
바스락
COULD IT BE...?
YOU'VE COME AT LAST.
OH...

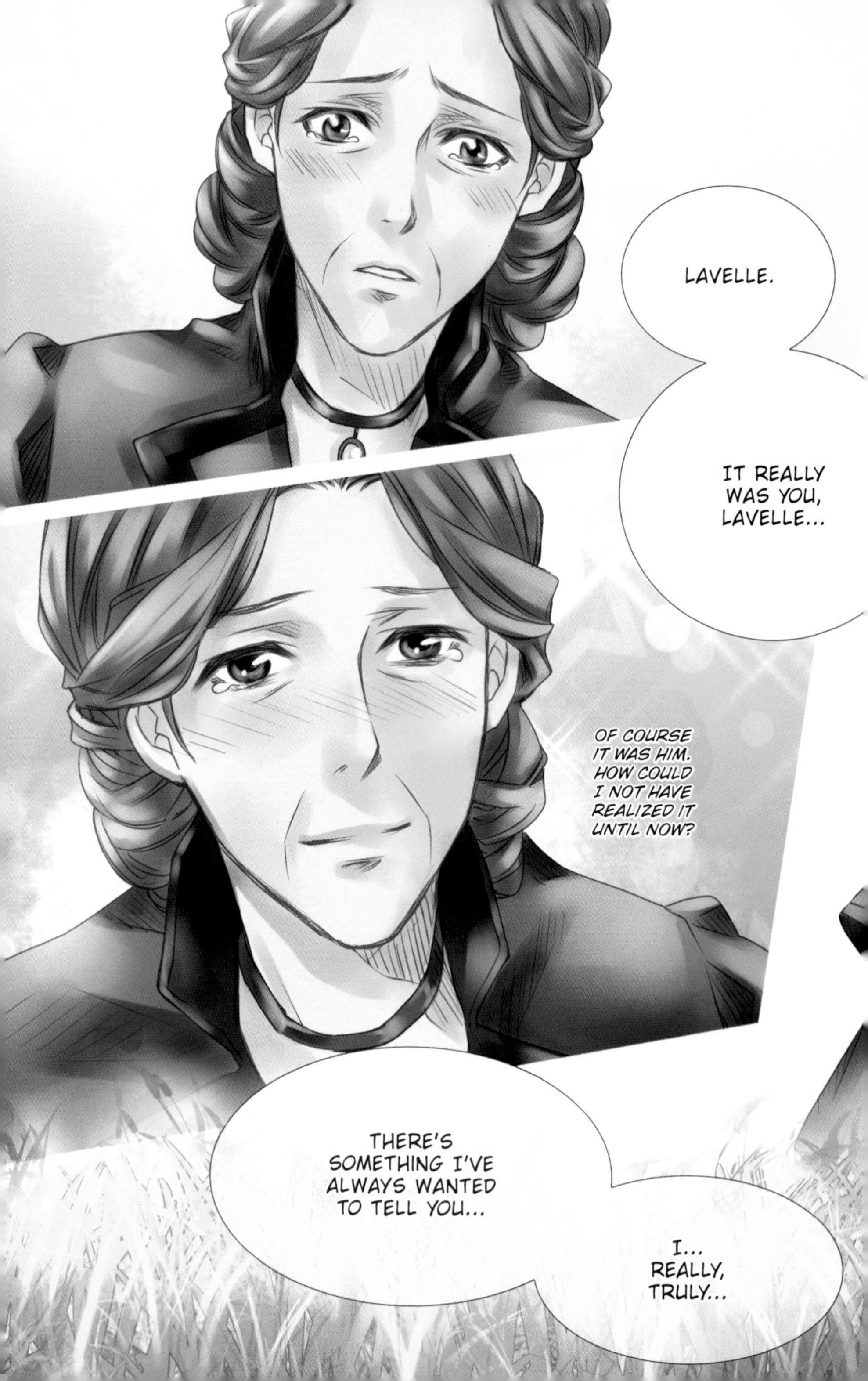
LAVELLE.
IT REALLY WAS YOU, LAVELLE...
OF COURSE IT WAS HIM. HOW COULD I NOT HAVE REALIZED IT UNTIL NOW?
THERE'S SOMETHING I'VE ALWAYS WANTED TO TELL YOU...
I... REALLY, TRULY...

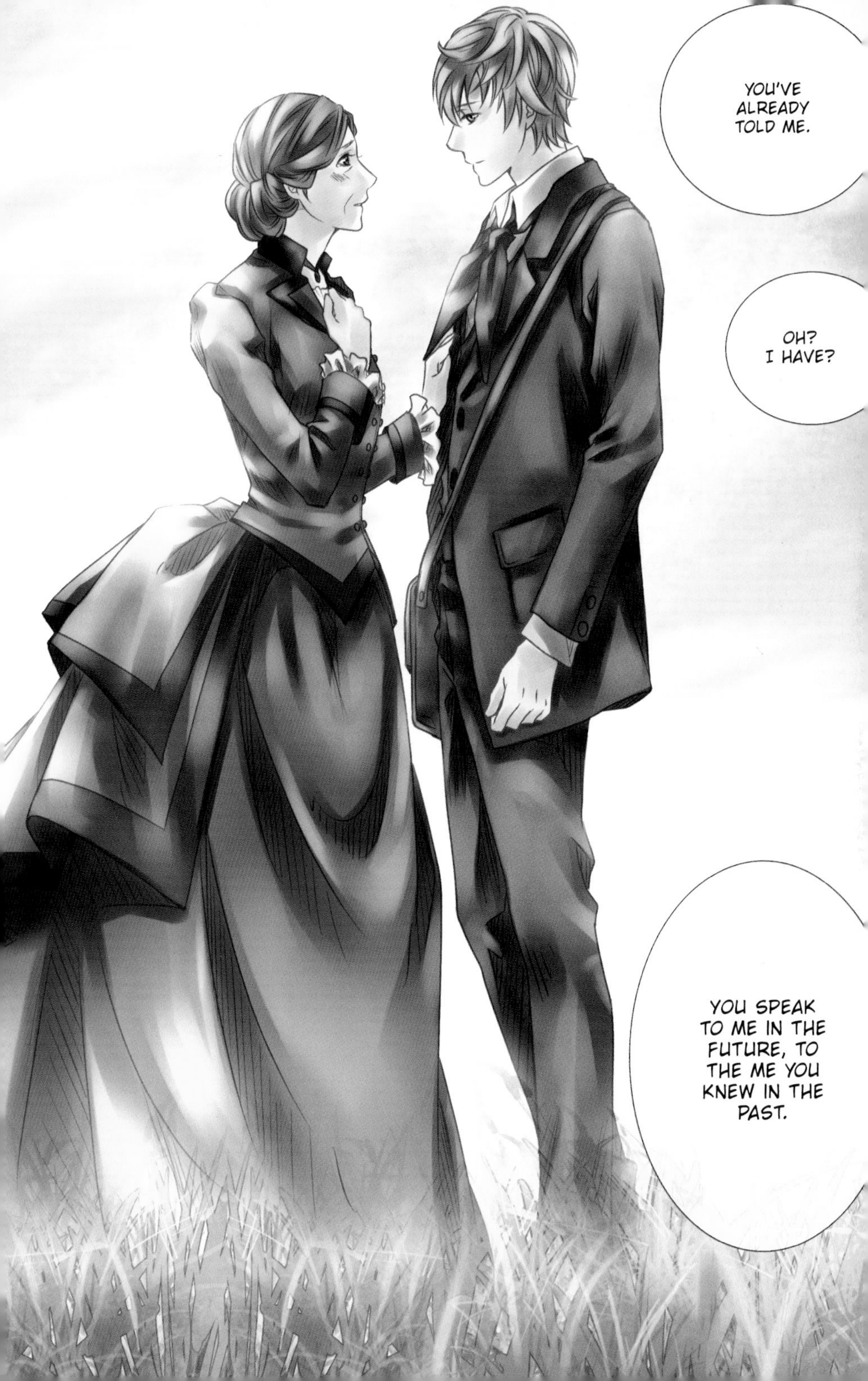
YOU'VE ALREADY TOLD ME.
OH? I HAVE?
YOU SPEAK TO ME IN THE FUTURE, TO THE ME YOU KNEW IN THE PAST.

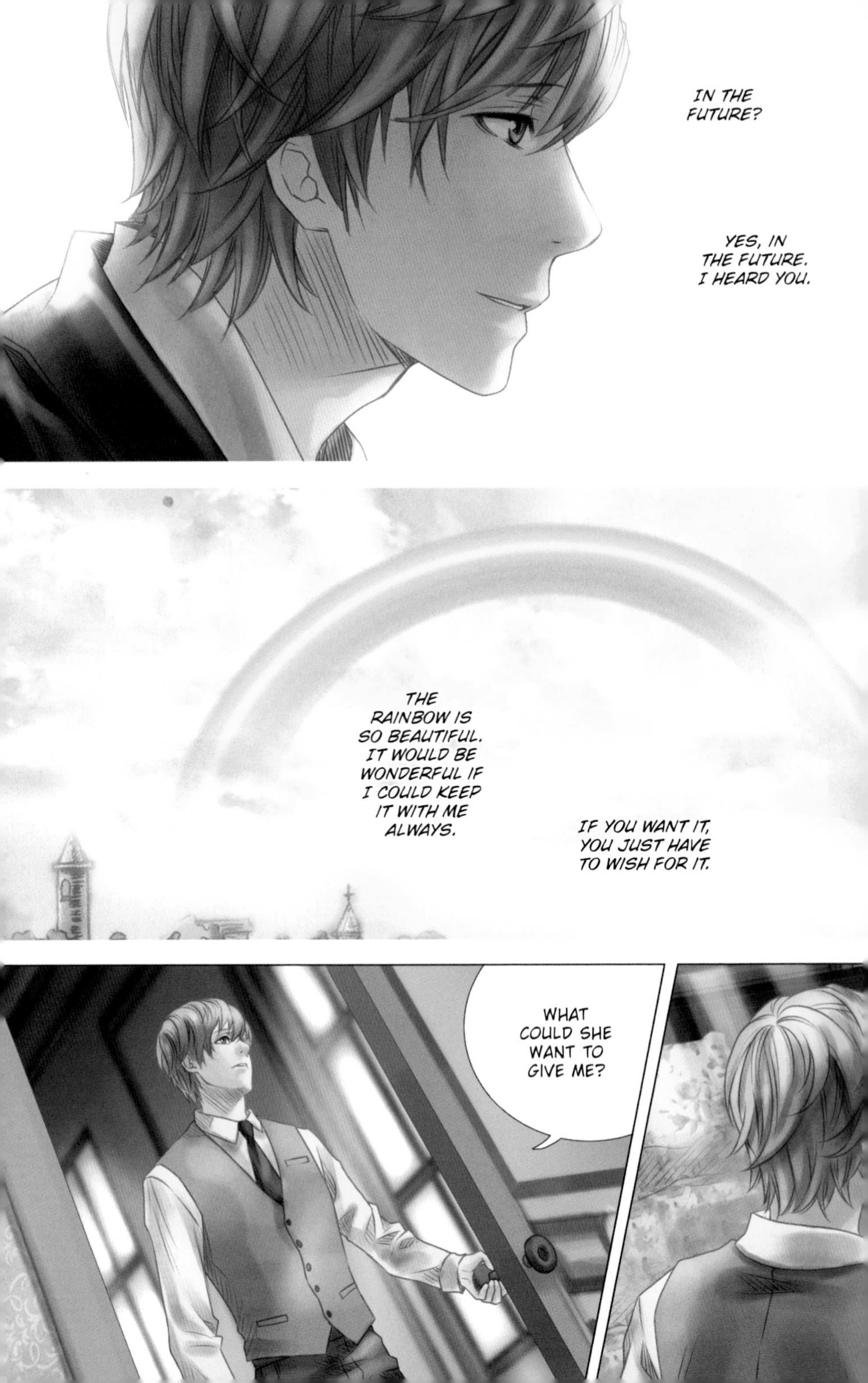
IN THE FUTURE?
YES, IN THE FUTURE. I HEARD YOU.
THE RAINBOW IS SO BEAUTIFUL. IT WOULD BE WONDERFUL IF I COULD KEEP IT WITH ME ALWAYS.
IF YOU WANT IT, YOU JUST HAVE TO WISH FOR IT.
WHAT COULD SHE WANT TO GIVE ME?

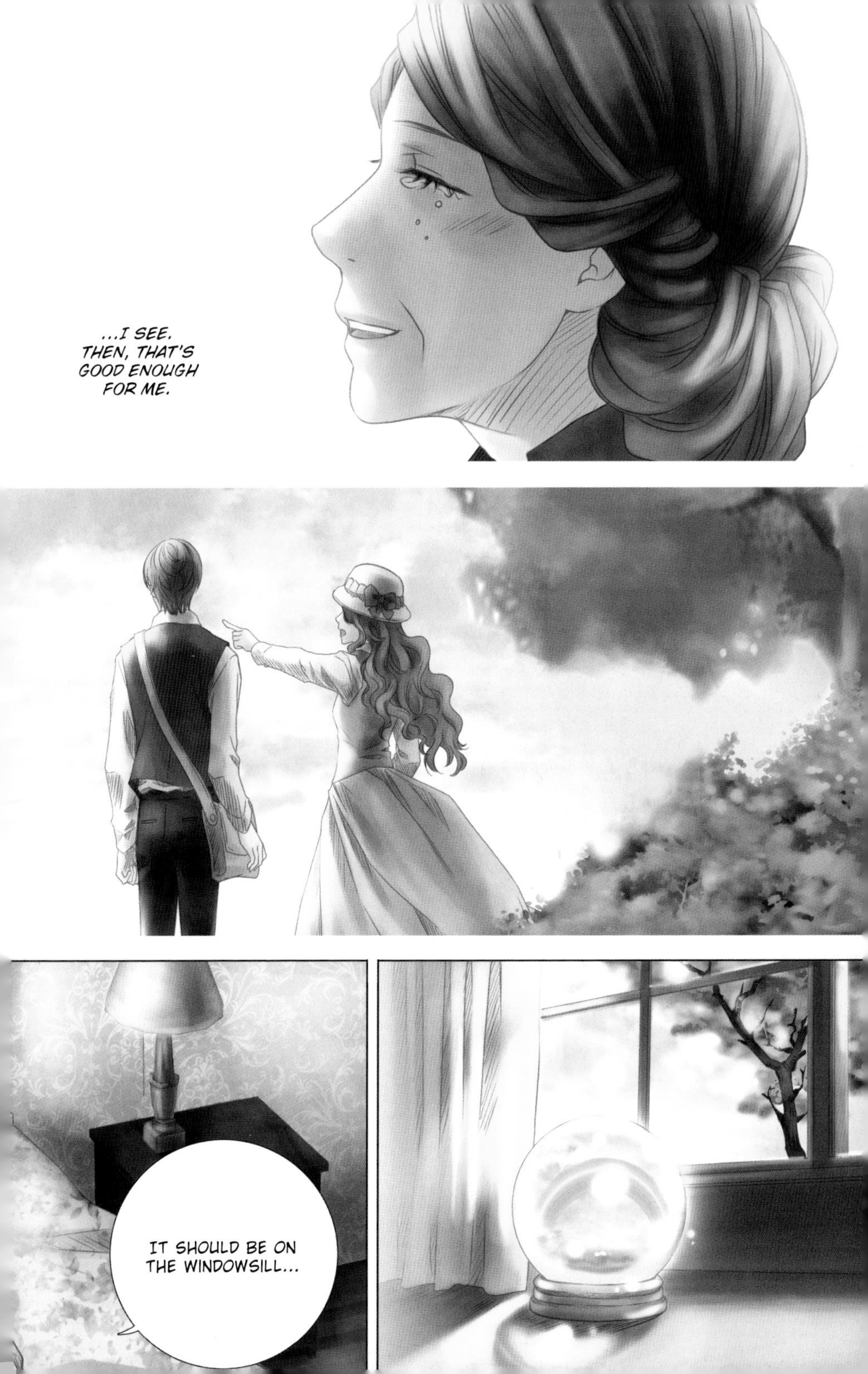
...I SEE. THEN, THAT'S GOOD ENOUGH FOR ME.
IT SHOULD BE ON THE WINDOWSILL...

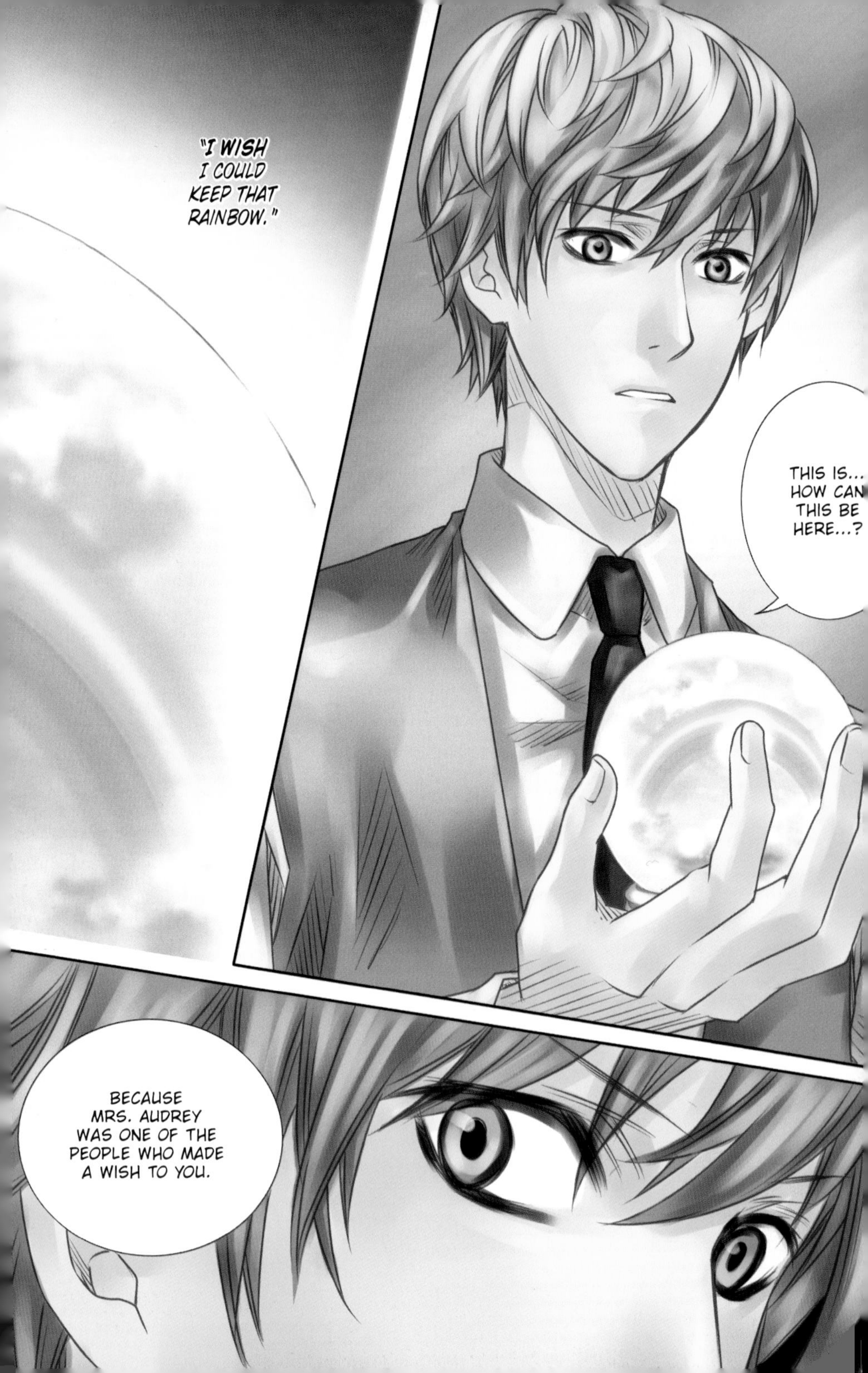
"I WISH I COULD KEEP THAT RAINBOW."
THIS IS... HOW CAN THIS BE HERE...?
BECAUSE MRS. AUDREY WAS ONE OF THE PEOPLE WHO MADE A WISH TO YOU.

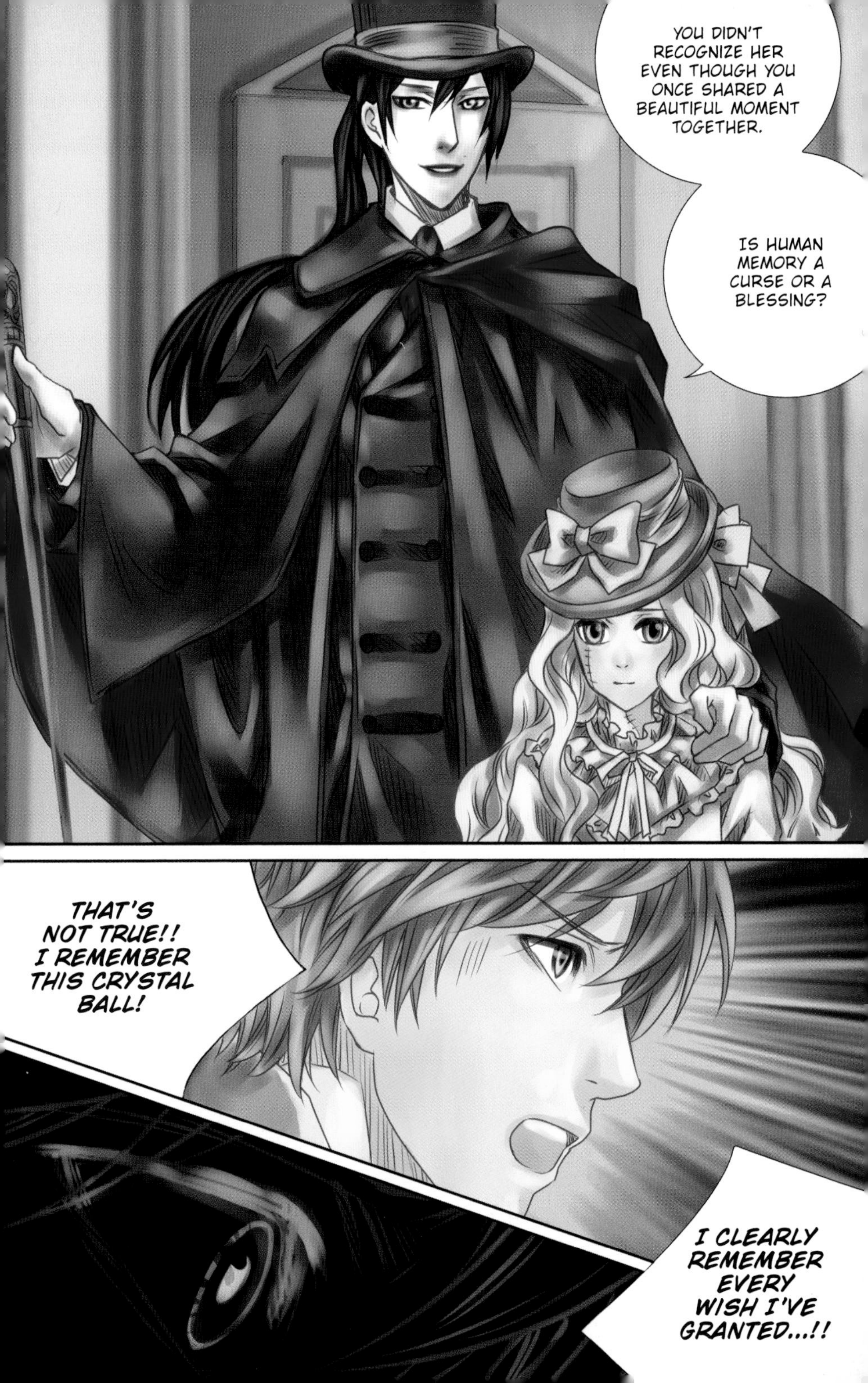
YOU DIDN'T RECOGNIZE HER EVEN THOUGH YOU ONCE SHARED A BEAUTIFUL MOMENT TOGETHER.
IS HUMAN MEMORY A CURSE OR A BLESSING?
THAT'S NOT TRUE!! I REMEMBER THIS CRYSTAL BALL!
I CLEARLY REMEMBER EVERY WISH I'VE GRANTED...!!

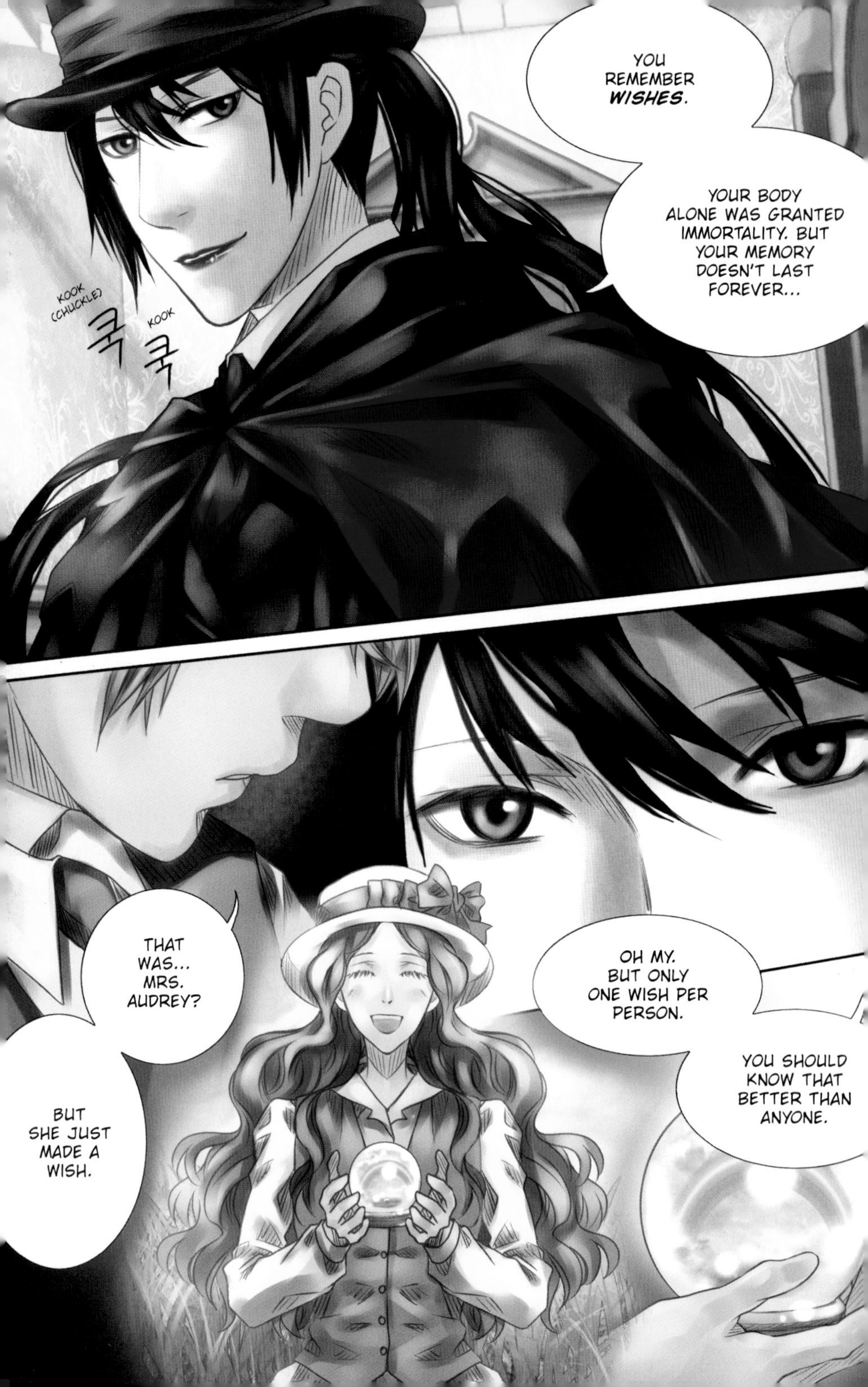
YOU REMEMBER ***WISHES***.
YOUR BODY ALONE WAS GRANTED IMMORTALITY. BUT YOUR MEMORY DOESN'T LAST FOREVER...
KOOK (CHUCKLE)
쿡
KOOK
쿡
THAT WAS... MRS. AUDREY?
BUT SHE JUST MADE A WISH.
OH MY. BUT ONLY ONE WISH PER PERSON.
YOU SHOULD KNOW THAT BETTER THAN ANYONE.

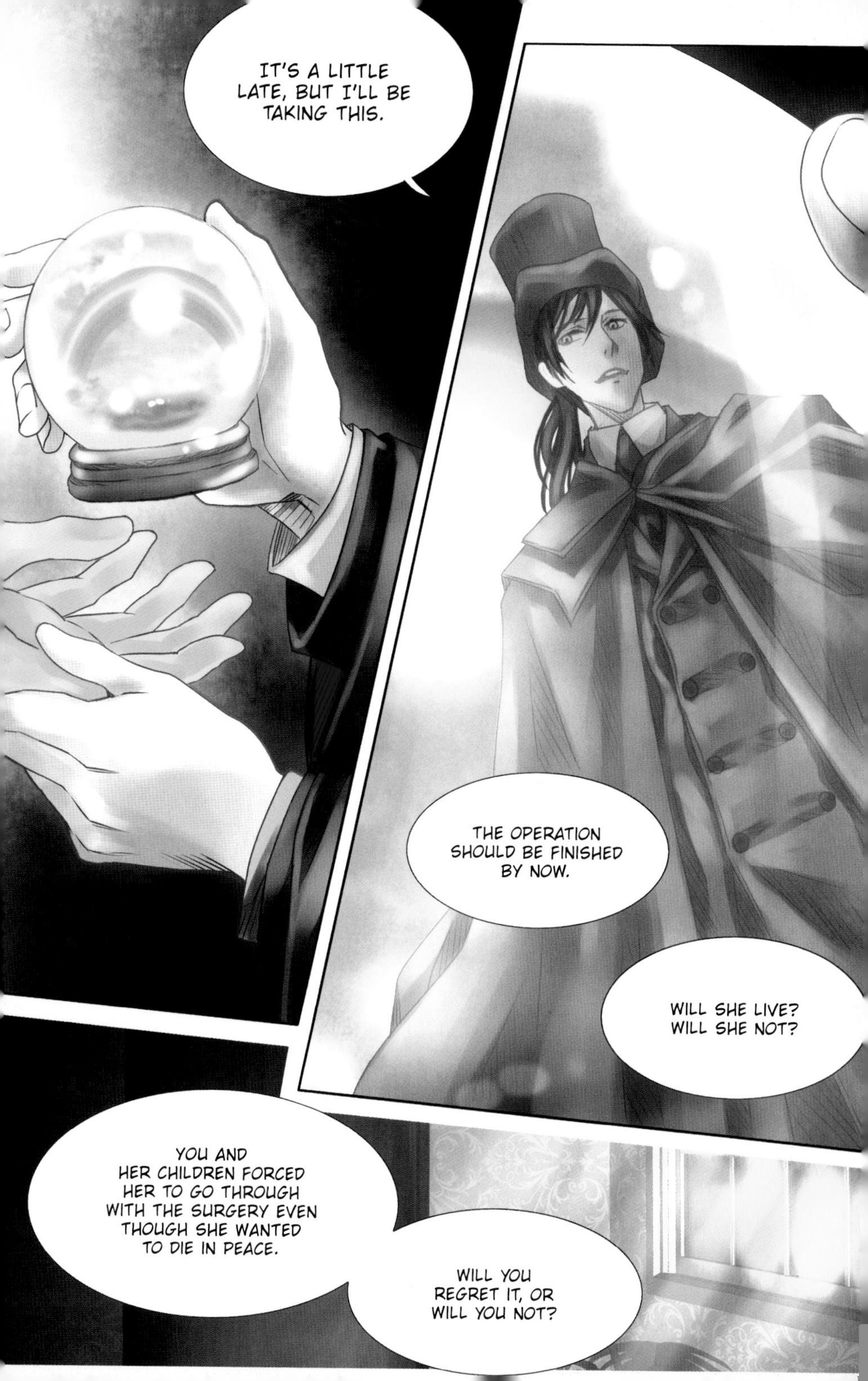
IT'S A LITTLE LATE, BUT I'LL BE TAKING THIS.
THE OPERATION SHOULD BE FINISHED BY NOW.
WILL SHE LIVE? WILL SHE NOT?
YOU AND HER CHILDREN FORCED HER TO GO THROUGH WITH THE SURGERY EVEN THOUGH SHE WANTED TO DIE IN PEACE.
WILL YOU REGRET IT, OR WILL YOU NOT?

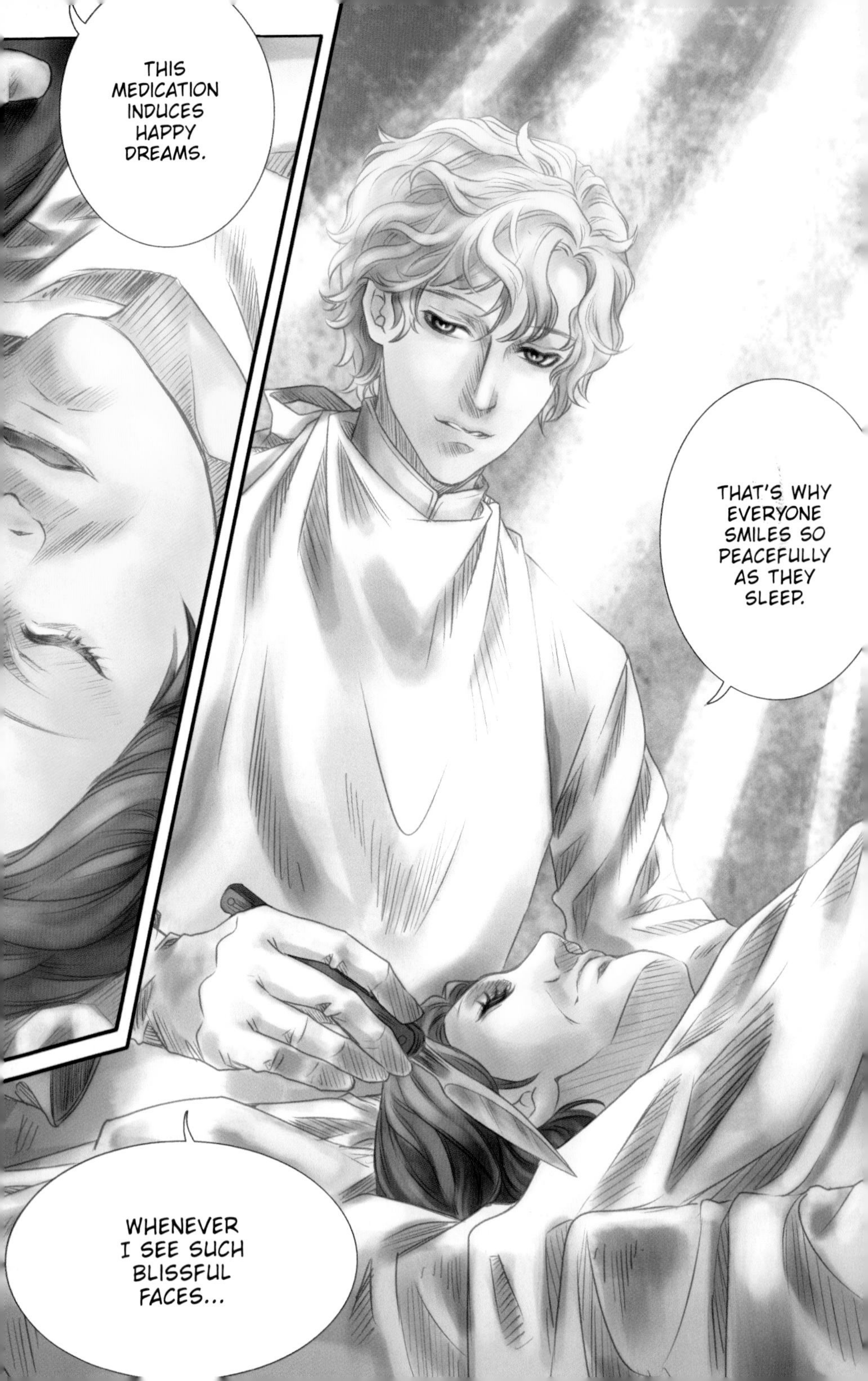
THIS MEDICATION INDUCES HAPPY DREAMS.
THAT'S WHY EVERYONE SMILES SO PEACEFULLY AS THEY SLEEP.
WHENEVER I SEE SUCH BLISSFUL FACES...

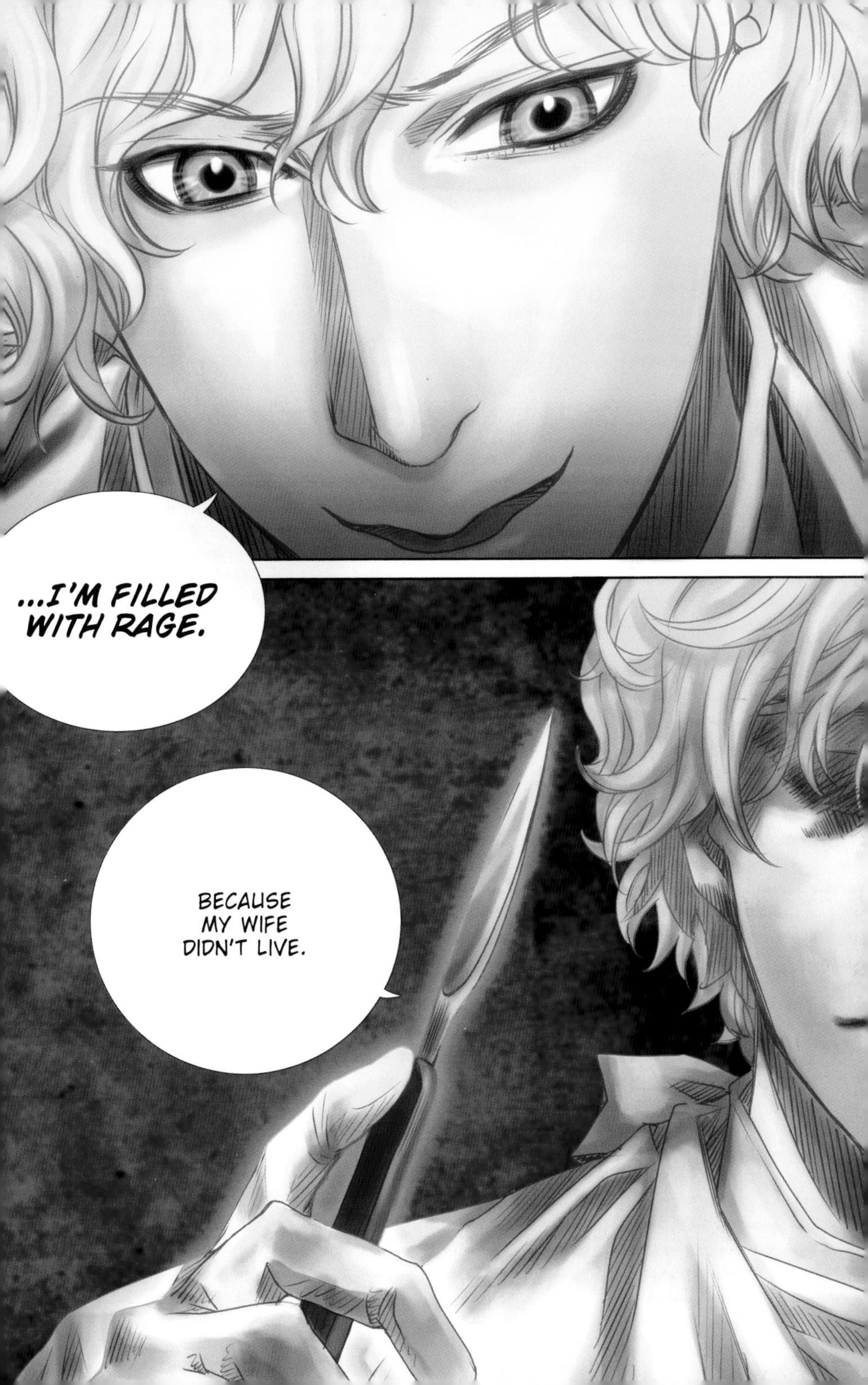
...I'M FILLED WITH RAGE.
BECAUSE MY WIFE DIDN'T LIVE.

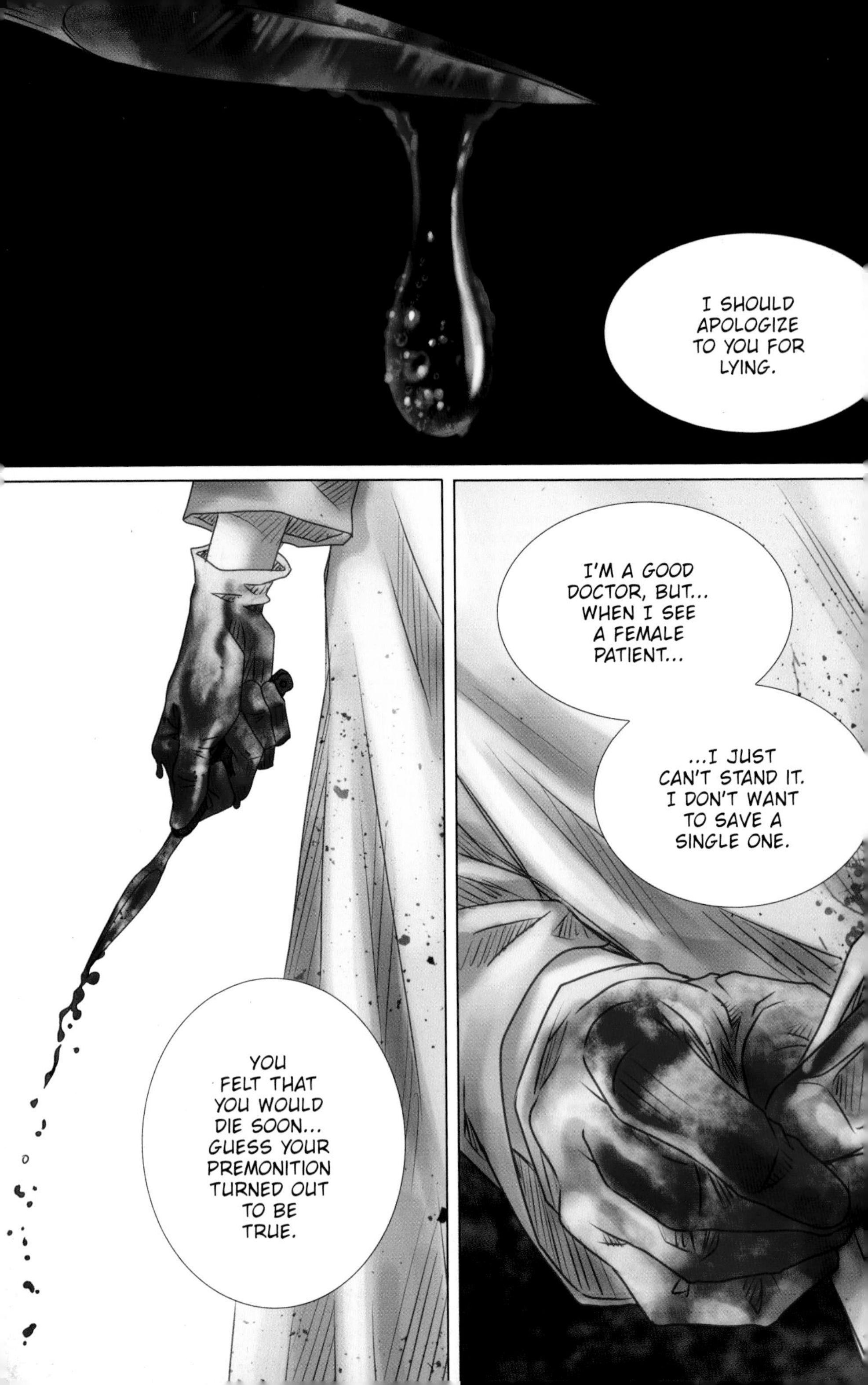
I SHOULD APOLOGIZE TO YOU FOR LYING.
YOU FELT THAT YOU WOULD DIE SOON... GUESS YOUR PREMONITION TURNED OUT TO BE TRUE.
I'M A GOOD DOCTOR, BUT... WHEN I SEE A FEMALE PATIENT...
...I JUST CAN'T STAND IT. I DON'T WANT TO SAVE A SINGLE ONE.

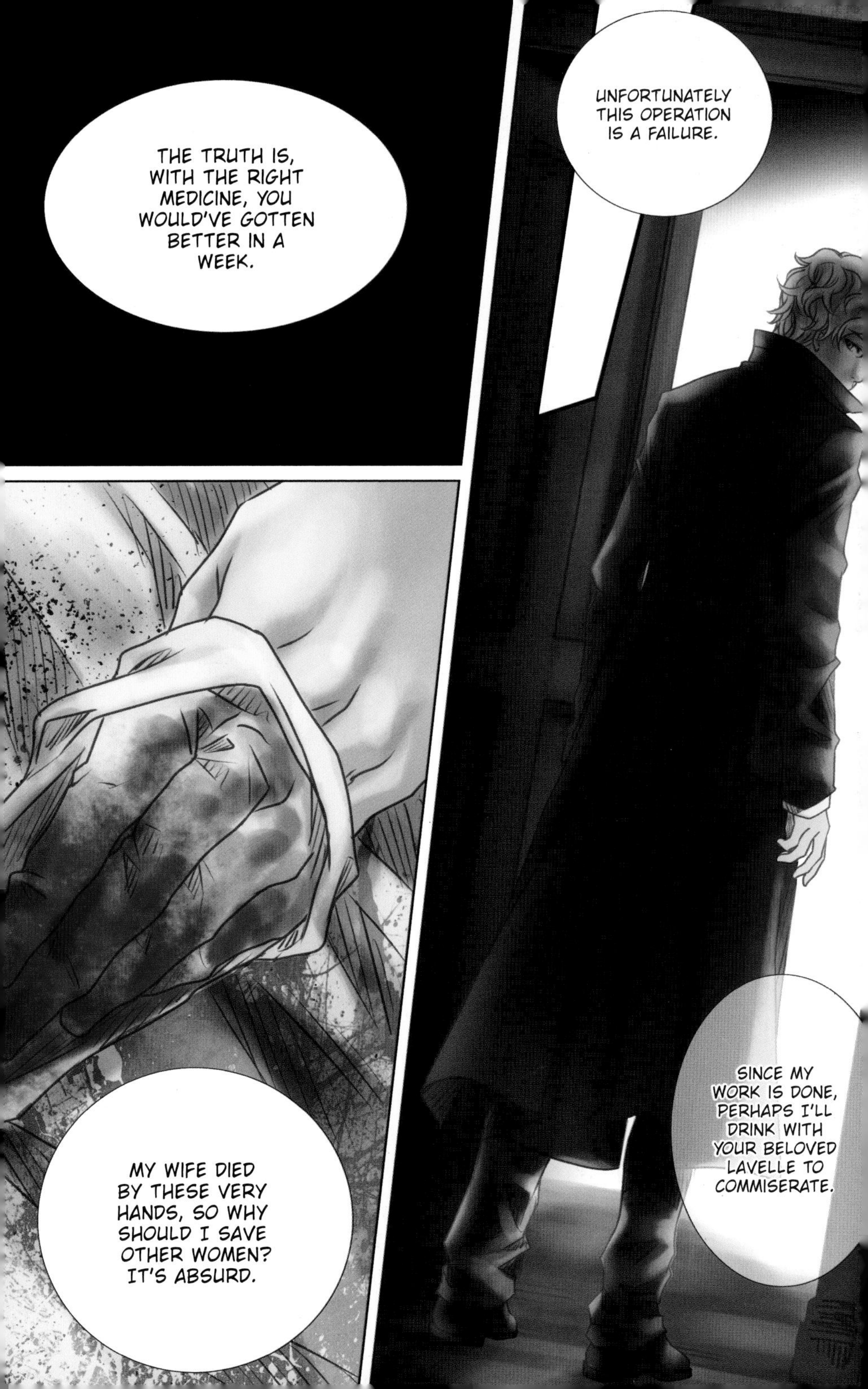
THE TRUTH IS, WITH THE RIGHT MEDICINE, YOU WOULD'VE GOTTEN BETTER IN A WEEK.
MY WIFE DIED BY THESE VERY HANDS, SO WHY SHOULD I SAVE OTHER WOMEN? IT'S ABSURD.
UNFORTUNATELY THIS OPERATION IS A FAILURE.
SINCE MY WORK IS DONE, PERHAPS I'LL DRINK WITH YOUR BELOVED LAVELLE TO COMMISERATE.

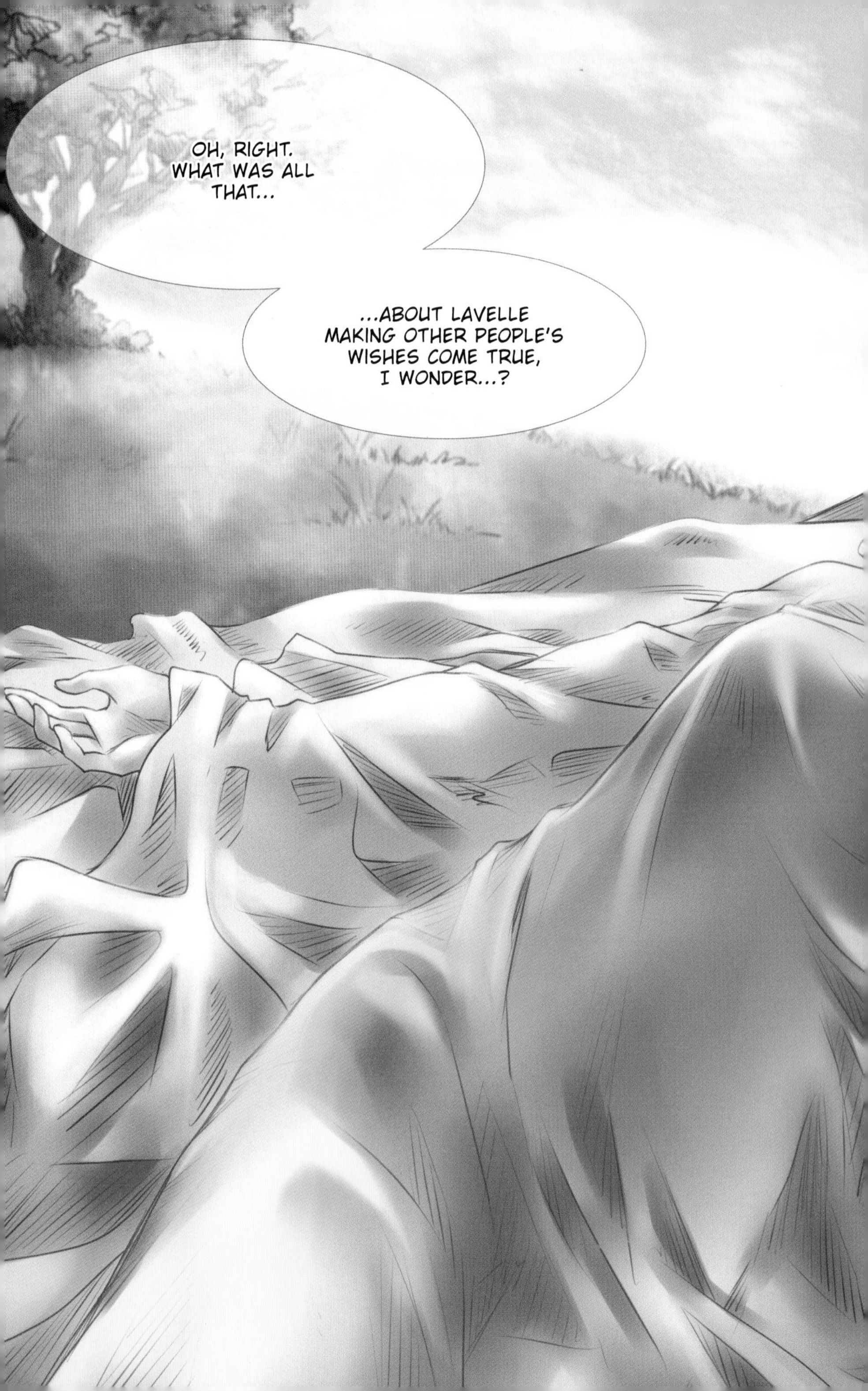
OH, RIGHT. WHAT WAS ALL THAT...
...ABOUT LAVELLE MAKING OTHER PEOPLE'S WISHES COME TRUE, I WONDER...?

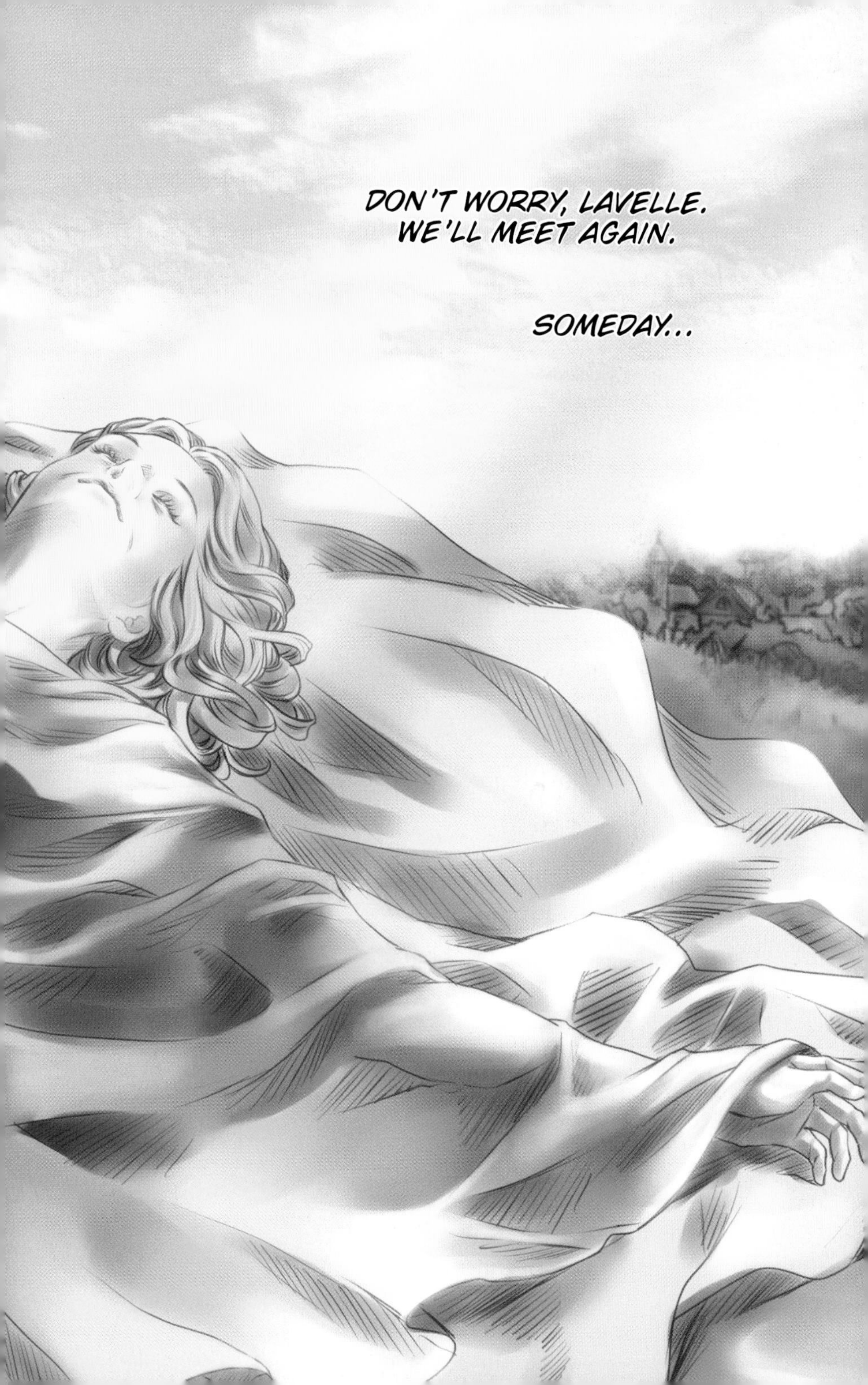
DON'T WORRY, LAVELLE. WE'LL MEET AGAIN.
SOMEDAY...

Void's Enigmatic Mansion

"

I'll make a wish
for him instead.

"

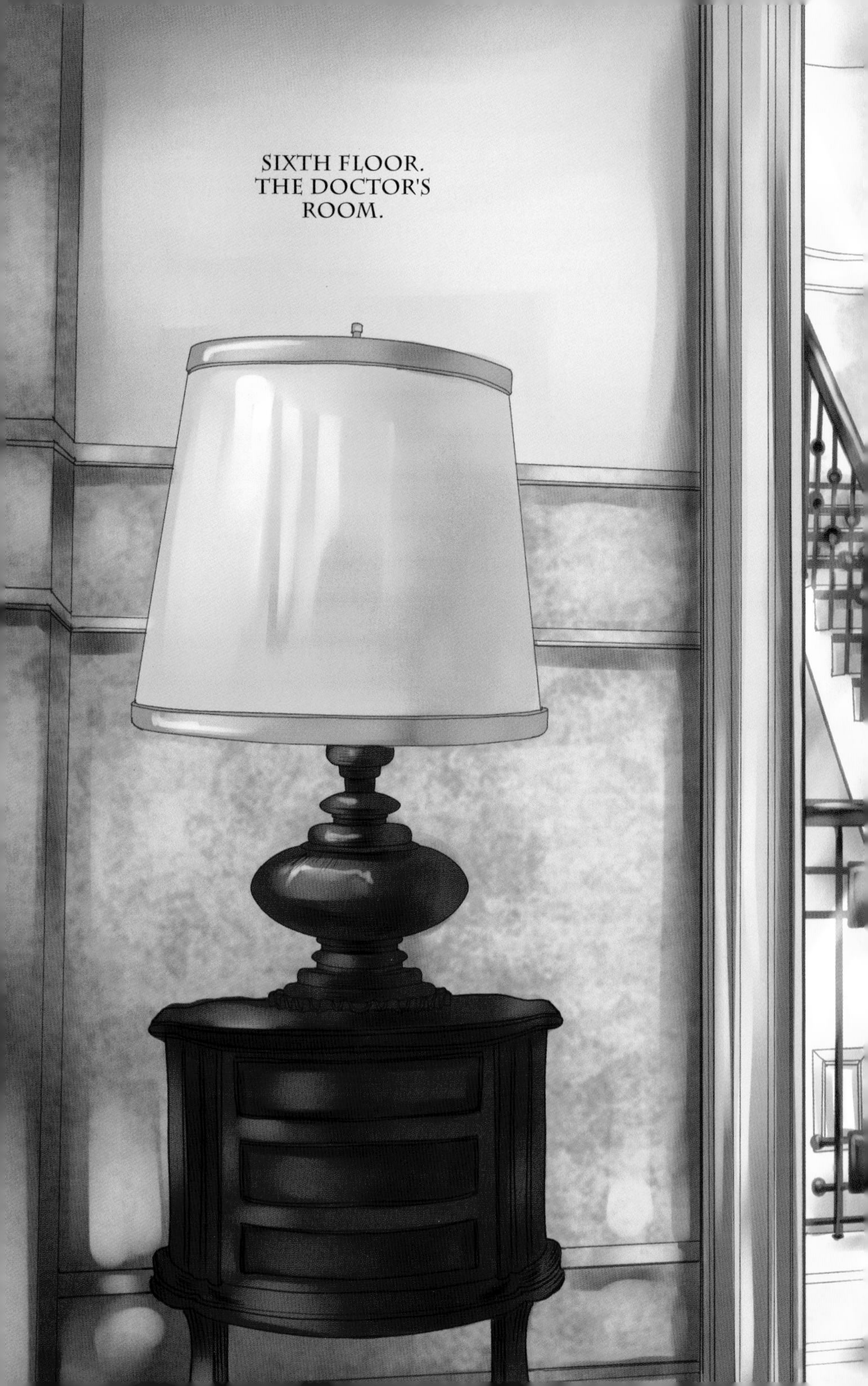
SIXTH FLOOR. THE DOCTOR'S ROOM.

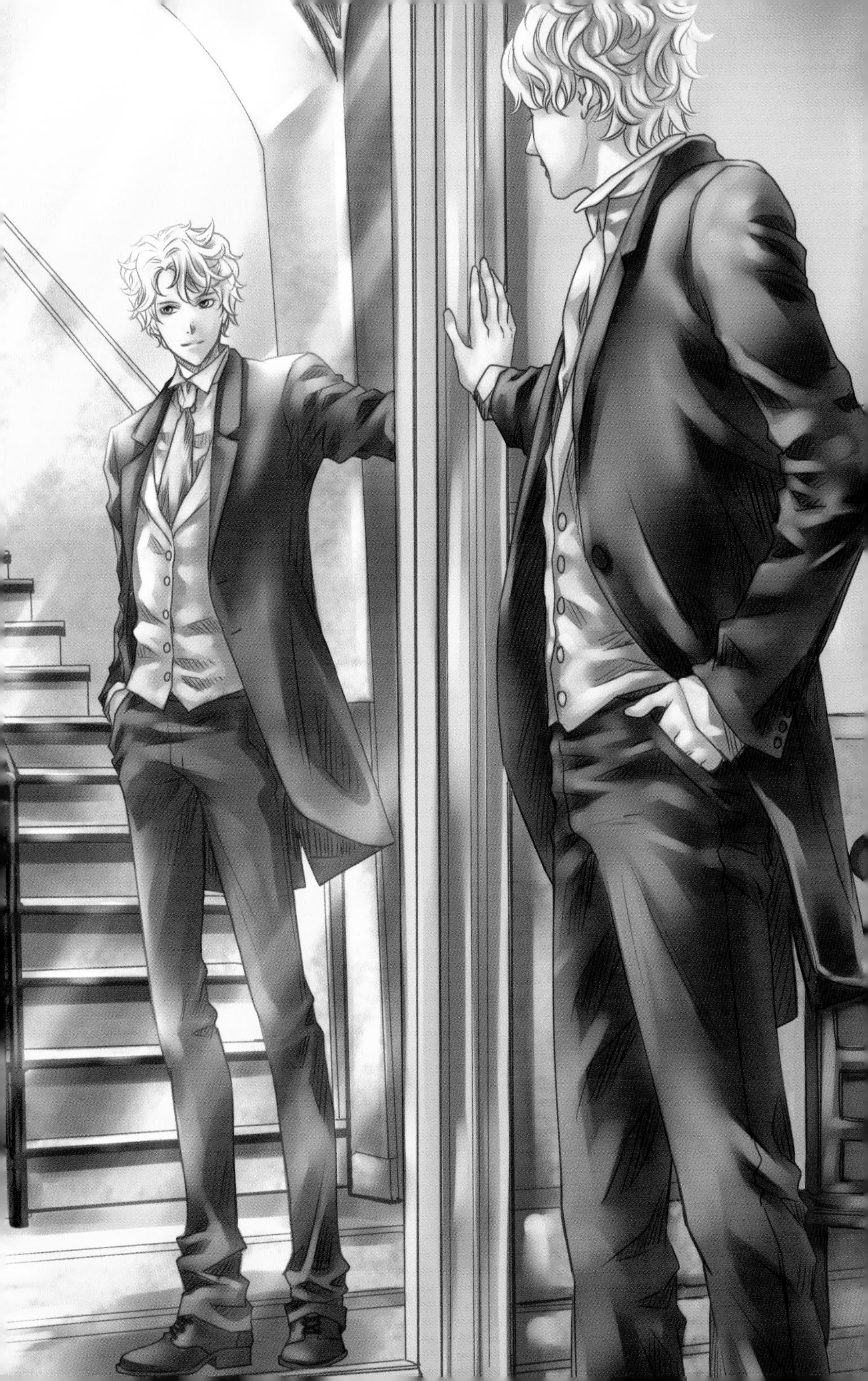

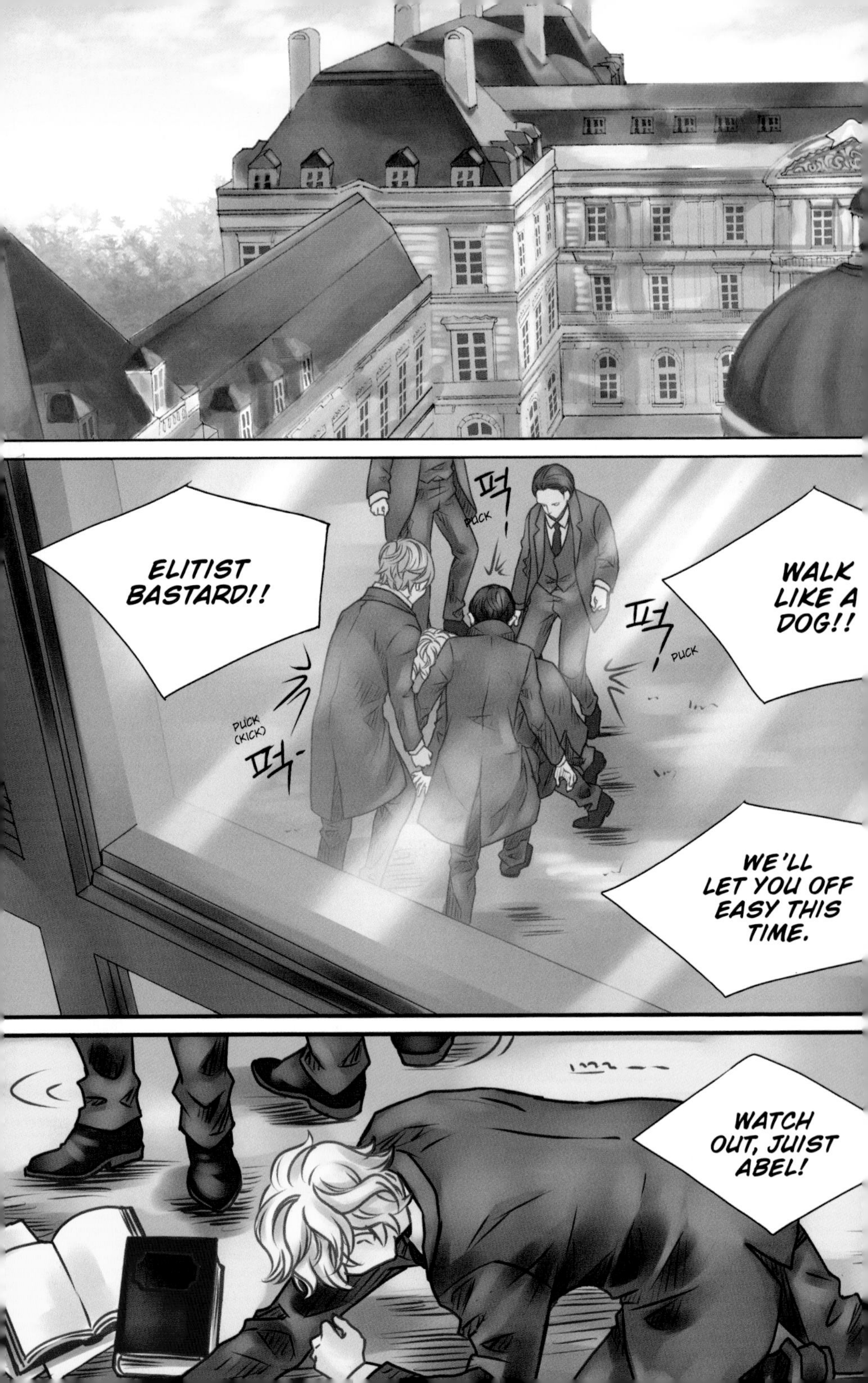
퍽
PUCK
ELITIST BASTARD!!
WALK LIKE A DOG!!
퍽
PUCK
PUCK (KICK)
퍽
WE'LL LET YOU OFF EASY THIS TIME.
WATCH OUT, JUIST ABEL!

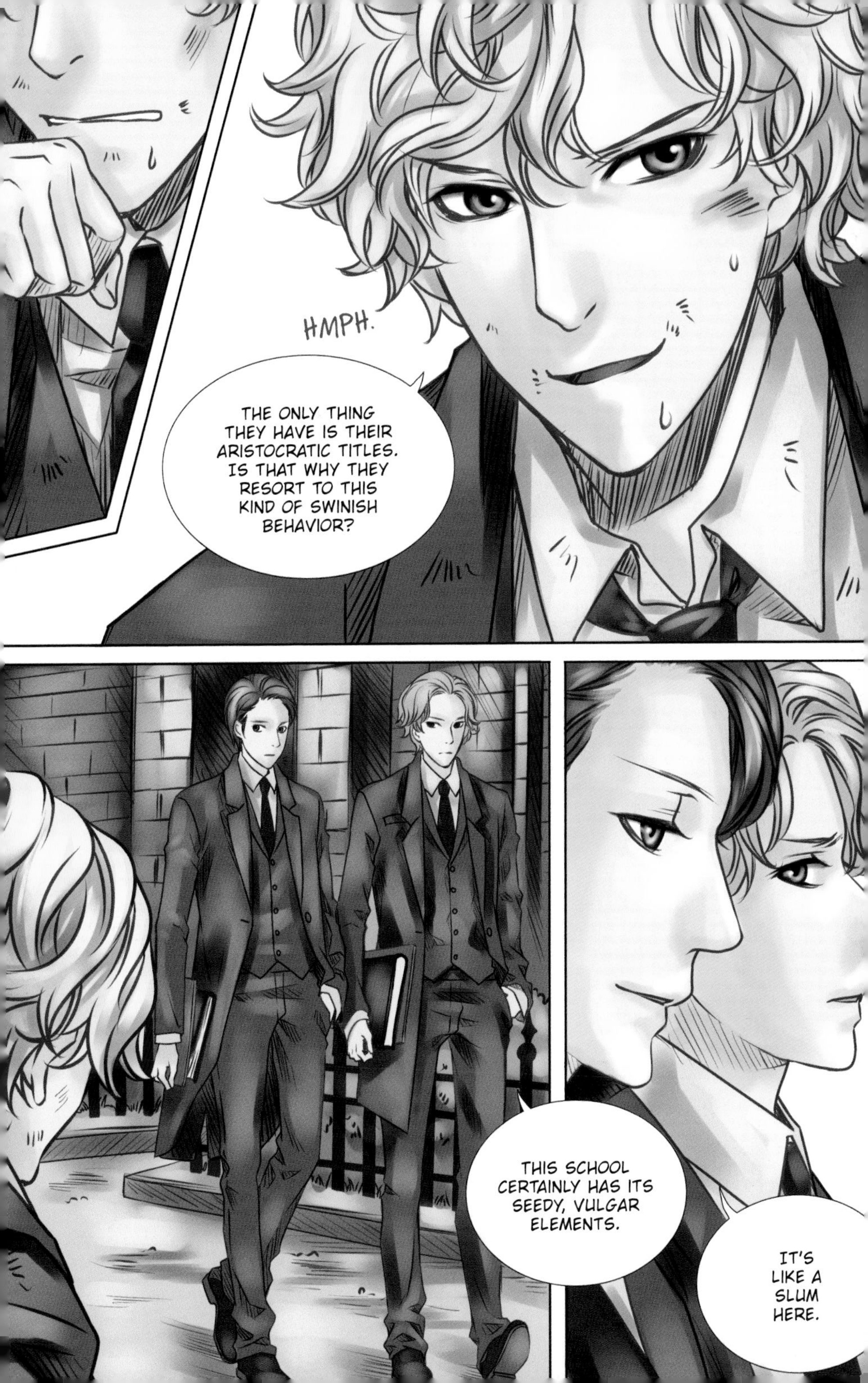
HMPH.
THE ONLY THING THEY HAVE IS THEIR ARISTOCRATIC TITLES. IS THAT WHY THEY RESORT TO THIS KIND OF SWINISH BEHAVIOR?
THIS SCHOOL CERTAINLY HAS ITS SEEDY, VULGAR ELEMENTS.
IT'S LIKE A SLUM HERE.

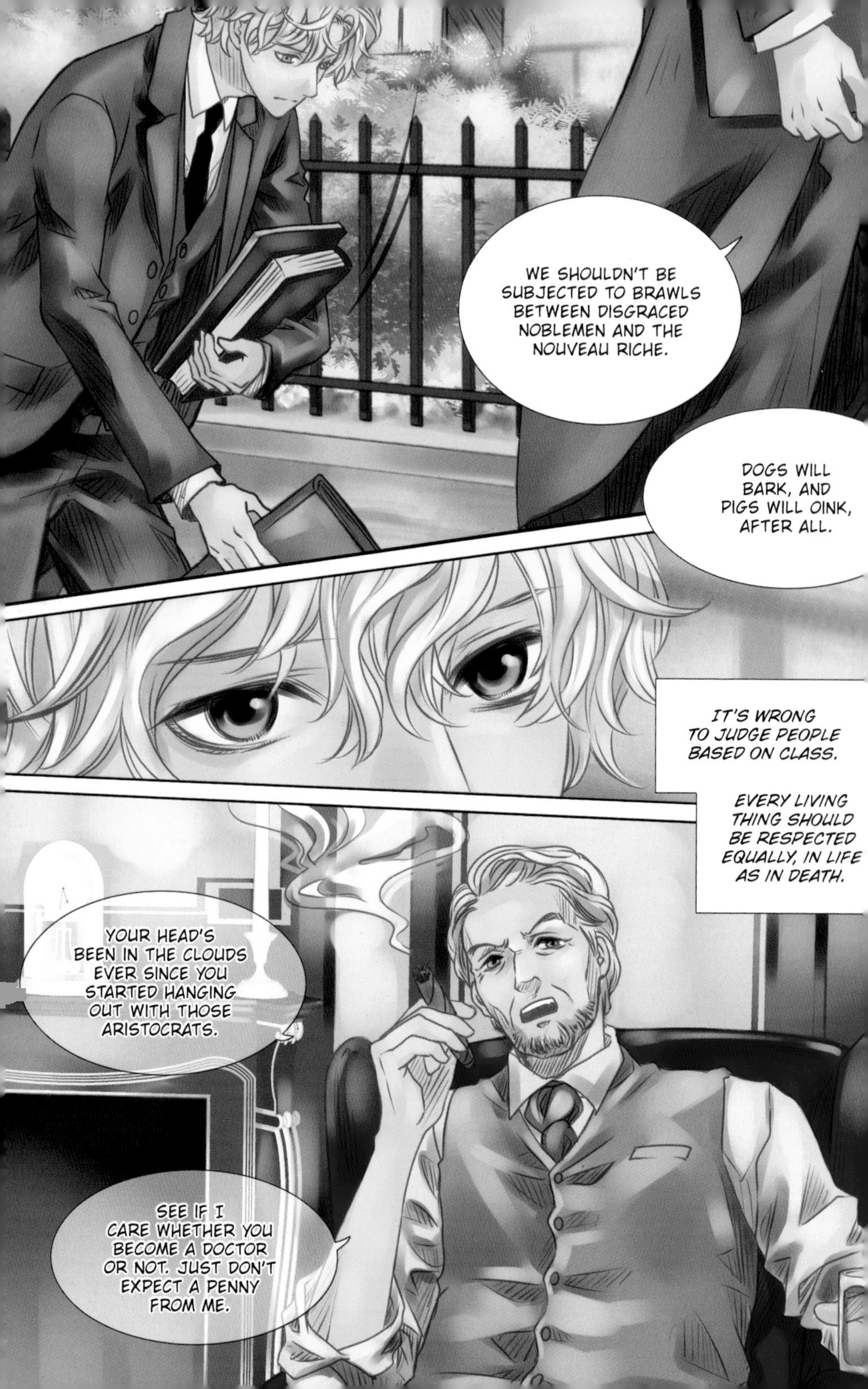
WE SHOULDN'T BE SUBJECTED TO BRAWLS BETWEEN DISGRACED NOBLEMEN AND THE NOUVEAU RICHE.
DOGS WILL BARK, AND PIGS WILL OINK, AFTER ALL.
IT'S WRONG TO JUDGE PEOPLE BASED ON CLASS.
EVERY LIVING THING SHOULD BE RESPECTED EQUALLY, IN LIFE AS IN DEATH.
YOUR HEAD'S BEEN IN THE CLOUDS EVER SINCE YOU STARTED HANGING OUT WITH THOSE ARISTOCRATS.
SEE IF I CARE WHETHER YOU BECOME A DOCTOR OR NOT. JUST DON'T EXPECT A PENNY FROM ME.

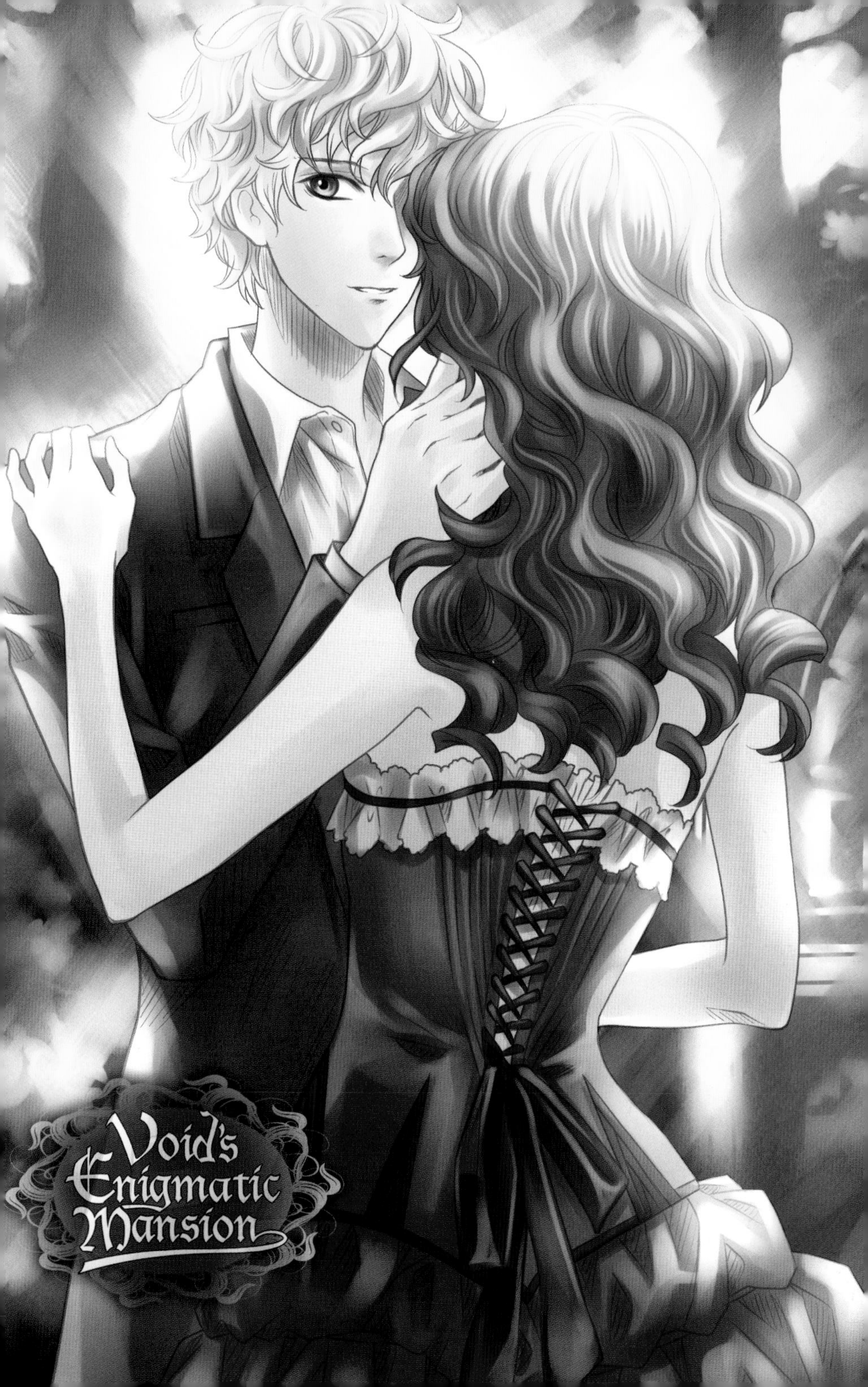
Void's Enigmatic Mansion

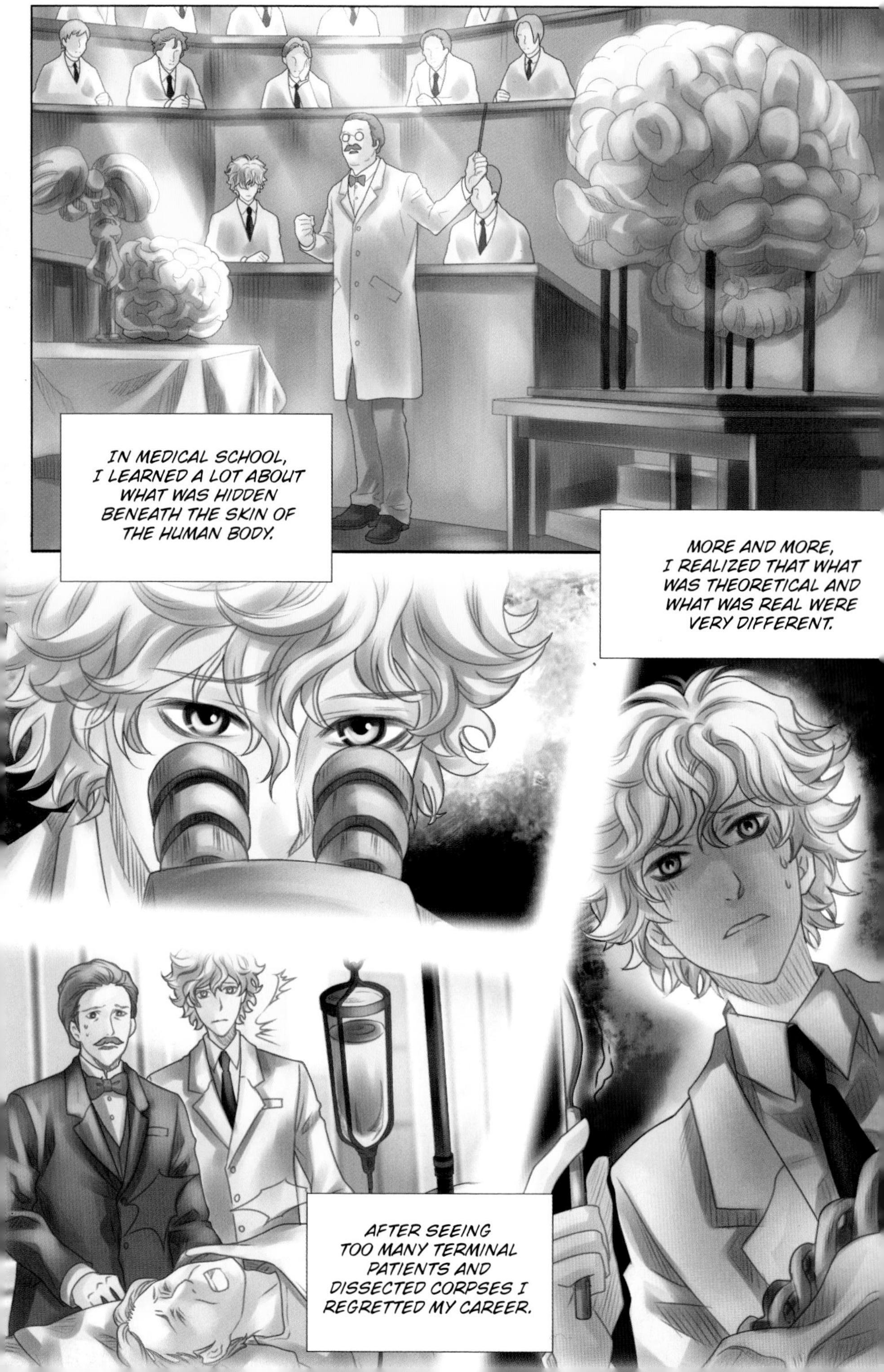
IN MEDICAL SCHOOL, I LEARNED A LOT ABOUT WHAT WAS HIDDEN BENEATH THE SKIN OF THE HUMAN BODY.
MORE AND MORE, I REALIZED THAT WHAT WAS THEORETICAL AND WHAT WAS REAL WERE VERY DIFFERENT.
AFTER SEEING TOO MANY TERMINAL PATIENTS AND DISSECTED CORPSES I REGRETTED MY CAREER.

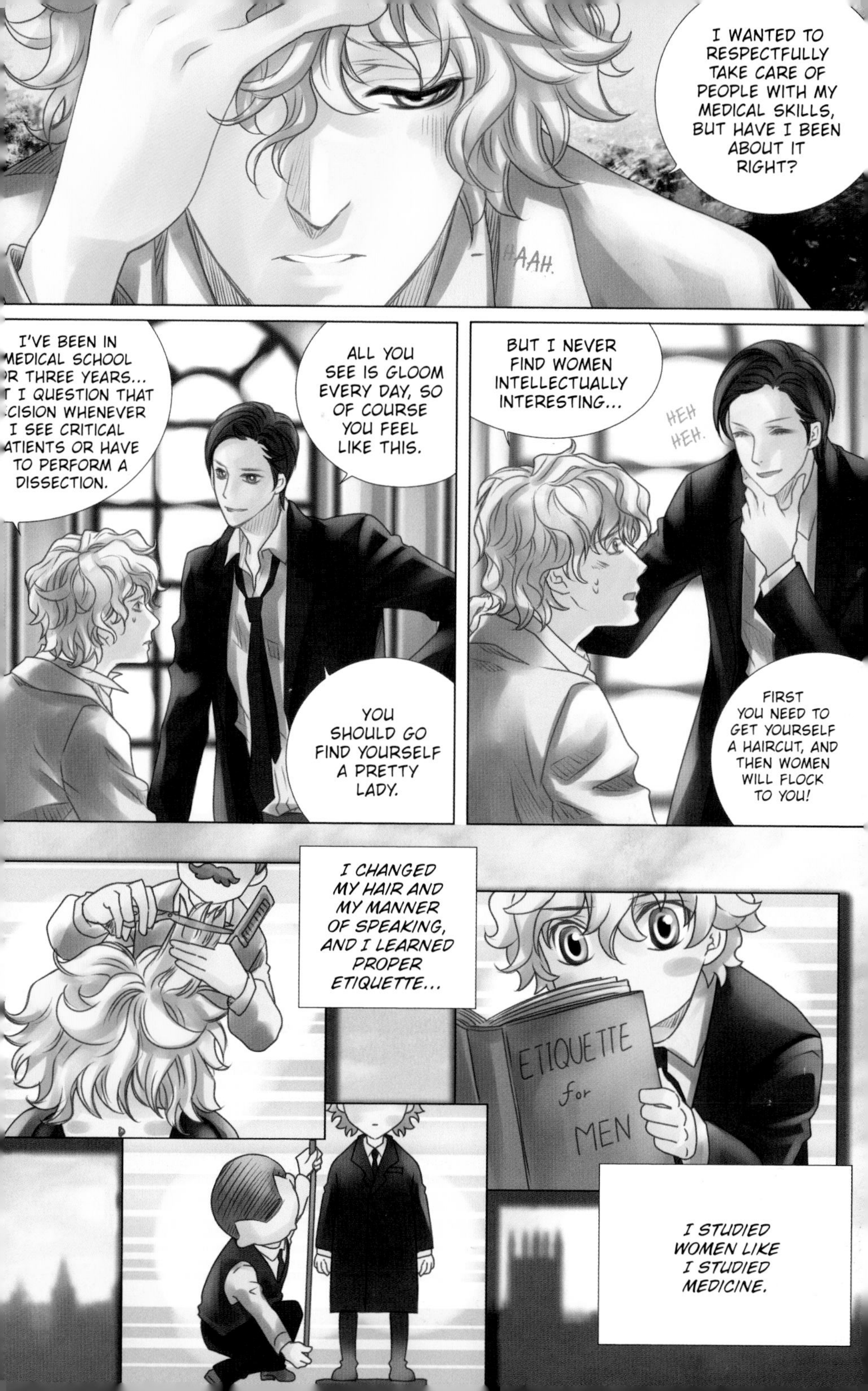
I WANTED TO RESPECTFULLY TAKE CARE OF PEOPLE WITH MY MEDICAL SKILLS, BUT HAVE I BEEN ABOUT IT RIGHT?
HAAH.
I'VE BEEN IN MEDICAL SCHOOL R THREE YEARS... T I QUESTION THAT CISION WHENEVER I SEE CRITICAL ATIENTS OR HAVE TO PERFORM A DISSECTION.
ALL YOU SEE IS GLOOM EVERY DAY, SO OF COURSE YOU FEEL LIKE THIS.
YOU SHOULD GO FIND YOURSELF A PRETTY LADY.
BUT I NEVER FIND WOMEN INTELLECTUALLY INTERESTING...
HEH HEH.
FIRST YOU NEED TO GET YOURSELF A HAIRCUT, AND THEN WOMEN WILL FLOCK TO YOU!
I CHANGED MY HAIR AND MY MANNER OF SPEAKING, AND I LEARNED PROPER ETIQUETTE...
ETIQUETTE for MEN
I STUDIED WOMEN LIKE I STUDIED MEDICINE.

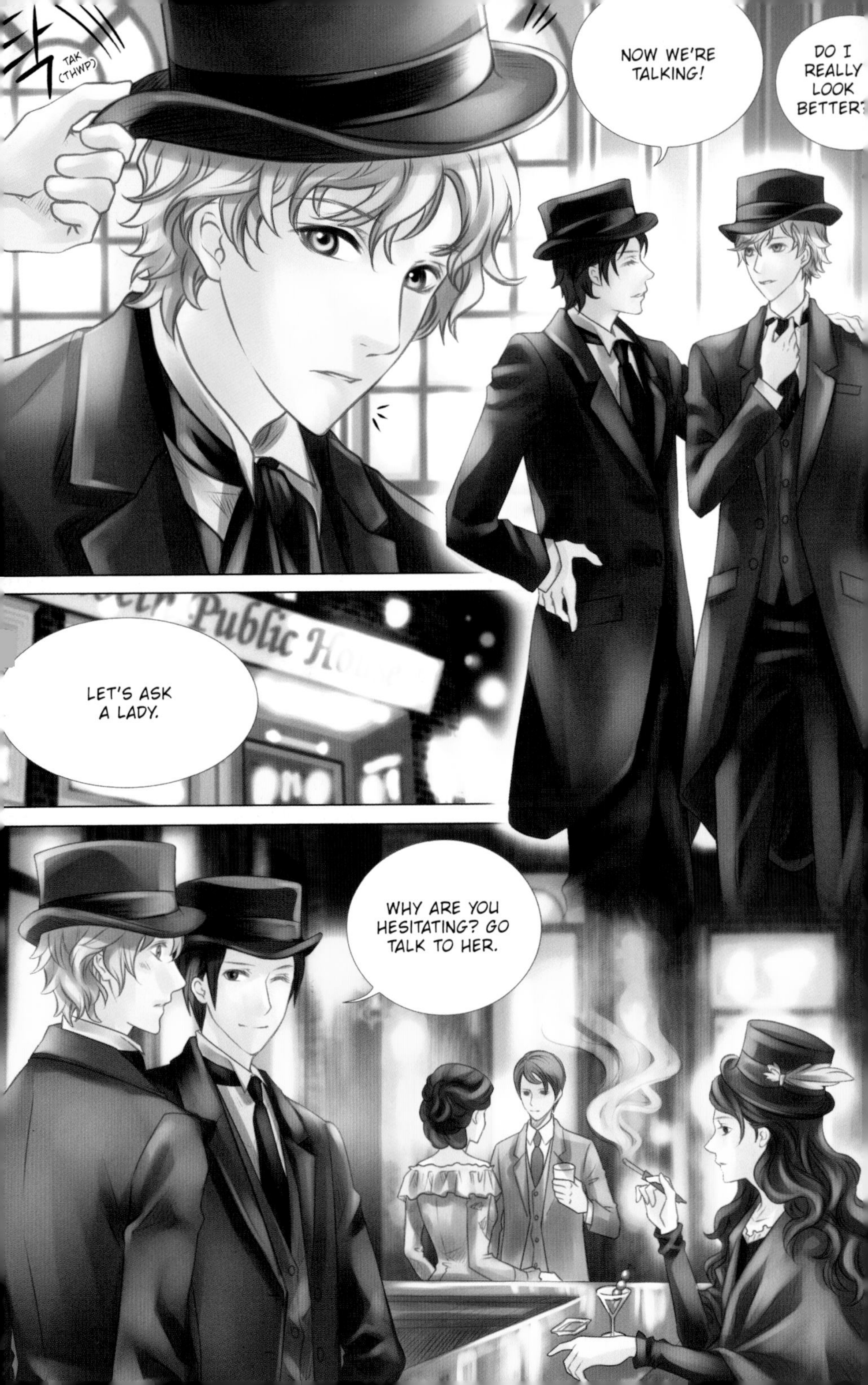
TAK (THWP)
NOW WE'RE TALKING!
DO I REALLY LOOK BETTER?
LET'S ASK A LADY.
Public Ho
WHY ARE YOU HESITATING? GO TALK TO HER.

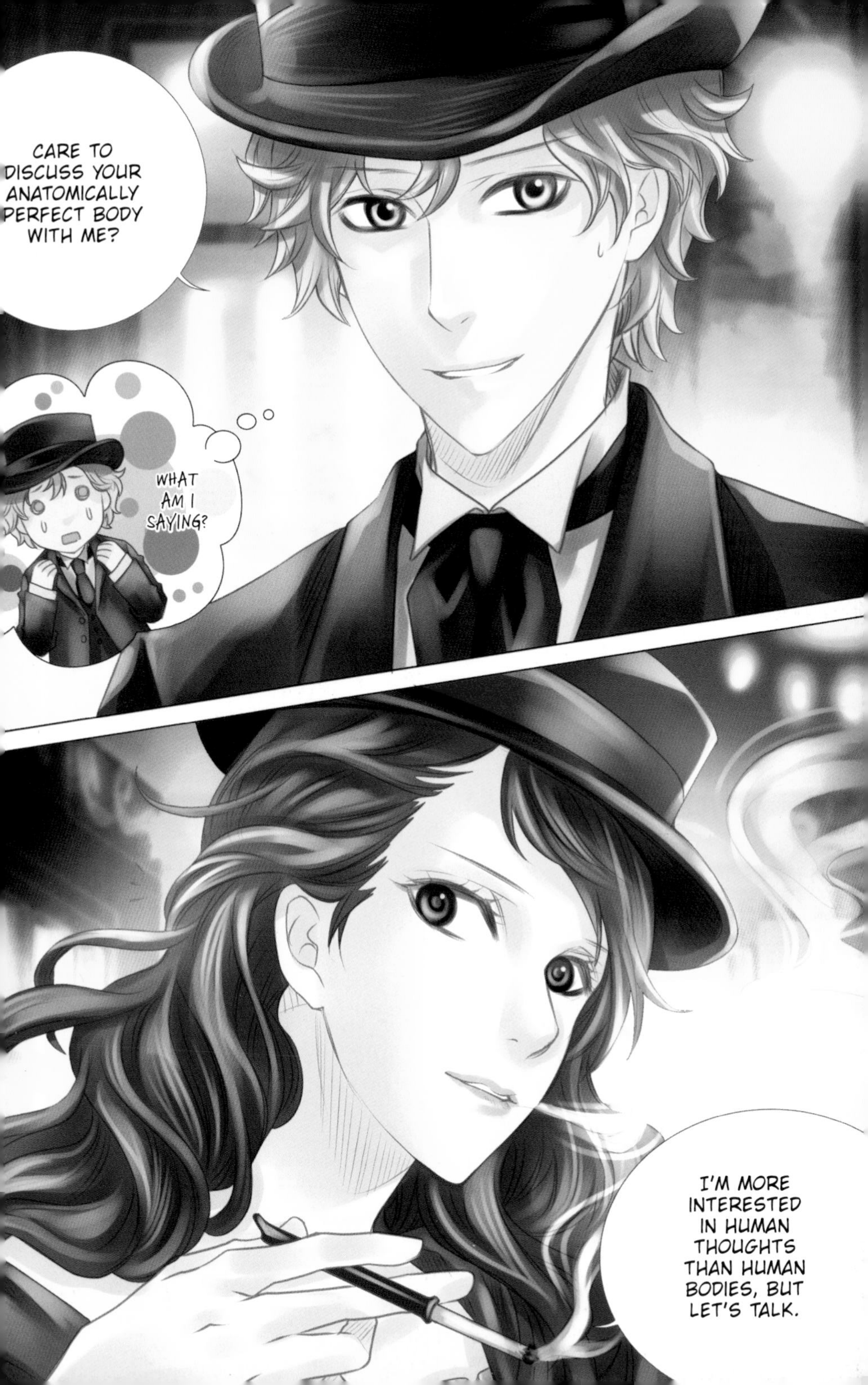
CARE TO DISCUSS YOUR ANATOMICALLY PERFECT BODY WITH ME?
WHAT AM I SAYING?
I'M MORE INTERESTED IN HUMAN THOUGHTS THAN HUMAN BODIES, BUT LET'S TALK.

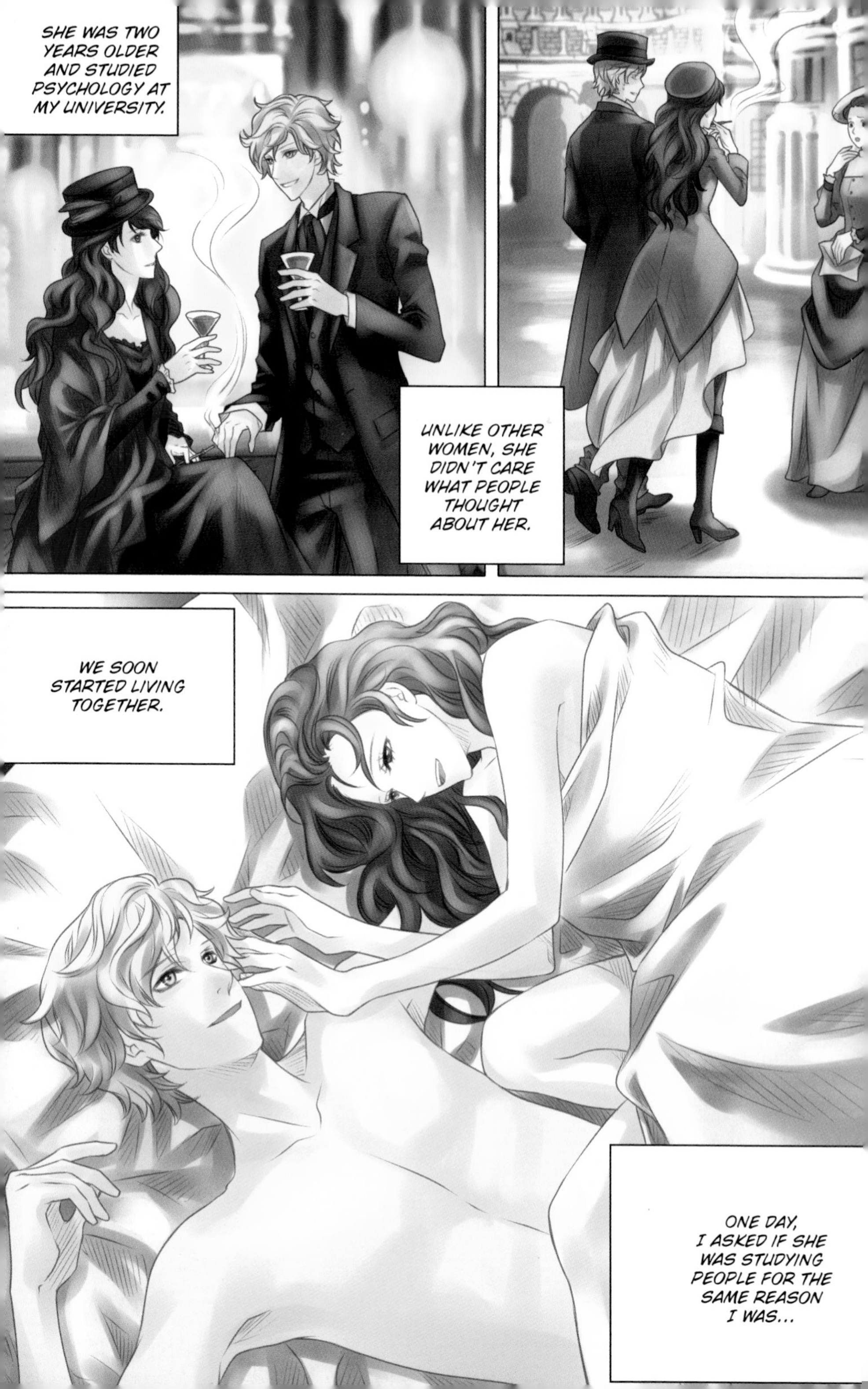
SHE WAS TWO YEARS OLDER AND STUDIED PSYCHOLOGY AT MY UNIVERSITY.
UNLIKE OTHER WOMEN, SHE DIDN'T CARE WHAT PEOPLE THOUGHT ABOUT HER.
WE SOON STARTED LIVING TOGETHER.
ONE DAY, I ASKED IF SHE WAS STUDYING PEOPLE FOR THE SAME REASON I WAS...

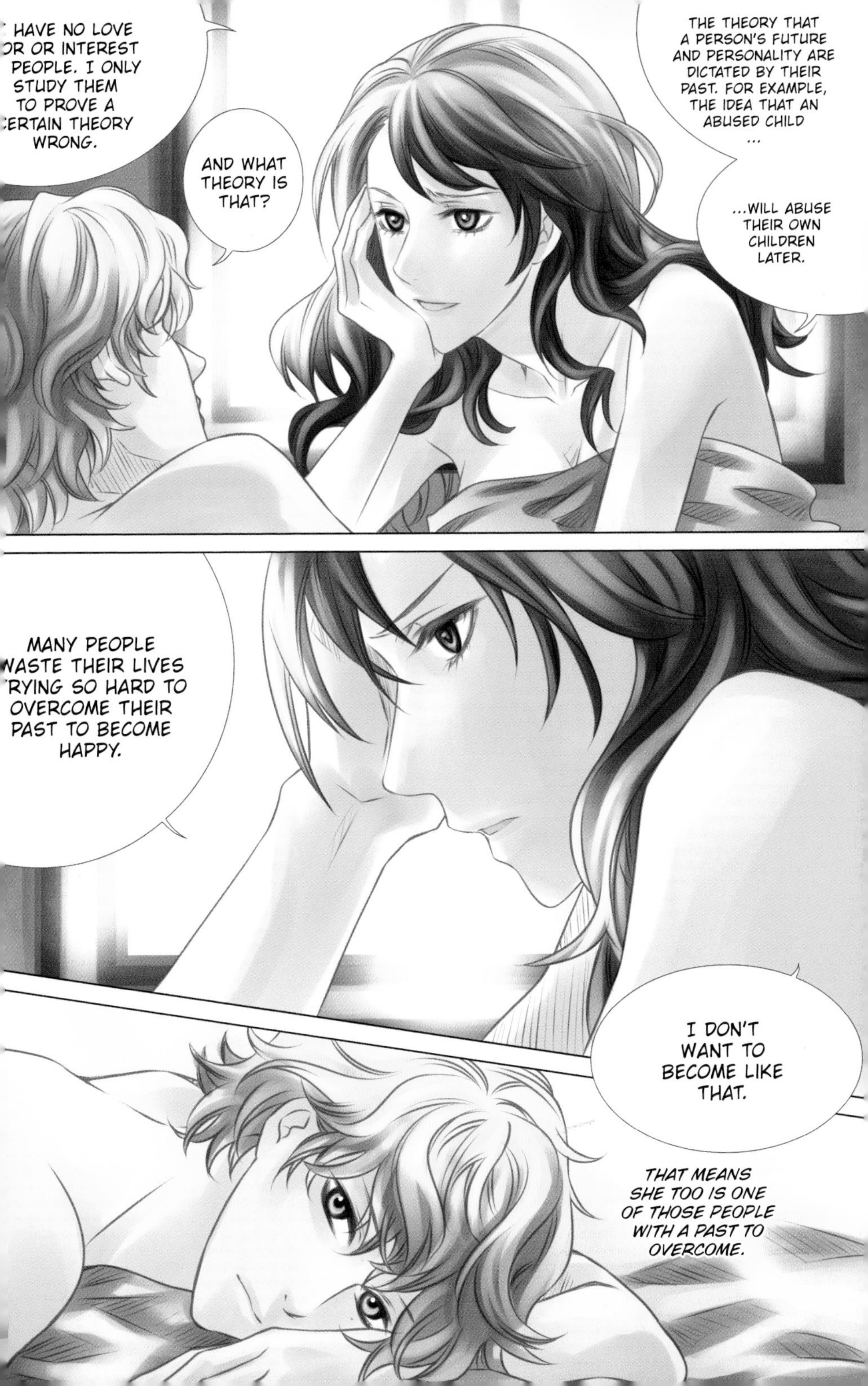
HAVE NO LOVE OR OR INTEREST PEOPLE. I ONLY STUDY THEM TO PROVE A ERTAIN THEORY WRONG.
AND WHAT THEORY IS THAT?
THE THEORY THAT A PERSON'S FUTURE AND PERSONALITY ARE DICTATED BY THEIR PAST. FOR EXAMPLE, THE IDEA THAT AN ABUSED CHILD ...
...WILL ABUSE THEIR OWN CHILDREN LATER.
MANY PEOPLE ASTE THEIR LIVES RYING SO HARD TO OVERCOME THEIR PAST TO BECOME HAPPY.
I DON'T WANT TO BECOME LIKE THAT.
THAT MEANS SHE TOO IS ONE OF THOSE PEOPLE WITH A PAST TO OVERCOME.

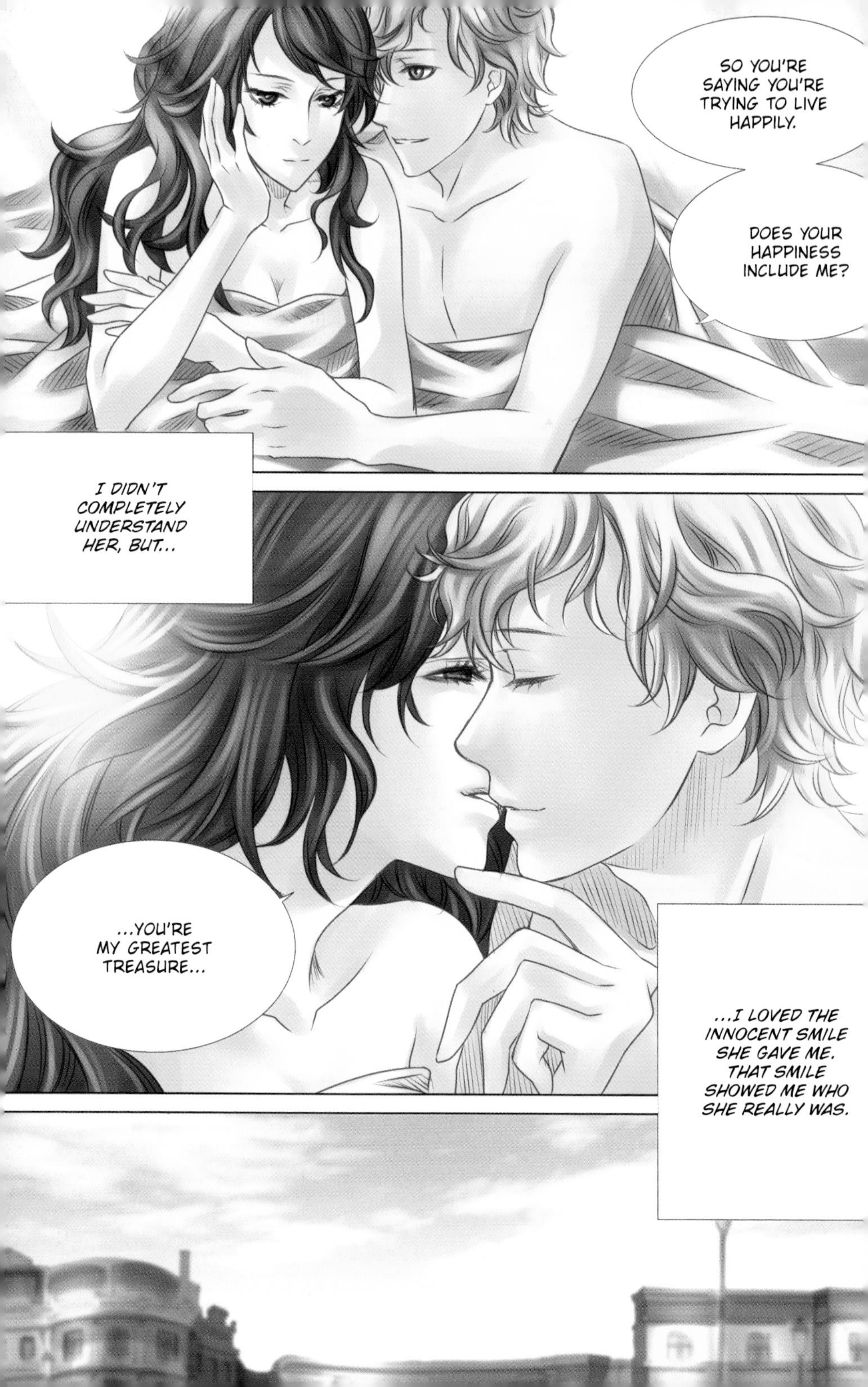
SO YOU'RE SAYING YOU'RE TRYING TO LIVE HAPPILY.
DOES YOUR HAPPINESS INCLUDE ME?
I DIDN'T COMPLETELY UNDERSTAND HER, BUT...
...YOU'RE MY GREATEST TREASURE...
...I LOVED THE INNOCENT SMILE SHE GAVE ME. THAT SMILE SHOWED ME WHO SHE REALLY WAS.

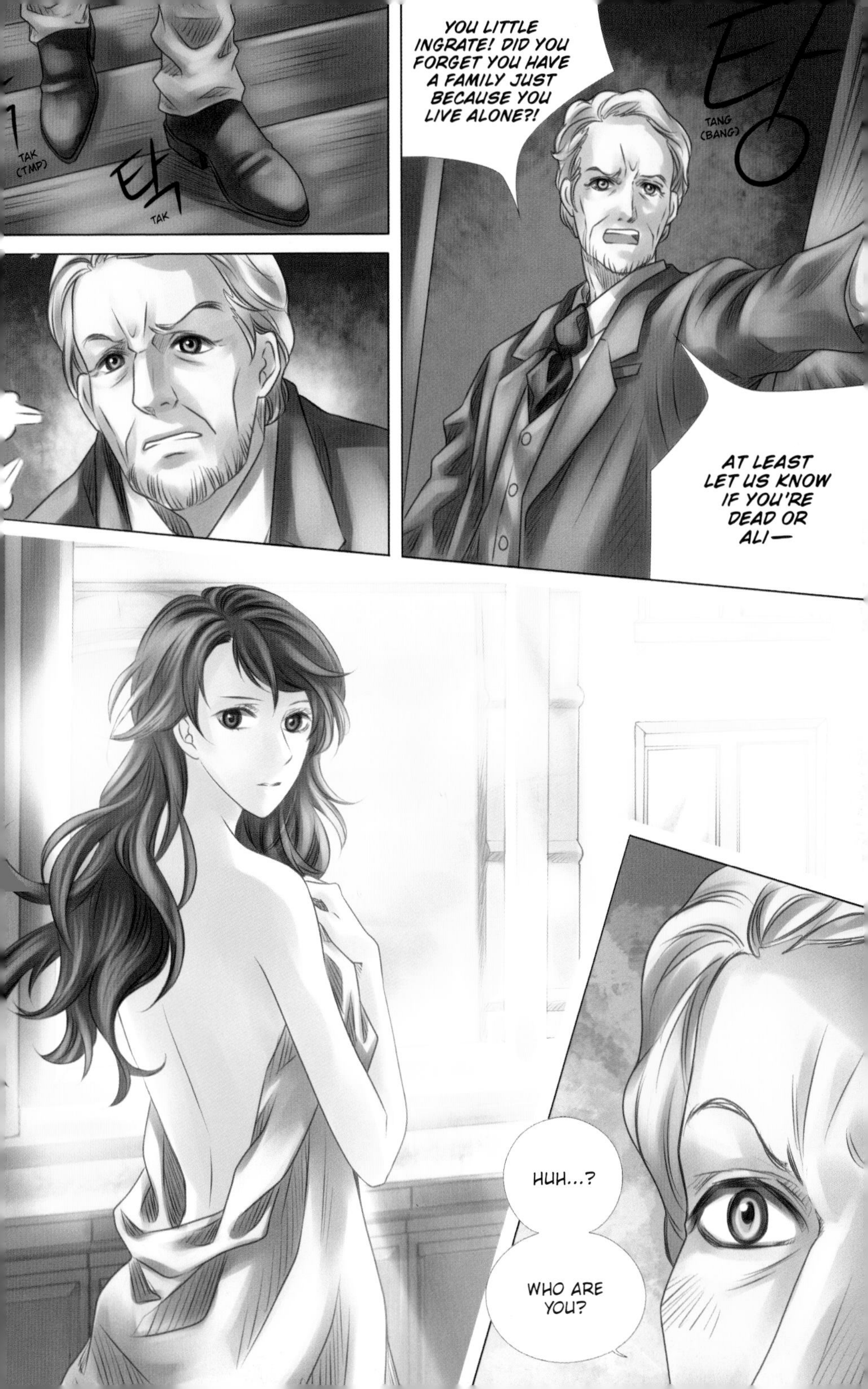

TAK (TMP)
TAK
YOU LITTLE INGRATE! DID YOU FORGET YOU HAVE A FAMILY JUST BECAUSE YOU LIVE ALONE?!
TANG (BANG)
AT LEAST LET US KNOW IF YOU'RE DEAD OR ALI—
HUH...?
WHO ARE YOU?

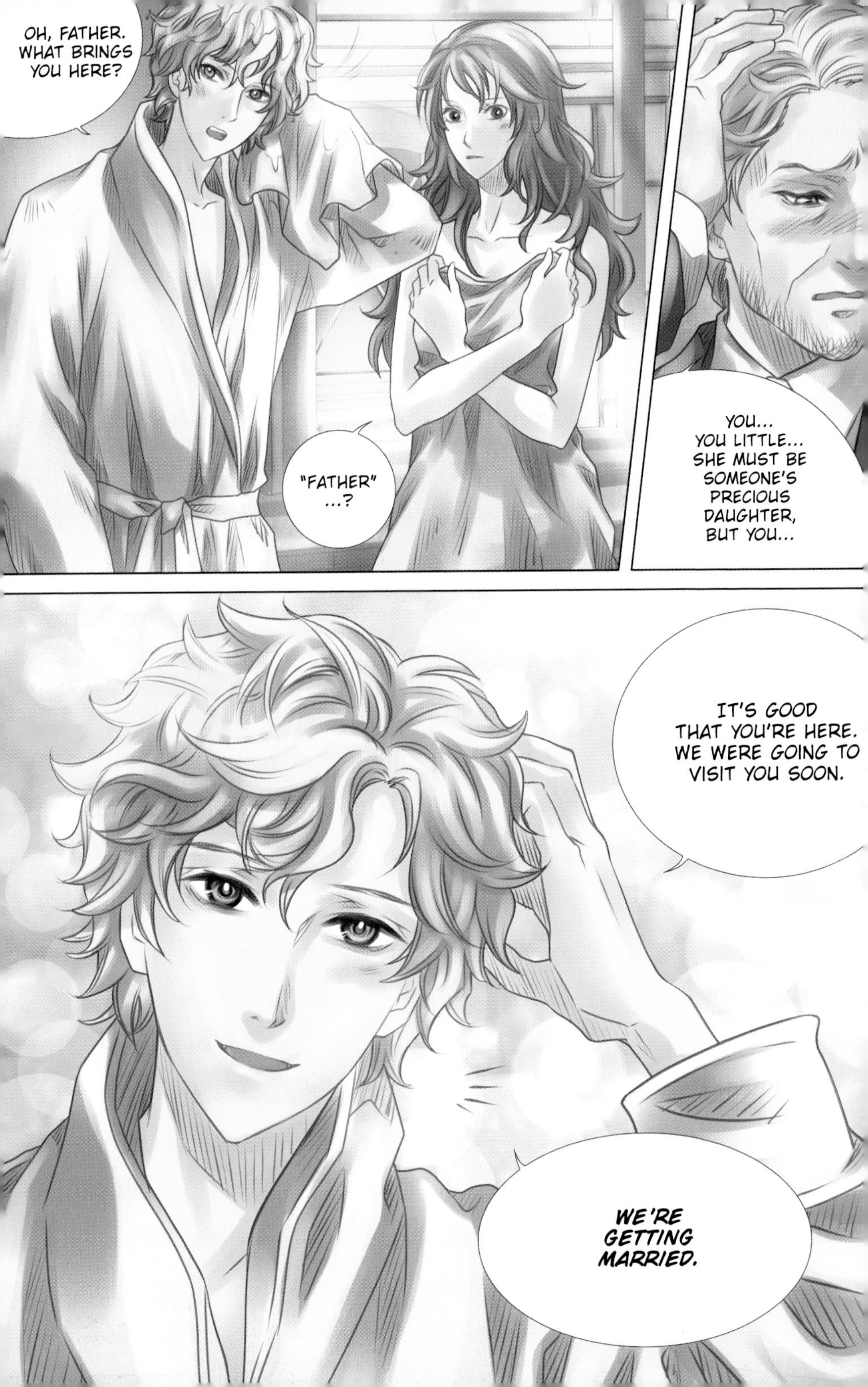
OH, FATHER. WHAT BRINGS YOU HERE?
"FATHER" ...?
YOU... YOU LITTLE... SHE MUST BE SOMEONE'S PRECIOUS DAUGHTER, BUT YOU...
IT'S GOOD THAT YOU'RE HERE. WE WERE GOING TO VISIT YOU SOON.
WE'RE GETTING MARRIED.

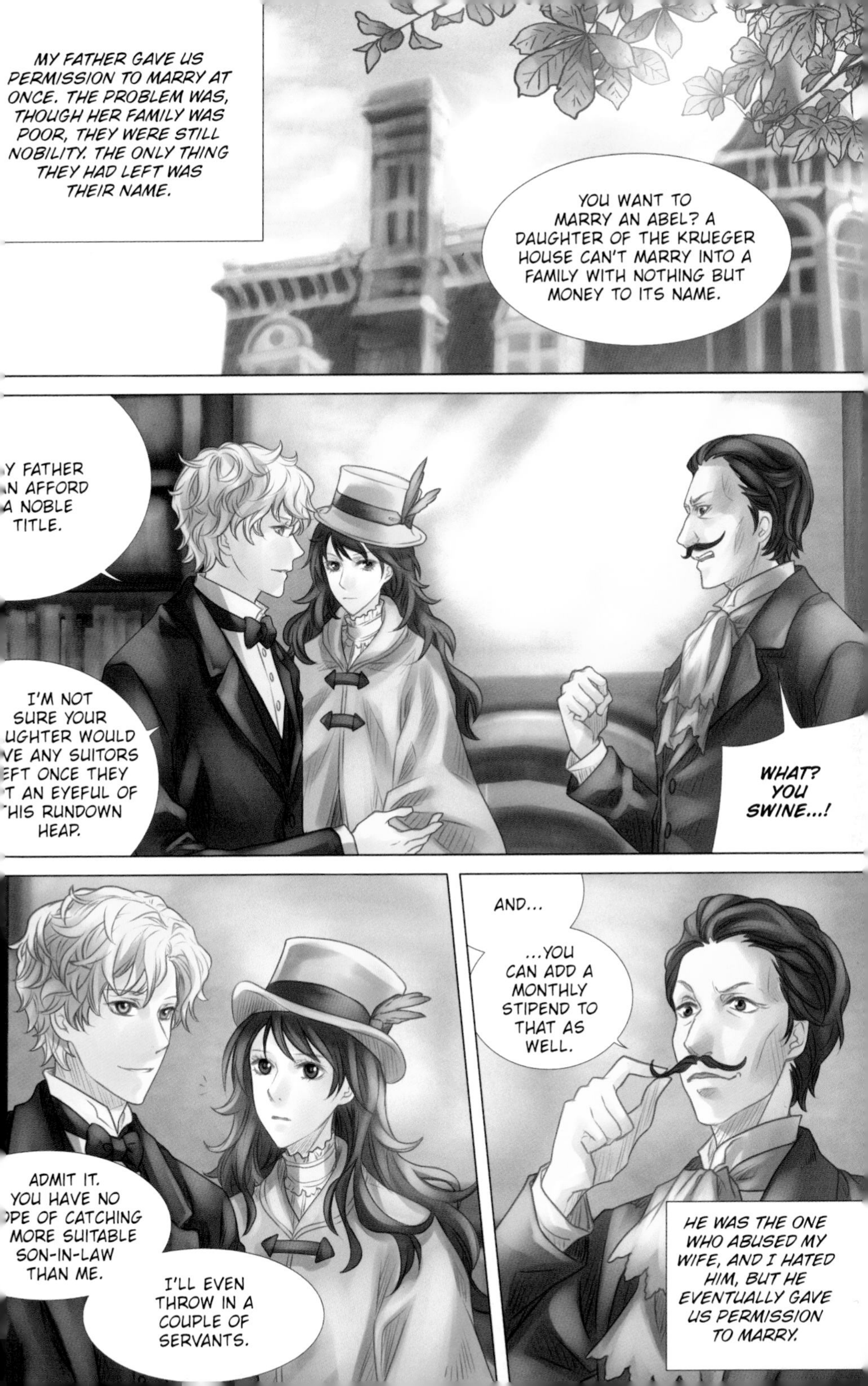

MY FATHER GAVE US PERMISSION TO MARRY AT ONCE. THE PROBLEM WAS, THOUGH HER FAMILY WAS POOR, THEY WERE STILL NOBILITY. THE ONLY THING THEY HAD LEFT WAS THEIR NAME.
YOU WANT TO MARRY AN ABEL? A DAUGHTER OF THE KRUEGER HOUSE CAN'T MARRY INTO A FAMILY WITH NOTHING BUT MONEY TO ITS NAME.
Y FATHER N AFFORD A NOBLE TITLE.
I'M NOT SURE YOUR UGHTER WOULD VE ANY SUITORS EFT ONCE THEY T AN EYEFUL OF THIS RUNDOWN HEAP.
WHAT? YOU SWINE...!
ADMIT IT. YOU HAVE NO PE OF CATCHING MORE SUITABLE SON-IN-LAW THAN ME.
I'LL EVEN THROW IN A COUPLE OF SERVANTS.
AND...
...YOU CAN ADD A MONTHLY STIPEND TO THAT AS WELL.
HE WAS THE ONE WHO ABUSED MY WIFE, AND I HATED HIM, BUT HE EVENTUALLY GAVE US PERMISSION TO MARRY.

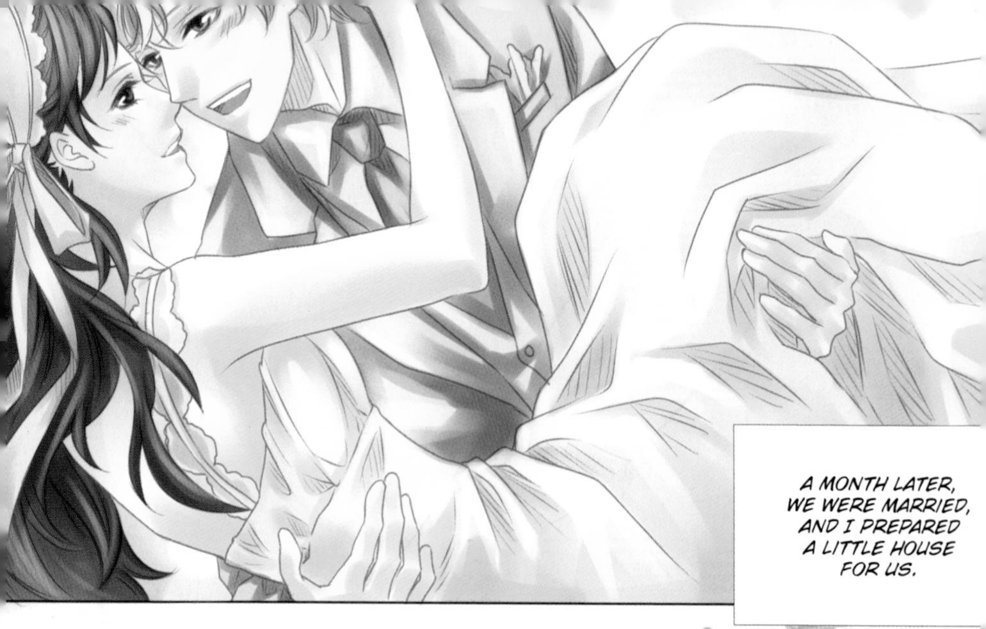
A MONTH LATER, WE WERE MARRIED, AND I PREPARED A LITTLE HOUSE FOR US.
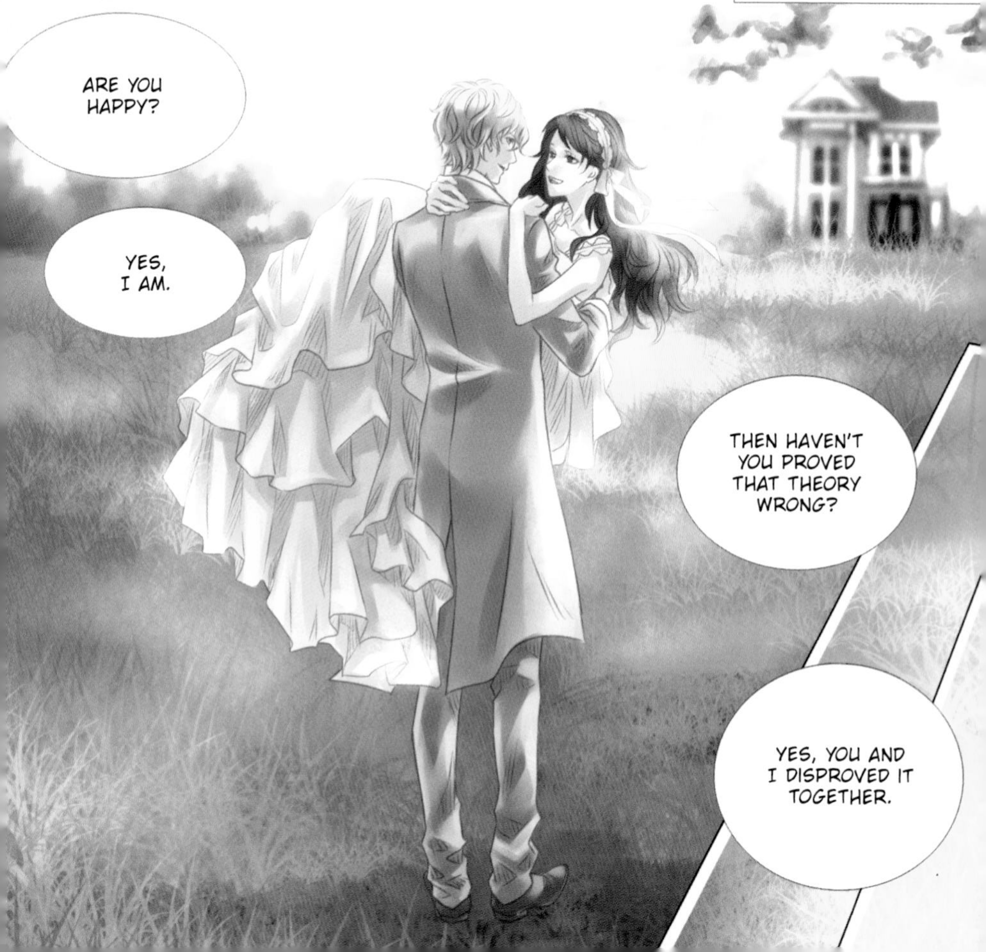
ARE YOU HAPPY?
YES, I AM.
THEN HAVEN'T YOU PROVED THAT THEORY WRONG?
YES, YOU AND I DISPROVED IT TOGETHER.

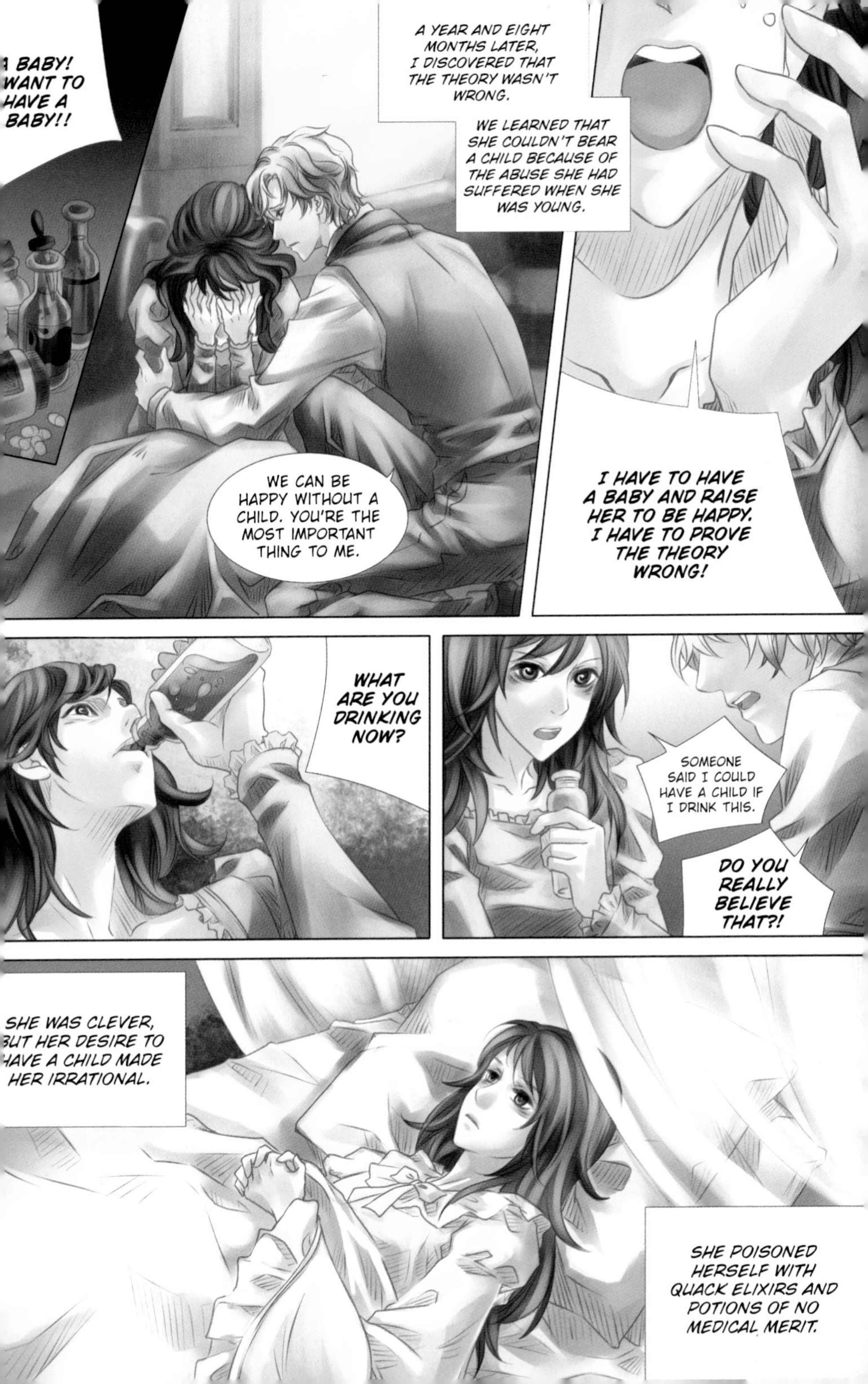

A BABY! WANT TO HAVE A BABY!!
A YEAR AND EIGHT MONTHS LATER, I DISCOVERED THAT THE THEORY WASN'T WRONG.
WE LEARNED THAT SHE COULDN'T BEAR A CHILD BECAUSE OF THE ABUSE SHE HAD SUFFERED WHEN SHE WAS YOUNG.
WE CAN BE HAPPY WITHOUT A CHILD. YOU'RE THE MOST IMPORTANT THING TO ME.
I HAVE TO HAVE A BABY AND RAISE HER TO BE HAPPY. I HAVE TO PROVE THE THEORY WRONG!
WHAT ARE YOU DRINKING NOW?
SOMEONE SAID I COULD HAVE A CHILD IF I DRINK THIS.
DO YOU REALLY BELIEVE THAT?!
SHE WAS CLEVER, BUT HER DESIRE TO HAVE A CHILD MADE HER IRRATIONAL.
SHE POISONED HERSELF WITH QUACK ELIXIRS AND POTIONS OF NO MEDICAL MERIT.

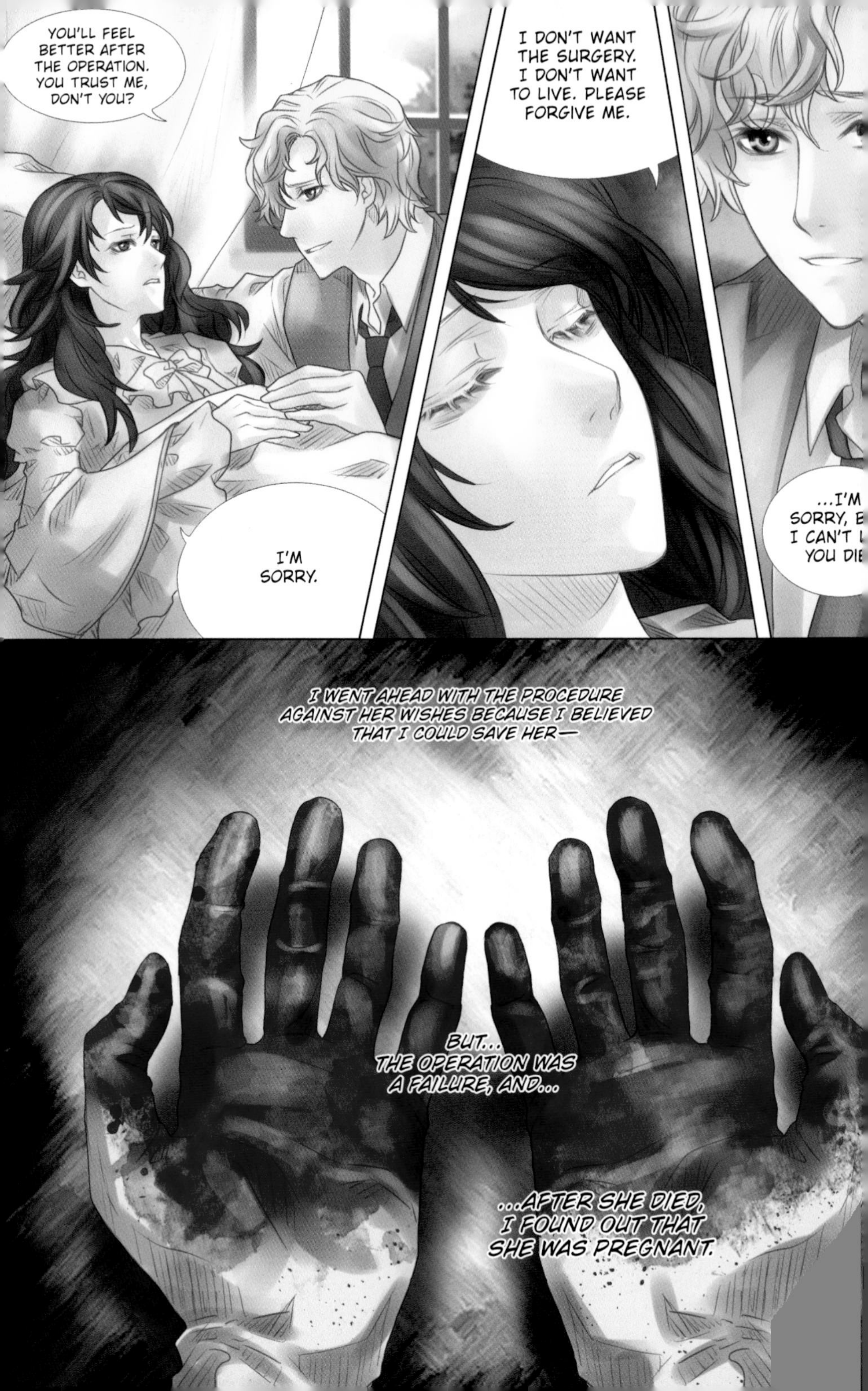
YOU'LL FEEL BETTER AFTER THE OPERATION. YOU TRUST ME, DON'T YOU?
I'M SORRY.
I DON'T WANT THE SURGERY. I DON'T WANT TO LIVE. PLEASE FORGIVE ME.
...I'M SORRY,
I WENT AHEAD WITH THE PROCEDURE AGAINST HER WISHES BECAUSE I BELIEVED THAT I COULD SAVE HER—
BUT... THE OPERATION WAS A FAILURE, AND...
...AFTER SHE DIED, I FOUND OUT THAT SHE WAS PREGNANT.

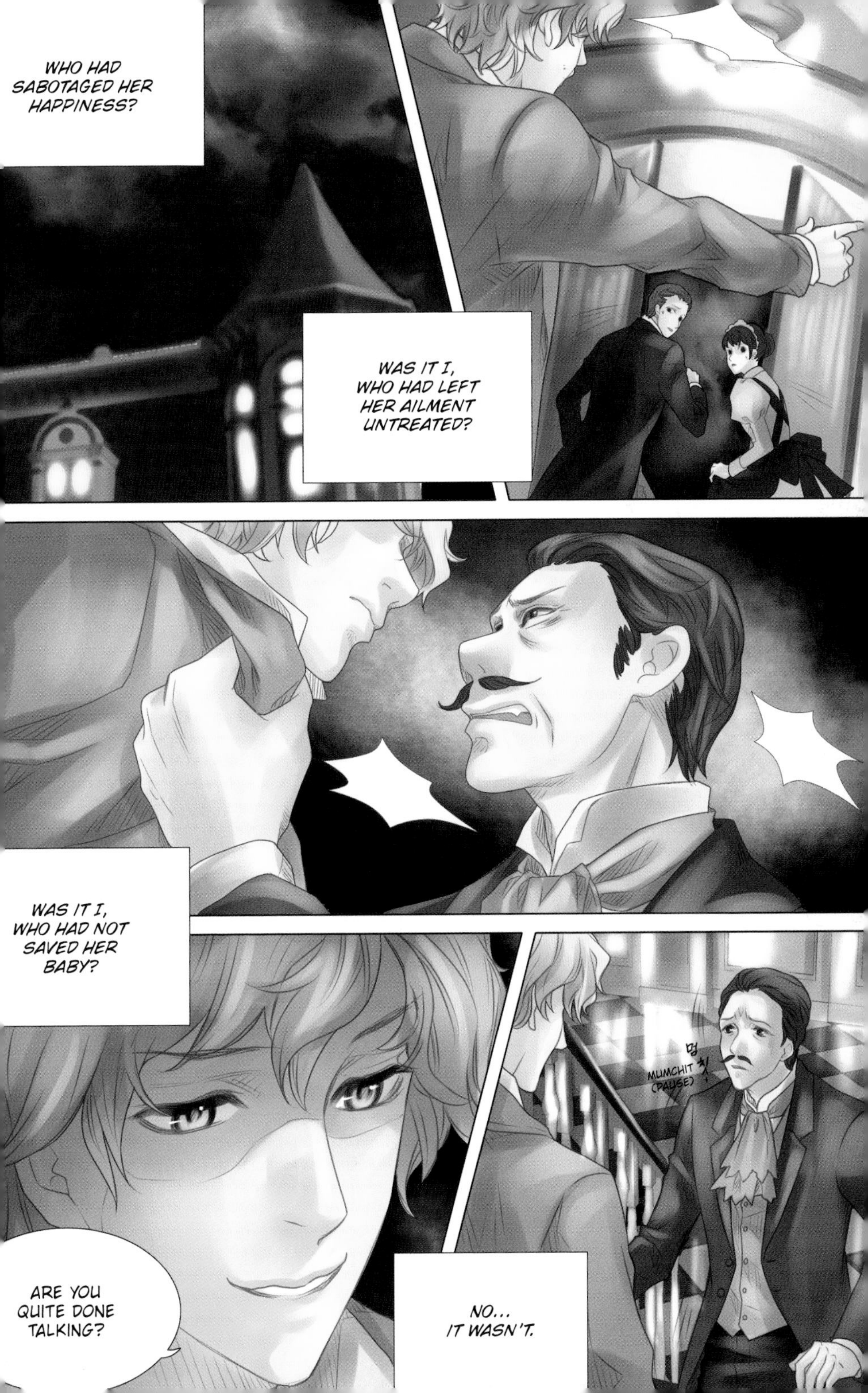
WHO HAD SABOTAGED HER HAPPINESS?
WAS IT I, WHO HAD LEFT HER AILMENT UNTREATED?
WAS IT I, WHO HAD NOT SAVED HER BABY?
ARE YOU QUITE DONE TALKING?
멈칫 MUMCHIT (PAUSE)
NO... IT WASN'T.

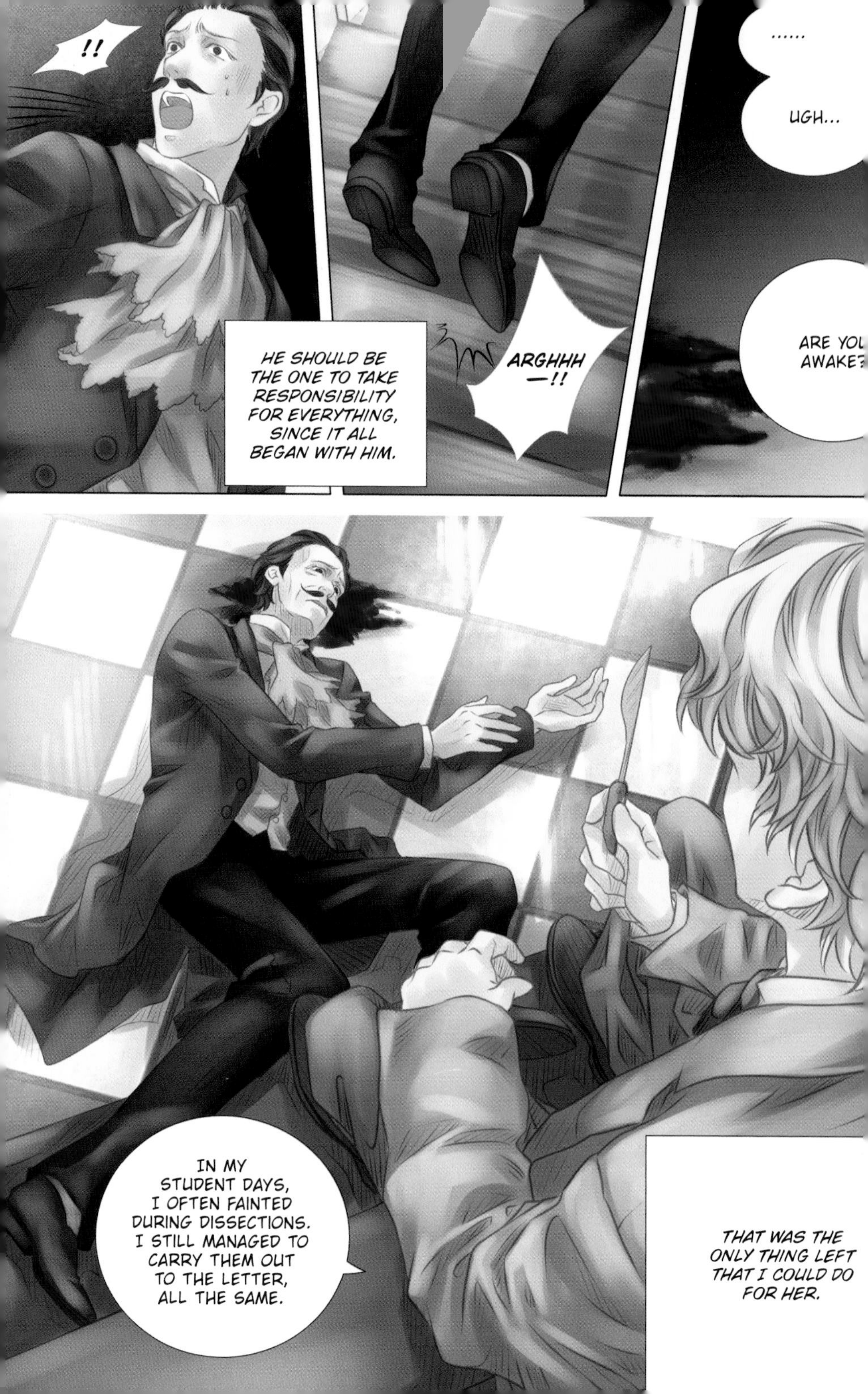
!!
HE SHOULD BE THE ONE TO TAKE RESPONSIBILITY FOR EVERYTHING, SINCE IT ALL BEGAN WITH HIM.
ARGHHH—!!
......
UGH...
ARE YOU AWAKE?
IN MY STUDENT DAYS, I OFTEN FAINTED DURING DISSECTIONS. I STILL MANAGED TO CARRY THEM OUT TO THE LETTER, ALL THE SAME.
THAT WAS THE ONLY THING LEFT THAT I COULD DO FOR HER.

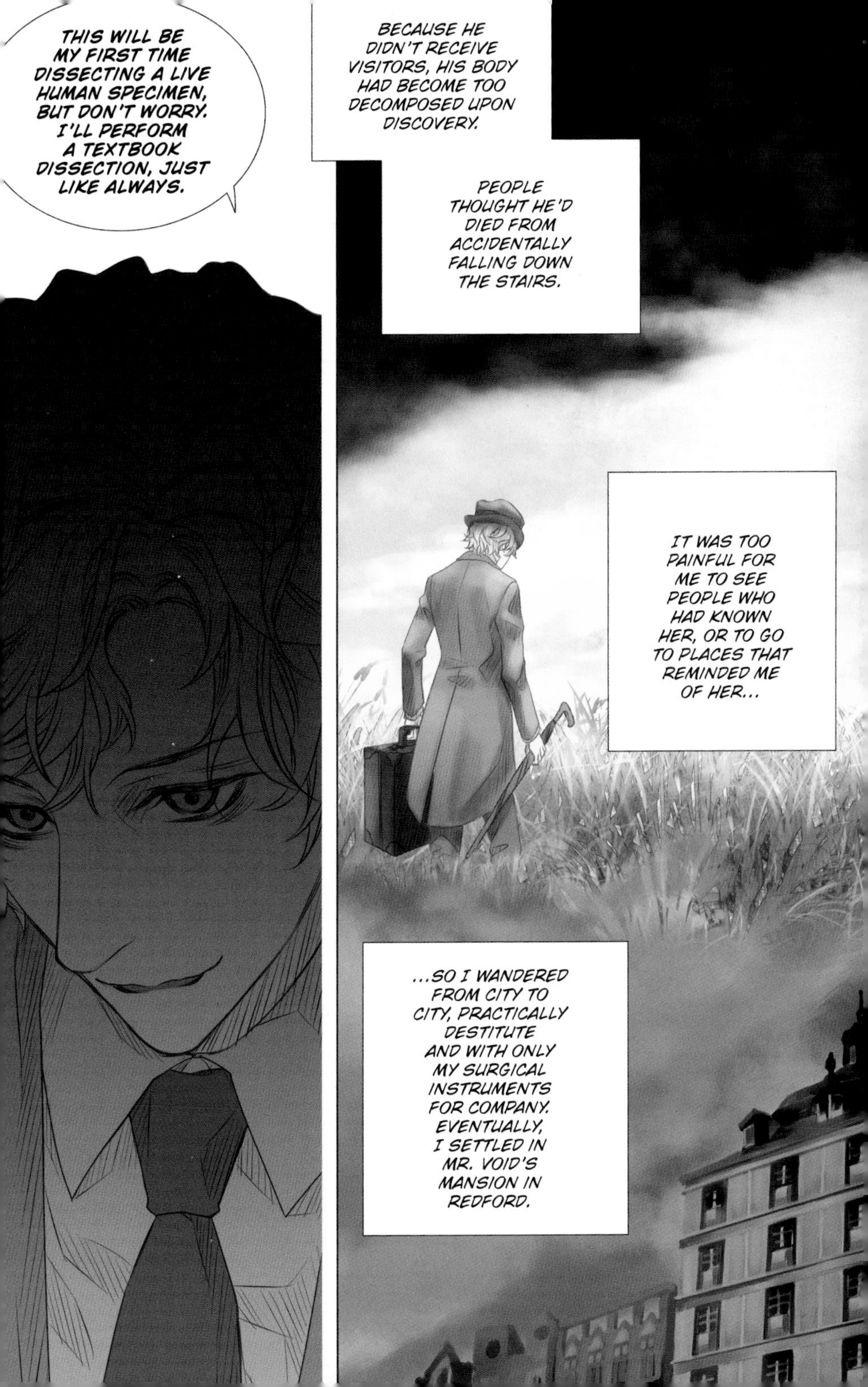
THIS WILL BE MY FIRST TIME DISSECTING A LIVE HUMAN SPECIMEN, BUT DON'T WORRY. I'LL PERFORM A TEXTBOOK DISSECTION, JUST LIKE ALWAYS.
BECAUSE HE DIDN'T RECEIVE VISITORS, HIS BODY HAD BECOME TOO DECOMPOSED UPON DISCOVERY.
PEOPLE THOUGHT HE'D DIED FROM ACCIDENTALLY FALLING DOWN THE STAIRS.
IT WAS TOO PAINFUL FOR ME TO SEE PEOPLE WHO HAD KNOWN HER, OR TO GO TO PLACES THAT REMINDED ME OF HER...
...SO I WANDERED FROM CITY TO CITY, PRACTICALLY DESTITUTE AND WITH ONLY MY SURGICAL INSTRUMENTS FOR COMPANY. EVENTUALLY, I SETTLED IN MR. VOID'S MANSION IN REDFORD.

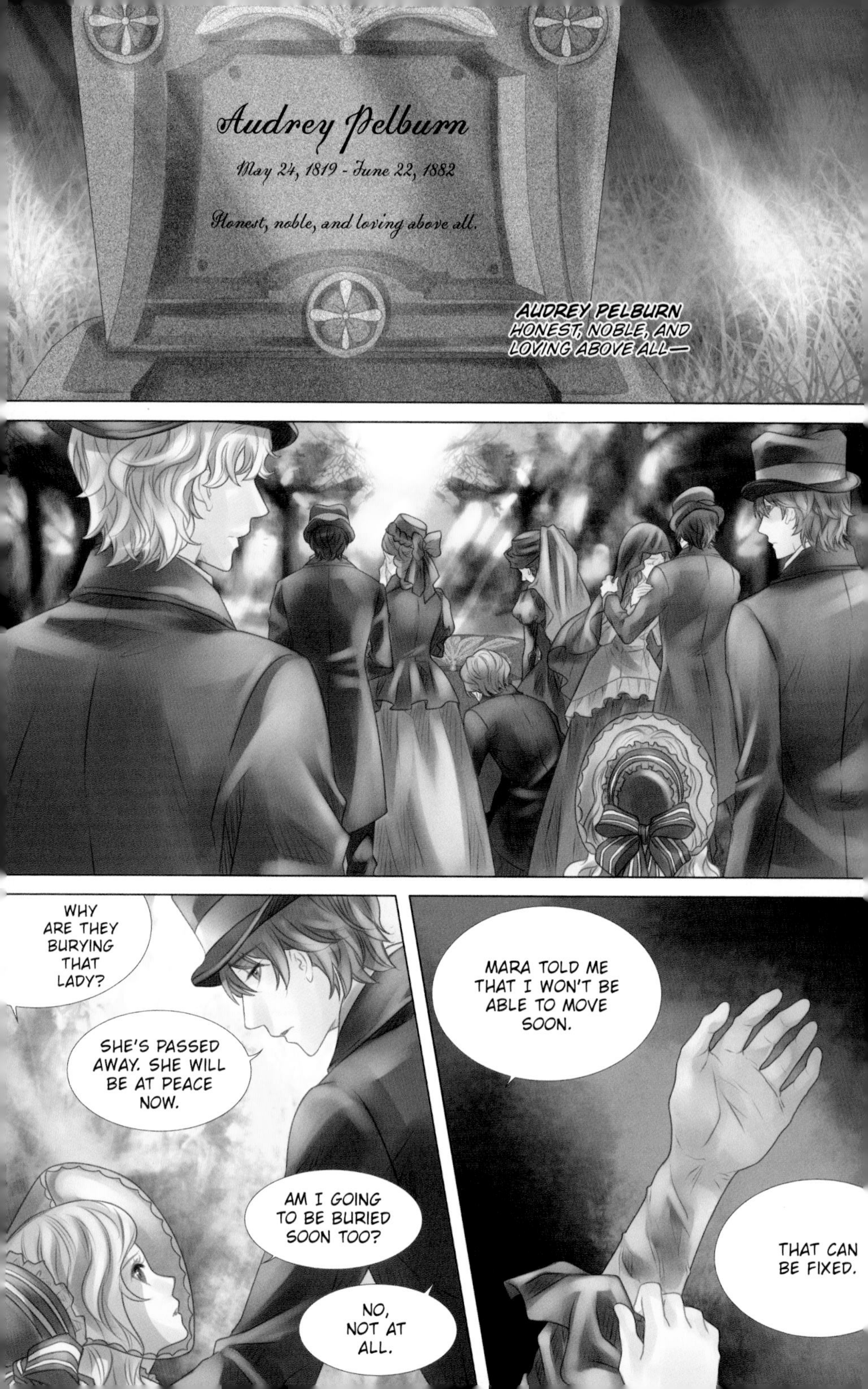
Audrey Pelburn
May 24, 1819 - June 22, 1882
Honest, noble, and loving above all.
AUDREY PELBURN HONEST, NOBLE, AND LOVING ABOVE ALL—
WHY ARE THEY BURYING THAT LADY?
SHE'S PASSED AWAY. SHE WILL BE AT PEACE NOW.
AM I GOING TO BE BURIED SOON TOO?
NO, NOT AT ALL.
MARA TOLD ME THAT I WON'T BE ABLE TO MOVE SOON.
THAT CAN BE FIXED.

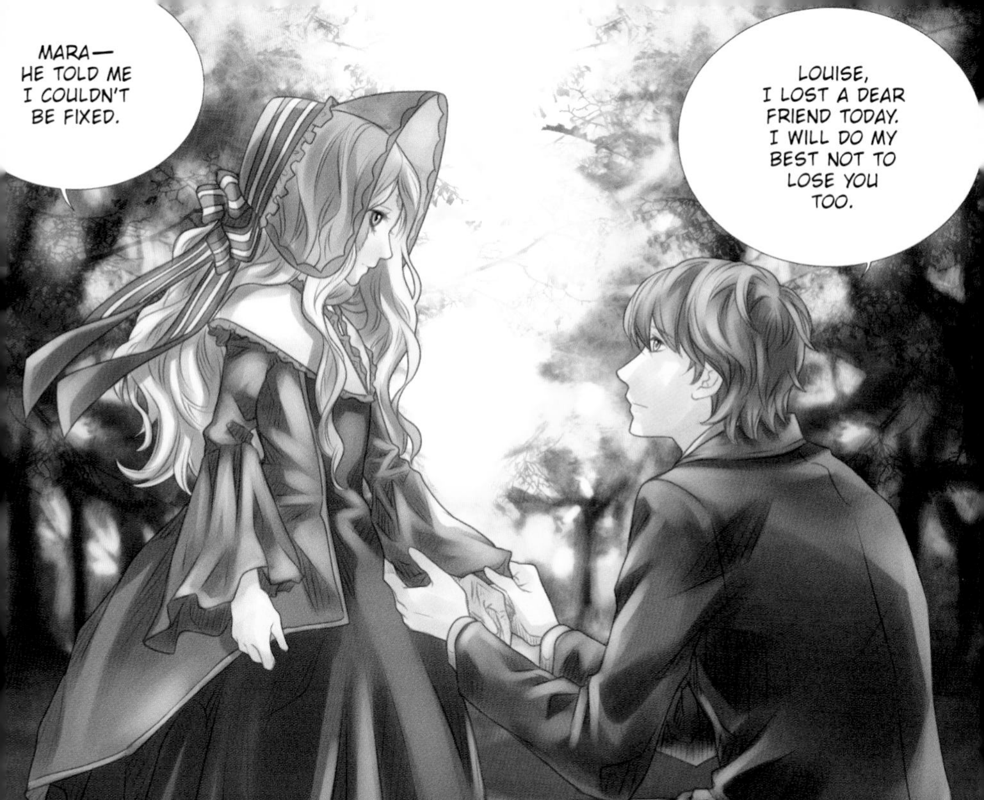
MARA— HE TOLD ME I COULDN'T BE FIXED.
LOUISE, I LOST A DEAR FRIEND TODAY. I WILL DO MY BEST NOT TO LOSE YOU TOO.
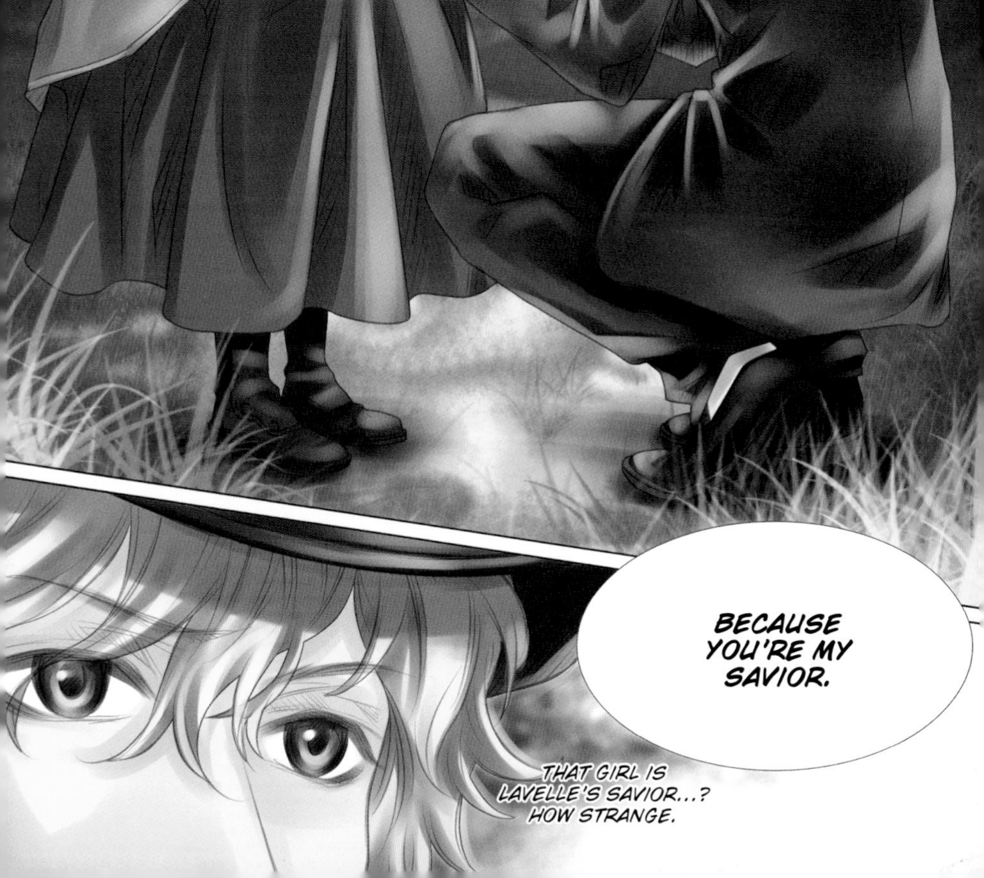
BECAUSE YOU'RE MY SAVIOR.
THAT GIRL IS LAVELLE'S SAVIOR...? HOW STRANGE.

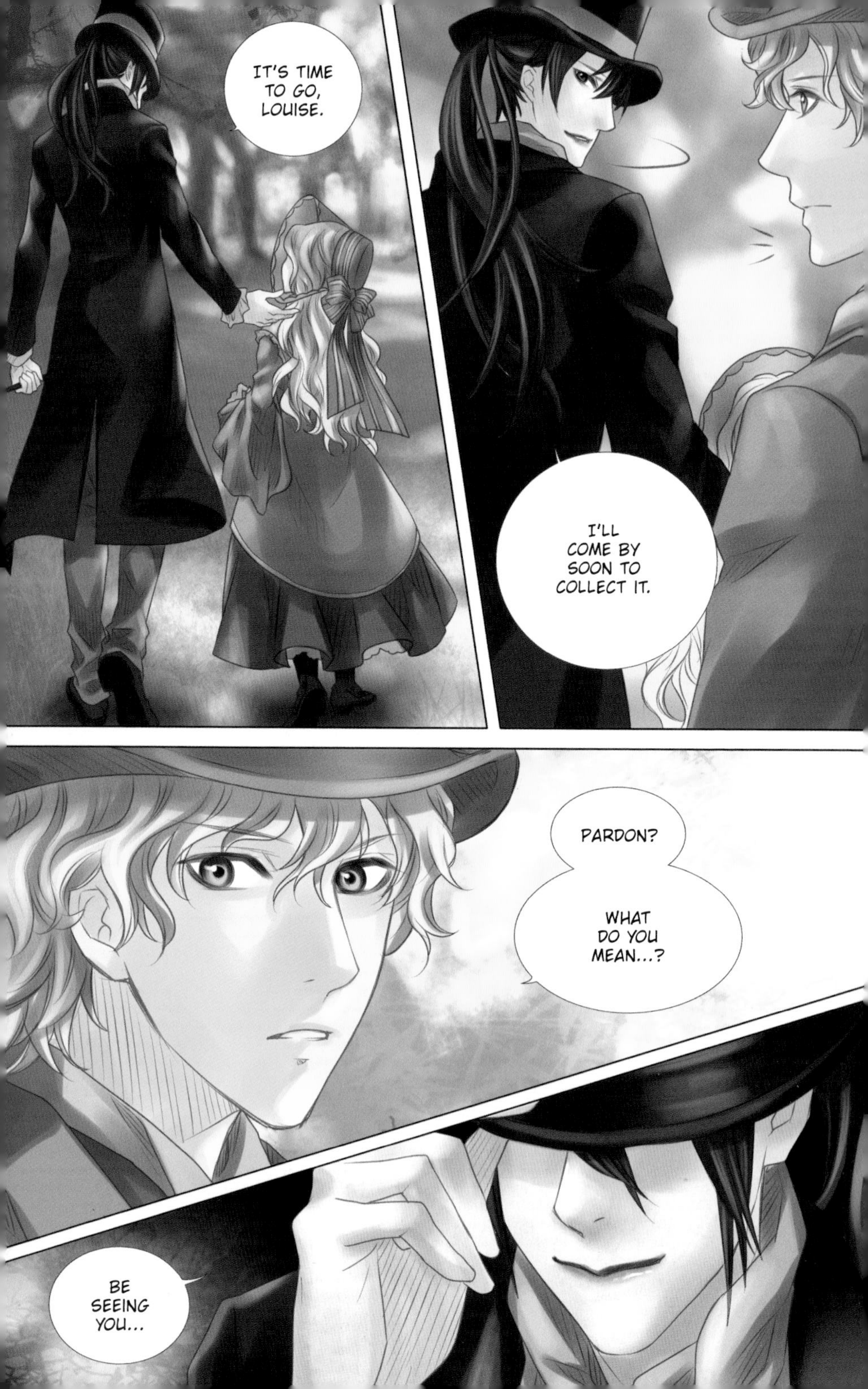
IT'S TIME TO GO, LOUISE.
I'LL COME BY SOON TO COLLECT IT.
PARDON?
WHAT DO YOU MEAN...?
BE SEEING YOU...

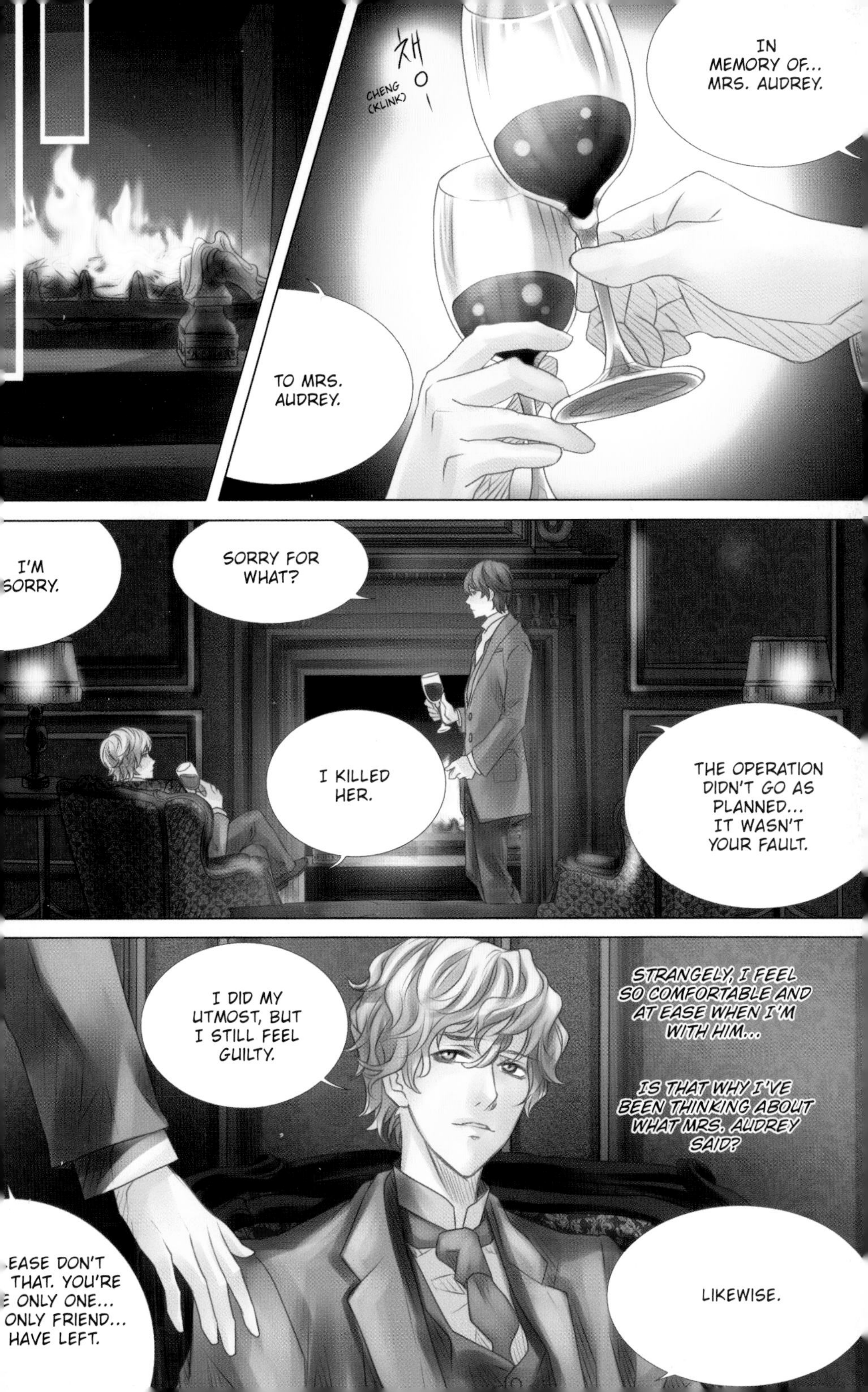

채
ㅇ
CHENG (KLINK)
IN MEMORY OF... MRS. AUDREY.
TO MRS. AUDREY.
I'M SORRY.
SORRY FOR WHAT?
I KILLED HER.
THE OPERATION DIDN'T GO AS PLANNED... IT WASN'T YOUR FAULT.
I DID MY UTMOST, BUT I STILL FEEL GUILTY.
STRANGELY, I FEEL SO COMFORTABLE AND AT EASE WHEN I'M WITH HIM...
IS THAT WHY I'VE BEEN THINKING ABOUT WHAT MRS. AUDREY SAID?
EASE DON'T THAT. YOU'RE ONLY ONE... ONLY FRIEND... HAVE LEFT.
LIKEWISE.

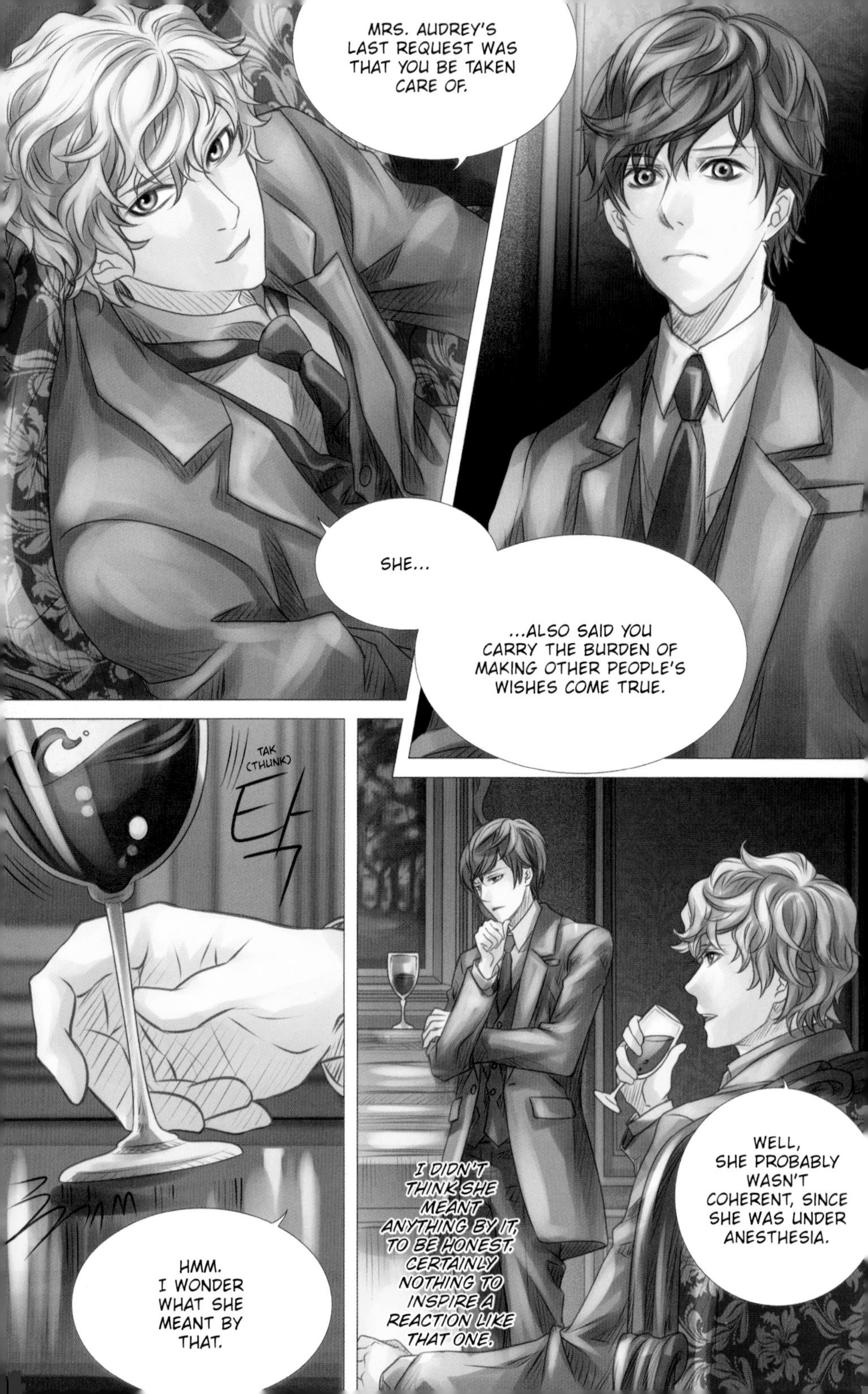
MRS. AUDREY'S LAST REQUEST WAS THAT YOU BE TAKEN CARE OF.
SHE...
...ALSO SAID YOU CARRY THE BURDEN OF MAKING OTHER PEOPLE'S WISHES COME TRUE.
TAK (THUNK)
HMM. I WONDER WHAT SHE MEANT BY THAT.
I DIDN'T THINK SHE MEANT ANYTHING BY IT, TO BE HONEST. CERTAINLY NOTHING TO INSPIRE A REACTION LIKE THAT ONE.
WELL, SHE PROBABLY WASN'T COHERENT, SINCE SHE WAS UNDER ANESTHESIA.

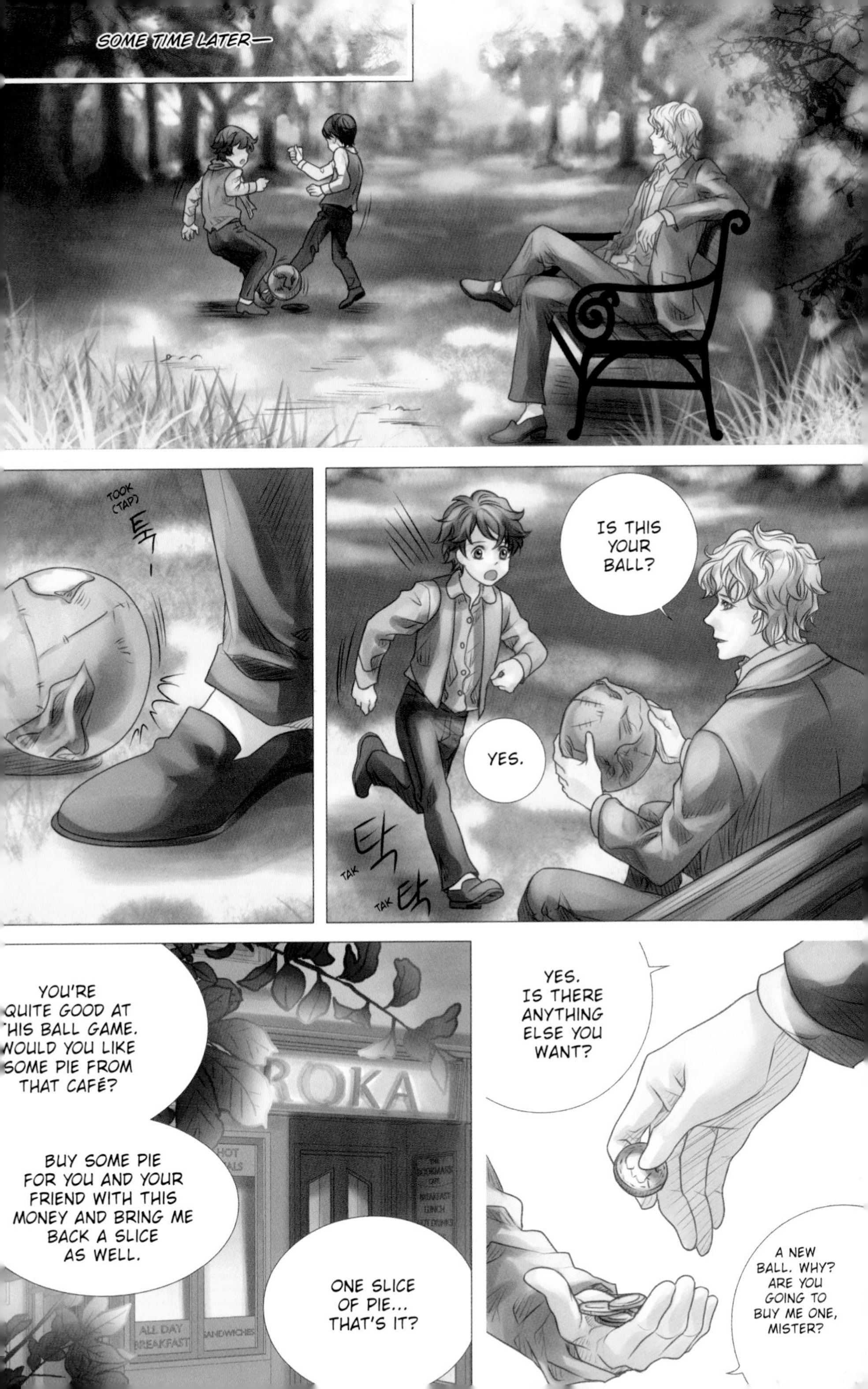
SOME TIME LATER—
TOOK (TAP)
톡
IS THIS YOUR BALL?
YES.
탁
TAK
탁
TAK
YOU'RE QUITE GOOD AT THIS BALL GAME. WOULD YOU LIKE SOME PIE FROM THAT CAFÉ?
ROKA
BUY SOME PIE FOR YOU AND YOUR FRIEND WITH THIS MONEY AND BRING ME BACK A SLICE AS WELL.
ALL DAY BREAKFAST
SANDWICHES
ONE SLICE OF PIE... THAT'S IT?
YES. IS THERE ANYTHING ELSE YOU WANT?
A NEW BALL. WHY? ARE YOU GOING TO BUY ME ONE, MISTER?

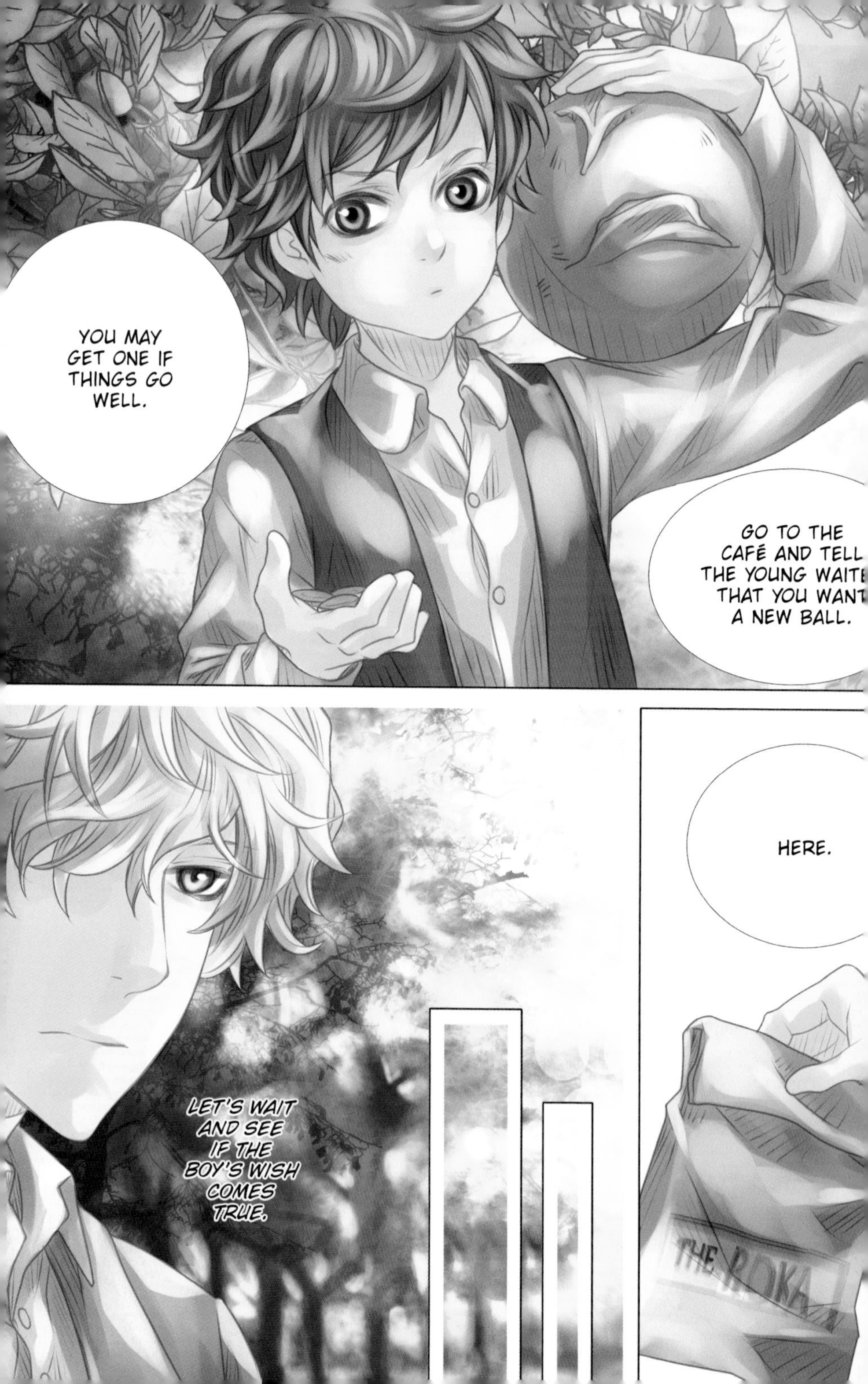
YOU MAY GET ONE IF THINGS GO WELL.
GO TO THE CAFÉ AND TELL THE YOUNG WAITE THAT YOU WANT A NEW BALL.
LET'S WAIT AND SEE IF THE BOY'S WISH COMES TRUE.
HERE.
THE ROKA

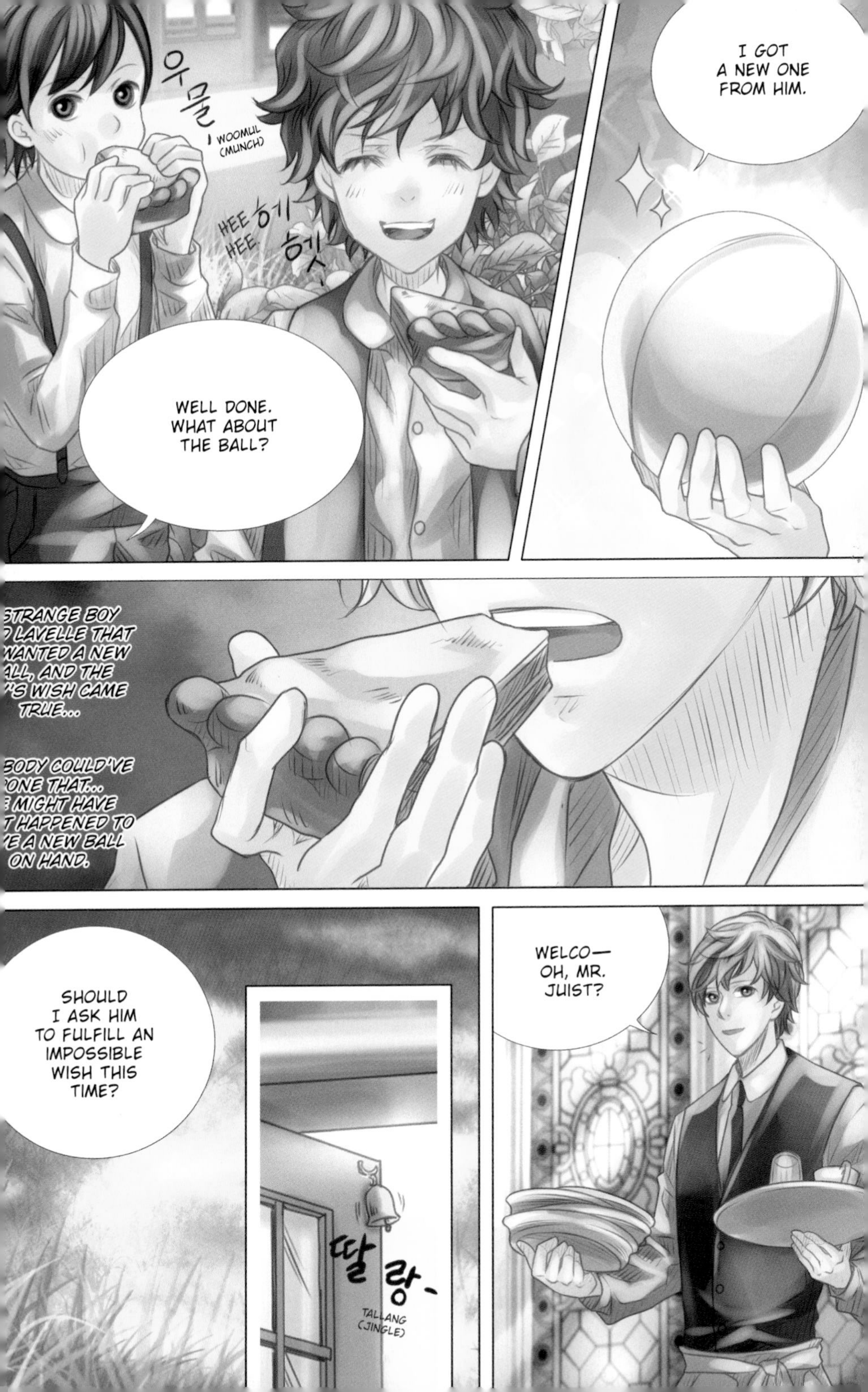

우물
WOOMUL (MUNCH)
HEE HEE
헤헷
WELL DONE. WHAT ABOUT THE BALL?
I GOT A NEW ONE FROM HIM.
STRANGE BOY
LAVELLE THAT
WANTED A NEW
ALL, AND THE
'S WISH CAME
TRUE...
BODY COULD'VE
DONE THAT...
E MIGHT HAVE
T HAPPENED TO
VE A NEW BALL
ON HAND.
SHOULD I ASK HIM TO FULFILL AN IMPOSSIBLE WISH THIS TIME?
딸랑~
TALLANG (JINGLE)
WELCO— OH, MR. JUIST?

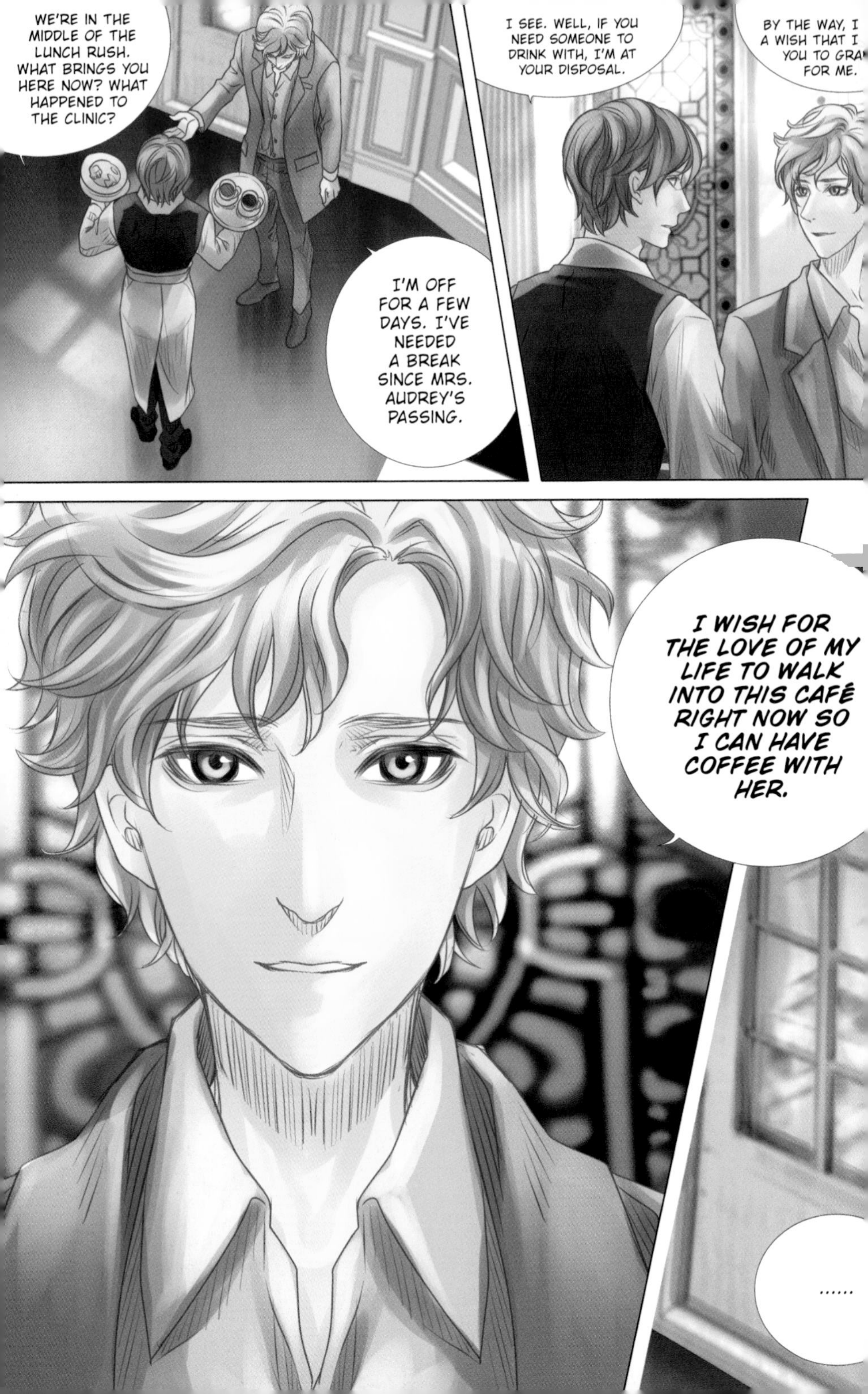
WE'RE IN THE MIDDLE OF THE LUNCH RUSH. WHAT BRINGS YOU HERE NOW? WHAT HAPPENED TO THE CLINIC?
I'M OFF FOR A FEW DAYS. I'VE NEEDED A BREAK SINCE MRS. AUDREY'S PASSING.
I SEE. WELL, IF YOU NEED SOMEONE TO DRINK WITH, I'M AT YOUR DISPOSAL.
BY THE WAY, A WISH THAT YOU TO GRA FOR ME.
I WISH FOR THE LOVE OF MY LIFE TO WALK INTO THIS CAFÉ RIGHT NOW SO I CAN HAVE COFFEE WITH HER.
......

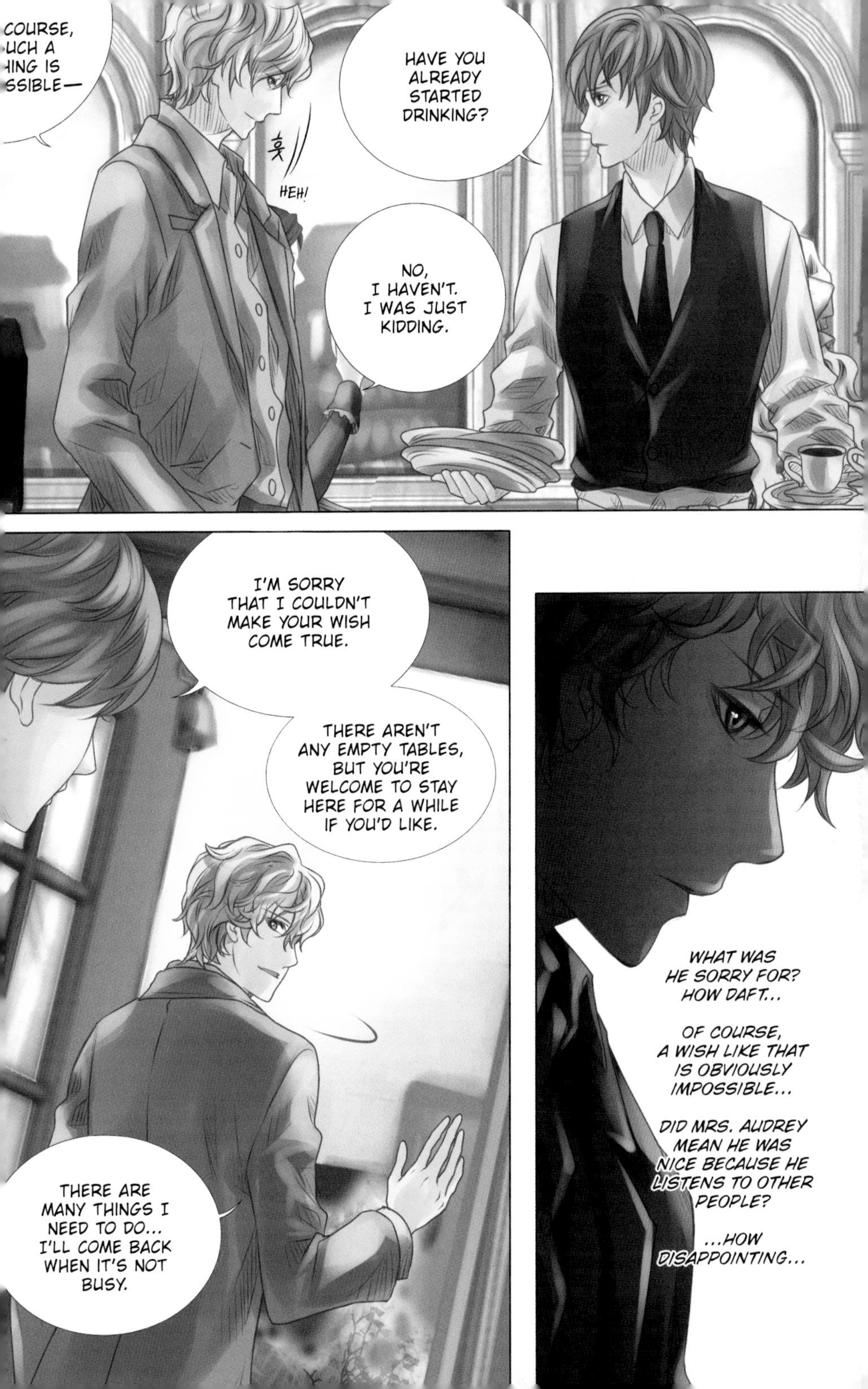
COURSE, UCH A IING IS SSIBLE—
흣 HEH!
HAVE YOU ALREADY STARTED DRINKING?
NO, I HAVEN'T. I WAS JUST KIDDING.
I'M SORRY THAT I COULDN'T MAKE YOUR WISH COME TRUE.
THERE AREN'T ANY EMPTY TABLES, BUT YOU'RE WELCOME TO STAY HERE FOR A WHILE IF YOU'D LIKE.
THERE ARE MANY THINGS I NEED TO DO... I'LL COME BACK WHEN IT'S NOT BUSY.
WHAT WAS HE SORRY FOR? HOW DAFT...
OF COURSE, A WISH LIKE THAT IS OBVIOUSLY IMPOSSIBLE...
DID MRS. AUDREY MEAN HE WAS NICE BECAUSE HE LISTENS TO OTHER PEOPLE?
...HOW DISAPPOINTING...

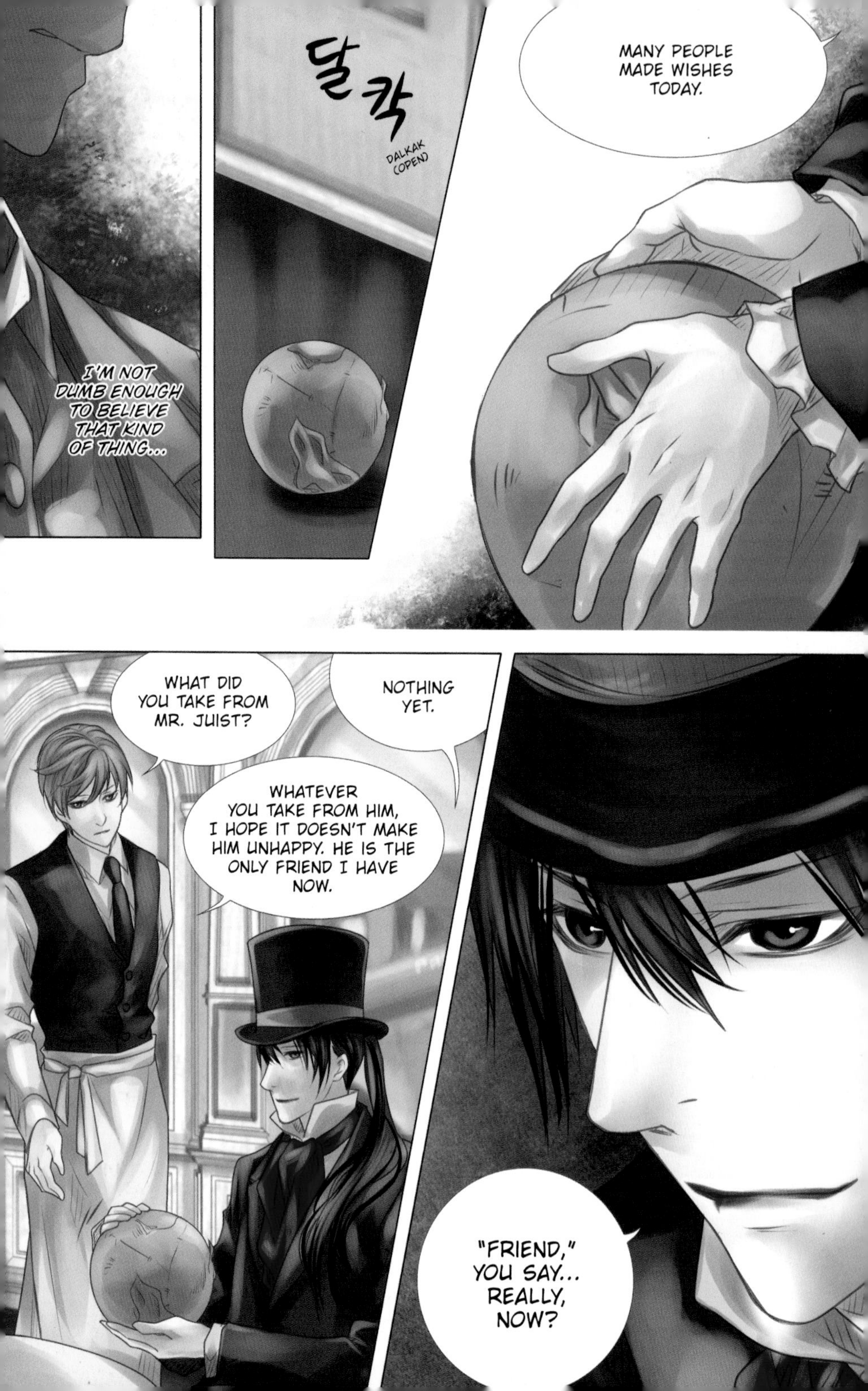
I'M NOT DUMB ENOUGH TO BELIEVE THAT KIND OF THING...
달칵
DALKAK (OPEN)
MANY PEOPLE MADE WISHES TODAY.
WHAT DID YOU TAKE FROM MR. JUIST?
NOTHING YET.
WHATEVER YOU TAKE FROM HIM, I HOPE IT DOESN'T MAKE HIM UNHAPPY. HE IS THE ONLY FRIEND I HAVE NOW.
"FRIEND," YOU SAY... REALLY, NOW?

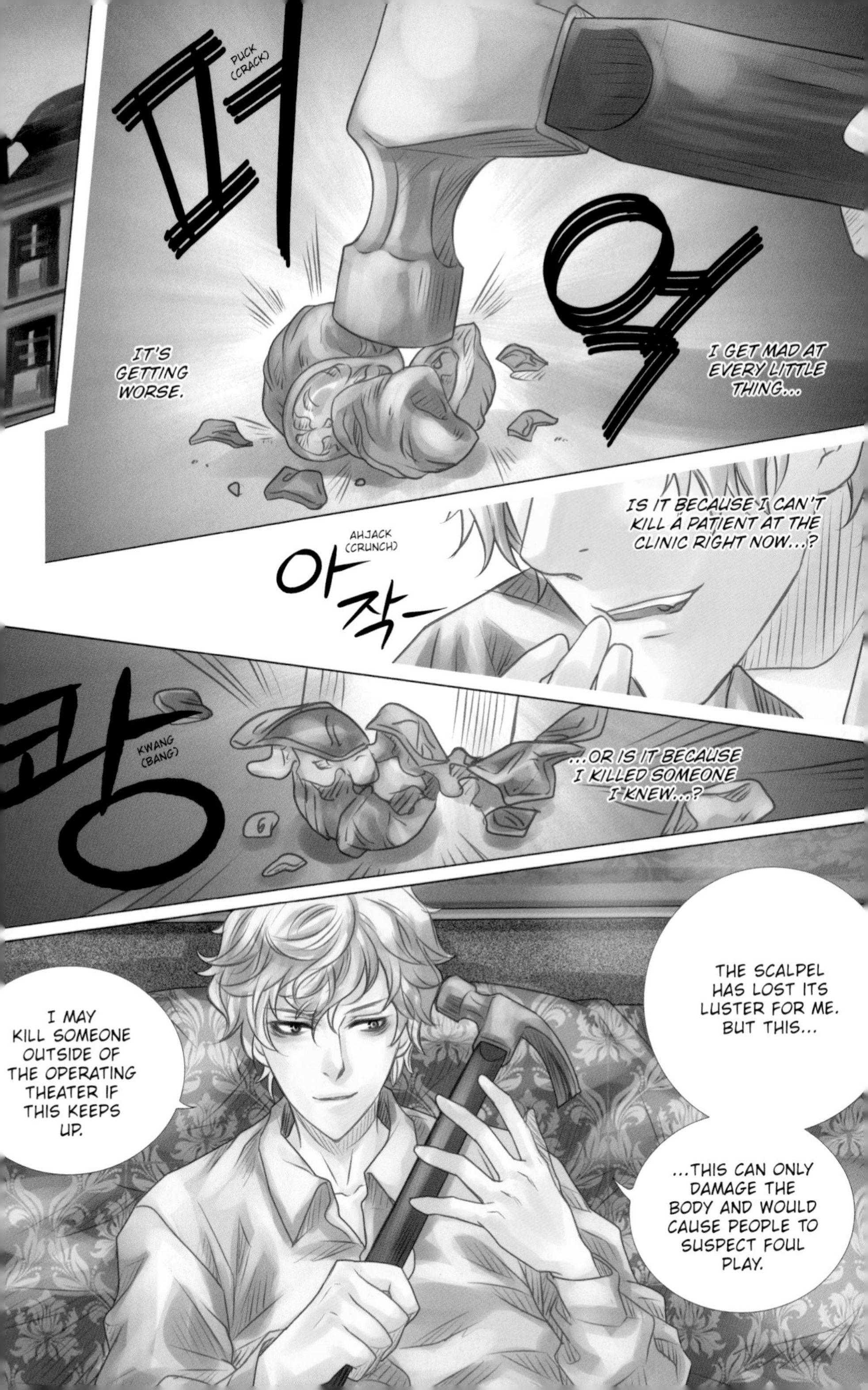

퍽
PUCK (CRACK)
IT'S GETTING WORSE.
I GET MAD AT EVERY LITTLE THING...
아작
AHJACK (CRUNCH)
IS IT BECAUSE I CAN'T KILL A PATIENT AT THE CLINIC RIGHT NOW...?
쾅
KWANG (BANG)
...OR IS IT BECAUSE I KILLED SOMEONE I KNEW...?
I MAY KILL SOMEONE OUTSIDE OF THE OPERATING THEATER IF THIS KEEPS UP.
THE SCALPEL HAS LOST ITS LUSTER FOR ME. BUT THIS...
...THIS CAN ONLY DAMAGE THE BODY AND WOULD CAUSE PEOPLE TO SUSPECT FOUL PLAY.

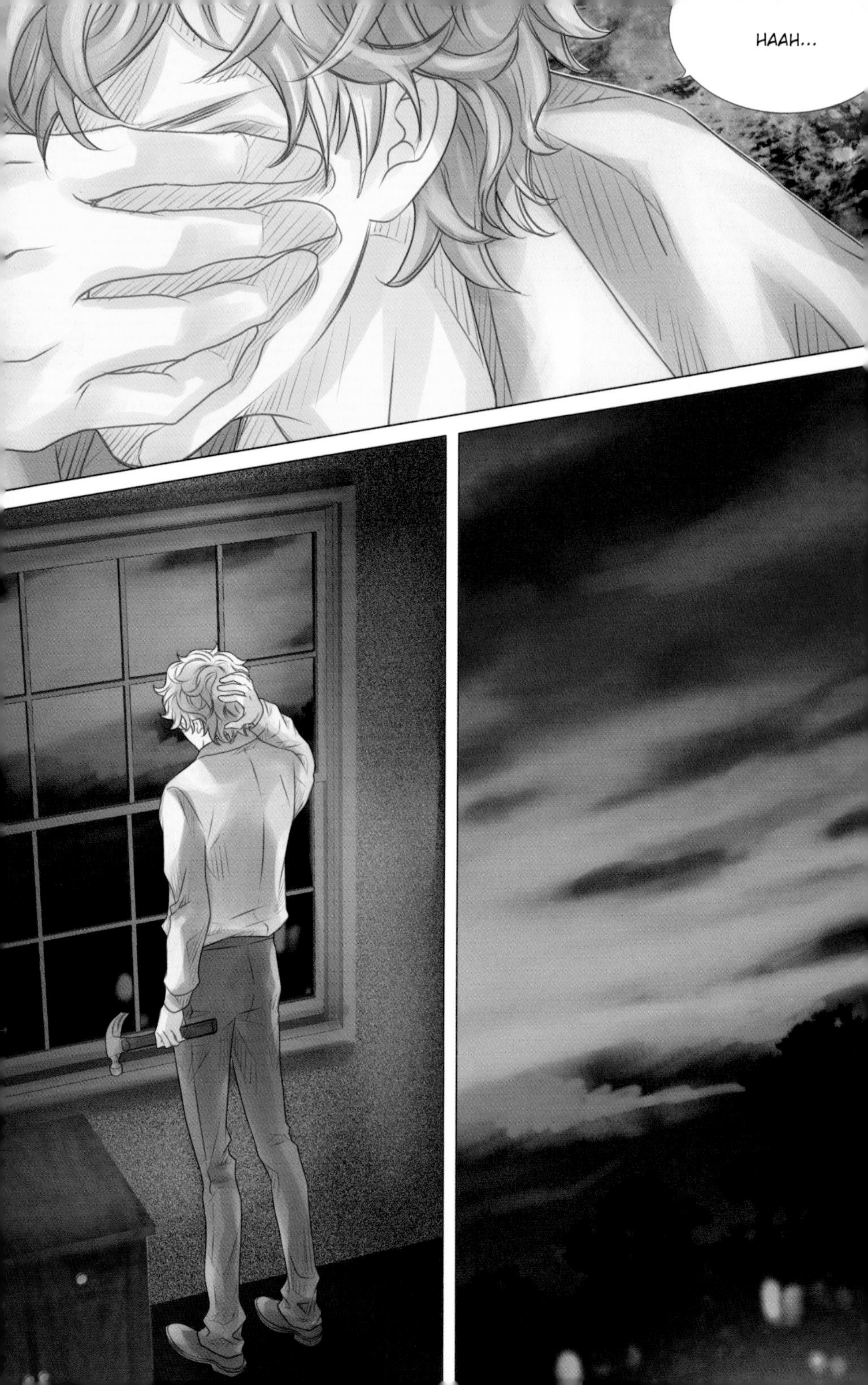
HAAH...

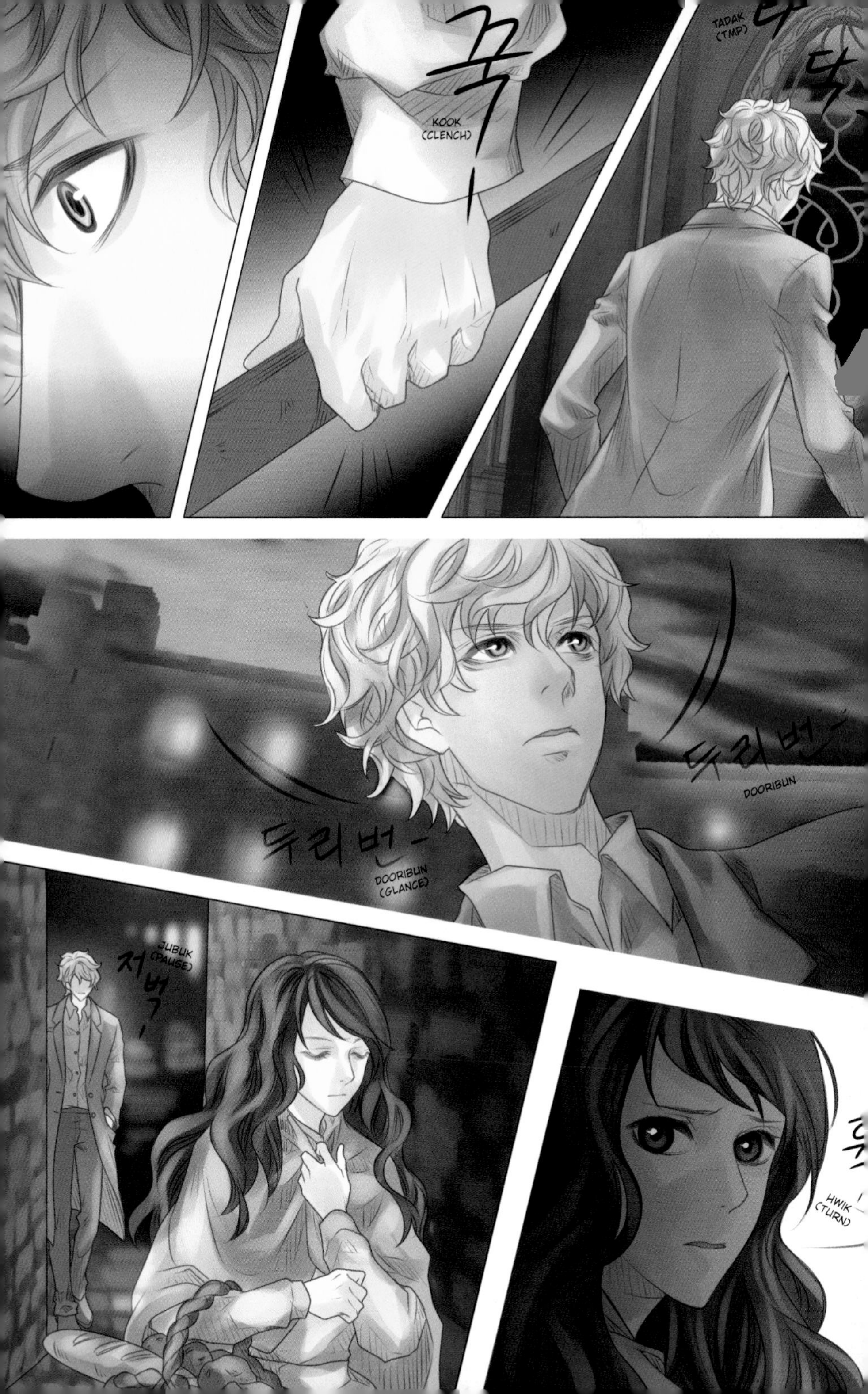
꾹
KOOK (CLENCH)
TADAK (TMP)
두리번
DOORIBUN
두리번
DOORIBUN (GLANCE)
JUBUK (PAUSE)
저벅
HWIK (TURN)

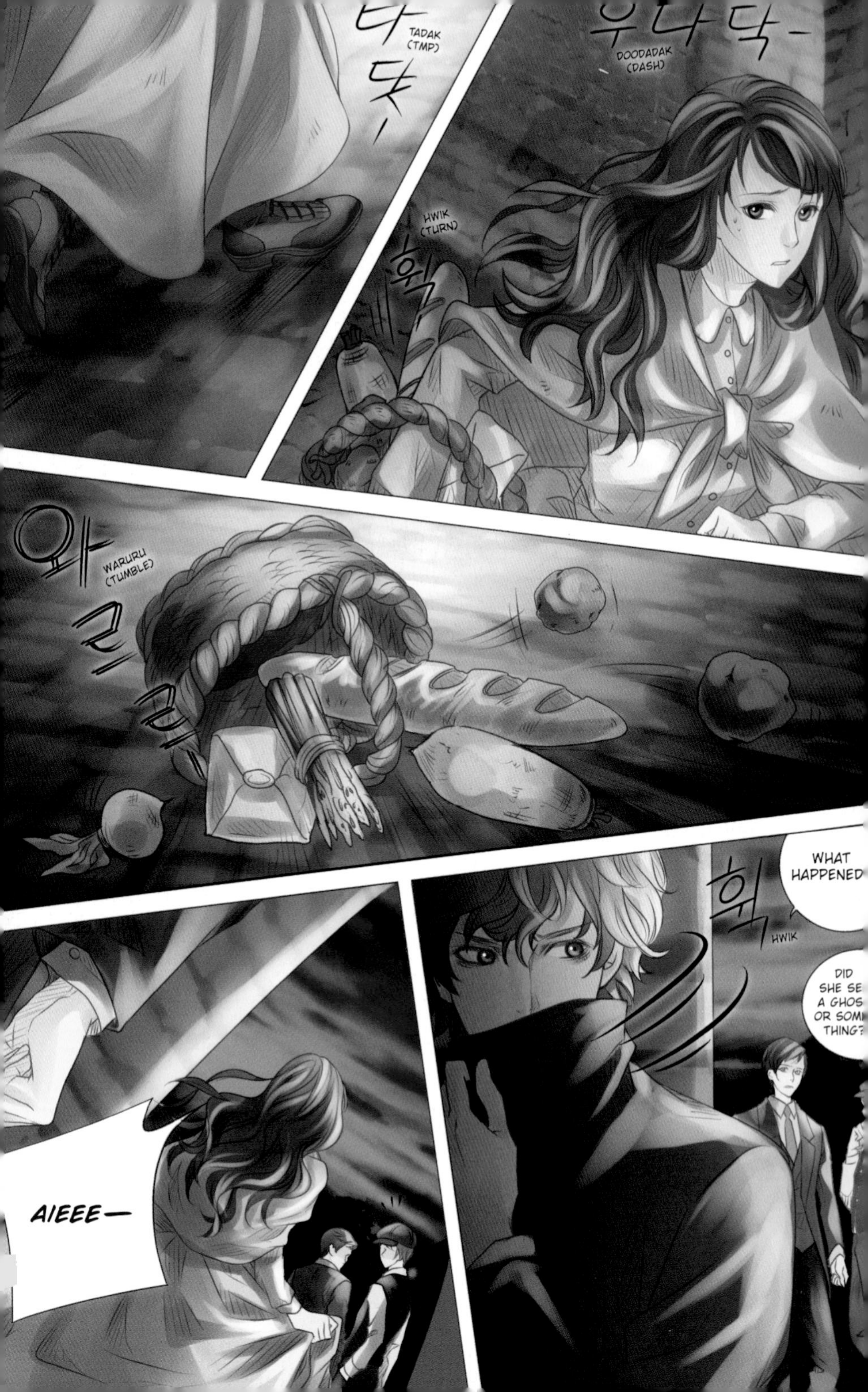
다닥
TADAK (TMP)
우다닥
DOODADAK (DASH)
휙
HWIK (TURN)
와르르
WARURU (TUMBLE)
AIEEE—
휙
HWIK
WHAT HAPPENED
DID SHE SE A GHOS OR SOM THING?

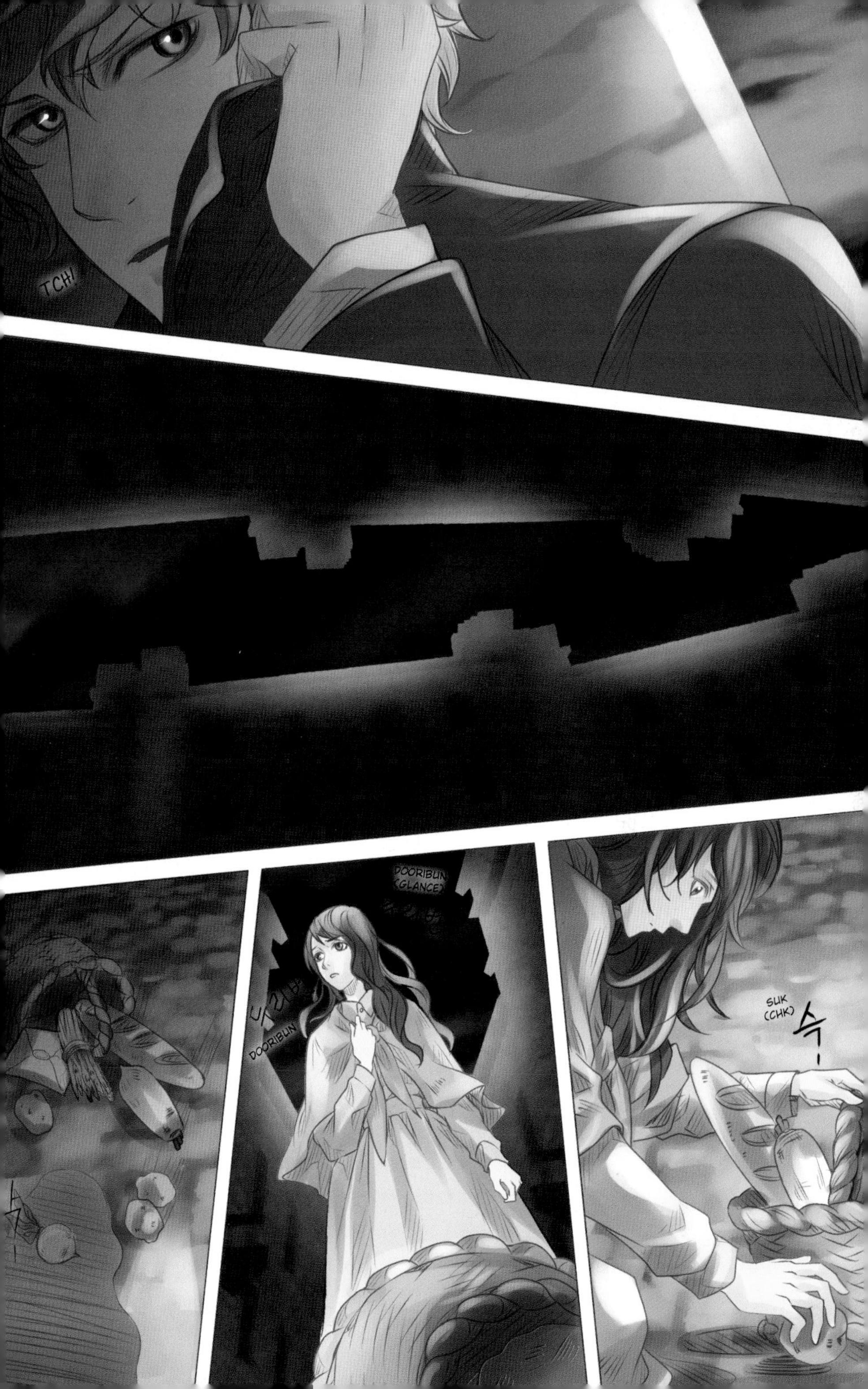
TCH!
DOORIBUN (GLANCE)
DOORIBUN
SUK (CHK)

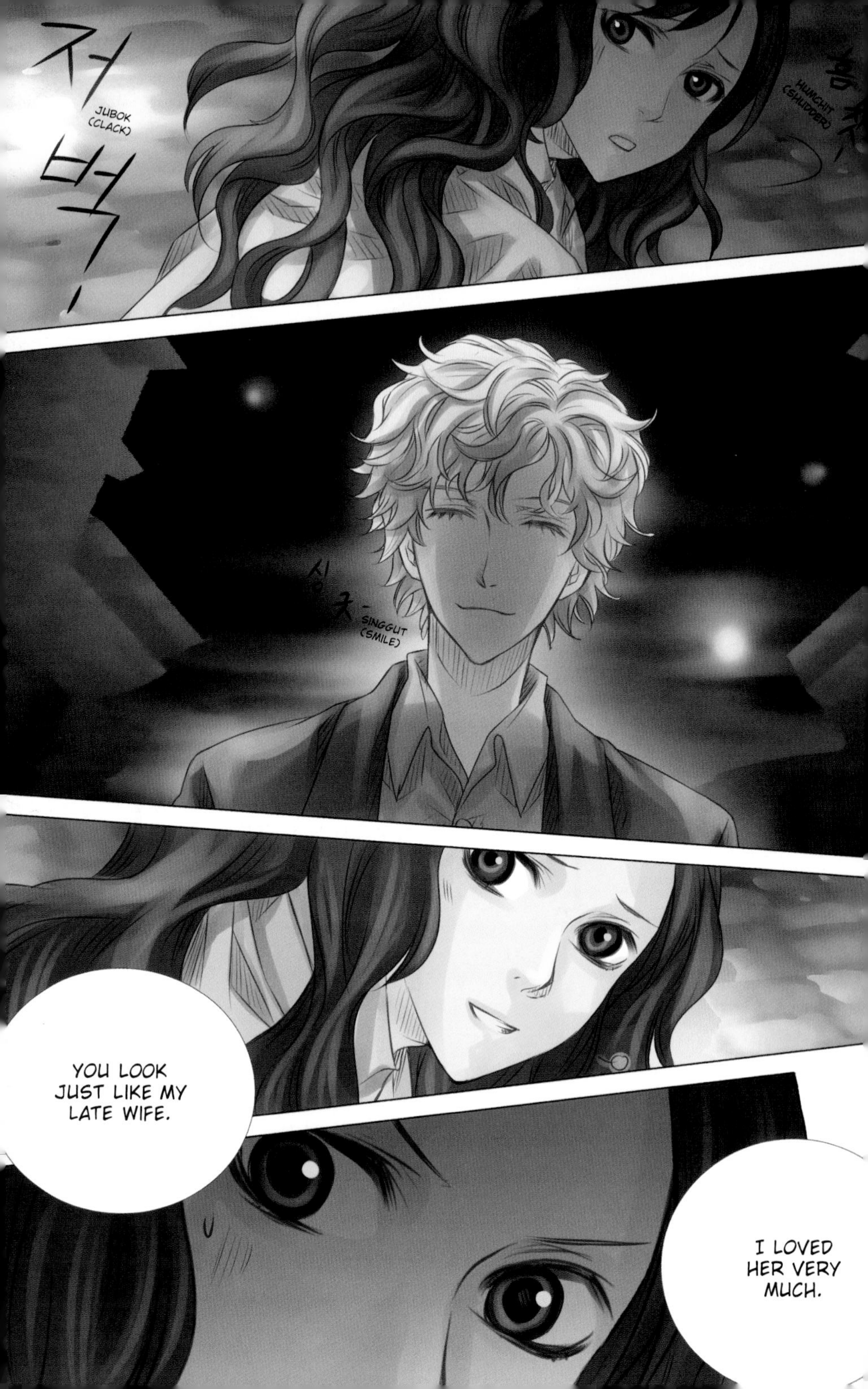
저벅-!
JUBOK (CLACK)
흠칫-
HUMCHIT (SHUDDER)
싱긋-
SINGGUT (SMILE)
YOU LOOK JUST LIKE MY LATE WIFE.
I LOVED HER VERY MUCH.

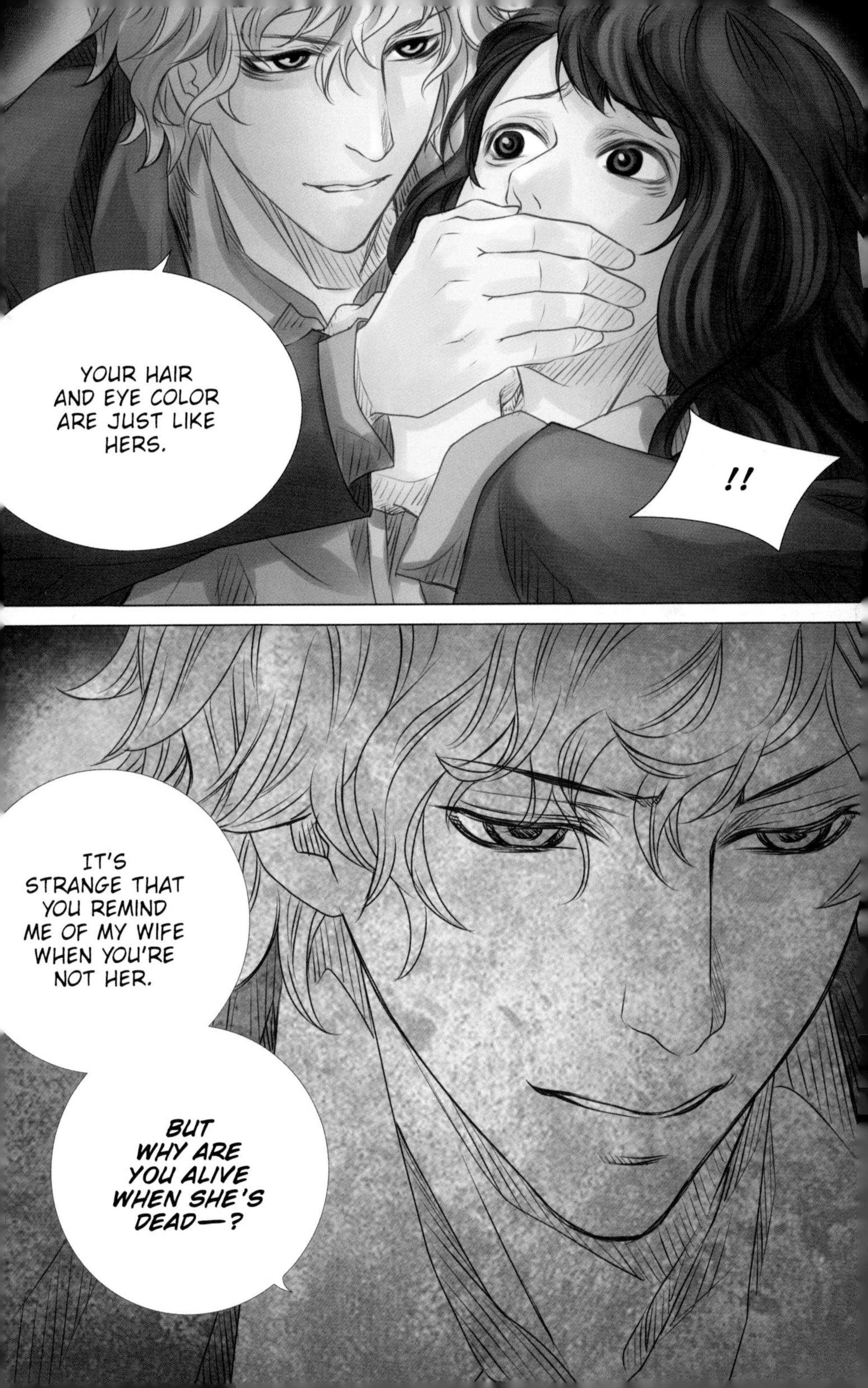
YOUR HAIR AND EYE COLOR ARE JUST LIKE HERS.
!!
IT'S STRANGE THAT YOU REMIND ME OF MY WIFE WHEN YOU'RE NOT HER.
BUT WHY ARE YOU ALIVE WHEN SHE'S DEAD—?

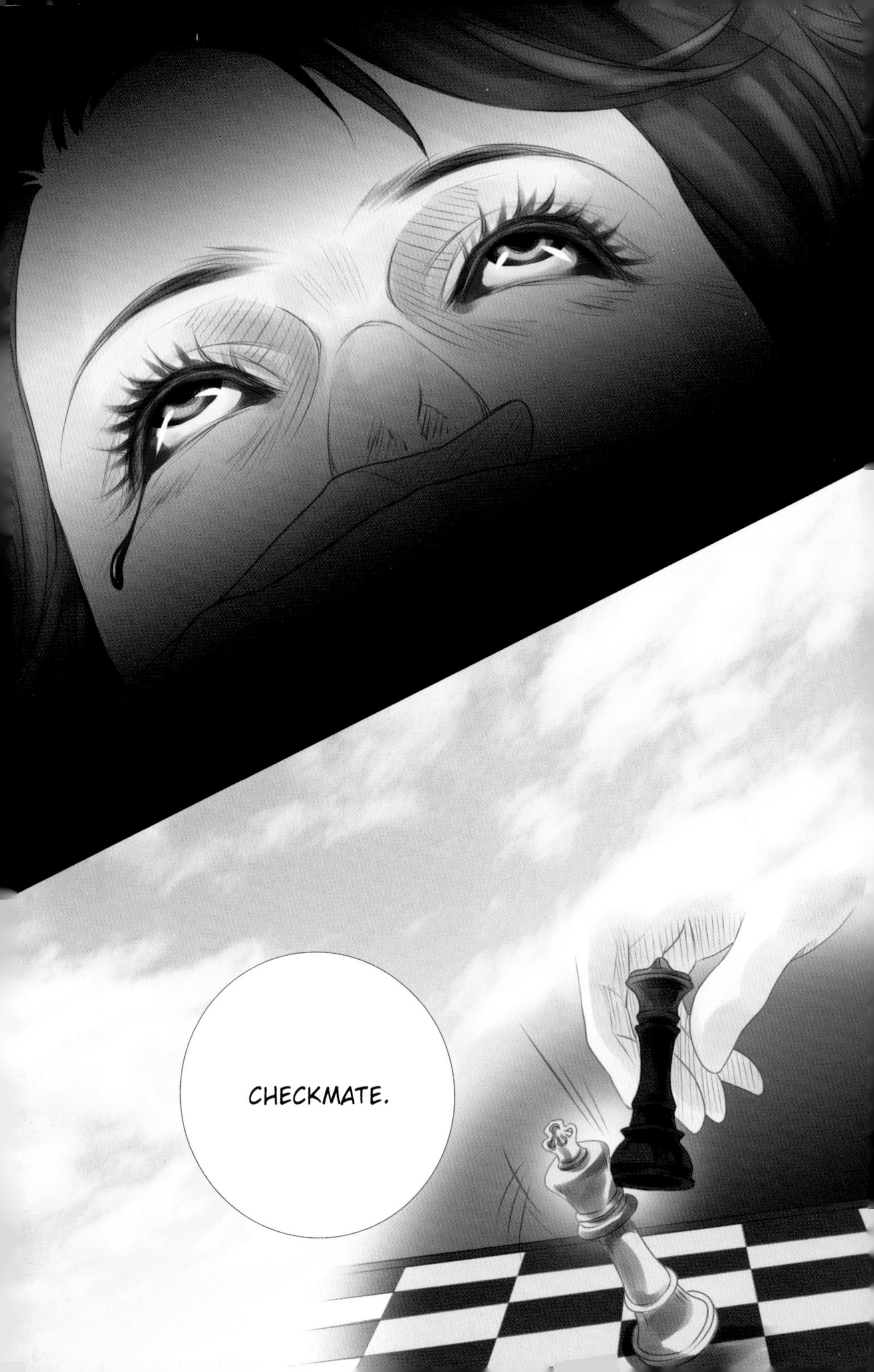
CHECKMATE.

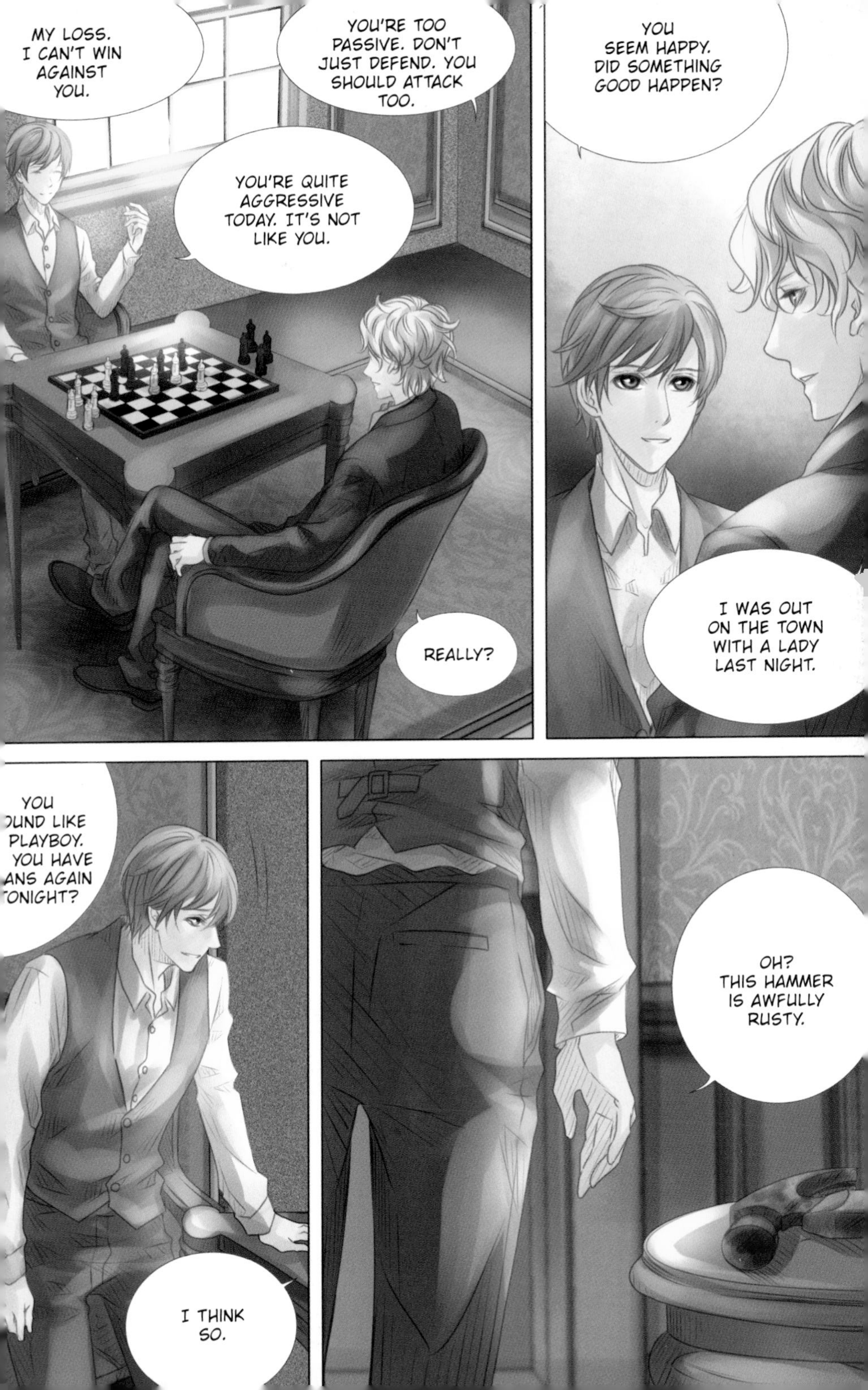
MY LOSS. I CAN'T WIN AGAINST YOU.
YOU'RE TOO PASSIVE. DON'T JUST DEFEND. YOU SHOULD ATTACK TOO.
YOU'RE QUITE AGGRESSIVE TODAY. IT'S NOT LIKE YOU.
REALLY?
YOU SEEM HAPPY. DID SOMETHING GOOD HAPPEN?
I WAS OUT ON THE TOWN WITH A LADY LAST NIGHT.
YOU OUND LIKE PLAYBOY. YOU HAVE ANS AGAIN TONIGHT?
I THINK SO.
OH? THIS HAMMER IS AWFULLY RUSTY.

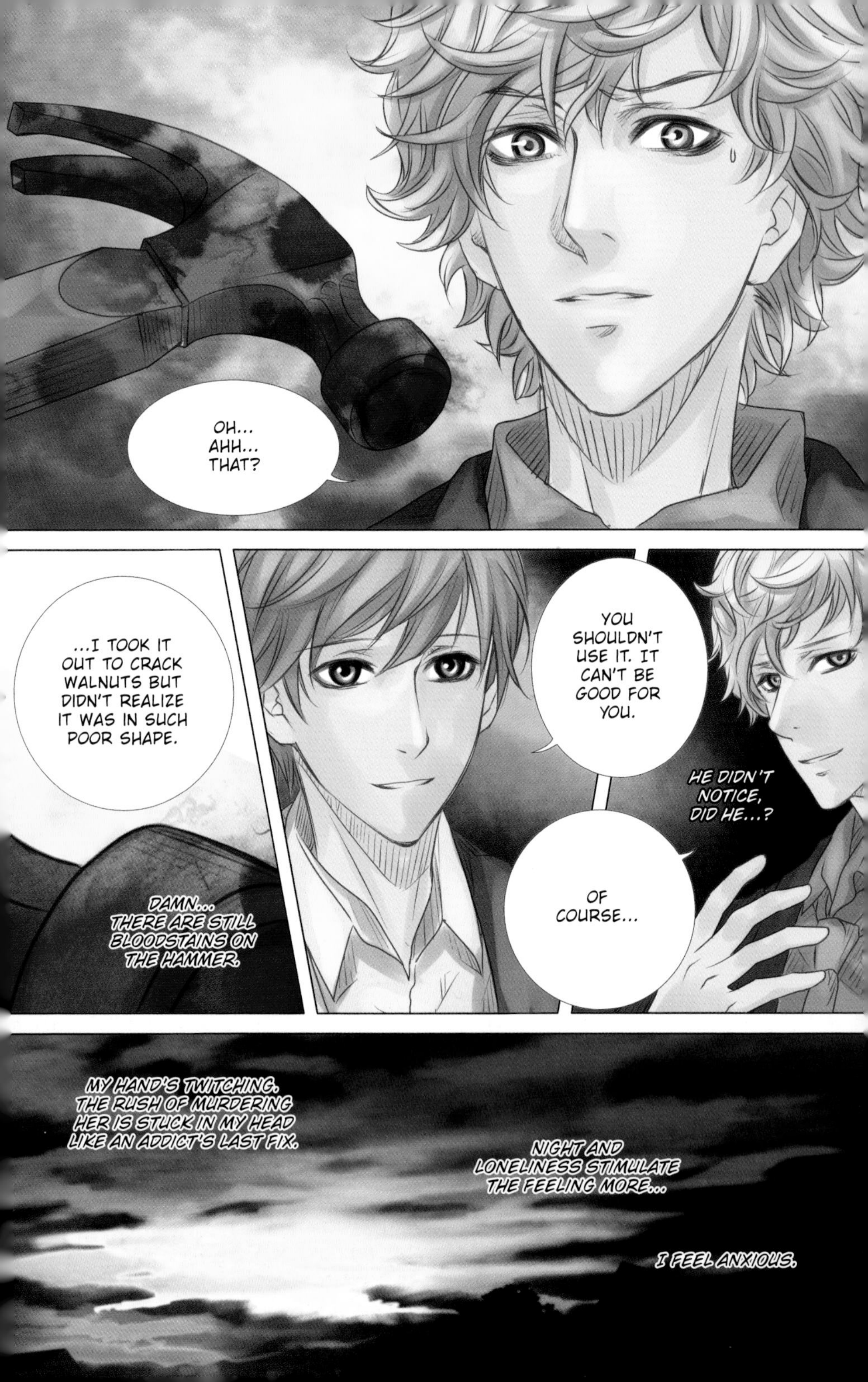
OH... AHH... THAT?
...I TOOK IT OUT TO CRACK WALNUTS BUT DIDN'T REALIZE IT WAS IN SUCH POOR SHAPE.
DAMN... THERE ARE STILL BLOODSTAINS ON THE HAMMER.
YOU SHOULDN'T USE IT. IT CAN'T BE GOOD FOR YOU.
OF COURSE...
HE DIDN'T NOTICE, DID HE...?
MY HAND'S TWITCHING. THE RUSH OF MURDERING HER IS STUCK IN MY HEAD LIKE AN ADDICT'S LAST FIX.
NIGHT AND LONELINESS STIMULATE THE FEELING MORE...
I FEEL ANXIOUS.

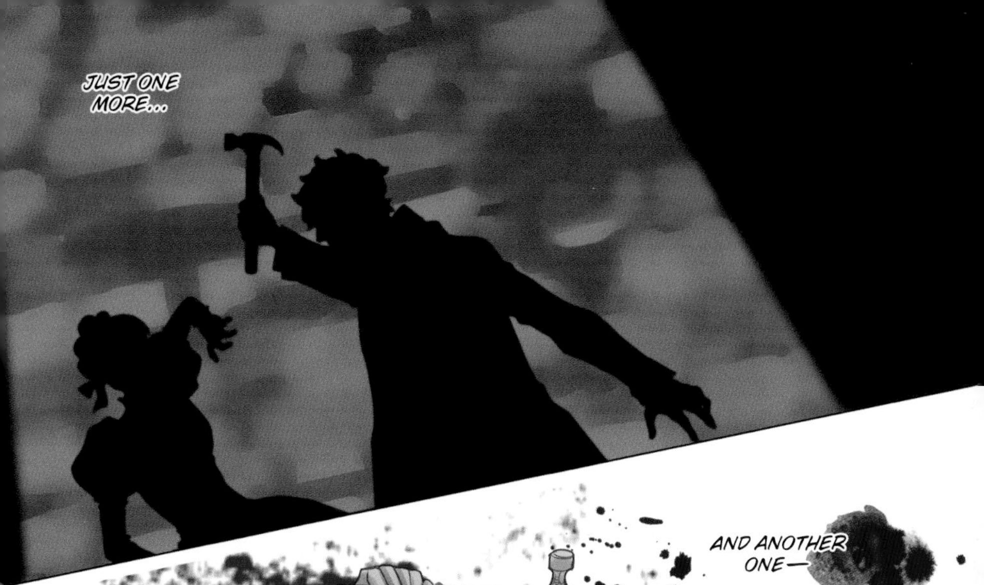
JUST ONE MORE...

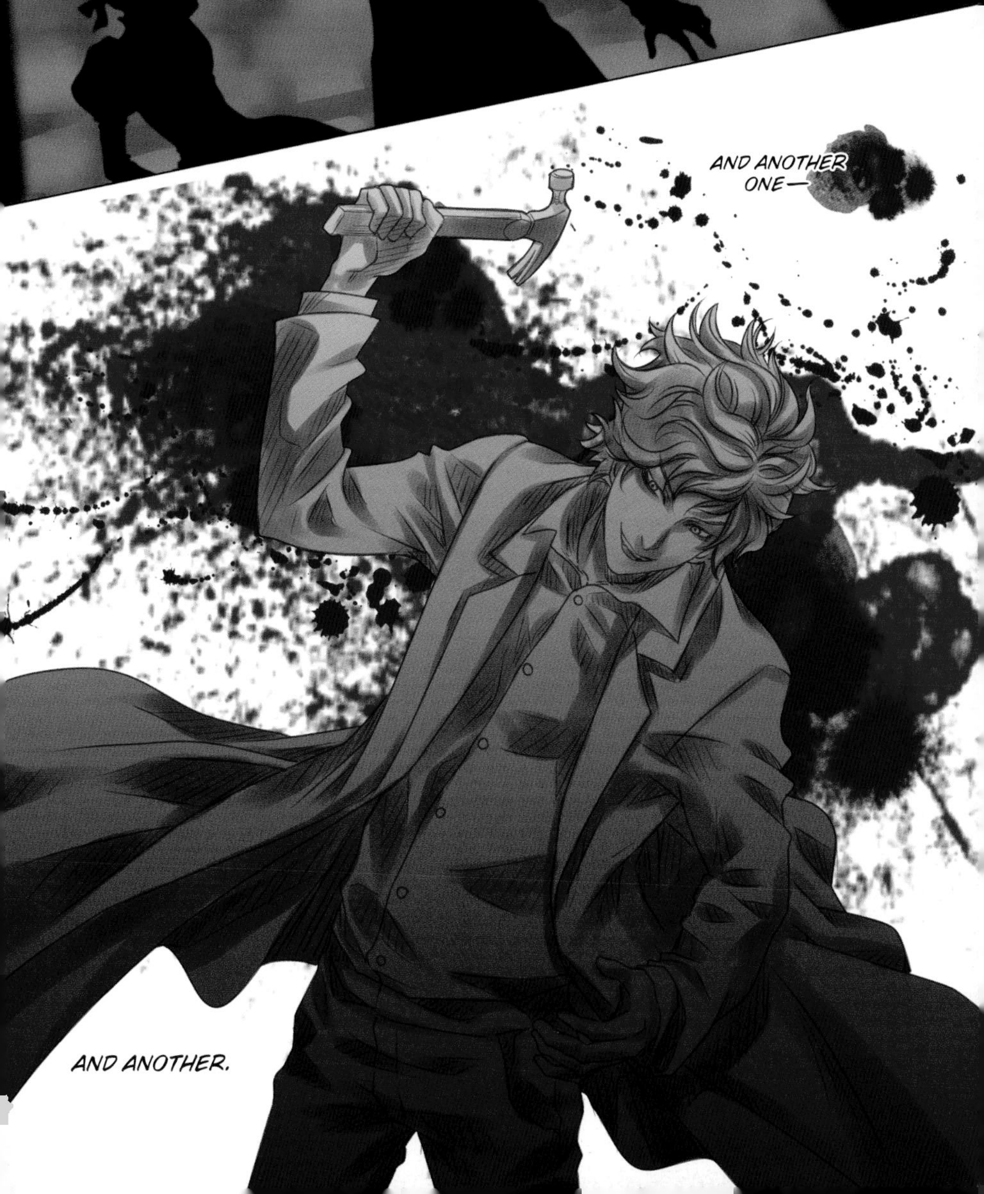
AND ANOTHER ONE—
AND ANOTHER.

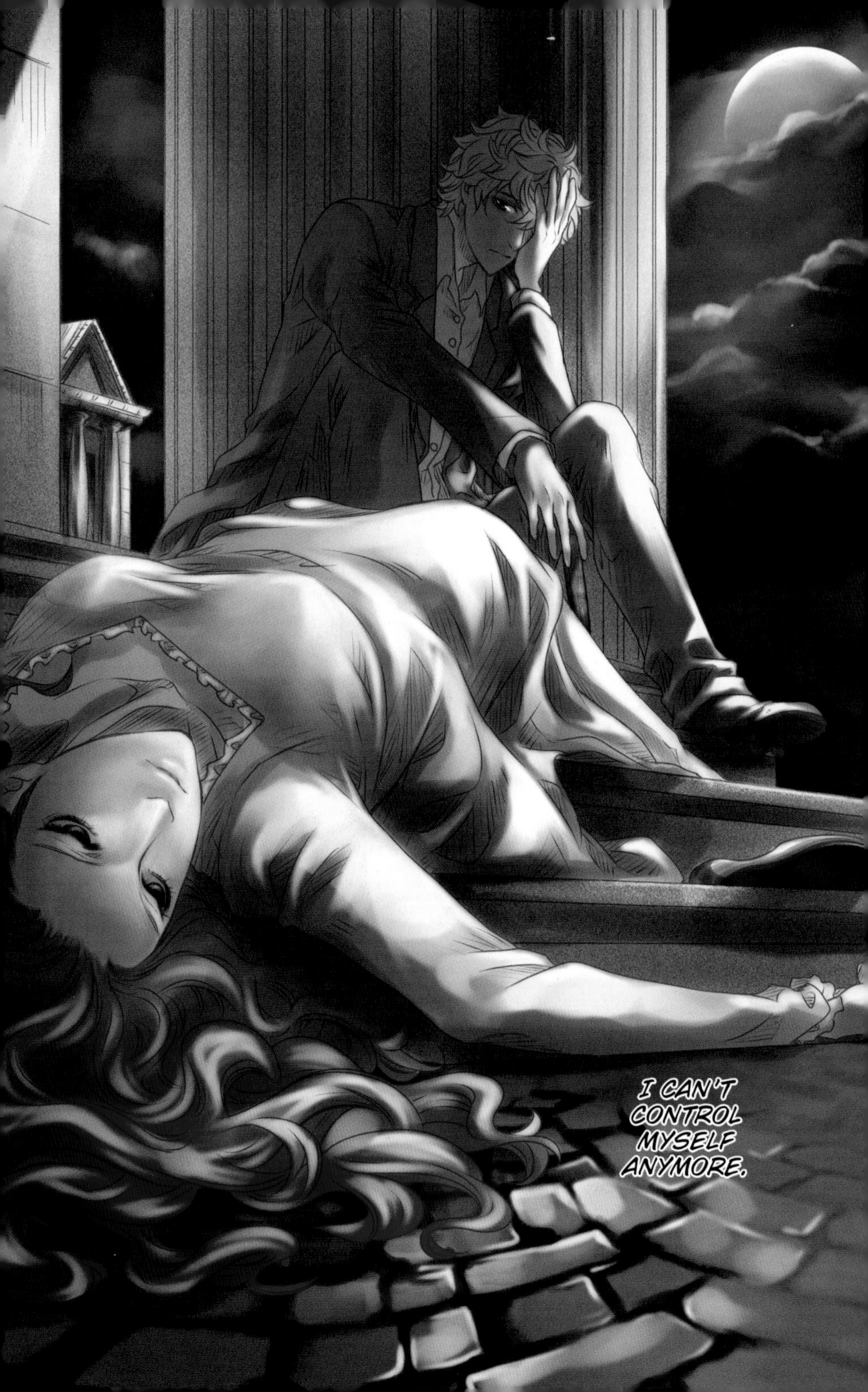
I CAN'T CONTROL MYSELF ANYMORE.

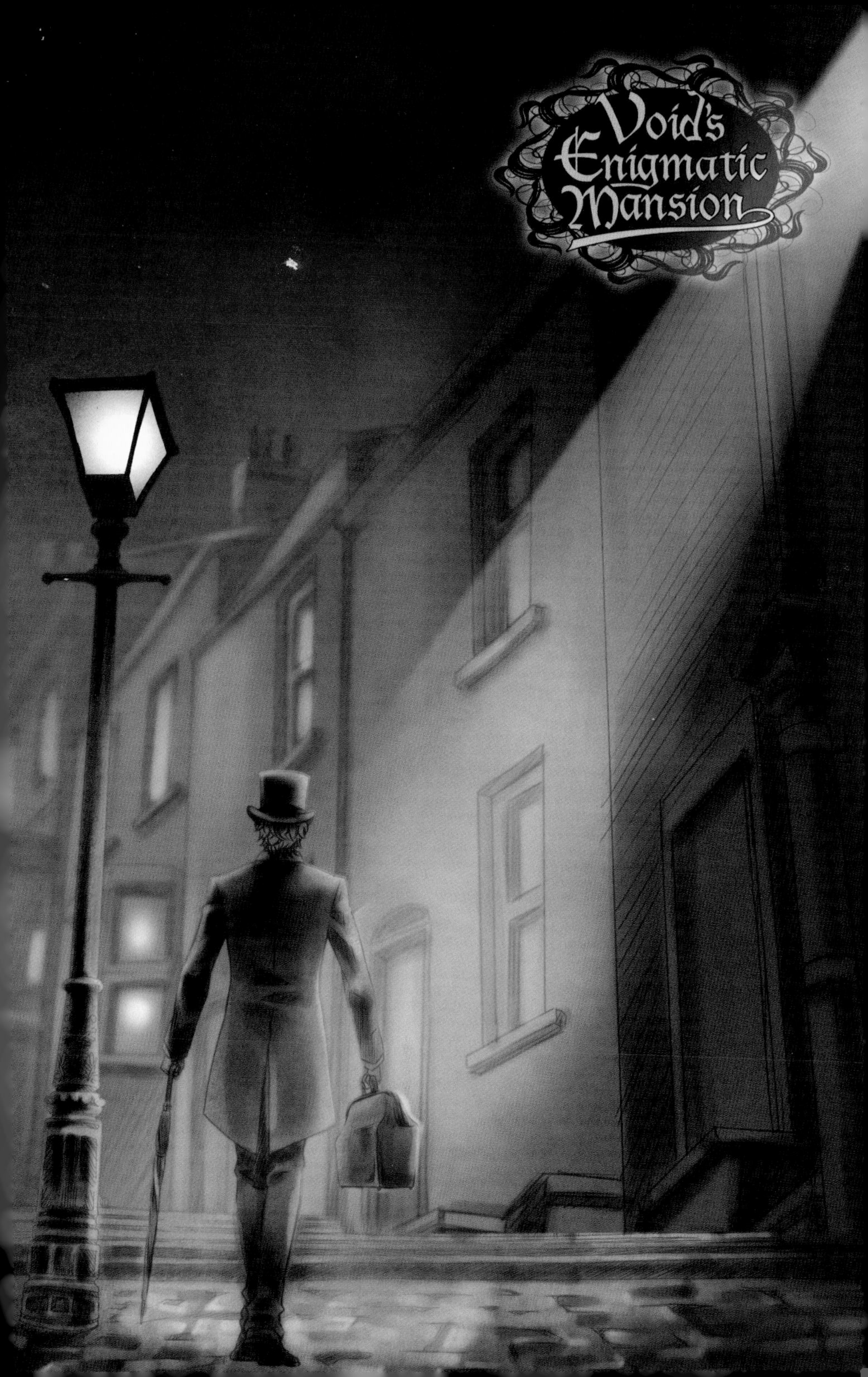
Void's Enigmatic Mansion

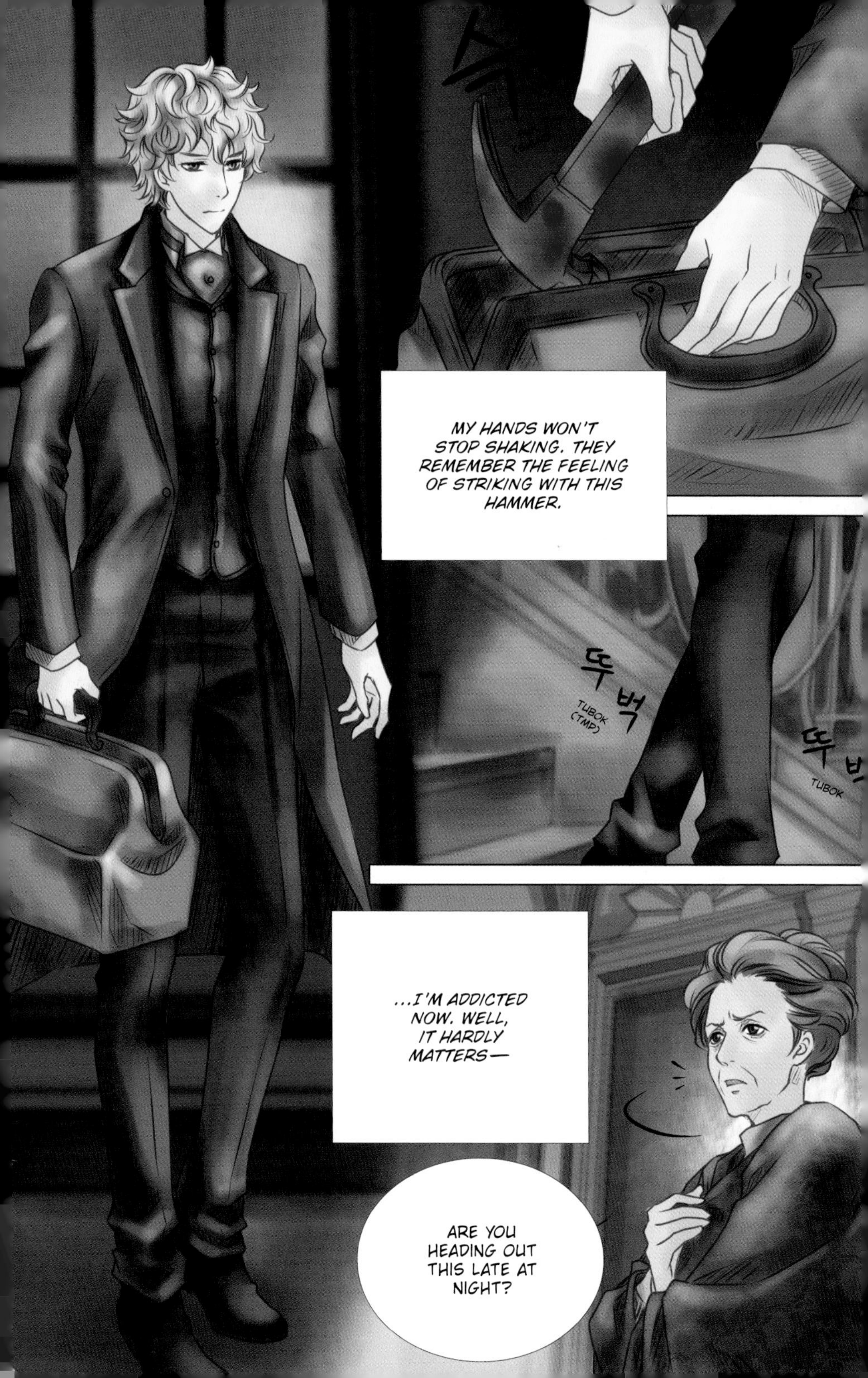
MY HANDS WON'T STOP SHAKING. THEY REMEMBER THE FEELING OF STRIKING WITH THIS HAMMER.
뚜벅
TUBOK (TMP)
뚜벅
TUBOK
...I'M ADDICTED NOW. WELL, IT HARDLY MATTERS—
ARE YOU HEADING OUT THIS LATE AT NIGHT?

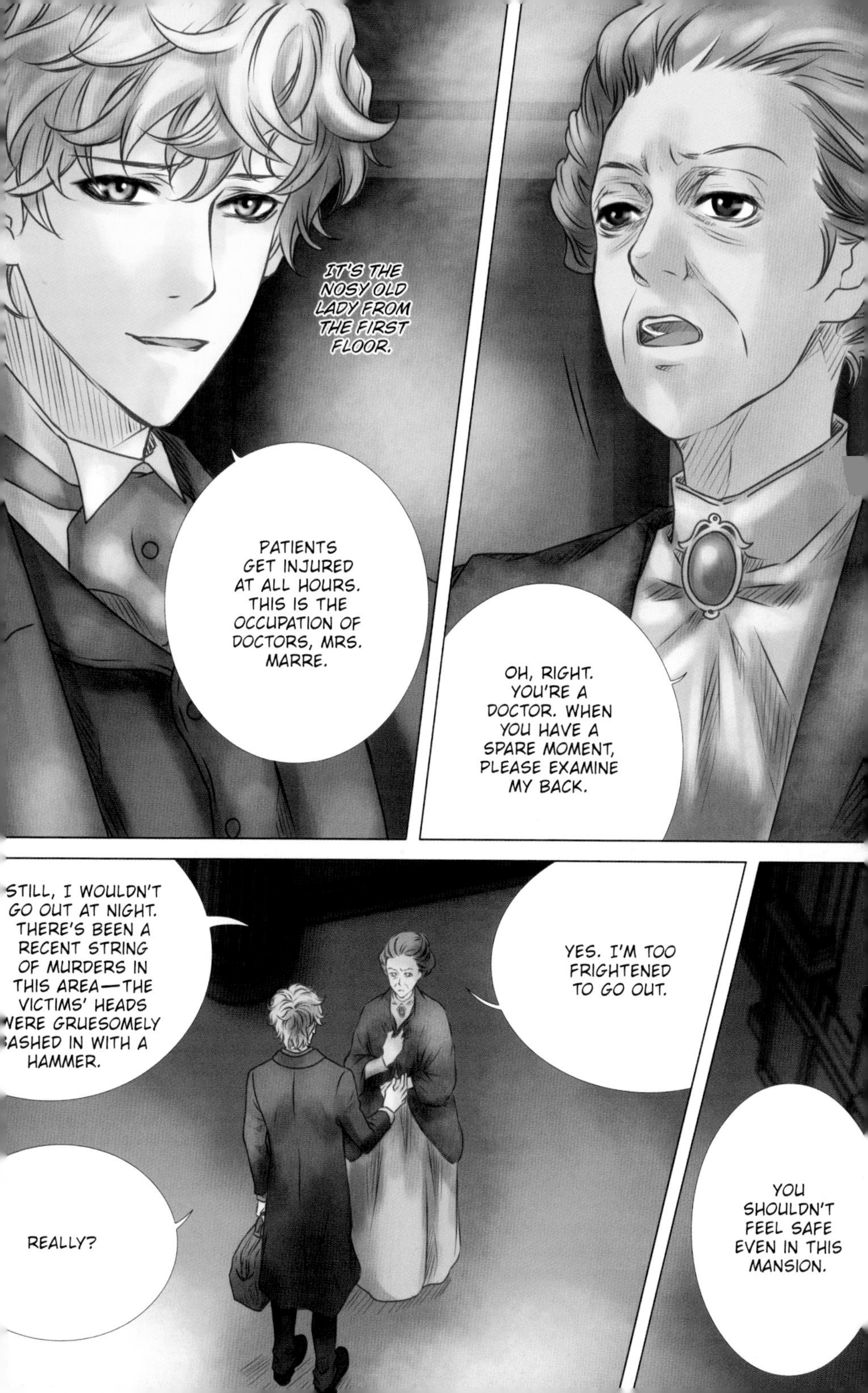
IT'S THE NOSY OLD LADY FROM THE FIRST FLOOR.
PATIENTS GET INJURED AT ALL HOURS. THIS IS THE OCCUPATION OF DOCTORS, MRS. MARRE.
OH, RIGHT. YOU'RE A DOCTOR. WHEN YOU HAVE A SPARE MOMENT, PLEASE EXAMINE MY BACK.
STILL, I WOULDN'T GO OUT AT NIGHT. THERE'S BEEN A RECENT STRING OF MURDERS IN THIS AREA—THE VICTIMS' HEADS WERE GRUESOMELY BASHED IN WITH A HAMMER.
YES. I'M TOO FRIGHTENED TO GO OUT.
REALLY?
YOU SHOULDN'T FEEL SAFE EVEN IN THIS MANSION.

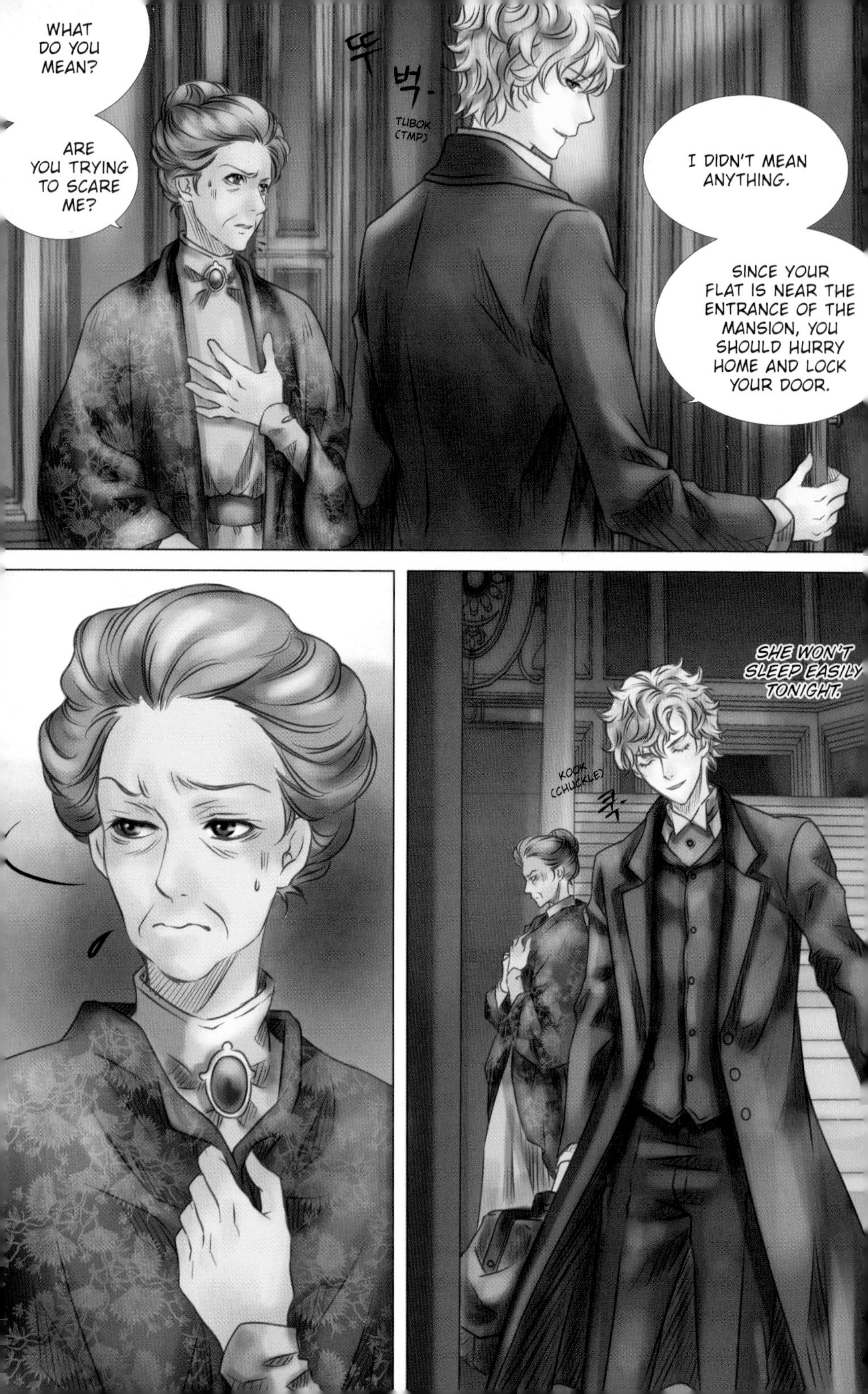
WHAT DO YOU MEAN?
ARE YOU TRYING TO SCARE ME?
뚜벅.
TUBOK (TMP)
I DIDN'T MEAN ANYTHING.
SINCE YOUR FLAT IS NEAR THE ENTRANCE OF THE MANSION, YOU SHOULD HURRY HOME AND LOCK YOUR DOOR.
SHE WON'T SLEEP EASILY TONIGHT.
KOOK (CHUCKLE)
쿡

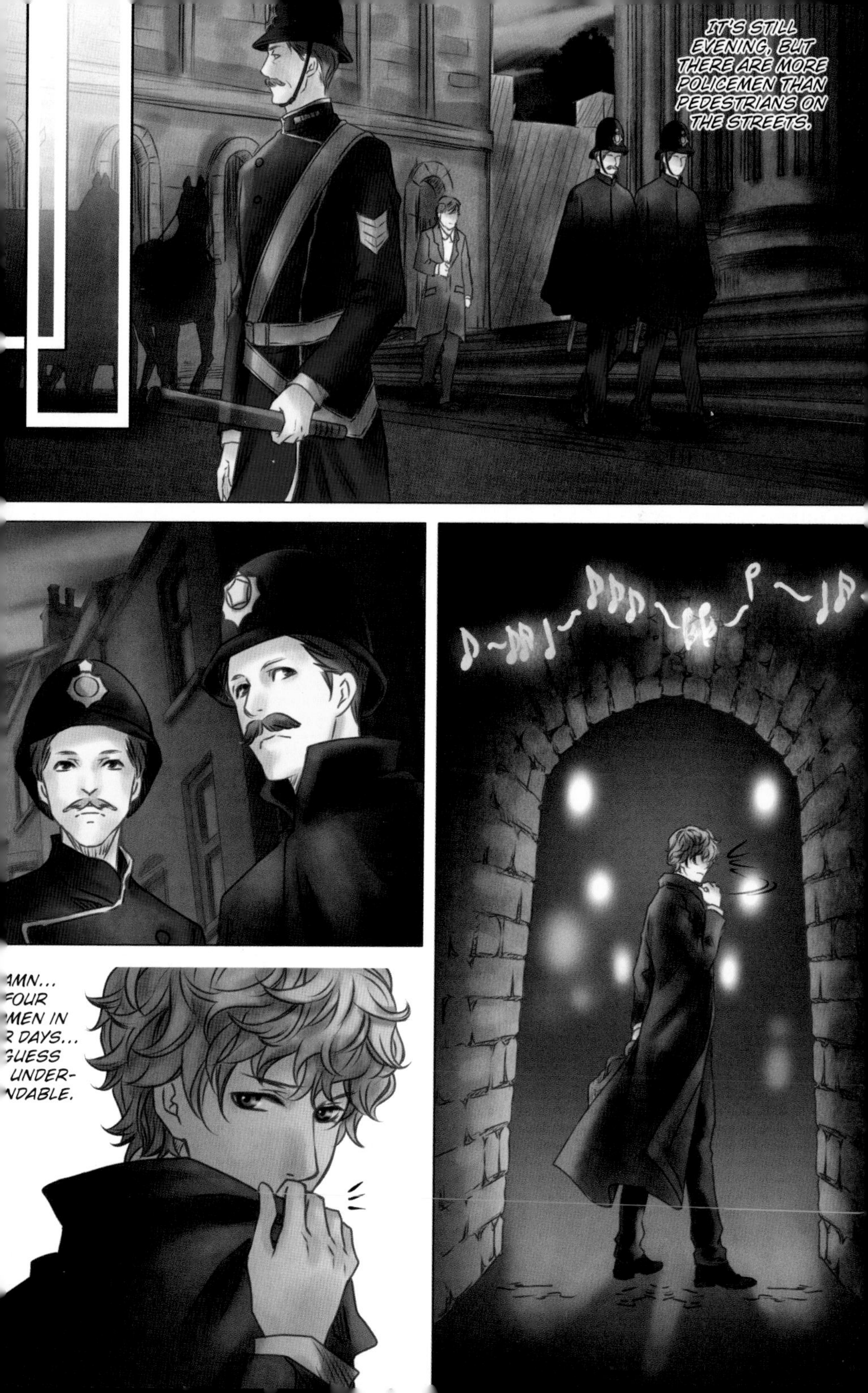
IT'S STILL EVENING, BUT THERE ARE MORE POLICEMEN THAN PEDESTRIANS ON THE STREETS.
AMN... FOUR MEN IN R DAYS... GUESS UNDER-NDABLE.

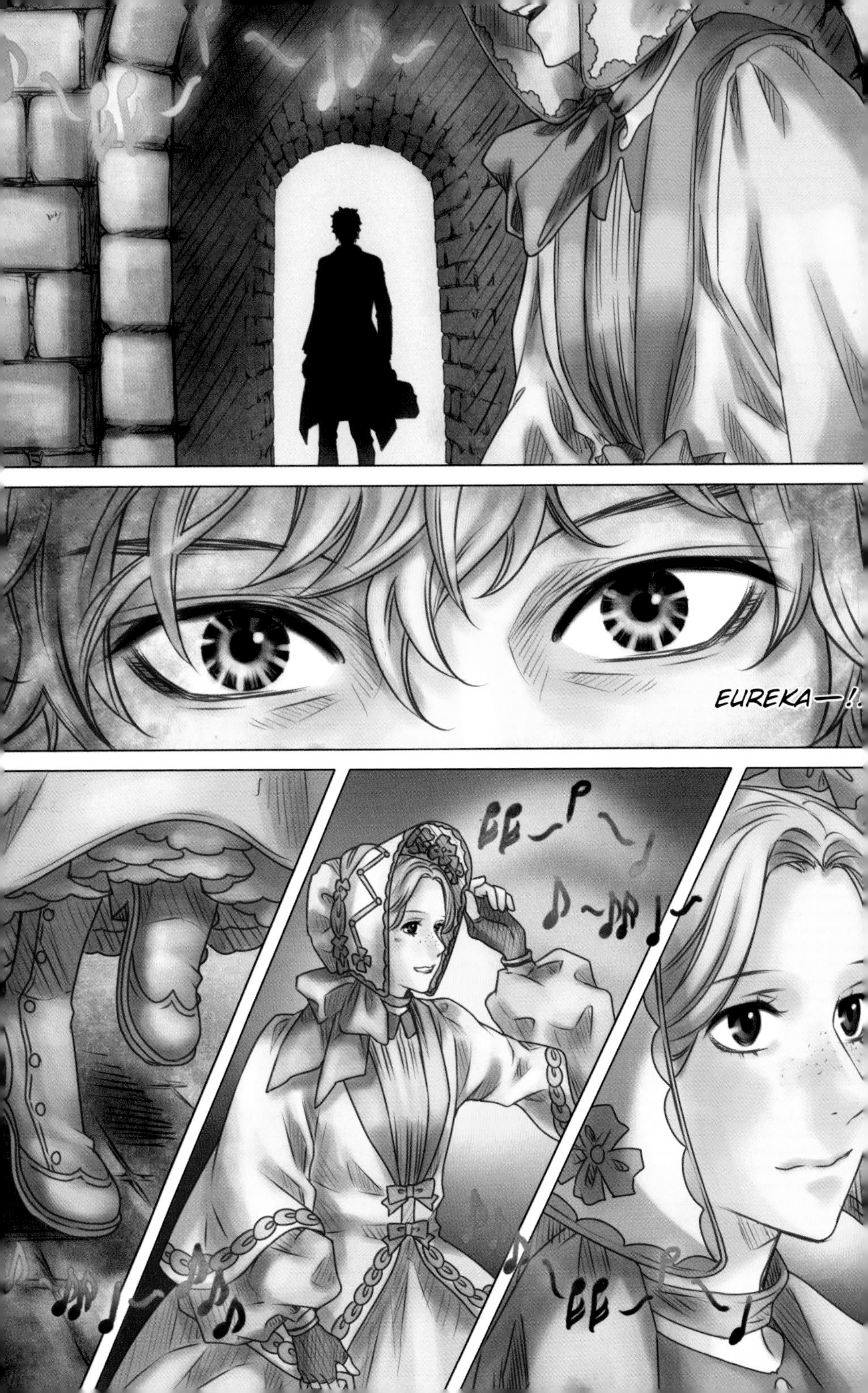
EUREKA—!!

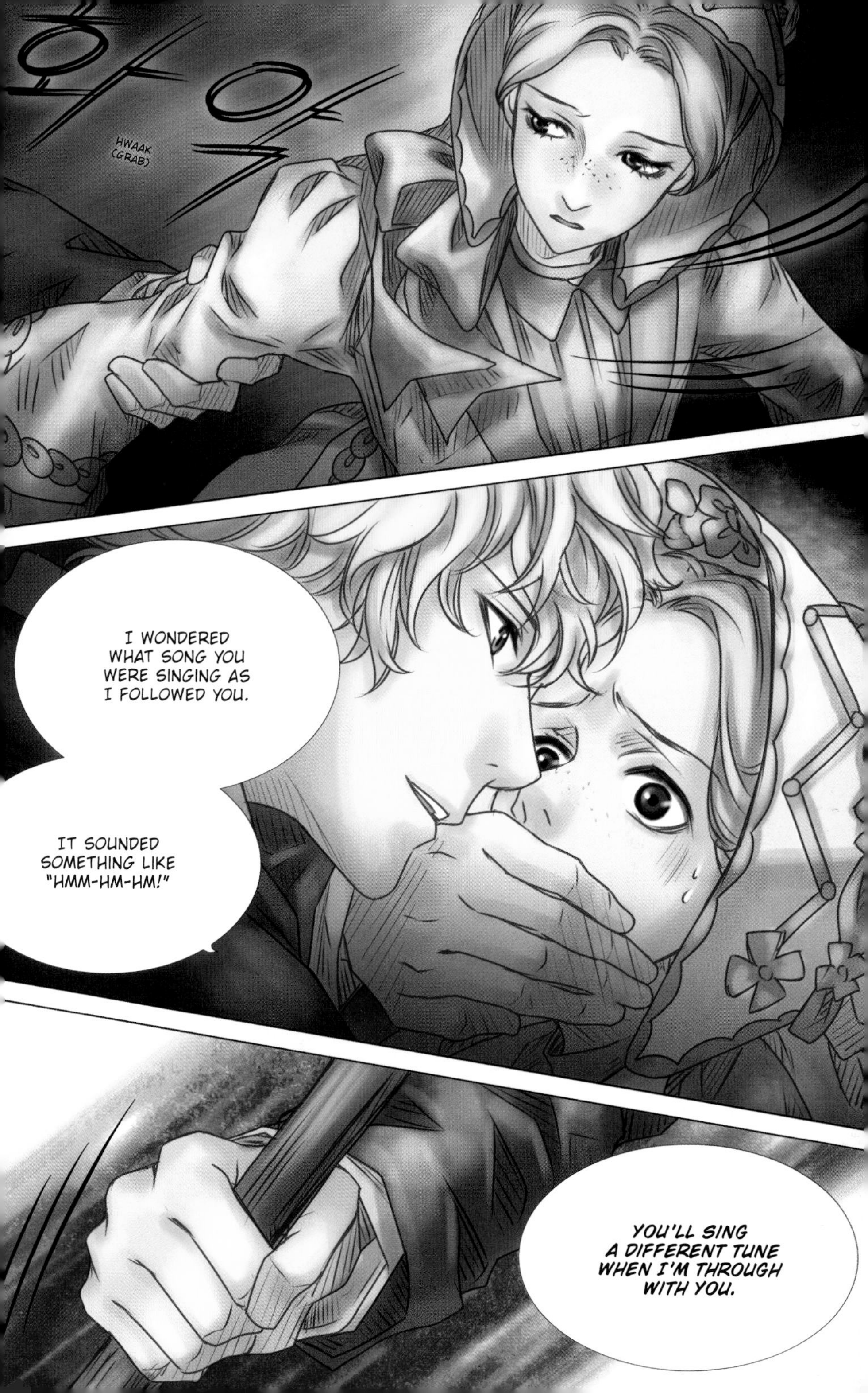
HWAAK (GRAB)
I WONDERED WHAT SONG YOU WERE SINGING AS I FOLLOWED YOU.
IT SOUNDED SOMETHING LIKE "HMM-HM-HM!"
YOU'LL SING A DIFFERENT TUNE WHEN I'M THROUGH WITH YOU.

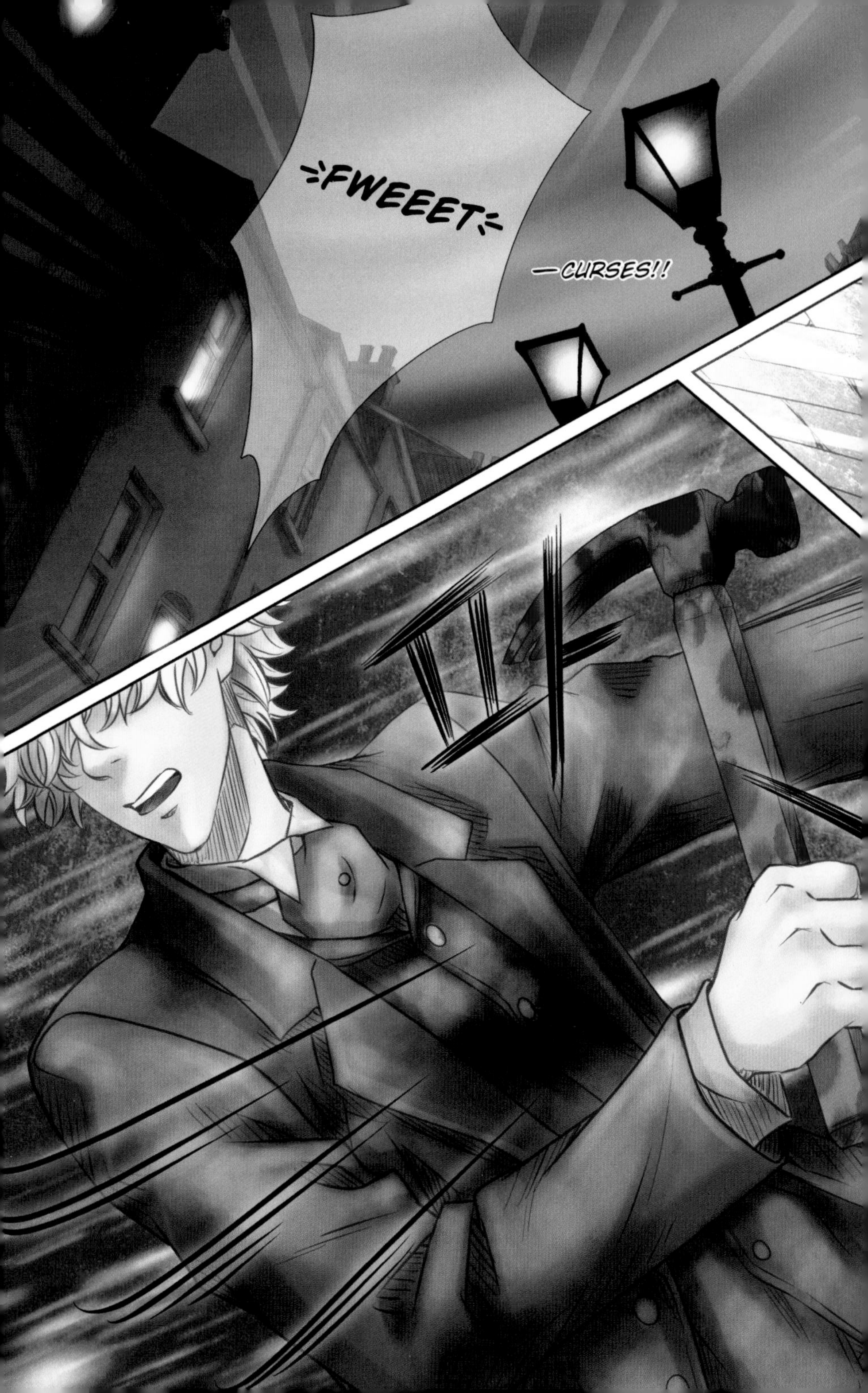
FWEEET
—CURSES!!

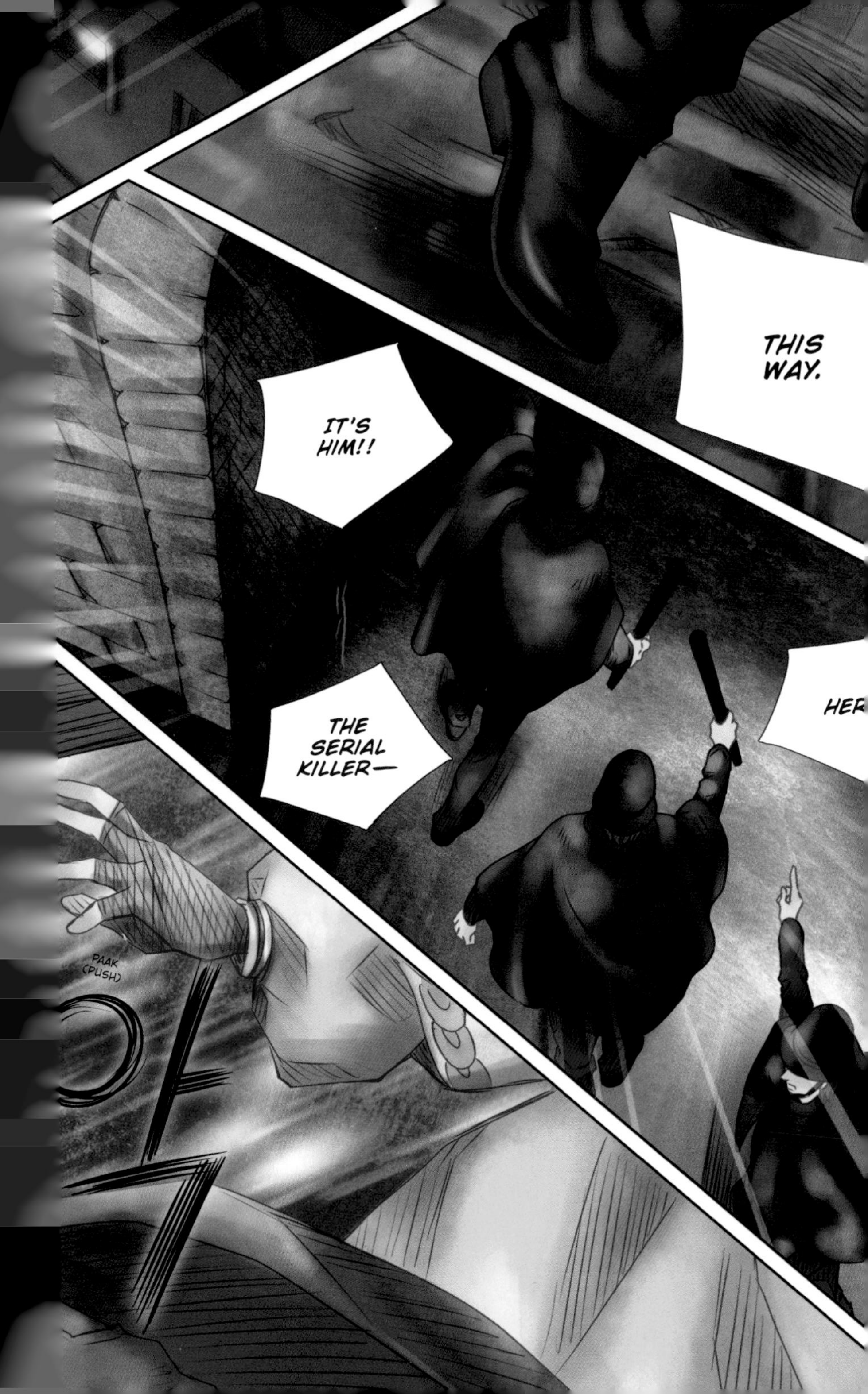
THIS WAY.
IT'S HIM!!
THE SERIAL KILLER—
HER
PAAK (PUSH)

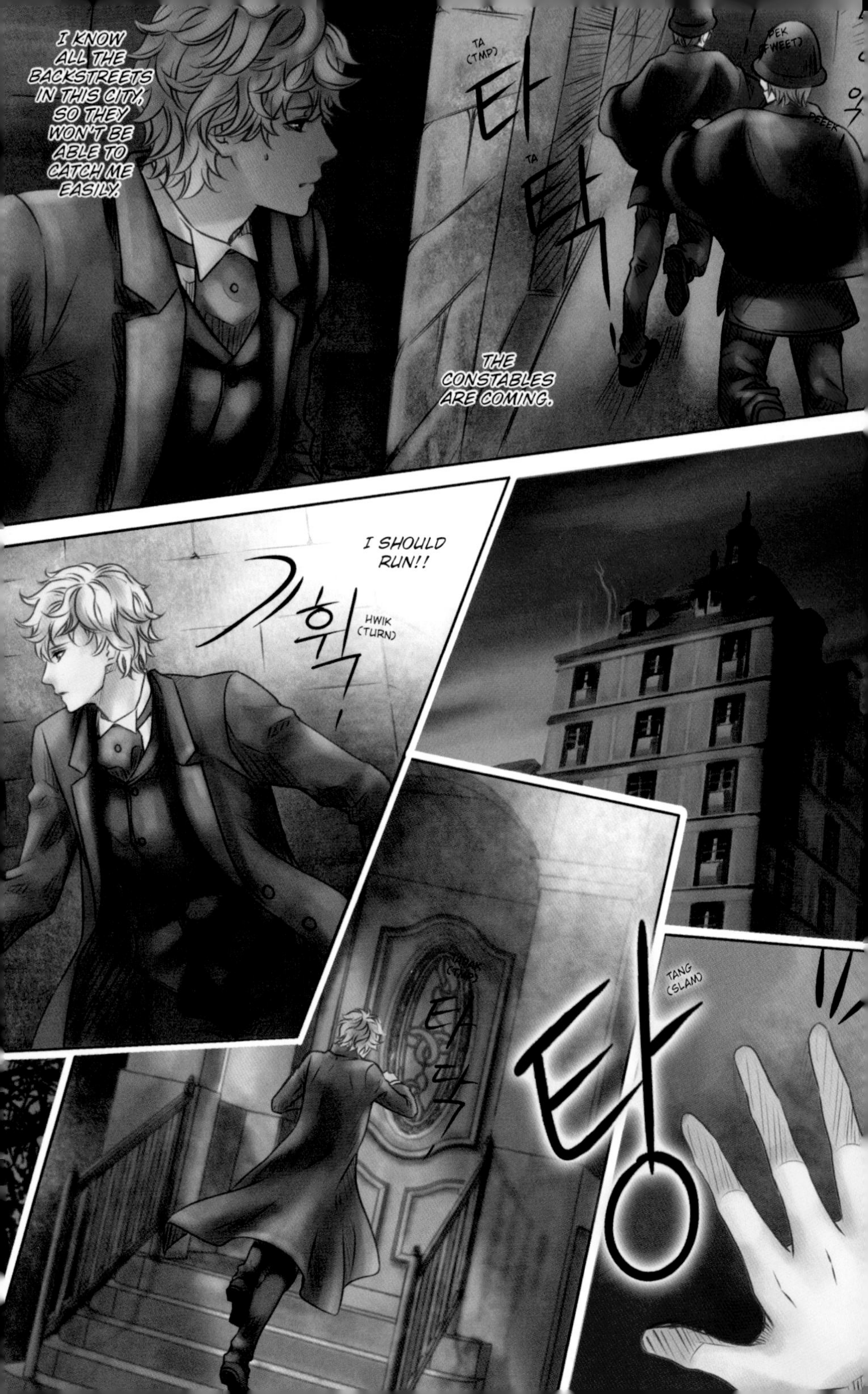
I KNOW ALL THE BACKSTREETS IN THIS CITY, SO THEY WON'T BE ABLE TO CATCH ME EASILY.
TA (TMP)
타
TA
탁
PEK (FWEET)
PEEEK
THE CONSTABLES ARE COMING.
I SHOULD RUN!!
휙
HWIK (TURN)
TARAK (TMP)
타닥
TANG (SLAM)
탕

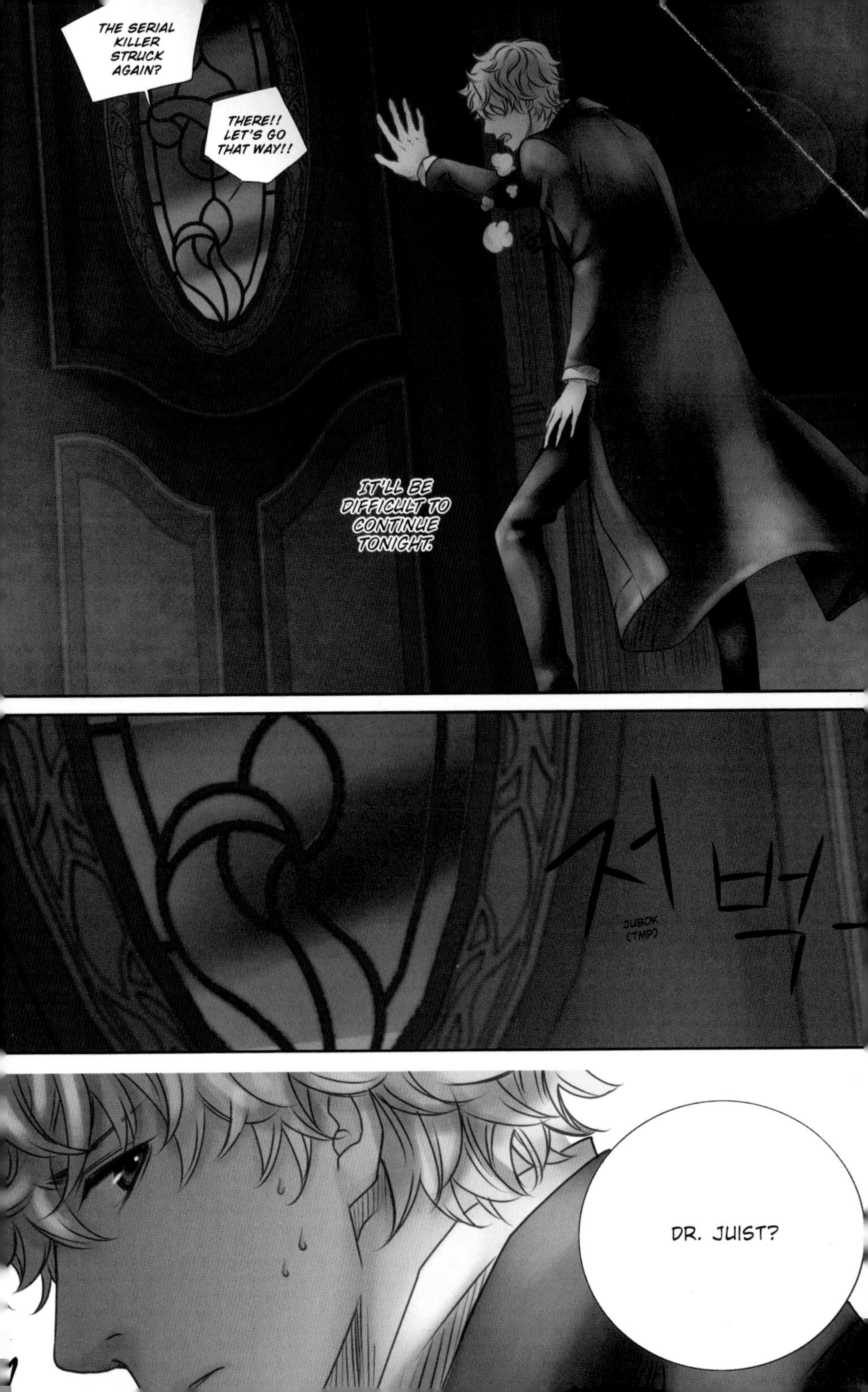
THE SERIAL KILLER STRUCK AGAIN?
THERE!! LET'S GO THAT WAY!!
IT'LL BE DIFFICULT TO CONTINUE TONIGHT.
저벅
JUBOK (TMP)
DR. JUIST?

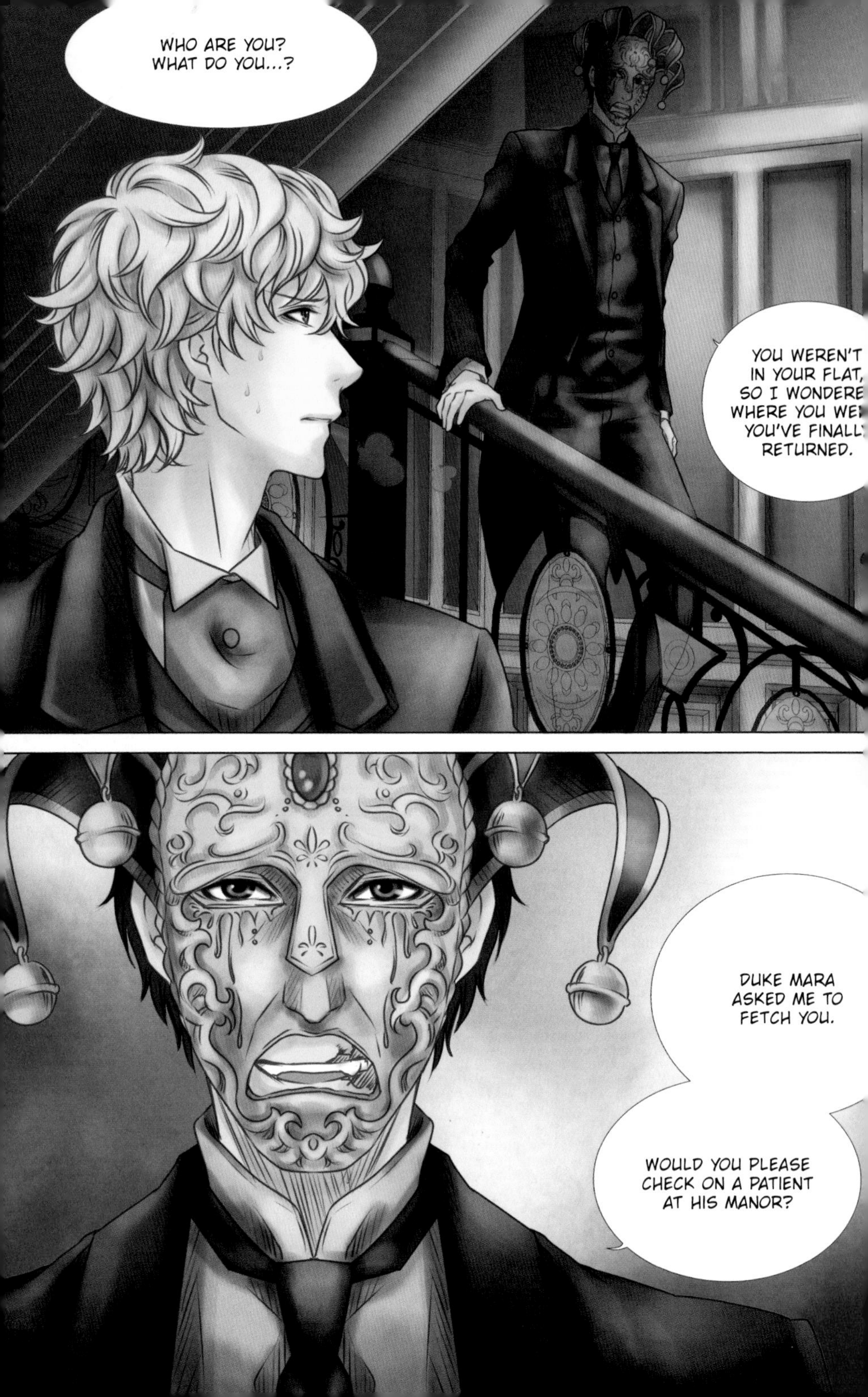
WHO ARE YOU? WHAT DO YOU...?
YOU WEREN'T IN YOUR FLAT, SO I WONDERE WHERE YOU WE YOU'VE FINALL RETURNED.
DUKE MARA ASKED ME TO FETCH YOU.
WOULD YOU PLEASE CHECK ON A PATIENT AT HIS MANOR?

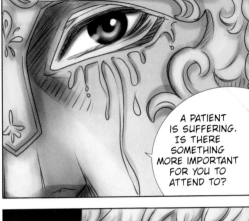

I'M ON HOLIDAY, SO I DON'T THINK I CAN DO THAT.

I UNDERSTAND, BUT THE DUKE INSISTED. HE SAID HE WOULD PAY YOU HANDSOMELY.

A PATIENT IS SUFFERING. IS THERE SOMETHING MORE IMPORTANT FOR YOU TO ATTEND TO?

WELL... THAT...

YES... ENDING SOMEONE ELSE'S LIFE.

I EVEN WANT TO SMASH IN YOUR LAUGHING JESTER'S HEAD.

THERE IS A LADY IN MUCH PAIN. PLEASE COME WITH ME.

...HOW FORTUNATE.

I MAY HAVE YET ANOTHER OPPORTUNITY TO KILL TONIGHT...

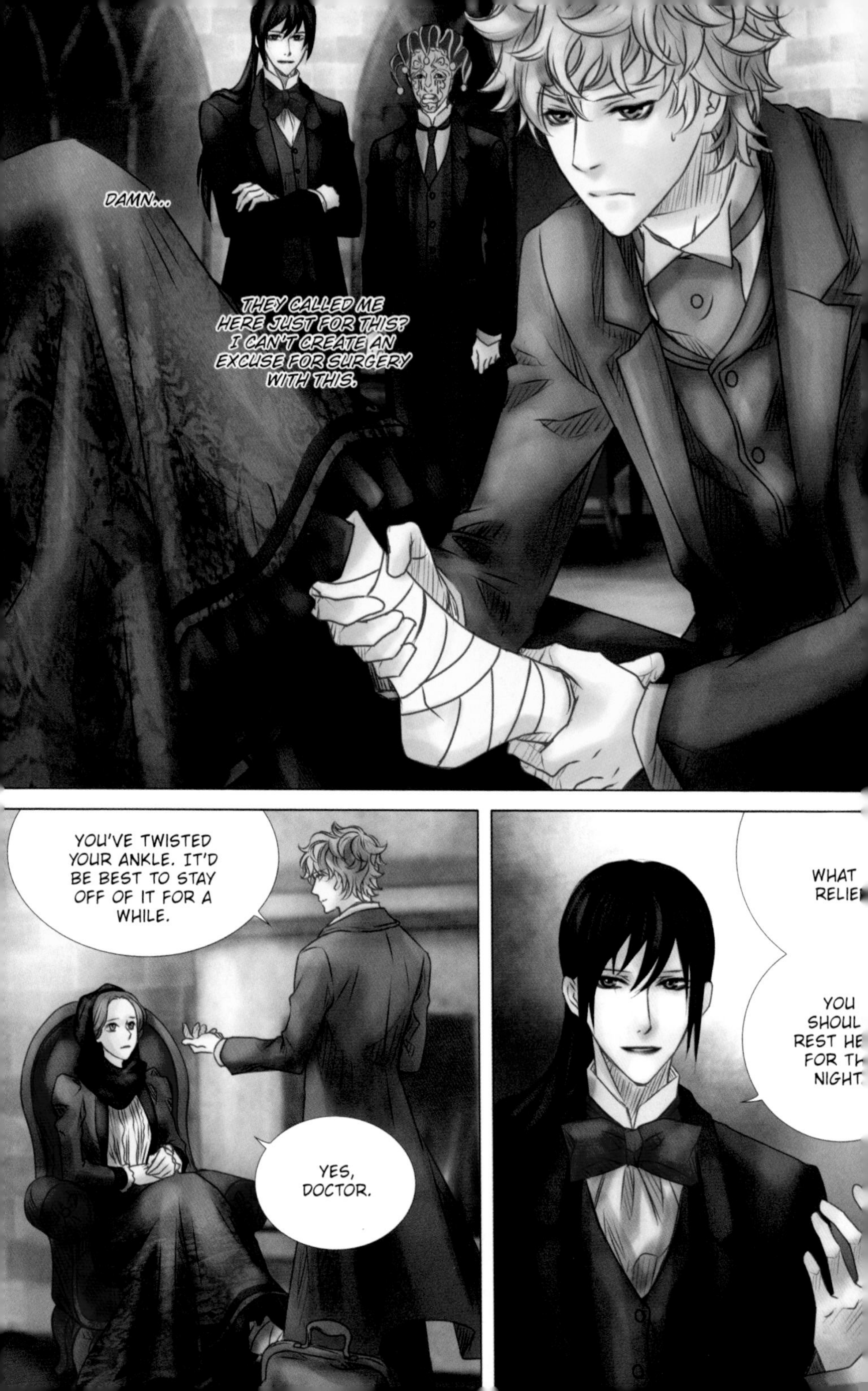
DAMN...
THEY CALLED ME HERE JUST FOR THIS? I CAN'T CREATE AN EXCUSE FOR SURGERY WITH THIS.
YOU'VE TWISTED YOUR ANKLE. IT'D BE BEST TO STAY OFF OF IT FOR A WHILE.
YES, DOCTOR.
WHAT RELIE
YOU SHOUL REST HE FOR TH NIGHT.

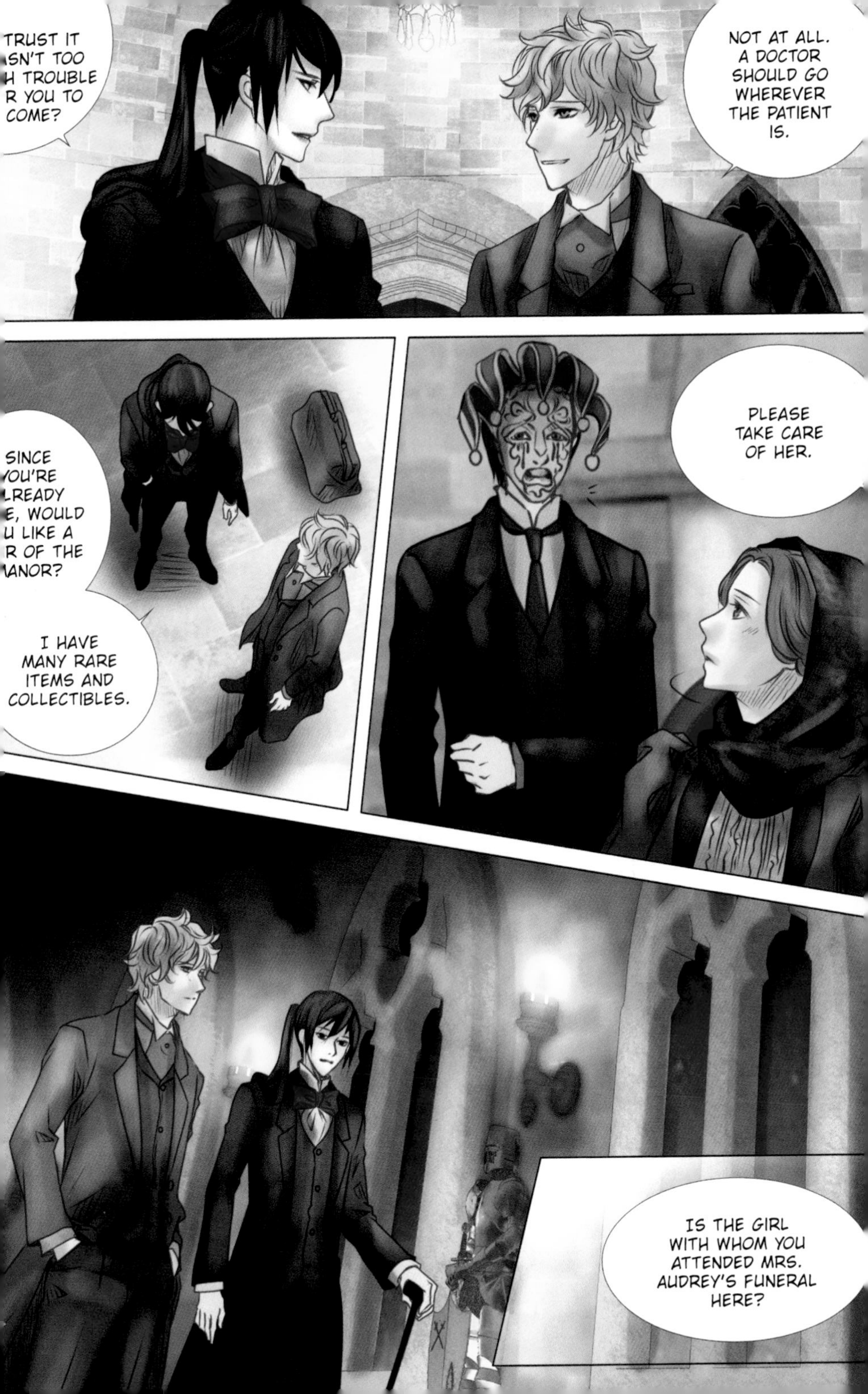
TRUST IT
ISN'T TOO
H TROUBLE
R YOU TO
COME?
NOT AT ALL. A DOCTOR SHOULD GO WHEREVER THE PATIENT IS.
SINCE
YOU'RE
LREADY
E, WOULD
U LIKE A
R OF THE
ANOR?
I HAVE MANY RARE ITEMS AND COLLECTIBLES.
PLEASE TAKE CARE OF HER.
IS THE GIRL WITH WHOM YOU ATTENDED MRS. AUDREY'S FUNERAL HERE?

SHE WENT TO VISIT LAVELLE.

I WANT HER TO BE WITH HIM, AS IT APPEARS SHE DOESN'T HAVE MUCH TIME LEFT.

WHEN I MET HER THE OTHER DAY, SHE DIDN'T LOOK TO BE IN THE BEST CONDITION.

...EVERYONE'S TIME IS LIMITED.

WELL... THERE ARE SOME EXCEPTIONS THOUGH.

IF LAVELLE LOSES THIS GIRL SO SOON AFTER MRS. AUDREY, HE'LL BE DEVASTATED.

YOU'RE CLOSE TO LAVELLE TOO, RIGHT?

WELL, YES. HE'S THE ONLY PERSON IN THE MANSION WHO SHARES MY INTERESTS.

I THOUGH I COULD B HIS FRIEN AT ONE POI AS WELL

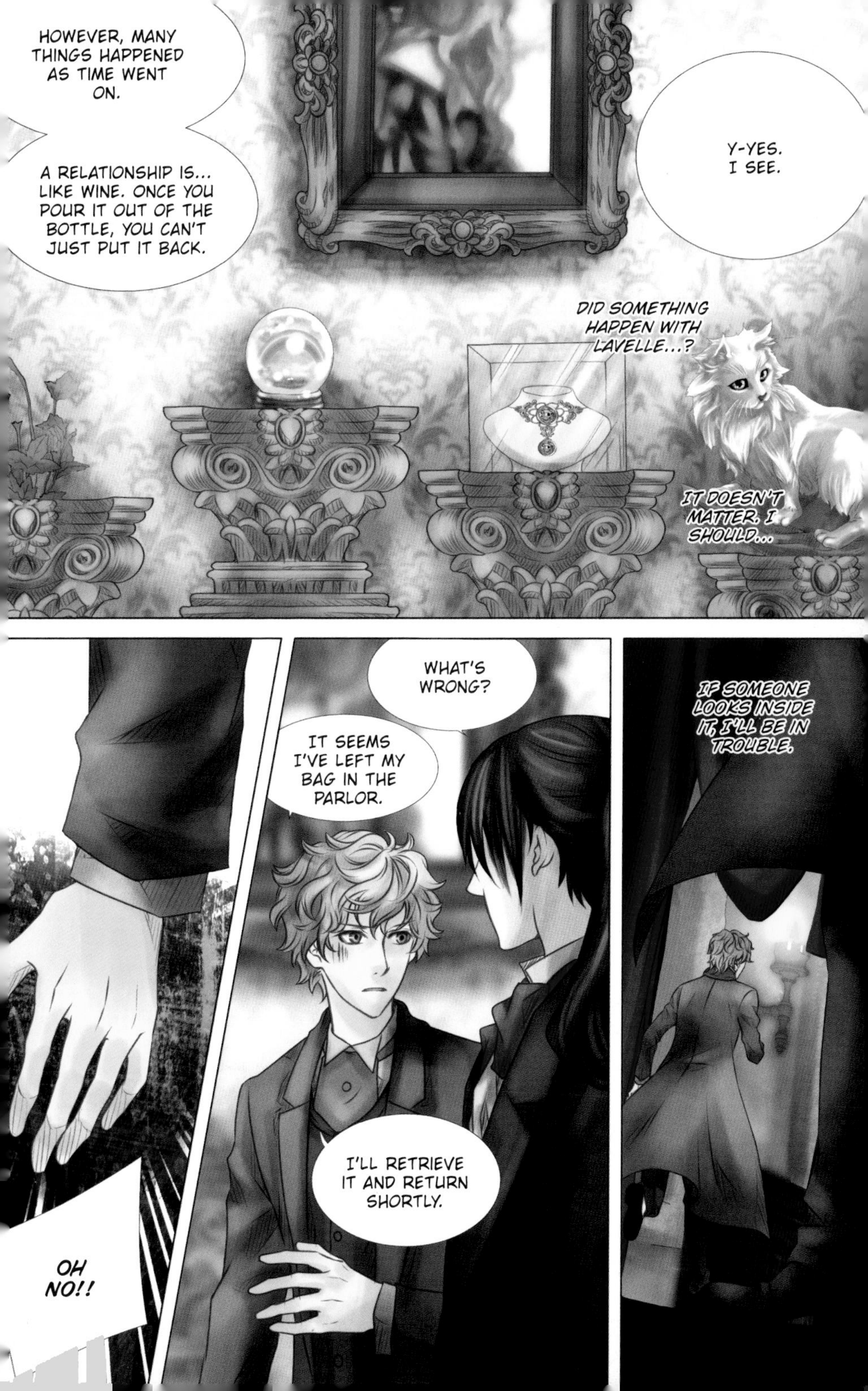
HOWEVER, MANY THINGS HAPPENED AS TIME WENT ON.
A RELATIONSHIP IS... LIKE WINE. ONCE YOU POUR IT OUT OF THE BOTTLE, YOU CAN'T JUST PUT IT BACK.
Y-YES. I SEE.
DID SOMETHING HAPPEN WITH LAVELLE...?
IT DOESN'T MATTER. I SHOULD...
OH NO!!
WHAT'S WRONG?
IT SEEMS I'VE LEFT MY BAG IN THE PARLOR.
I'LL RETRIEVE IT AND RETURN SHORTLY.
IF SOMEONE LOOKS INSIDE IT, I'LL BE IN TROUBLE.

FOR YOU, I ABANDONED MY HUSBAND, MY TITLE, AND EVEN MY FRIENDS...

I LEFT EVERYTHING BEHIND AND CAME HERE.

I NEVER ASKED YOU TO DO THAT.

I KNOW. I WANTED TO DO IT BECAUSE I LOVE YOU. I COULDN'T LET YOU CRY ALONE.

I'LL MAKE YOU HAPPY. LET'S LEAVE THE CITY TOGETHER.

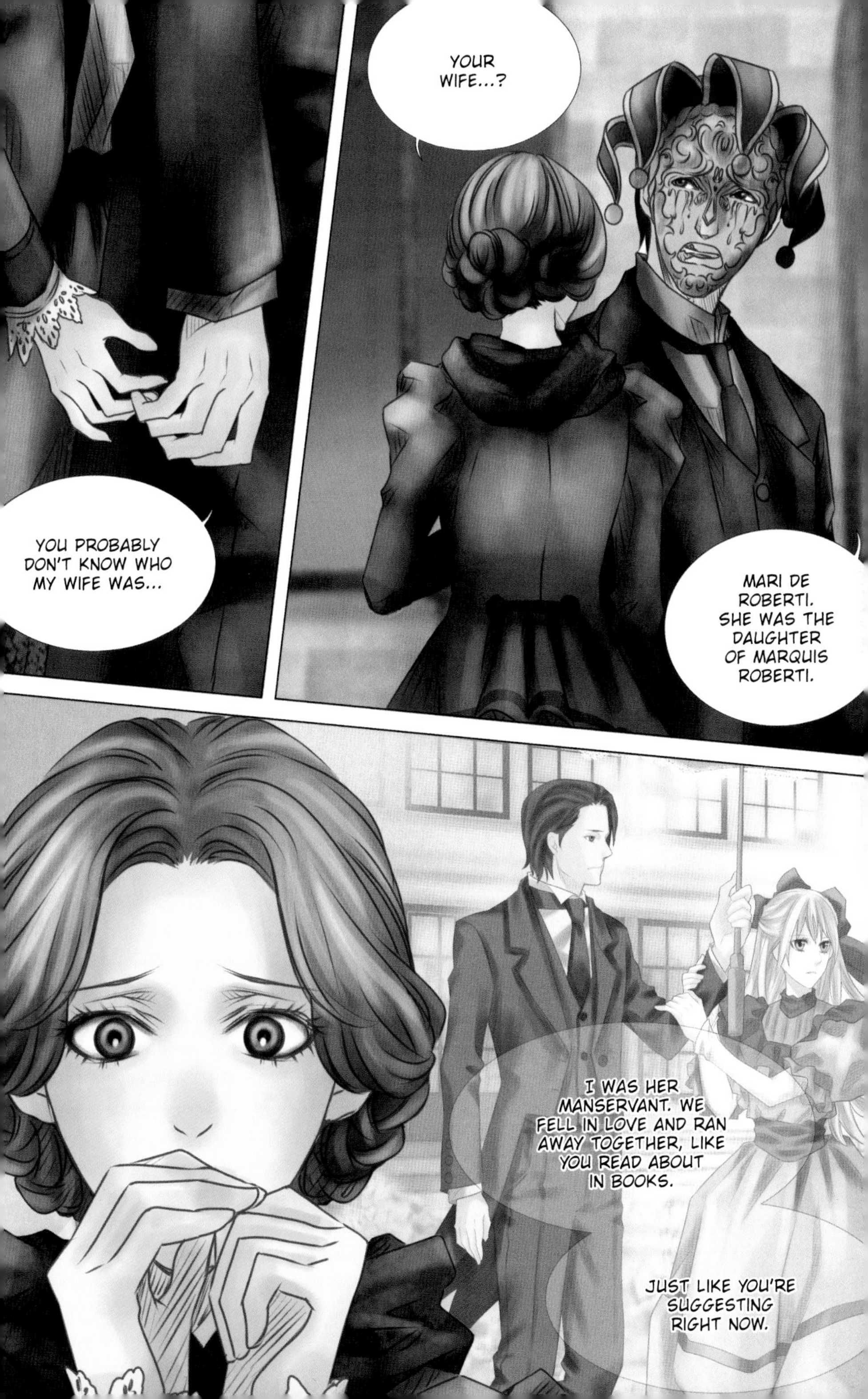
YOU PROBABLY DON'T KNOW WHO MY WIFE WAS...
YOUR WIFE...?
MARI DE ROBERTI. SHE WAS THE DAUGHTER OF MARQUIS ROBERTI.
I WAS HER MANSERVANT. WE FELL IN LOVE AND RAN AWAY TOGETHER, LIKE YOU READ ABOUT IN BOOKS.
JUST LIKE YOU'RE SUGGESTING RIGHT NOW.

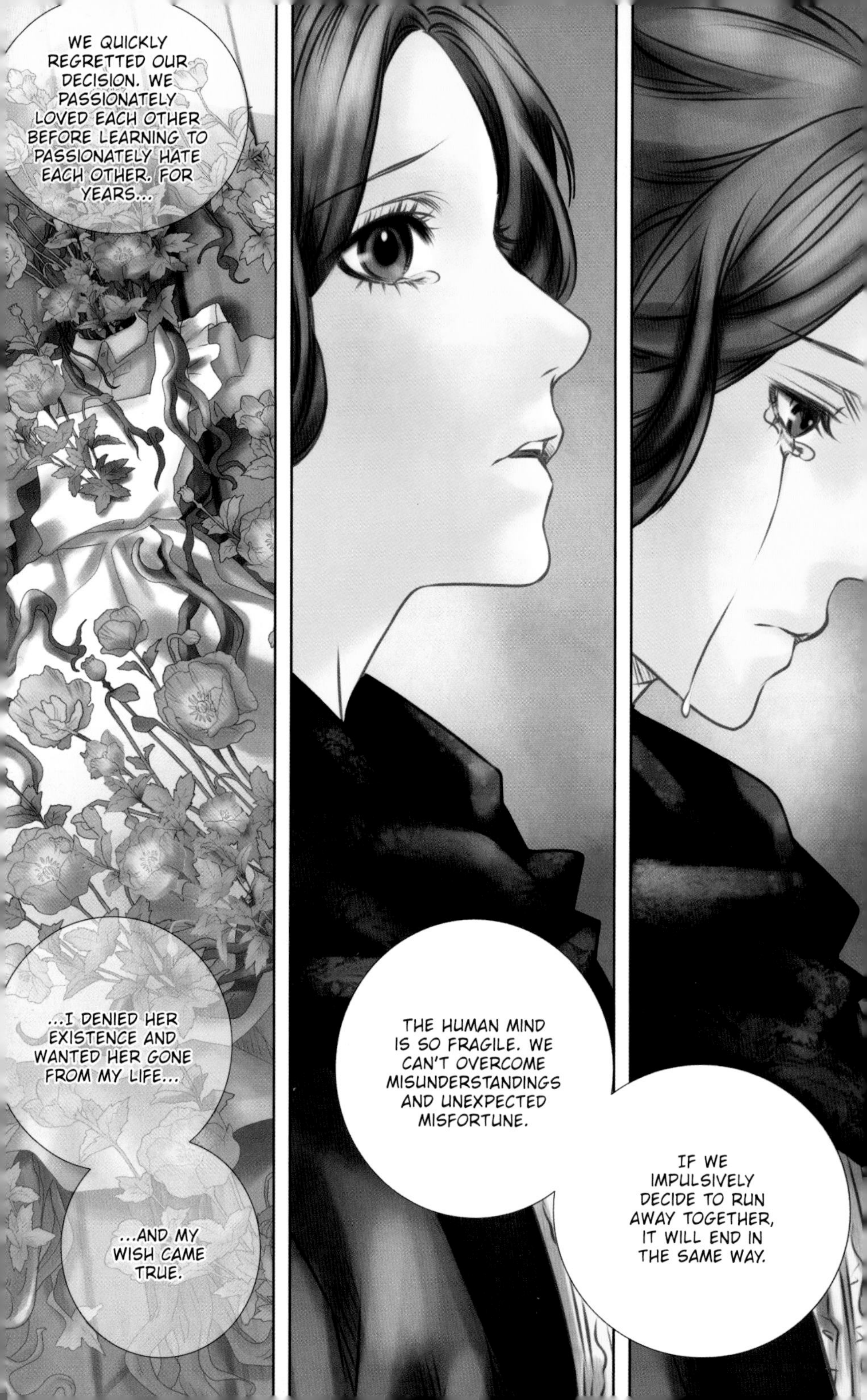
WE QUICKLY REGRETTED OUR DECISION. WE PASSIONATELY LOVED EACH OTHER BEFORE LEARNING TO PASSIONATELY HATE EACH OTHER. FOR YEARS...
...I DENIED HER EXISTENCE AND WANTED HER GONE FROM MY LIFE...
...AND MY WISH CAME TRUE.
THE HUMAN MIND IS SO FRAGILE. WE CAN'T OVERCOME MISUNDERSTANDINGS AND UNEXPECTED MISFORTUNE.
IF WE IMPULSIVELY DECIDE TO RUN AWAY TOGETHER, IT WILL END IN THE SAME WAY.

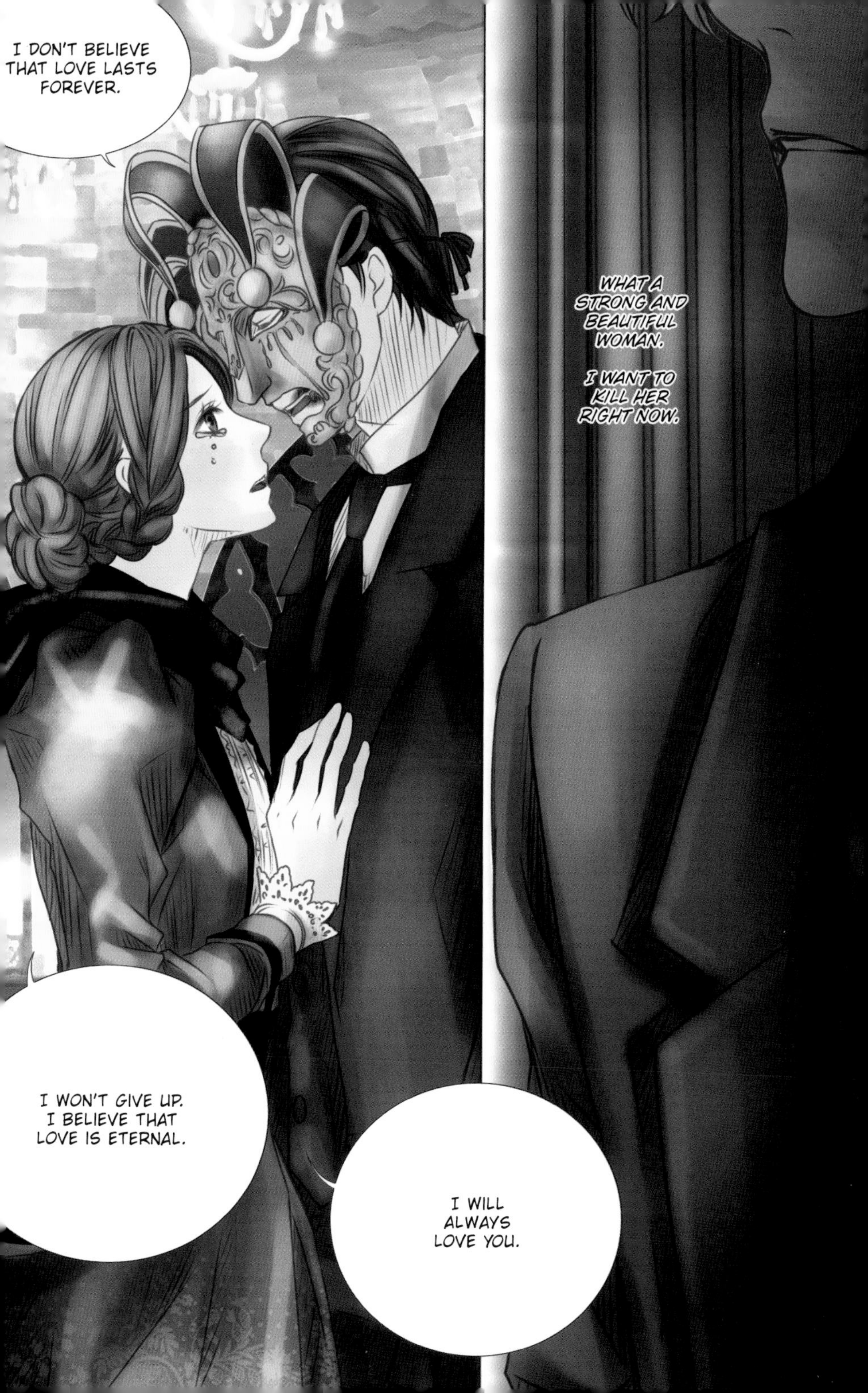
I DON'T BELIEVE THAT LOVE LASTS FOREVER.
I WON'T GIVE UP. I BELIEVE THAT LOVE IS ETERNAL.
I WILL ALWAYS LOVE YOU.
WHAT A STRONG AND BEAUTIFUL WOMAN.
I WANT TO KILL HER RIGHT NOW.

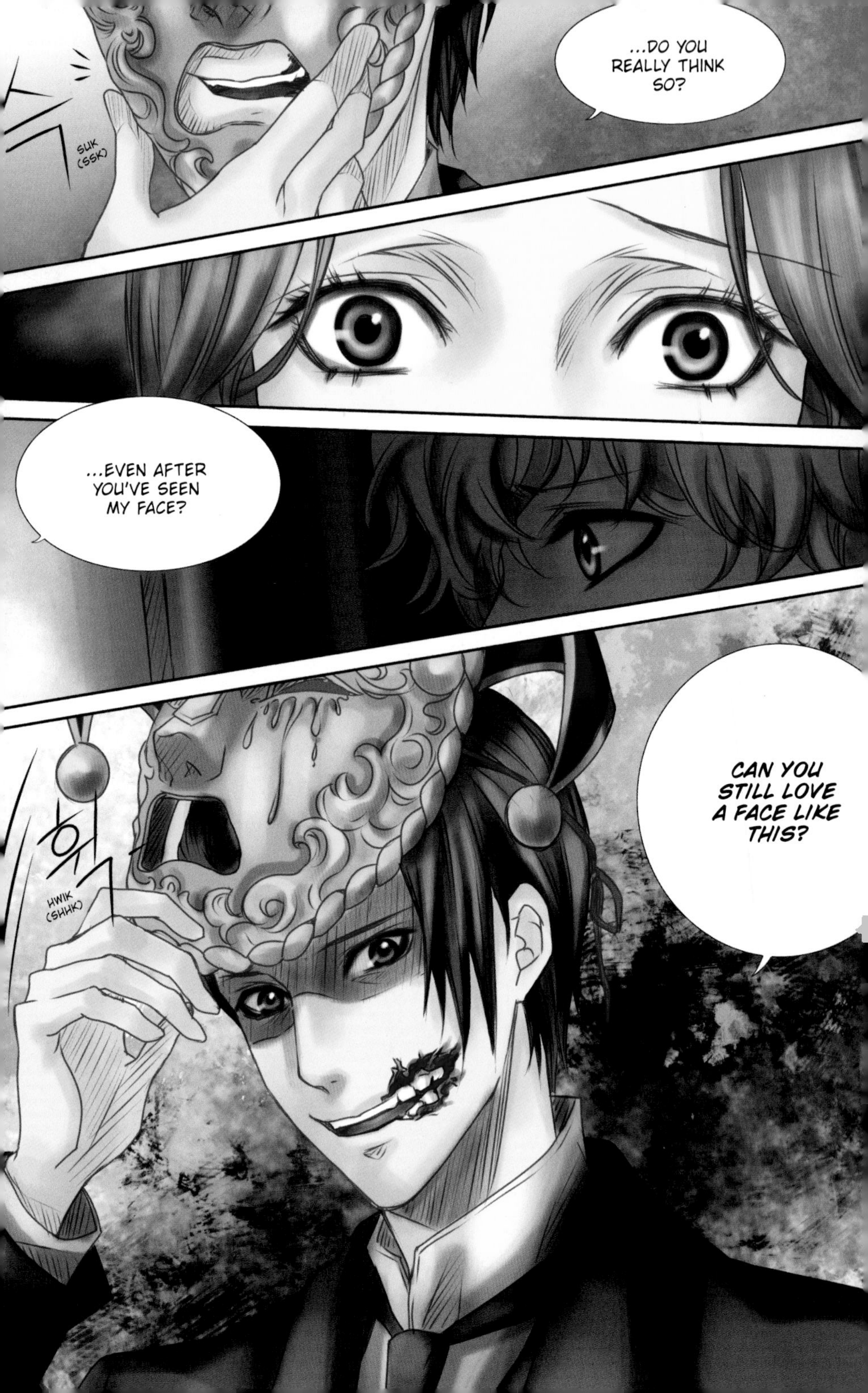
SUK (SSK)
...DO YOU REALLY THINK SO?
...EVEN AFTER YOU'VE SEEN MY FACE?
휙
HWIK (SHHK)
CAN YOU STILL LOVE A FACE LIKE THIS?

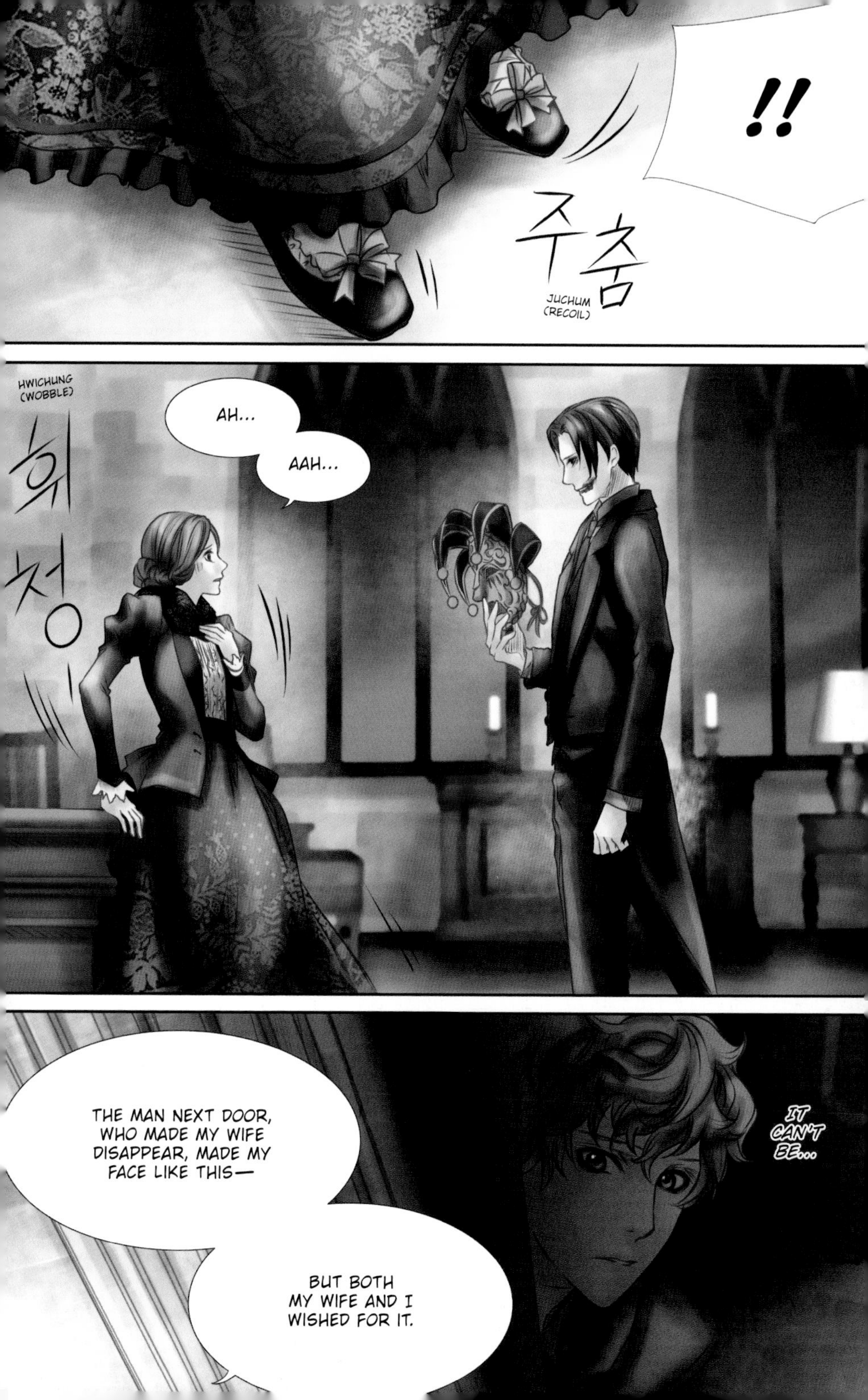
!!
주춤
JUCHUM (RECOIL)
HWICHUNG (WOBBLE)
휘청
AH...
AAH...
THE MAN NEXT DOOR, WHO MADE MY WIFE DISAPPEAR, MADE MY FACE LIKE THIS—
IT CAN'T BE...
BUT BOTH MY WIFE AND I WISHED FOR IT.

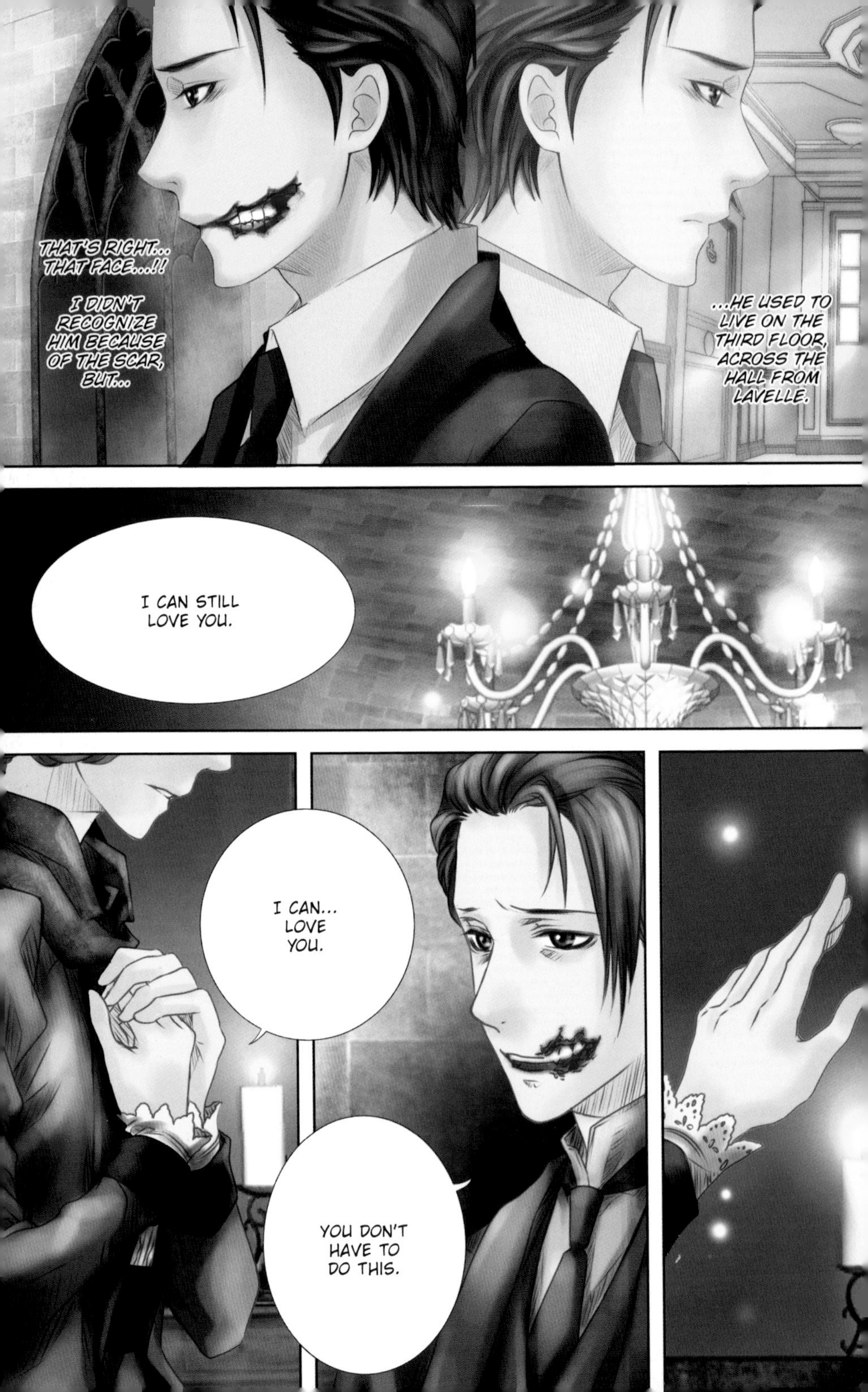
THAT'S RIGHT... THAT FACE...!!
I DIDN'T RECOGNIZE HIM BECAUSE OF THE SCAR, BUT...
...HE USED TO LIVE ON THE THIRD FLOOR, ACROSS THE HALL FROM LAVELLE.
I CAN STILL LOVE YOU.
I CAN... LOVE YOU.
YOU DON'T HAVE TO DO THIS.

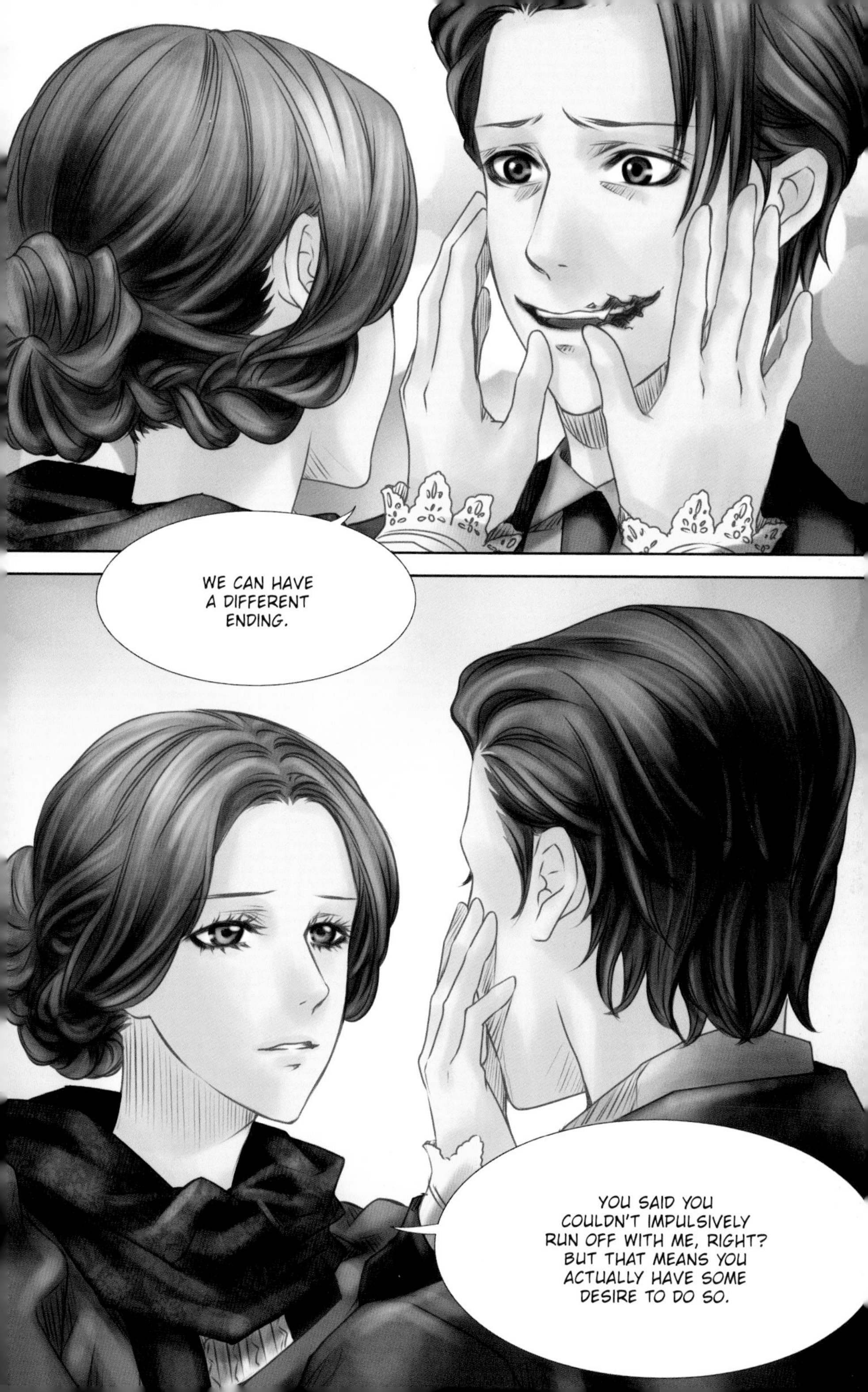
WE CAN HAVE A DIFFERENT ENDING.
YOU SAID YOU COULDN'T IMPULSIVELY RUN OFF WITH ME, RIGHT? BUT THAT MEANS YOU ACTUALLY HAVE SOME DESIRE TO DO SO.

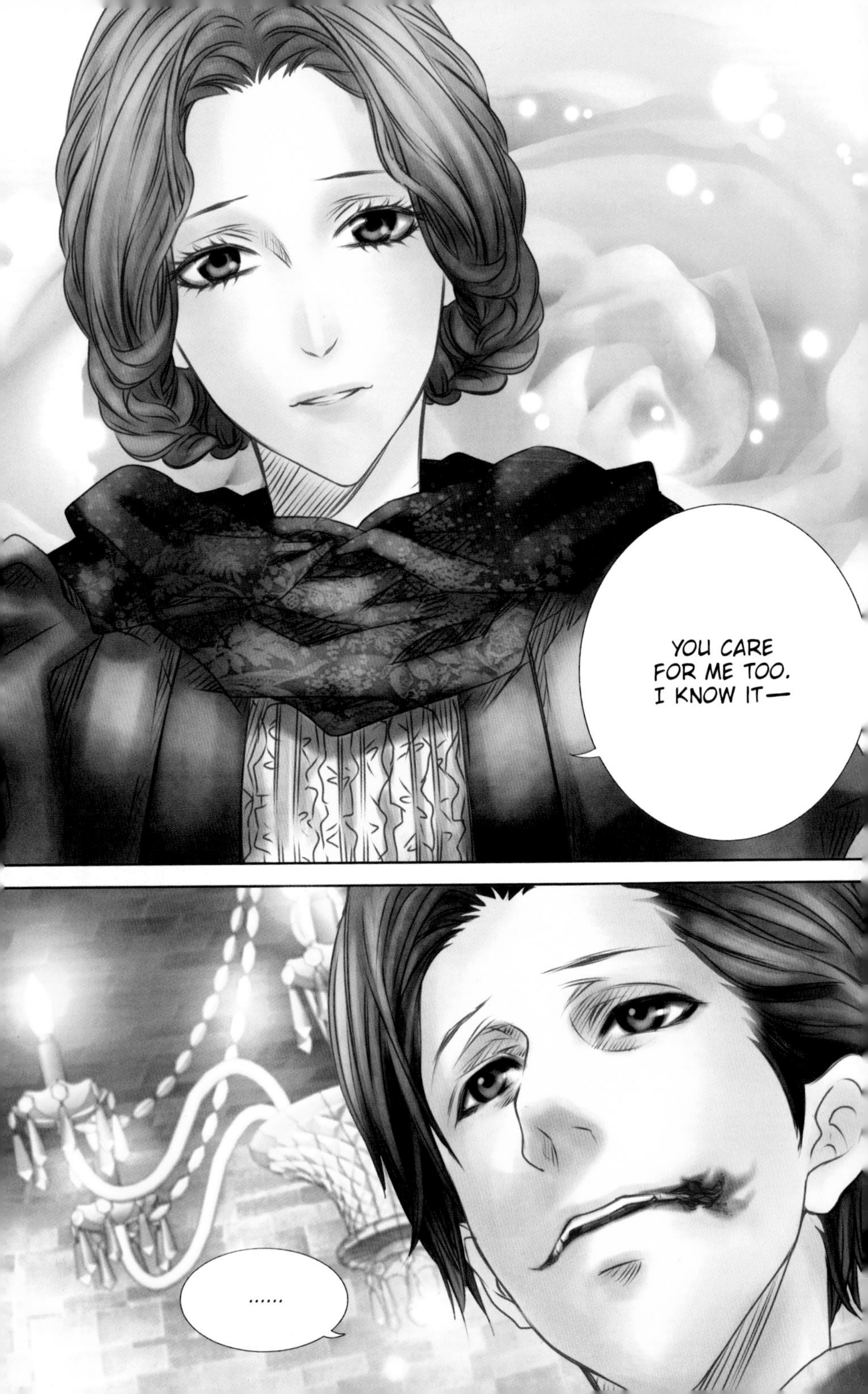
YOU CARE FOR ME TOO. I KNOW IT—
......

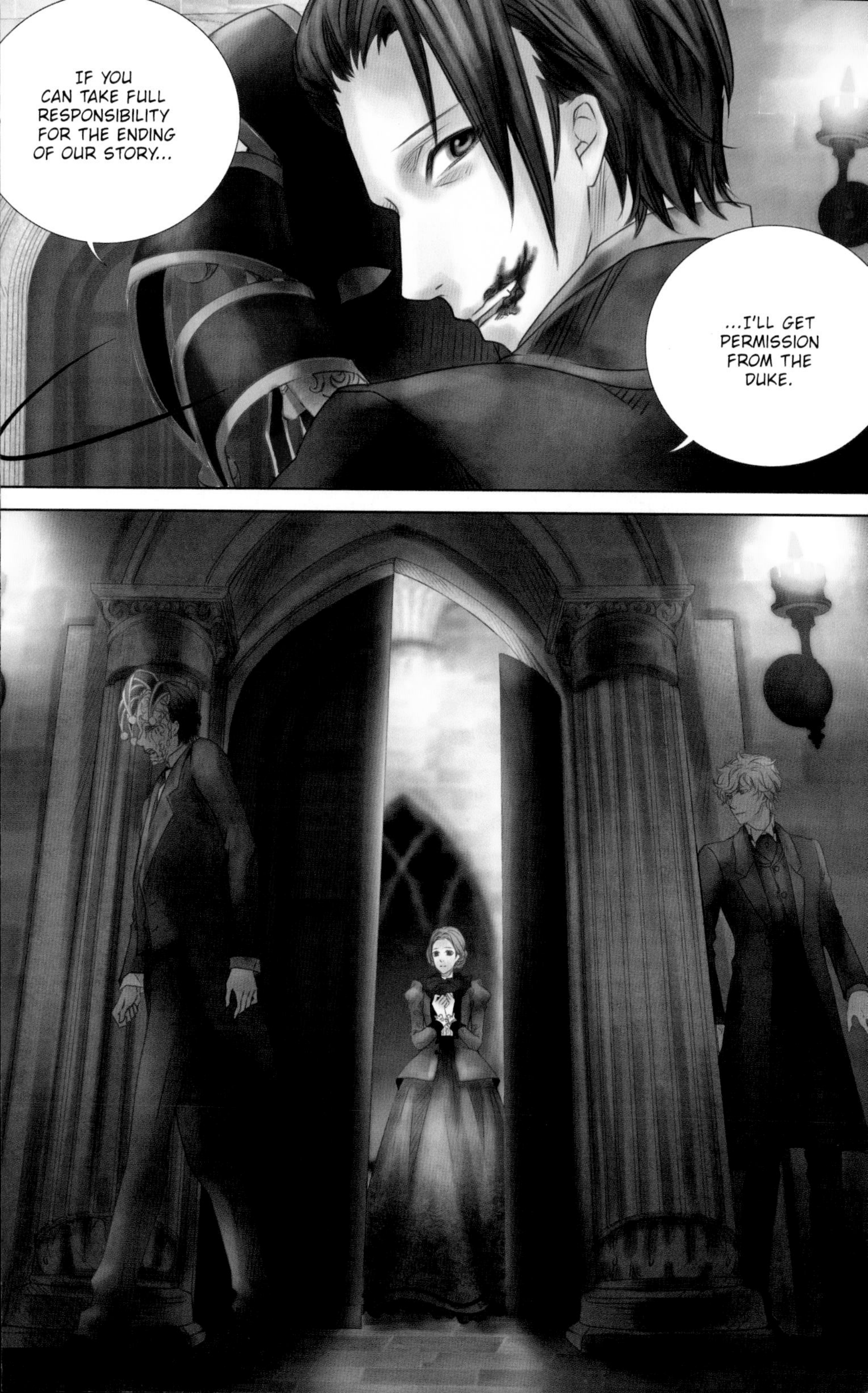
IF YOU CAN TAKE FULL RESPONSIBILITY FOR THE ENDING OF OUR STORY...
...I'LL GET PERMISSION FROM THE DUKE.

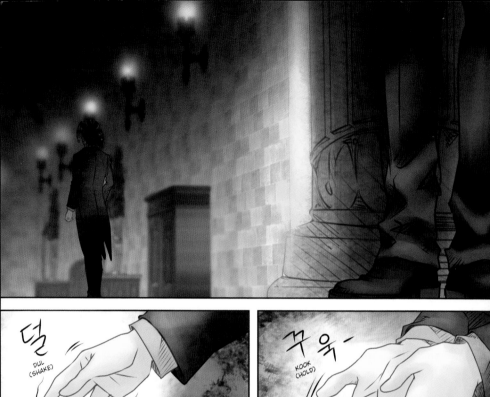

덜
DUL
(SHAKE)

덜
DUL

덜
DUL

꾸욱-
KOOK
(HOLD)

뚜벅
TUBOK
(TMP)

OH...
DOCTOR?

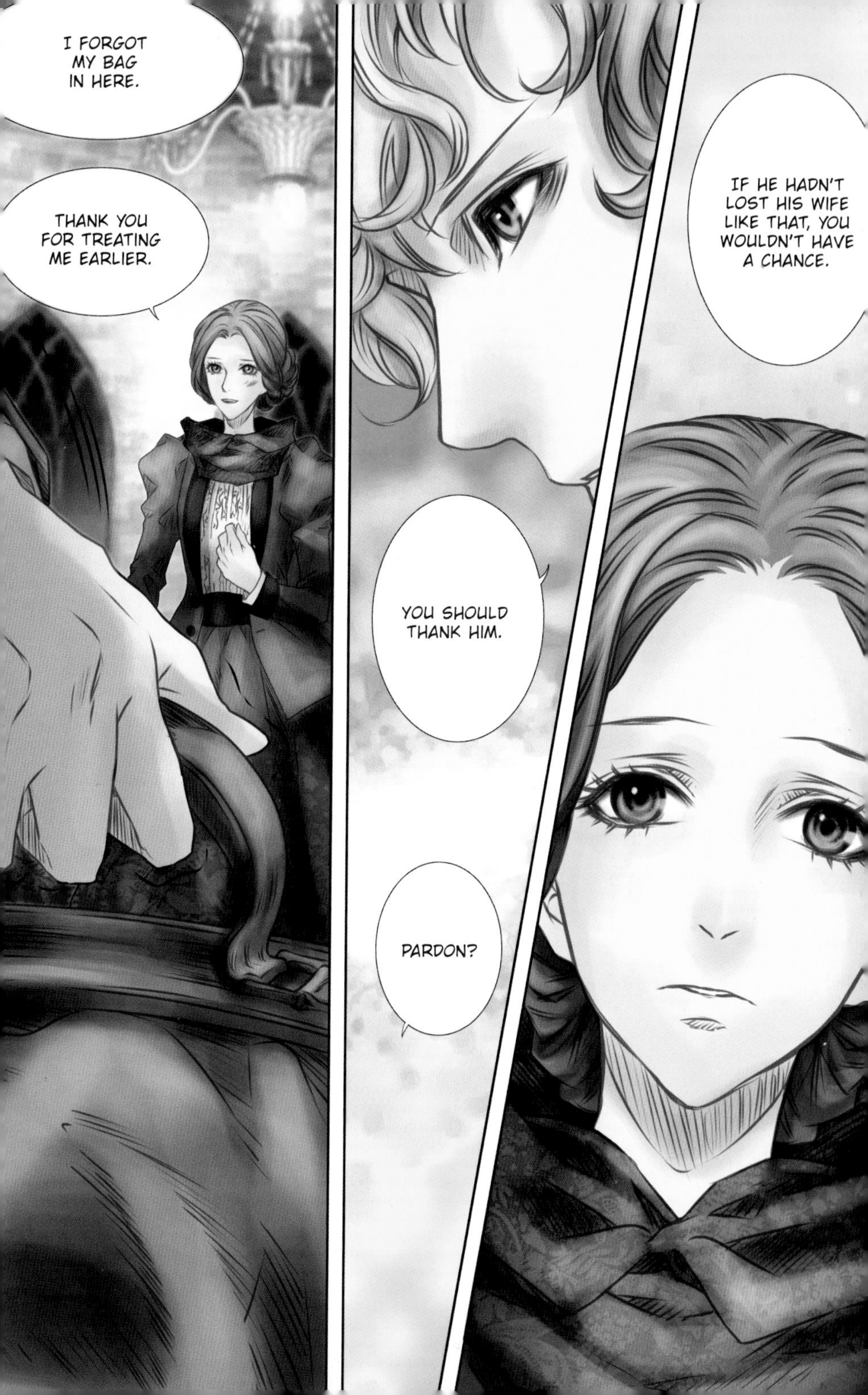
I FORGOT MY BAG IN HERE.
THANK YOU FOR TREATING ME EARLIER.
YOU SHOULD THANK HIM.
PARDON?
IF HE HADN'T LOST HIS WIFE LIKE THAT, YOU WOULDN'T HAVE A CHANCE.

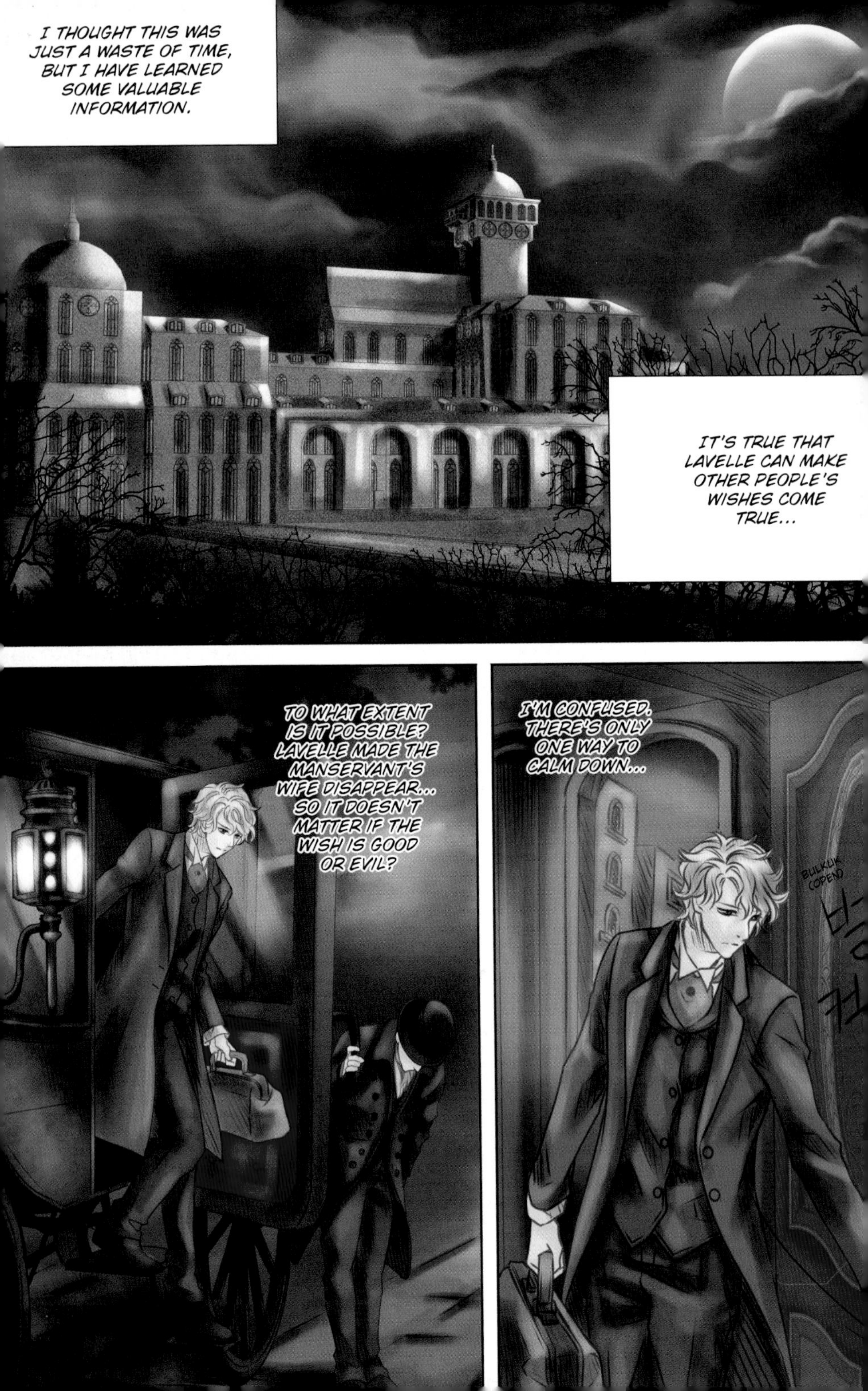
I THOUGHT THIS WAS JUST A WASTE OF TIME, BUT I HAVE LEARNED SOME VALUABLE INFORMATION.
IT'S TRUE THAT LAVELLE CAN MAKE OTHER PEOPLE'S WISHES COME TRUE...
TO WHAT EXTENT IS IT POSSIBLE? LAVELLE MADE THE MANSERVANT'S WIFE DISAPPEAR... SO IT DOESN'T MATTER IF THE WISH IS GOOD OR EVIL?
I'M CONFUSED. THERE'S ONLY ONE WAY TO CALM DOWN...
BULKUK (OPEN)

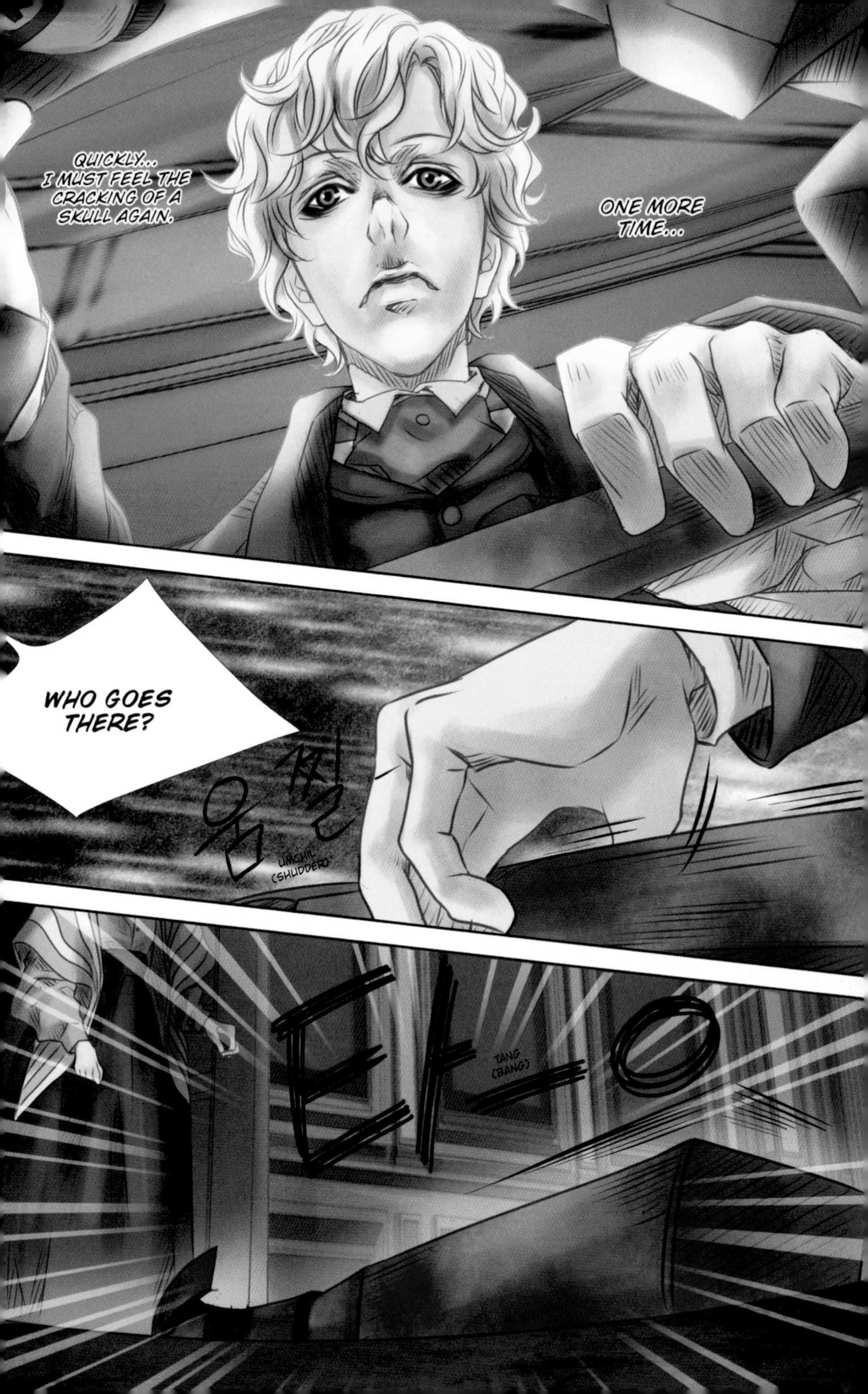
QUICKLY... I MUST FEEL THE CRACKING OF A SKULL AGAIN.
ONE MORE TIME...
WHO GOES THERE?
움찔
UMCHIL (SHUDDER)
타앙
TANG (BANG)

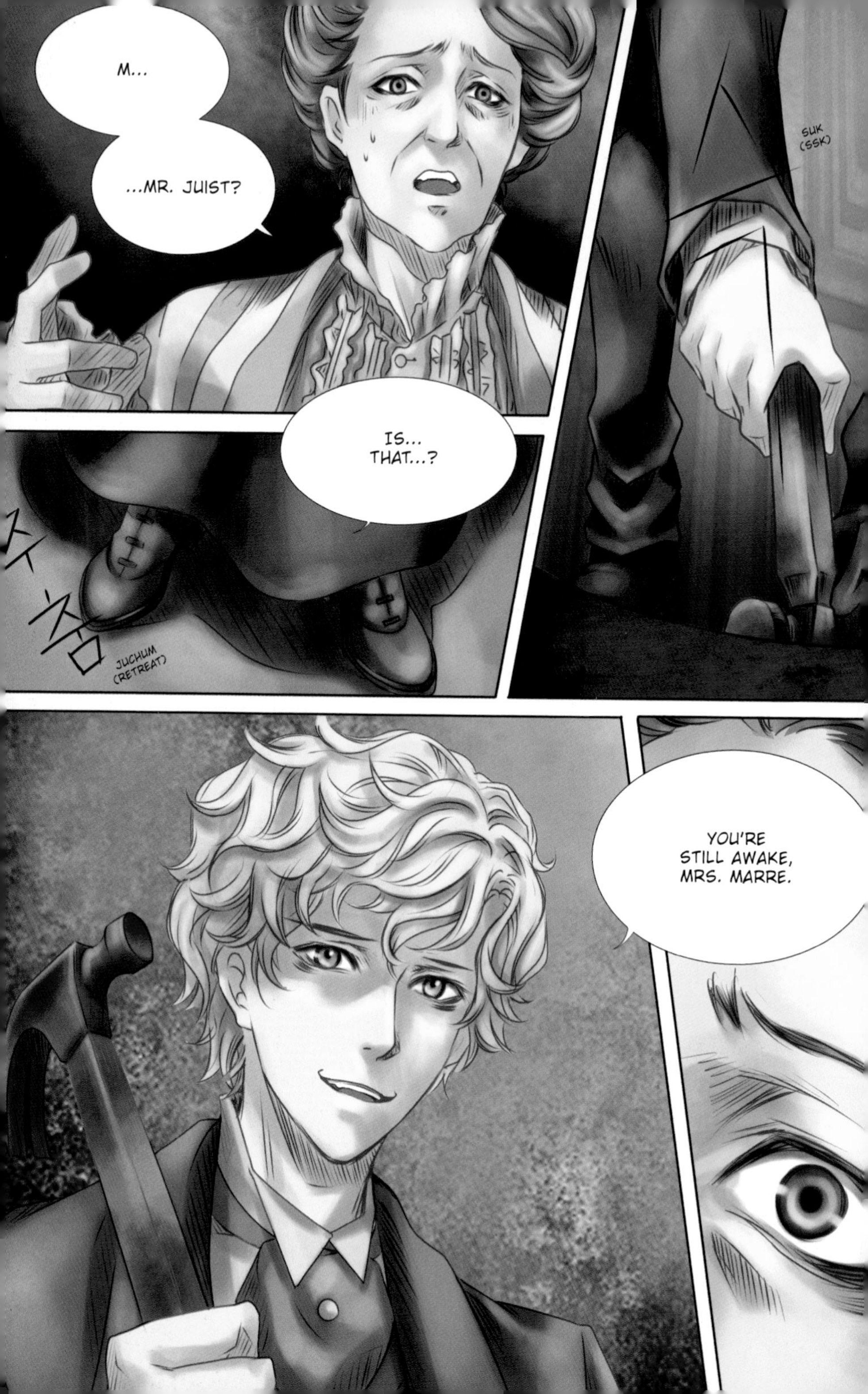
M...
...MR. JUIST?
IS... THAT...?
JUCHUM (RETREAT)
SUK (SSK)
YOU'RE STILL AWAKE, MRS. MARRE.

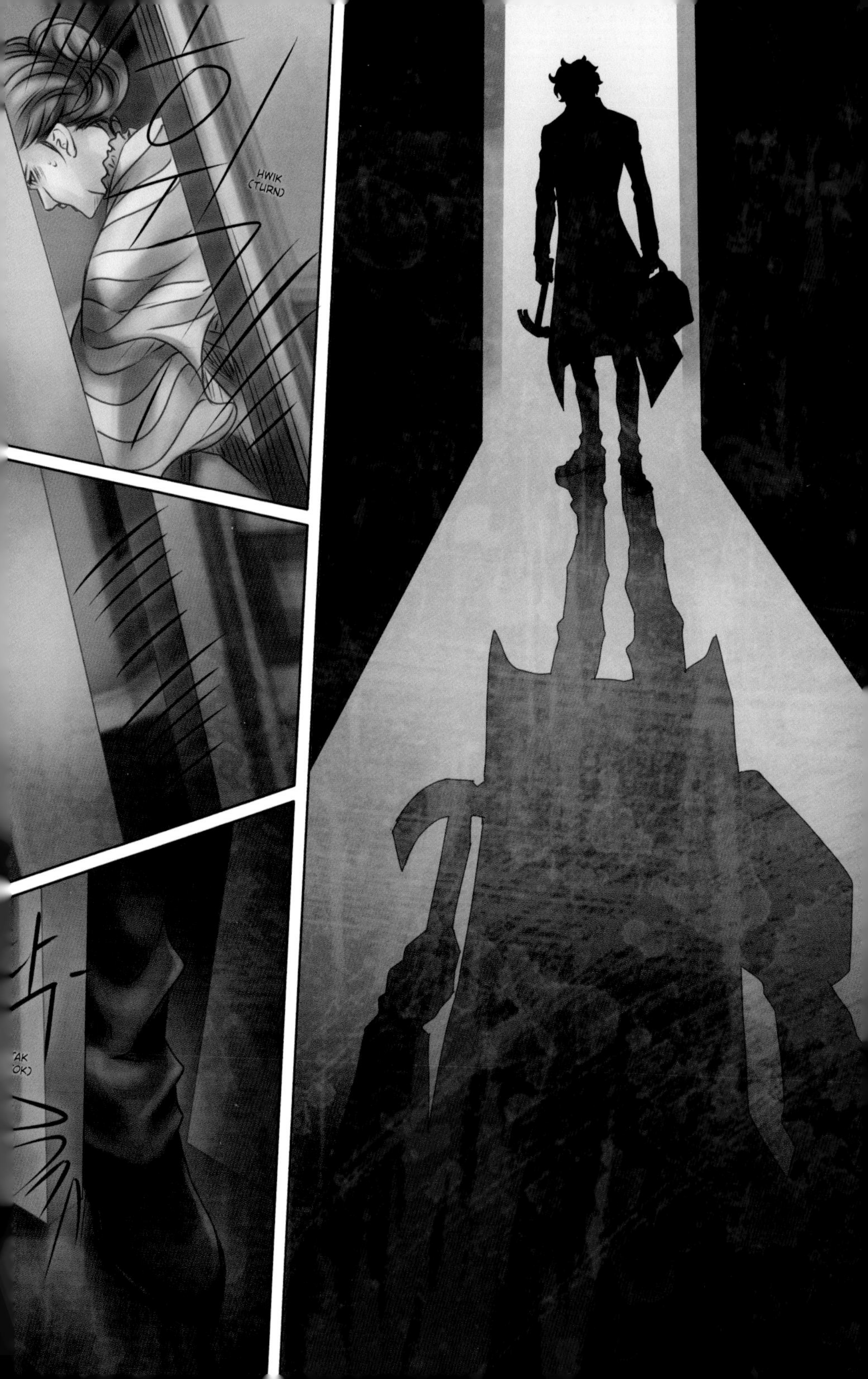
HWIK
(TURN)
TAK
OK)

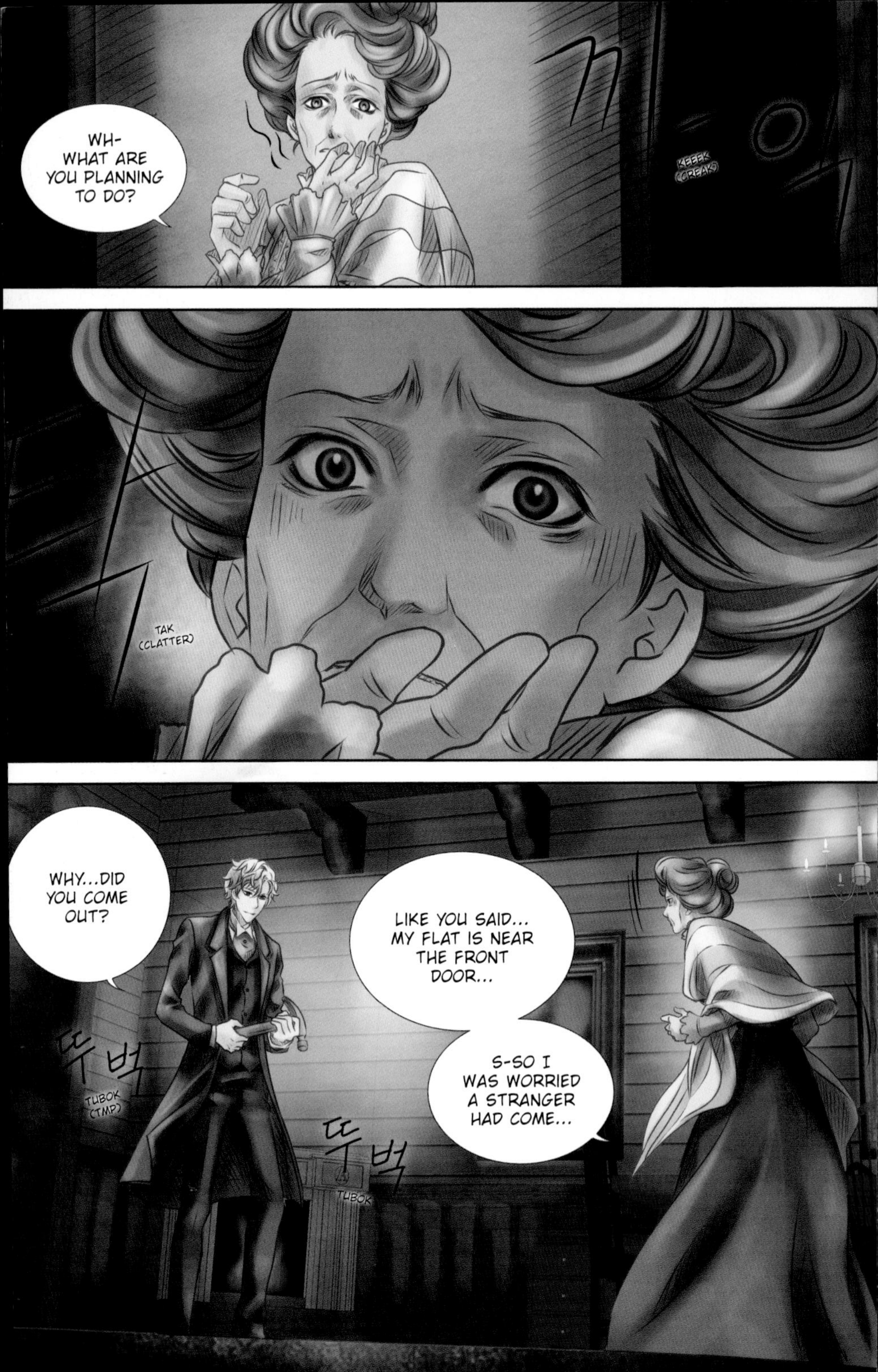

WH- WHAT ARE YOU PLANNING TO DO?
KEEEK (CREAK)
TAK (CLATTER)
WHY...DID YOU COME OUT?
LIKE YOU SAID... MY FLAT IS NEAR THE FRONT DOOR...
S-SO I WAS WORRIED A STRANGER HAD COME...
뚜벅
TUBOK (TMP)
뚜벅
TUBOK

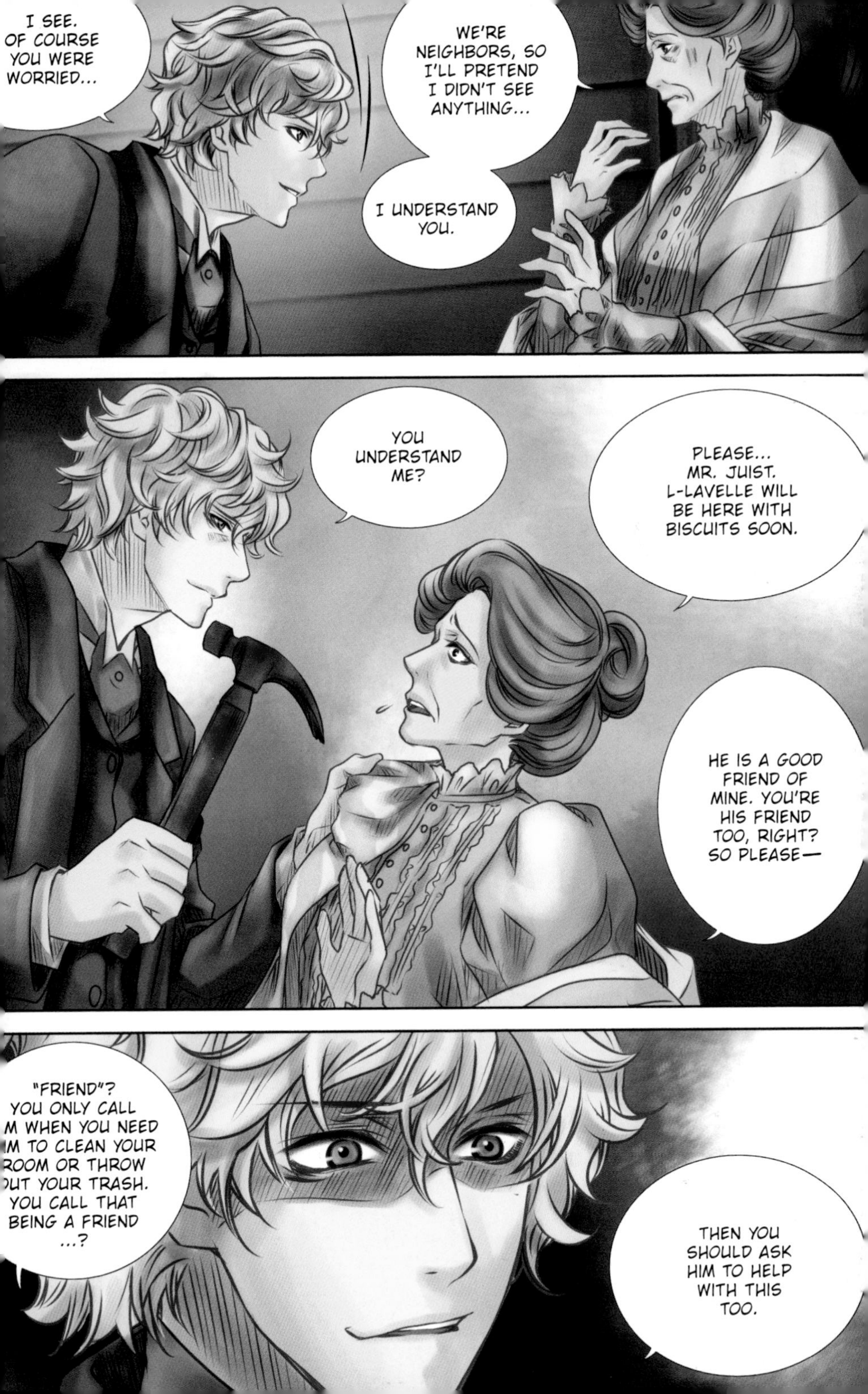
I SEE. OF COURSE YOU WERE WORRIED...
WE'RE NEIGHBORS, SO I'LL PRETEND I DIDN'T SEE ANYTHING...
I UNDERSTAND YOU.
YOU UNDERSTAND ME?
PLEASE... MR. JUIST. L-LAVELLE WILL BE HERE WITH BISCUITS SOON.
HE IS A GOOD FRIEND OF MINE. YOU'RE HIS FRIEND TOO, RIGHT? SO PLEASE—
"FRIEND"? YOU ONLY CALL M WHEN YOU NEED IM TO CLEAN YOUR ROOM OR THROW UT YOUR TRASH. YOU CALL THAT BEING A FRIEND ...?
THEN YOU SHOULD ASK HIM TO HELP WITH THIS TOO.

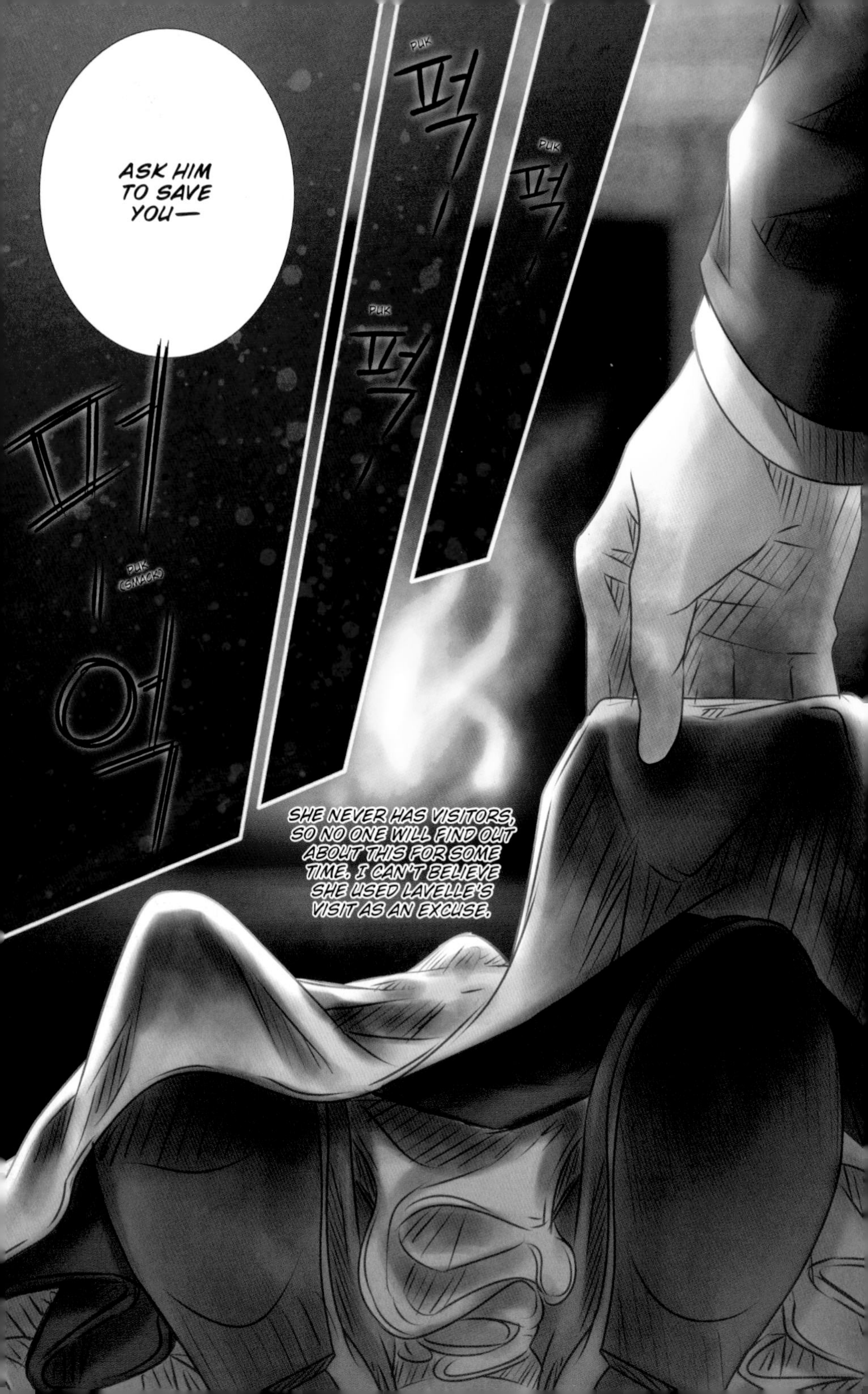
ASK HIM TO SAVE YOU—
PUK
퍽
PUK
퍽
PUK
퍽
PUK (SMACK)
퍼억
SHE NEVER HAS VISITORS, SO NO ONE WILL FIND OUT ABOUT THIS FOR SOME TIME. I CAN'T BELIEVE SHE USED LAVELLE'S VISIT AS AN EXCUSE.

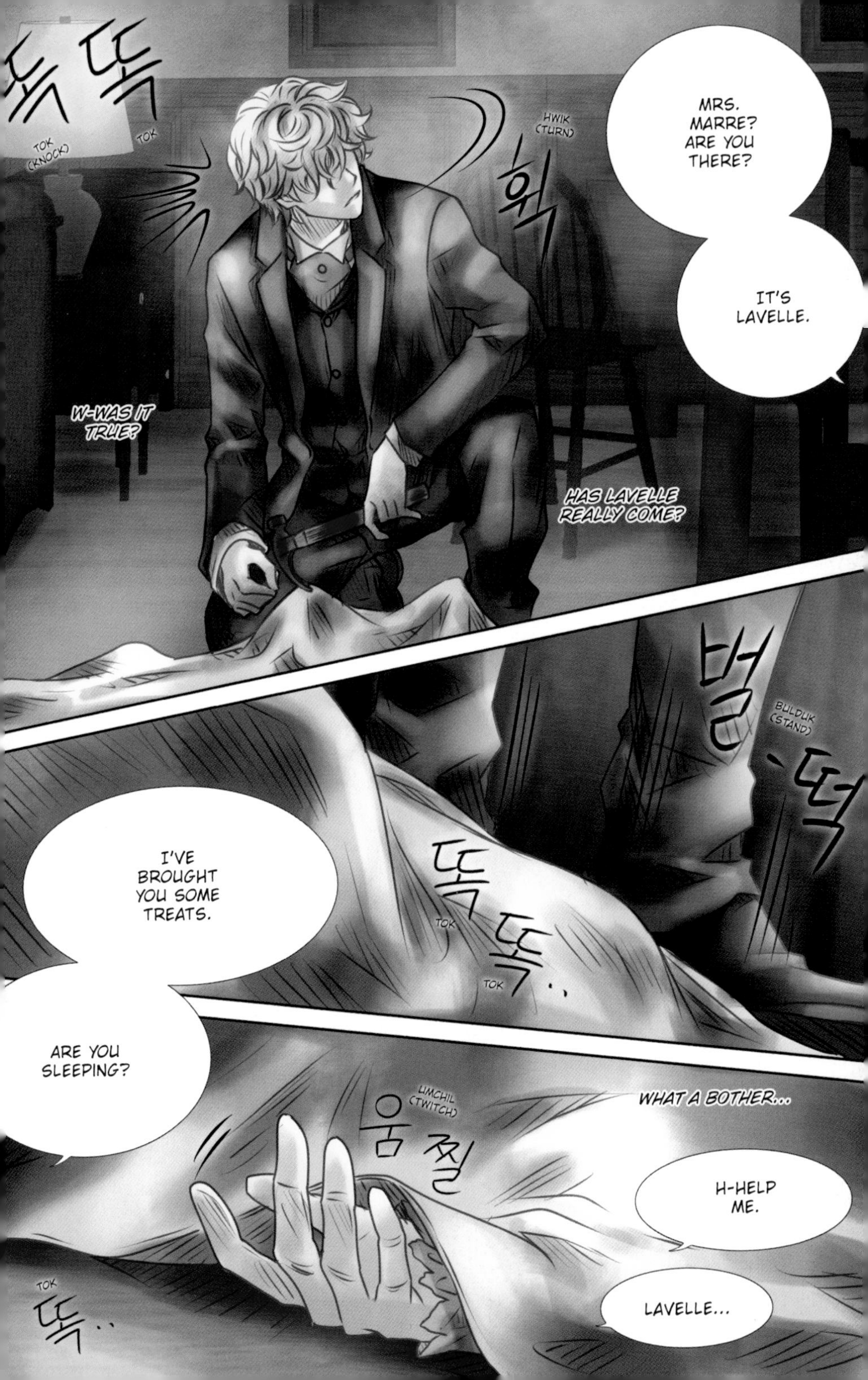
똑 똑
TOK (KNOCK)
TOK
HWIK (TURN)
휙
MRS. MARRE? ARE YOU THERE?
IT'S LAVELLE.
W-WAS IT TRUE?
HAS LAVELLE REALLY COME?
I'VE BROUGHT YOU SOME TREATS.
똑
TOK
똑..
TOK
BULDUK (STAND)
벌떡
ARE YOU SLEEPING?
UMCHIL (TWITCH)
움찔
WHAT A BOTHER...
H-HELP ME.
LAVELLE...
TOK
똑..

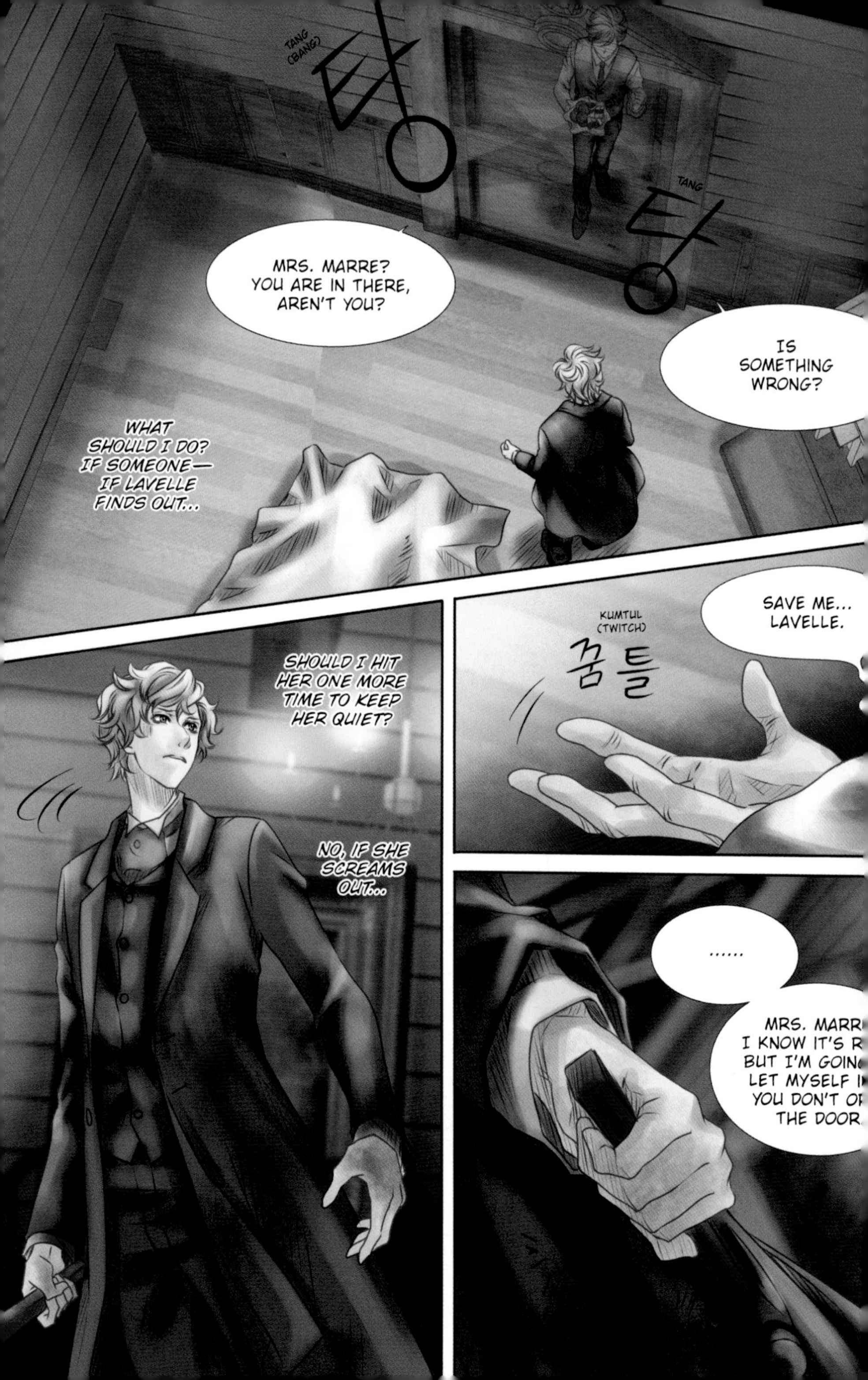

TANG (BANG)
탕
TANG
탕
MRS. MARRE? YOU ARE IN THERE, AREN'T YOU?
IS SOMETHING WRONG?
WHAT SHOULD I DO? IF SOMEONE— IF LAVELLE FINDS OUT...
SHOULD I HIT HER ONE MORE TIME TO KEEP HER QUIET?
NO, IF SHE SCREAMS OUT...
KUMTUL (TWITCH)
꿈틀
SAVE ME... LAVELLE.
......

SURUK
(SHIK)

...MR. JUIST?

OH, IT'S YOU, LAVELLE.

ARE YOU HERE TO VISIT MRS. MARRE?

I'VE BROUGHT SOME COOKIES FOR HER.

WHAT BRINGS YOU HERE, MR. JUIST?

I GUESS I CAME DOWN TOO LATE. I'LL LEAVE THOSE TO YOU, THEN.

MRS. MARRE AND I WERE CHATTING, BUT SHE JUST RETIRED TO BED. I'LL GIVE HER THE COOKIES.

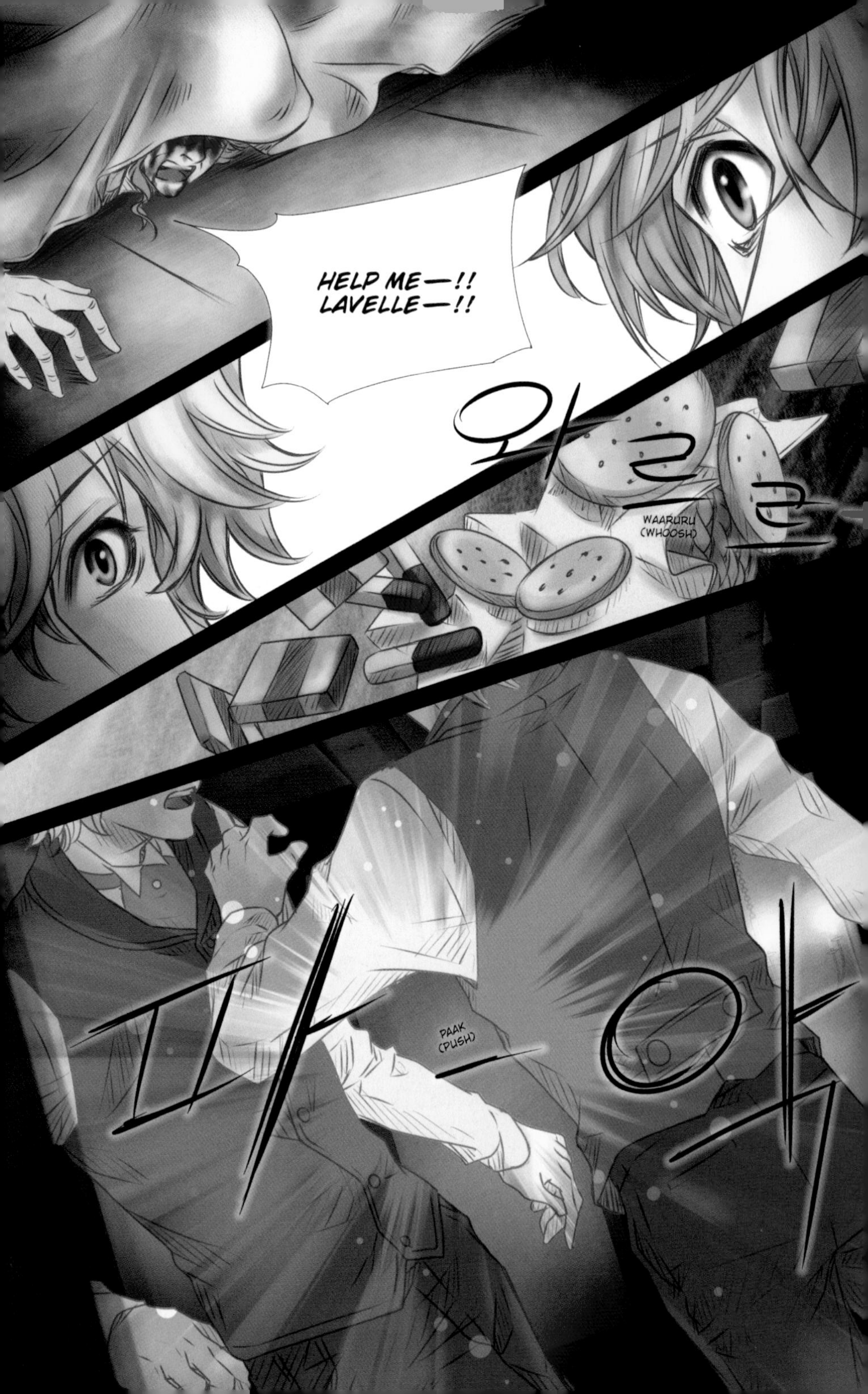
HELP ME—!!
LAVELLE—!!
와르르
WAARURU
(WHOOSH)
파-악
PAAK
(PUSH)

Void's Enigmatic Mansion

To be continued in Volume 5...

Void's Enigmatic Mansion

Visit artist HeeEun Kim's blog at http://blog.naver.com/kimnoran!

Void's Enigmatic Mansion

VOID'S ENIGMATIC MANSION

Can't wait for the next volume? Read the rest of the story digitally now!

CHAPTERS AVAILABLE
FROM YOUR FAVORITE E-BOOK RETAILER
AND IN THE YEN PRESS APP!

www.YenPress.com

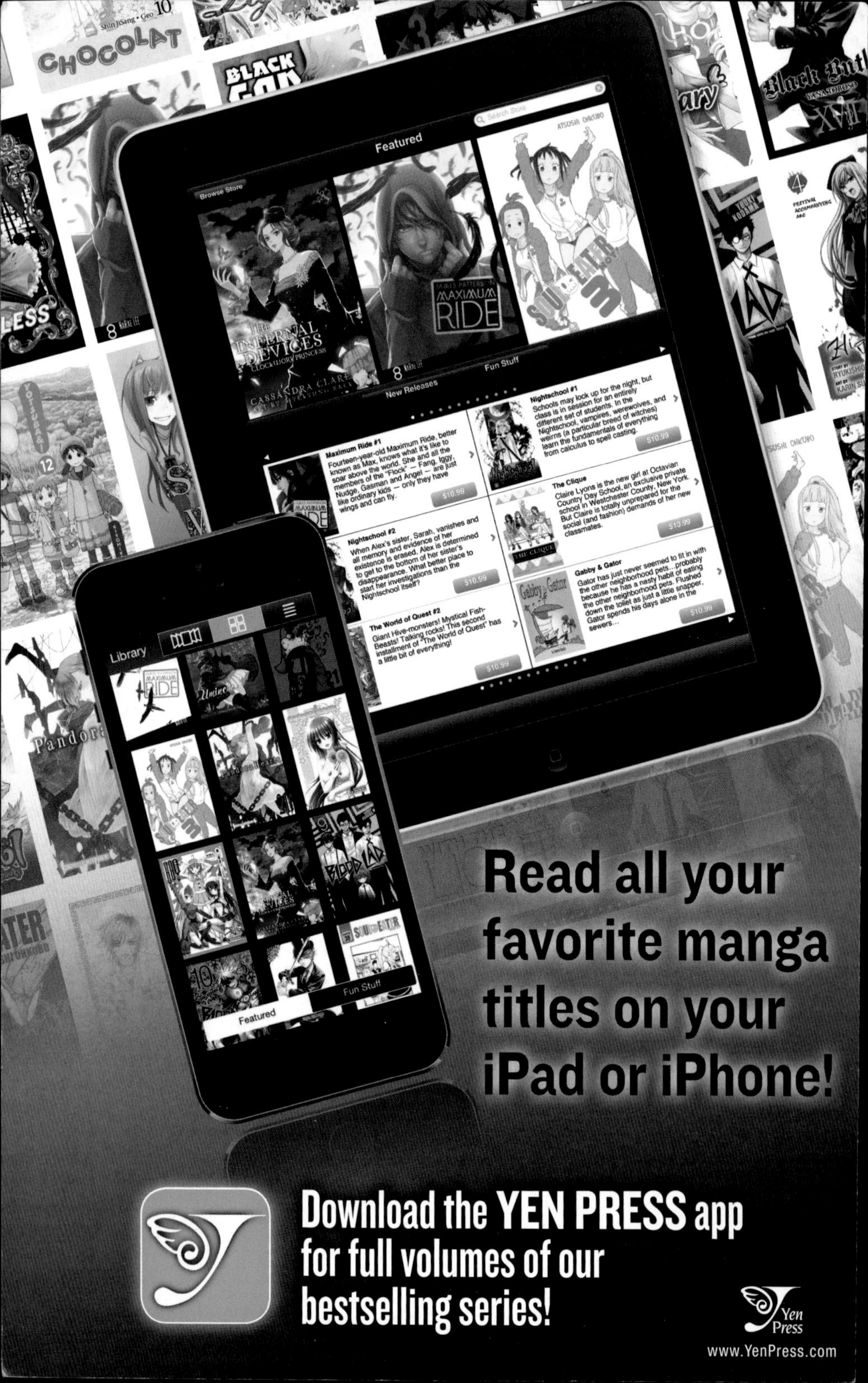
Read all your favorite manga titles on your iPad or iPhone!
Download the YEN PRESS app for full volumes of our bestselling series!
Yen Press
www.YenPress.com

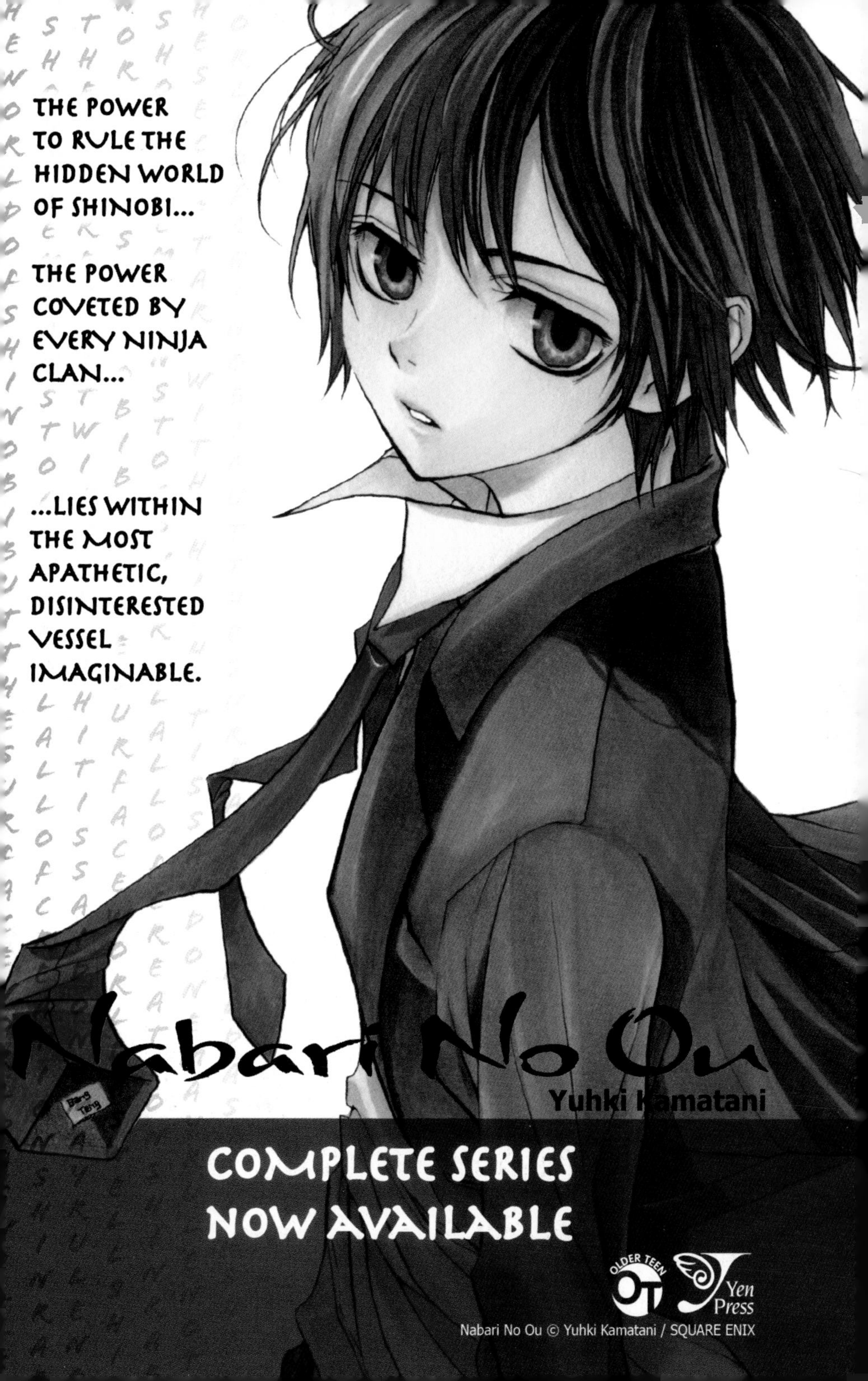
THE POWER TO RULE THE HIDDEN WORLD OF SHINOBI...
THE POWER COVETED BY EVERY NINJA CLAN...
...LIES WITHIN THE MOST APATHETIC, DISINTERESTED VESSEL IMAGINABLE.
Nabari No Ou
Yuhki Kamatani
COMPLETE SERIES NOW AVAILABLE
OLDER TEEN OT
Yen Press
Nabari No Ou © Yuhki Kamatani / SQUARE ENIX

You oughtn't keep a lady waiting...

GAIL CARRIGER

SOULLESS

REM

Yen
Press

VOID'S ENIGMATIC MANSION 4

HeeEun Kim
JiEun Ha

Translation: HyeYoung Im
English Adaptation: J. Torres
Lettering: Stephanie Lee

VOID'S ENIGMATIC MANSION, Vol. 4
©2015 HeeEun Kim
©2015 JiEun Ha
All rights reserved.
First published in Korea in 2015 by Haksan Publishing Co., Ltd.

English translation rights in U.S.A., Canada, UK and Republic of Ireland arranged with Haksan Publishing Co., Ltd.

English translation © 2014, 2015 by Yen Press, LLC

Yen Press
1290 Avenue of the Americas
New York, NY 10104
Visit us at yenpress.com
facebook.com/yenpress
twitter.com/yenpress
yenpress.tumblr.com

First Yen Press Print Edition: July 2016
The chapters in this volume were originally published as ebooks by Yen Press.

Yen Press is an imprint of Yen Press, LLC.
The Yen Press name and logo are trademarks of Yen Press, LLC.

Library of Congress Control Number: 2015952617

ISBN: 978-0-316-36027-2

10 9 8 7 6 5 4 3 2 1

WOR

Printed in the United States of America